The Occult Madonna

The Occult Madonna

Douglas D. Hawk

A Critic's Choice paperback
from Lorevan Publishing, Inc.
New York, New York

ISBN: 1-55547-282-6

First Critic's Choice edition: 1988

From LOREVAN PUBLISHING, INC.

Critic's Choice Paperbacks
31 E. 28th St.
New York, New York 10016

Manufactured in the United States of America

This is for Jean. Her faith is unshakeable, her support unwaivering, her love without question. Few men are so blessed.

PART ONE
THE CEMETERY

She is the mother of all things
  By the world's engines outcast thrown:
Where they are she is: hope she brings
  To those beneath the Nether Stone:
Incorporate with the air and mould,
  She moves through regions manifold.

—J.C. Powys

ONE

Vince Cassidy turned his battered Toyota pickup truck from the street and onto the graveled driveway leading to the huge iron gates that barred the way into the cemetery. The windows of the truck were shut against the pouring, late summer rain and the defroster had made the cramped interior muggy and warm.

"They're chained shut, Vince," Mary Renata said, as she sat across from him, peering out through the foggy, rain splattered windshield. "Wasn't what's-his-name supposed to meet us here?"

Vince glanced at her and nodded his head. "That's what he said. I sure as hell hope he hasn't forgotten. We're down to about five bucks and an eighth of a tank of gas. I'll get out and take a look."

"You'll get soaked," Mary protested as he yanked open the door and climbed out into the downpour.

"Won't be the first time," he answered sourly, putting up the collar of his faded jean jacket. Huge drops of water immediately soaked his coat and jeans and matted his brown hair. He glanced at the heavy plastic tarp covering their belongings, glad he had decided to take the time to secure it.

He ran to the shelter of a huge oak tree flanking the stone columns which supported the iron gates. Looking into the cemetery grounds, he could see no one nor any cars. The sodden ground was washed smooth and there were no tire tracks. The caretaker's stone cottage with its ivy covered walls and eighteenth century English design, sat silent and empty fifty yards from the gate.

Cursing, Vince hurried down the fifty-foot driveway to look up and down the street for some sign of the agent who handled the affairs of the cemetery. But the rain-slick sidewalk was empty and even the normally busy street had only a couple of cars crawling along it.

Vince studied the iron fence surrounding Mansfield Memorial Cemetery. It stretched for three blocks in either direction from the massive, rusty gates. Ten feet high, the spiked shafts, which rested on slabs of quarried stone, jutted menacingly toward the overcast sky. The spikes were set only six inches apart, preventing all but cats, small dogs and rodents access to the rolling, monument-strewn hills.

The beep of the truck's horn jarred him out of his reverie and, realizing he was getting drenched, he ran back to the pickup.

"You'll catch pneumonia," Mary scolded as he climbed back inside. Her dark, almond-shaped eyes fixed him with a harsh stare. "You're in no condition to be out in this kind of weather."

"Just a little water," he said, raising his voice to be heard above the rain thundering on the truck's roof. Running his hand through his dripping hair, he flung the beads of water at her. Squealing, Mary pulled back and brought her hands up to protect her face, expecting another shower.

"Very funny, Diggerman," she laughed, reaching across the seat to jab him playfully in the ribs.

"Ain't no Diggerman no mo'," he entoned, a trace of bitterness in his voice.

Mary smiled sadly as a strand of her raven black hair

fell across her face. Brushing it back, she again reached for him, this time touching his arm lightly. "You will be. There'll be jobs coming along soon."

Vince sighed and nodded.

A trained archaeologist, Vince Cassidy had not been on a dig for over six months. The last one had been a short-term exploration on land near Castle Rock, south of Denver, which a developer was planning to turn into yet another bedroom community. Prior to building, however, the environmental impact statement required that trained archaeologists survey and study the land for possible archaeological sites and artifacts.

Since that job ended, Vince had expended all of his savings trying to keep a roof over his head and food on his table while he looked for another dig. He had finally gone to work in a Vicker's gas station in the north end of Colorado Springs. The long hours on the night shift and the equally long days scanning the employment ads and contacting various archaeological teams in a fruitless search for work had taken their toll.

Mary Renata, with whom he had lived for a year and a half, had found him semi-coonscious in their bedroom when she had returned home from her partime job waitressing at Curly's Truckstop. He was running a high fever and was almost totally incoherent. She managed to get him to a hospital where the doctors diagnosed low blood pressure compounded by fatigue.

He emerged from the hospital five days later, weak, thin and in debt for two thousand dollars. With no insurance, he had looked at the bill as yet another insurmountable obstacle on his road to independence.

"I talked to a guy at Curly's the other day who told me about a pretty decent job," Mary had told him on the way home.

He had been too tired to do more than grunt, so she went on assuming he would be interested.

"This guy—have his name written down in my purse—is looking for a couple to be caretakers at a big old cemetery in Denver."

"A cemetery?" Vince asked, incredulously. "Like where they tuck away our dear departed brethren?"

Mary laughed. "Yeah. Be quiet."

"I'd think a job like that would be snapped up by some old retired folks."

"I asked him about that. You know: Why he just didn't advertise it and pick and chose from the people who apply and he said the man that oversees the place doesn't like to work that way. I guess he prefers to keep it quiet and fill it without much fuss." She shrugged.

Vince grimaced. "Probably filled by now any way. When did you talk to this guy?"

"Just this morning," she answered, pulling the truck into the parking lot behind their apartment building. "Might be worth a call."

"I guess I could call him," Vince agreed half-heartedly. "A cemetery, huh? Talk about the pits."

"You want me to help you to the apartment?" she asked, glancing at her books stacked on the seat between them. Mary was a senior at the University of Colorado at the Colorado Springs campus and Vince knew she was running late for class.

"I'm not crippled," he said with mock indignation. "Go study those dreary Victorian poets; just let me get that guy's name from you."

She fished a greasy order slip from her purse and handed it to him.

"And what if I *do* get this job? What about your school?"

She smiled knowingly. "I can transfer to CU in Denver. Don't worry, it won't be a problem. I'm sure as hell not leaving you to your own devices. Who'd take you to the hospital when you get sick?"

After Mary had driven away, Vince went into their apartment and placed a call to Denver. Much to his surprise, Henry Terrance, the man Mary met, was in his office. Once Vince explained who he was and how he learned about the job, the deep-voiced man on the other end of the line asked him to come to Denver for an interview the following day.

Vince agreed and drove the 70 miles to Denver the following morning. He met the man at a small office on Hampden Avenue in south Denver.

Terrance was a grotesquely large, football-shaped man. His round, fat bullet head sat on oddly slumped shoulders. His body expanded downward into an enormous waist which Vince had estimated to be at least 75 inches in girth. The huge gut narrowed to short, squat legs. He was wearing a black, three-piece suit, and Vince decided he looked like a human top.

The man had piercing black eyes which studied Vince the way an entomologist inspects an insect. His small mouth seldom smiled and when it did it struck his visitor as insincere and plastic.

"So you want to be the caretaker of Mansfield Memorial Cemetery, Mr. Cassidy," Terrance had said without preamble.

"I'm not sure. Mary . . . that is my girlfriend you spoke to yesterday . . . felt it was an interesting opportunity."

"It's not a cushy job, Mr. Cassidy," Terrance said sternly, leaning forward on his large dark oak desk, his fat, stubby hands clasped in front of him and his shiny eyes fixing Vince with a hard gaze. "There's plenty of work. It takes a certain dedication to keep up the cemetery. It's two and a half square miles. That's 1,600 acres and all filled with mausoleums, headstones, tombs and monuments. Filled to capacity, Mr. Cassidy. Some very famous and wealthy people are intered there."

"I'm not looking for a goldbricker's job," Vince had responded, trying not to sound as defensive as he suddenly felt. The obese man was rubbing him the wrong way as well as confusing him. On the telephone the day before he had been as friendly as anyone could be. Now he was acting as if Vince was some jerk right off the street.

The pseudo-smile suddenly appeared on Terrance's fat face. "Of course you're not, Mr. Cassidy. I didn't mean to imply you were. It's just that Mansfield is considered by many to be very historically significant. We have had some vandalism and theft and desperately need a fulltime person to watch over the place."

"What exactly does the job entail?" Vince asked.

"Mostly keeping an eye on the grounds. There's a crew of gardners who come once a week to mow and trim the grass and tend to the shrubs and flower beds."

"So you're looking for a security guard . . ."

Terrance cut him off, his tone again hard edged. "More than that. If we wanted a simple security guard, we could hire one from a contractor. No, we want someone who really *watches* the place; inspects it, makes sure it remains . . . shall I say . . . safe?"

Vince had thought about it for a moment, unclear of the man's meaning. "Safe? Safe from what? Kids? Vandals?"

"Of course," Terrance answered, too quickly Vince thought.

"Well . . ."

"Will your girlfriend be moving in with you?" The fatman's voice sounded very eager when he mentioned Mary.

Great, Vince had thought. The guy's a lech.

"If that won't be a problem."

"No. No problem at all. In fact, that would be preferable. She could help you and, of course, be paid for her time." Again, Terrance had sounded oddly anxious.

"Just exactly how much money are we talking about?" Vince braced himself.

The plastic smile appeared again. "Two thousand a month for you and an additional thousand for Ms. Renata. Plus, of course, the caretaker's cottage and all utilities paid."

Vince was speechless. He had expected to get a low-ball figure and be forced to negotiate or decline the offer altogether. Three thousand dollars a month for the two of them to watch over a fully-occupied cemetery? Amazing. A few months of that and they'd be out of debt and have a nice nestegg to boot. Mary could start on her master's degree right away.

"So, Mr. Cassidy? Do we have a deal?" Terrance's plastic smile had remained in place.

"Yes. Definitely. When do you want me to start?"

"We'd like you *both* to start next Monday. Can that be arranged?"

It was Thursday. He would have to let his apartment manager know he was moving out, get their stuff packed, find out if Mary could give short notice on her job and take care of a hundred other tedious details.

"I think so," Vince finally said.

"Excellent, Mr. Cassidy. You can meet my associate, Mr. Oscar Bedlow, at the north gate of the cemetery Monday afternoon at two. He will see that you get acquainted with the grounds and settled into the cottage." Terrance stood and extended a fat, puffy hand. Vince had taken it, gripping soft, spongy flesh that felt cold and clammy.

It wasn't until he was driving back to Colorado Springs that Vince wondered how Terrance had known Mary's last name. Maybe she had told him. It wasn't worth worrying about, he had decided. However, that evening he did mention to Mary that she had failed to tell him Terrance looked like Jabba the Hut.

Now, waiting in his truck, Vince turned to Mary and smiled, "Well, hell, maybe I can be a *grave*diggerman."

"Too creepy," she shivered, smoothing out her white skirt with her hands.

Although the money Terrance was offering was exceptional, given the job description, Vince felt a pang of regret that this was not an archaeology assignment. Mary wouldn't have been able to accompany him and that would have been a drag, but scraping the earth for ancient bones would be preferable to taking care of newer ones.

They both jumped involuntarily as someone rapped on Vince's window. Jerking around, Vince saw a gaunt, skull-like face peering through the glass. Shoulders hunched against the rain, the man studied the couple with cold, unblinking eyes.

"Sorry I'm late," he said, as Vince cranked down the glass. "I'm Oscar Bedlow. I'm afraid I got held up by a wreck on I-25. I'll open the gate. You drive on over to the cottage." The tall, stark man hurried to the iron gate and, producing a ring of keys from his trenchcoat, unlocked the large padlock securing the rusty chain. Vince put the truck in gear as Bedlow, with some effort, pushed open first one and then the other of the heavy gates.

The living room of the cottage was furnished with old heavy oak and walnut furniture, large fan-backed chairs, an intricately crafted secretary and a coffee table with brass talons gripping the crystal balls serving as its feet. The double-hung windows were covered with lace curtains which muffled the light filtering through them. It would have looked very much like a Victorian parlour had it not been for the walls. They were uniformly covered by a light blue paper with an erratic darker blue design. The effect of the room was at once soothing and vaguely unsettling.

As she stepped into the middle of the room, looking around curiously, Mary wrinkled her nose at the musty, closed-up smell. Vince, standing next to her, detected a more pungent odor; familiar, yet not readily identifiable.

"Now," said Bedlow, tugging off his dripping overcoat and hanging it on a halltree near the front door. "Shall we finalize the paperwork and, then if the rain lets up, we can then have a look around the grounds."

"Paperwork?" Vince asked curiously as the thin man pulled a wad of papers out of his inside jacket pocket.

Bedlow smiled apologetically. "Formalities. You know, just to make it all official." He moved into the small, cluttered living room, leaving wet footprints on the brown carpeting and sat down in one of the chairs surrounding the drop-leaf dining table. "Please, have a seat. This will only take a moment."

Exchanging glances, Mary and Vince joined Bedlow, sitting cross from each other and flanking him. He smiled at them, flashing a row of large, perfect teeth. His gaunt, pale face struck the couple as looking particularly unhealthy.

"I'll leave you these forms to fill out at your leisure," he began, pushing a set of papers toward them. "Insurance forms. There is an address where you can send them."

"This job includes insurance?" Vince asked, pleased and surprised.

"Of course. Didn't Mr. Terrance tell you? Well, of course he didn't. He's not concerned about such things." Bedlow sounded disdainful toward his colleague.

"Now this is the important document," he went on, handing each of them a single sheet of paper. A list was neatly typed on both sheets. "These are the requirements of the job. Please read it over and then ask any questions."

Vince glanced at the list. As he read down it, he became more mystified then enlightened.

1. The caretaker must walk the perimeter of the cemetery every morning after sunrise.
2. The caretaker must inspect all areas of the cemetery every morning before 10:00.
3. The caretaker must immediately report any damage, vandalism, desecrations or suspicious inconsistencies to his superiors immediately.
4. The caretaker must inspect the entryways of all mausoleums and crypts every morning to insure they are secured.
5. The caretaker will unlock the north gate promptly at 11:00 p.m. each month on the night of the full moon

to allow the tour group access to the grounds. All other gates will remain locked at all other times.

6. The caretaker will not permit anyone access to the cemetery other than the monthly tour group and the weekly visits by the groundskeepers.
7. The caretaker will not entertain at the cemetery cottage.
8. Under no circumstances is the caretaker to report any damage, vandalism and desecrations to anyone other than his superiors.

"The last one is the most important," said Bedlow evenly, his cadaverous face set and his cold eyes flinty and hard.

"Why don't you want the police notified if there is damage to the tombstones or crypts?" Mary asked.

"Publicity. We don't want any bad publicity. As I'm sure you are aware, Mansfield Memorial is an historical site and the monthly tour pays us a handsome fee. Bad publicity would drive away tourists."

Vince laughed nervously. "What kind of tour group shows up at a cemetery in the middle of the night?"

Bedlow smiled tightly, although his eyes remained unchanged, and spread his hands in a gesture of unconcern. "People who like to . . . experience the silence and beauty of Mansfield in the still of the night. And of course the full moon simply enhances that experience."

Vince doubted that. More likely a bunch of kooks trying to contact their dead relatives or conjure up some ghostly apparition. He didn't say anything, however.

"And why can't Vince and I entertain here?" Mary asked, scanning the list again.

Bedlow smiled patiently and answered her as if she was a child. "Again, we don't want strangers on the grounds other than the tours. Parties can get . . . well, shall I say, out of hand?"

"So much for the weekly orgy," Mary quipped, laughing. She quickly stifled her laugh when she saw Bedlow's disapproving glance. No sense of humor, she thought.

"Let me emphasize that these rules are no to be violated. To shirk these duties would result in immediate termination." Bedlow looked first at Vince and then at Mary, studying them to make certain they understood the gravity of their responsibilities.

Vince nodded. "I think we can handle this."

Bedlow let a fleeting smile play on his pale lips, but remained silent, watching Mary.

"Ah, sure, yes. This doesn't look too bad," she stammered when she realized he was waiting for her to speak.

Bedlow smiled, again showing those large even teeth. "Good." He glanced at one of the windows. "Still raining hard. Why don't I return tomorrow morning, say about six? We can look over the grounds and I can go over the duties with you."

"Six?" Vince said uncomfortably, finding the thought of climbing out of bed at five mildly appalling.

Bedlow fixed him with an even, steady gaze. "You have to get up early anyway to start your rounds. I'll just be along to accompany you."

Mary winked at Vince.

"And you'll join us, won't you?" Bedlow asked, turning quickly toward Mary, a salacious smile exposing his teeth.

"Ah, sure. Of course."

"Excellent." Bedlow got to his feet. "I'll leave you now to get unpacked and settled in. Here are the keys to the gate." He handed Vince a large ring with two keys on it. "I suggest you put one of those somewhere safe. It is a duplicate."

"Just one key? Is there a key to the cottage?"

Again, Bedlow smiled patiently. "No need to lock up the house if the main gate is always locked."

"What if Mary and I go out to a movie or dinner in the evening? Shouldn't the place be secured?"

The man gave them a knowing smile. "Don't worry about that. It'll be just fine. Now, I'll see you both at six o'clock. I can see myself out. Don't forget to lock up after me."

After the man had donned his overcoat and left, Mary and Vince looked at each other.

"Too damn spooky," Mary said. "You'd think this place attracted all sorts of kooky people. It's just a cemetery. And a full one at that."

"Bedlow makes Dr. Frankenstein seem like a Captain Kangaroo. Weird dude," Vince said, pulling his jacket back on. "Guess I'd better go lock the gate and then get the truck unloaded."

"I'll poke around the house and see what's where. Maybe after we get packed we can use that five bucks you have burning a hole in your pocket and get a bag of cheap burgers." Mary punched him playfully on the arm.

"Yeah. That'll be a great meal . . ."

A horn blared, cutting Vince off. "He must be waiting to make sure I lock up. Better do it. Can't get fired before I start"

If anything, it was raining harder. The sky was dark, filled with wind-swept black clouds. Vince dashed to the gates. He started to close one, when he saw Bedlow sitting in his Cadillac. The man motioned for him to come to the car.

"I almost forgot," Bedlow said, lowering the power window. "Your first month's pay." He shoved a fat brown envelope out the window. Vince took it, amazed at how quickly the rain soaked the paper. "It's all there. Count it when you get back inside. See you in the morning."

The window rose and Vince gave a quick wave, as he stuffed the envelope under his jacket and raced back to the gates. He shoved the heavy portals shut, wrapped the chain around the bars and affixed the padlock. Only then did Bedlow's Cadillac turn around in the driveway and pull into the street, disappearing in the torrential rain.

"Three thousand dollars? In cash?" Mary squealed, after Vince had opened the envelope and spread out the money, all in twenties and fifties, on the dining room table.

Vince grinned. "Some haul, huh? Guess we can do better than a bag of greasy burgers tonight, right?"

"That's no kidding. But, while you were outside, I checked the kitchen. It's crammed with food."

"What?" Vince stammered, as Mary grabbed his arm and fairly dragged him into the small, spacious kitchen. She began opening cupboards, revealing an array of canned and packaged foods.

"And look at this," she went on, beaming as she tugged open a huge freezer standing in one corner. "It's filled with steaks, roasts, chops, fish . . ."

"Jesus. Have we died and gone to heaven?" Vince asked, staring at the four full shelves.

"Nope, Diggerman. Just to Mansfield Memorial. And there's more." She shut the freezer door and moved to the refrigerator, opening it to show him that it was also amply stocked with fresh vegetables, butter, milk, eggs, two bottles of French wine, bottles of Corona beer and a variety of condiments.

"Amazing," was all he could say.

"And over here," Mary continued, acting like a game show hostess exhibiting the next prize, "is a fully-stocked wine cellar." She opened a cupboard door near the sink to reveal a rack filled with a variety of wines.

Vince whistled softly. "Three thousand clams, a furnished house and enough food and wine to make a glutton cry 'uncle.' What's the catch."

Something odd passed through Mary's eyes, fading her smile for an instant. Not wanting Vince to see her discomfort, which even she could not understand, she turned and pulled a bottle of burgundy from the rack. Her smile back, she held the bottle up for Vince to see.

"How about this with a couple of thick steaks and a nice salad?" she asked, her voice mildly strained.

"Yeah, sure. While you cook, I'll haul our stuff in before it floats away."

"Something stereotypic about that," Mary laughed, the strange, indefinable feeling gone.

Vince spread his arms in mock surrender. "Okay, I'll cook and you can go out into the monsoon."

Mary lifted the bottle over her head. "How about if I plant this up the side of your head?"

"Okay," Vince said, turning to leave the kitchen. "That clears up that."

The rain was still pouring down. Small rivers flowed down the graveled drives criss-crossing the cemetery, eventually rushing together in a tumbling confluence. Forming an inches-deep stream, the run-off flooded past the cottage and under the gates and down the drive to merge into the already full gutters. The grounds were shrouded by the deluge as sheets of rain swirled and danced among the monuments, crypts and headstones.

Vince wasted no time in tugging boxes and cartons from beneath the tarp, careful to keep the plastic covering in place. His feet sloshed through the stream as he carried his burdens into the cottage. It took a dozen trips to finally empty the truck's bed and by then he was cold and soaked to the skin. Tired, he realized that he was still very weak from his recent hospital stay.

When Mary emerged from the kitchen and saw him, she immediate sent him to the bathroom on the second floor and ordered him to strip off his wet clothes and climb into a hot shower.

"When you're done, it'll be time to eat," she said, as he turned on the water in the country-styled bathroom and stepped inside the oversized, white tub.

The musty smell in the house was effectively masked by the rich odors pouring from the kitchen. Vince, wrapped in one of the large towels he'd found in the bathroom, hurried back downstairs, opened his suitcase and pulled out clean clothes.

Mary had set two places at the dining room table and soon they were feasting on thick, rare T-bones, salad and the wine. When they finished, Vince helped her clean up and then, working until the cloud-covered sun was down, they unpacked their belongings.

Relatively settled in and armed with another bottle of the fine burgundy, they retired to the largest of the three bedrooms on the second floor.

The room was surprisingly spacious, with a high, pitched ceiling and tapered walls formed by the angle of the steep roof. Flocked mauve and gray wallpaper covered all four walls, blending well with the dusty rose carpeting and matching drapes. There was a massive wardrobe against one wall, a vanity and mirror against another and two handsome, velvet-covered Queen Anne chairs flanking a small table supporting the Tiffany lamp, which cast pale, soft light across the room. The centerpiece of the room was a king-sized, canopied bed with heavy curtains matching the drapes. Two small, gable-peaked windows looked out over the rain splattered cemetery.

In the wet darkness, Mary thought it looked surreal and totally alien, like something from a sick man's fever dream. Peering through the water-beaded glass, she tried to distinguish one tombstone from another, but it was all a confused blur.

She whirled from the window with a gasp when Vince popped the cork out of the bottle. Her hand over her heart, she sighed and laughed without mirth.

"Scared me to death."

Vince, bottle in one hand and two wine glasses from the kitchen in the other, flashed her a lacivious grin.

"How about some wine, little girl?" he entoned, doing an awful Peter Lorre imitation.

"Oh, I'd love some," she responded coquettishly.

He poured the wine and they sat on the edge of the huge

bed drinking and necking like teenagers, feeling more relaxed than either of them had in months. They were both giddy and lightheaded by the time the bottle was emptied. Mary slipped out of Vince's arms and stepped across the room to turn off the lamp. Before she twisted the switch, she glanced out the window, realizing the rain had stopped. Looking closer she shivered involuntary, fascinated by the fine, wispy mist that crept round the dark stones.

An inky black shadow moved near the hulking mausoleum standing scant yards on the opposite side of the driveway.

"Vince," she murmured, not taking her eyes from the spot. "I think someone's out there."

"Where?" he said, stepping across the room to stand beside her.

"There." She pointed at the spot, moving aside so he could peer into the gloom. He studied the spot for several seconds.

"I can't see anything. Are you sure you saw someone?"

"I'm sure I did," she said, irritated at his patronizing tone.

"Okay," he sighed. "I guess I'd better go check it out. That's what I'm being paid for."

Without another word, he left Mary and made his way down stairs in the dark. Flipping on a floor lamp in the living room, he took a flashlight he'd found earlier, out of a desk drawer, tested it and then, satisfied its batteries were strong, pulled on his jacket and went outside.

The night air smelled clean and wet and was mildly chilly. A gentle breeze stirred through the pines and elms, driving the dampness through the denim jacket.

Although the low gray clouds, now dispersing, reflected the amber lights of the city, they still obscured the nearly full moon which was only a bright spot against the eastern sky. Vince flipped on the flashlight and stepped cautiously across driveway. He glanced up at the bedroom window where Mary still stood watching him. He waved and she waved back.

The grass around the tombstone was spongy under his shoes and with each step there was a wet squishing, much like the sound a giant slug made when tromped upon. The thought sickened him.

He made his way carefully toward the crypt, coming up on it from behind. It squatted like an ancient, malevolent temple. Entangled ivy clung to it in thick, knotted strands, hiding the myriad of tiny fissures cracking the rough hewned brown stones. It's roof was peaked and in the light, he could see weatherstained figures crouched on each corner. Aiming the circle of light at one of the shapes, he gave a start. Instead of a cherub or angel, he stared at a horned gargoyle, its mouth gapping open, exposing sharp, chiseled stone teeth.

"Great," he muttered to himself. "A gargoyle as a grave watcher." He couldn't help wondering what sort of person in life would want gremlins guarding his body in death.

Turning the light away from the awful statue, Vince moved around the corner of the building. He paused and let the beam of light play over the nearby tombstones. It reflected off dozens of smooth, polished granite and marble surfaces, briefly passed over carved figures perched atop ostentations markers and occasionally illuminated a stone vase or brass urn.

Nothing stirred.

A sharp screech of metal on metal, like fingernails scraped across slate, caused Vince to jump and catch his breath. The back of his neck prickled. The sound came from the front of the crypt.

Now don't be stupid, Cassidy. This place is only filled with a lot of dusty old bones.

Gulping shallow breaths, his heart thudding in his ears, he moved slowly along the wall, the ivy clutching at his left arm, as if trying to grip him, hold him. He was vaguely aware of the icy sweat trickling down his sides and moistening his chest.

Get a grip on yourself. It's probably only something moving in the breeze.

Reaching the end of the wall, he pointed the flashlight directly in front of him, balled his right fist and stepped around the corner.

The heavy, iron banded door of the crypt hung open. As he crept nearer to it, he became aware of the noxious stench permeating the area; the fetid smell of mouldy earth and rotten meat.

Vandals. First night on the job and some asshole decides to play patty cake with a corpse.

Taking another deep breath, he stepped quickly in front of the opening, flashing the light inside. The yellow beam was swallowed up in blackness, unable to penetrate the interior and illuminating nothing.

What in the hell is wrong with this thing? Batteries must be going out . . .

As if a switch had been turned on, two bright red points appeared in the ebon gloom. Transfixed, Vince watched in horror as they shifted . . .

Damned animal in there. Some dog or rodent . . .

He felt his head swim as a wave of dizziness swept over him. Everything was out of focus and there was a painful, disorienting pounding in his head. The twin crimson points—*Eyes!*, his mind screamed—bored into him, seeming to pierce his flesh, his bone and burrow deep into his mind, his soul.

He backed away, keeping the now wavering light pointed into the unnatural blackness. The red, glistening orbs shifted again.

It's a dog. It has to be a dog! A fucking big dog!

The pounding in his head was worse and he feared he was about to pass out. Flashes of light darted at the corners of his eyes followed by fleeting, night-black shadows.

He whirled and started to run, only to bark his knee

painfully on a low tombstone. Tumbling to the wet grass, he clutched at the bruised, cut flesh under his jeans.

Something moved behind him.

There was the sharp crack of a dried tree limb snapping under someone's—*something's?*—heavy tread.

A blast of hot, stinking air—*breath?*—washed over him.

Wanting to scream and cry, feeling at once stupid and childish and foolish, he pushed himself to his feet and hobbled away.

Vince could sense a presence very close . . .

He was gasping, panting aware of the *thing* behind him, stalking him . . .

Mary Renata's terrified scream suddenly echoed through the darkness. Jerking his head up, Vince saw the bedroom light go out.

TWO

Mary stood at the window watching Vince cross the graveled drive and pick his way thorugh the mist-shrouded headstones. The further he walked, the more indistinct he became until he was only a black outline moving behind the dim circle of yellow light. She watched curiously when he paused behind the mausoleum and cast the light on something resting on one of the structure's corners. Then he was around the corner and out of her line of sight.

A shiver passed through her and she crossed her arms, trying to stave off the sudden chill in the room. The light cotton blouse did little to warm her.

Although she could no longer see him, Mary saw the beam of Vince's flashlight momentarily probe the cemetery surrounding the crypt. Then it abruptly vanished from her view. A shadow, like a cloud moving across the moon, blotted out the crypt and all of the surrounding tombstones. Almost pressing her face against the glass she glanced upward, attempting to discover the source of the shadow. But the moonless sky held only a few clouds, the last reminants of the rain storm.

Looking back toward the crypt, she sucked in her breath as a black, formless shadow, not unlike the one she had witnessed earlier, moved about the headstones. The crypt was still obscured.

"Damn it," she hissed, turning from the window. She was alarmed and frightened and worried about Vince. There was a gnawing panic clutching at her heart as she started across the bedroom, intent on going outside to find him . . .

Something moved in the hallway outside the door. There was the unmistakable creak of a loose floorboard as something heavy moved across it, followed by a dull thud on the door.

Mary frozen, her mouth dry and her heart racing.

"Who . . . who's there?" she stammered, her voice barely above a whisper.

She backed away from the door as something sharp and hard clawed the wood on the opposite side. There was the sound of the veneer splintering.

"My God . . ." Mary backed further away. Her arms hung loosely at her sides, her hands clenched in fists, her long nails biting into the soft flesh of her palms.

The scratching and clawing continued and Mary was sure the door would split open at any second under the wood-rending pressure.

Suddenly, as her head bumped the wall opposite the door, the already pale light from the Tiffany lamp grew dimmer, barely illuminating the room. Mary looked at it in wide-eyed terror. She sensed if the light was extinguished, whatever clawed at the door would be able to reach her, touch her, shred her flesh as it was even now shredding the wood . . .

"Pull yourself together, Renata," she said aloud, shaking away the nightmare images playing behind her eyes. "Don't be such a wimp." She looked around for something with which to defend herself.

The clawing at the door continued, louder, more frantic and intense now.

Mary turned to scan the top of the vanity where her small assortment of perfumes and cosmetics were carefully arrayed in front of the mirror. She stepped quickly to it, searched among the bottles and jars for something sharp and heavy to use as a weapon.

The light was growing dimmer and it was hard to see. Her hand moved among the objects. At last she grabbed a conical shaped bottle of perfume, a gift from Vince, with a sharply pointed plastic cap. Grabbing it by the base, she held it in front of her, her eyes returning to the door where the clawing and scraping was now so loud and furious, Mary knew the door would soon collapse.

She fought to control her panic and the terror which brought a tremble to her hands and sent a chill coursing down her spine.

She moved to the center of the room. Instinctively she knew if she gave in to her fear everything would be lost. Gripping the bottle—such a poor, inadequate weapon—in both her sweaty, shaking hands, she held it out before her.

There was a ripping and screeching of wood and Mary saw, in the ever dimming light, four massive black talons groove a path through the door. They glistened in the paling light, flexing as if struggling to disengage themselves from the thick panel.

Her resolve broke. She was unaware of the bottle dropping from her limp hands to clatter to the floor and roll beneath the massive bed. Her eyes fixed on those evil, dark claws, she did not know she was backing away; was unconscious of the screams tearing from her throat.

She only knew that those razor sharp talons wanted her. She could visualize them slashing into her soft flesh, tearing her body, extinguishing her life . . .

I don't want to die. Not this way! Not here. Not now. Not alone.

Suddenly Mary felt herself stumbling, falling. Bright flashes exploded in her head and she then was crashing heavily to the floor amid the sound of breaking glass.

As a merciful black void swallowed her consciousness, she was vaguely aware of a black shape hovering over her; of slime-encrusted, rough hands working their way up her thigh.

Vince limped frantically across the graveled drive and through the door of the cottage. His leg was throbbing painfully and he prayed it wouldn't give out on him.

In the dark, he ran into the hat tree, sending it tumbling to the floor. Cursing, he groped for the light switch just beyond the foyer. The overhead light dispersed the blackness and he limped to the stairs, gasping with each step as he climbed them.

"Mary!" He called to her frantically, an icy dread filling his heart, sending a shudder through his soul.

In the second floor hallway, he again searched for the light switch, flicked it on and hobbled to the master bedroom. The door hung slightly ajar. Pushing it open, he called to Mary. Inside it was dark. He paused momentarily as he was assailed by a stench of mould and decay. It was not unlike the stink he had encountered at the mausoleum.

Bracing himself, he entered the room, trying to see Mary in the darkness. Flipping on the overhead light, he could see her bare legs jutting out from the opposite side of the bed.

"Mary!" he cried, limping to her. She lay on her back, her skirt bunched up around her hips. Her eyes were closed and a trickle of blood was running down her forehead from a cut just below her hairline. The wound was surrounded by a dark bruise. One of the Queen Anne chairs was shoved back, the small table rested on its side and shards from the Tiffany lamp were shattered over the carpeting.

Kneeling beside her, Vince carefully avoided the piece of broken glass and gently touched her throat, sighing as he felt the strong pulse. Carefully, his leg aching under the weight, he lifted her up and placed her on the bed.

As he straightened her legs he noticed the streaks of grimy black mud traced over her thighs.

She moaned softly and her eyes fluttered. Suddenly she gasped and pulled away from him.

"NO!" she screamed.

"Mary? Mary, it's me. You're okay now. You're okay." Her eyes opened wide with fright. She searched his face and then with a choking sob, she clutched at him, pulling him to her.

"Oh God, Vince, it was awful. It . . . it tried to get me. It . . . was . . . oh God . . ."

Mary pressed her face against his shoulder and sobbed, her body shaking. He held her close, confused and alarmed, not knowing what to tell her nor even what he should think.

After a time, between dry sobs, she told him what had happened.

"It ripped the door apart," she gasped. Vince looked at the door hanging open and intact. Mary's eyes followed his and she stared at it, her mouth agape.

"It can't be. It was ripped apart, Vince." There was a pleading hysteria edging her voice that scared Vince. Mary was not given to emotional excesses nor histrionics. She was, if anything, in too much control of her passions.

She pulled away from him and made to climb off the bed, only to be stopped by an explosion of pain from her bruised head.

"Don't," Vince told her, forcing her to lay back down. "Let me get something to fix that cut."

"Vince," she whispered, her eyes closed against the pain as her fingers gently probed her cut forehead. "I'm not lying. I am not imagining what I saw."

He thought about his experience at the mausoleum. "No, I don't think you're imagining it. Now lie still while I go get a bandage."

He hurried to the bathroom and searched the medicine chest above the sink where he found an unopened bottle of hydrogen peroxide, a box of Band-Aids, a packet of cotton and a bottle of aspirin. Returning to their room, he found Mary standing next to the door, inspecting it with her fingers and shaking her head.

"It was destroyed, Vince," she said to him, not taking her eyes off the polished, dark surface of the door.

"Maybe it was a nightmare, Mary," he responded lamely, not really wanting to believe any of it. "Maybe you tripped and fell and banged your head and had a nightmare, a hallucination."

She looked at him, her expression telling him she was unconvinced.

"A hallucination? Then explain this," she snapped, hiking her skirt, exposing the muddy marks on her thigh.

Vince shrugged and shook his head. "Baby, I just don't know. Come on. You shouldn't be standing around. Sit down and let me fix that cut."

Reluctantly, she sat in one of the chairs and let Vince clean and dress the cut. She winced and gasped when he carefully dabbed at it with a piece of cotton soaked in the peroxide, waiting until the watery liquid had ceased bubbling before he covered the wound with a large Band-Aid.

"There," he said, smiling weakly. "As good as new. I don't even think there'll be a scar . . ."

"Damn it, Vince," she said in irritation. "Don't patronize me. I'm not a child. Something happened in here. I don't understand it, but I . . I wasn't dreaming!"

He stood and looked around helplessly, not knowing what to say. He reached for one of the wine glasses sitting on the night stand.

"I'll get you some water for the aspirin," he told her, heading for the bathroom. When he returned, she was stepping out of the wrinkled, dirty white skirt.

"And what happened out there?" she asked, tossing the skirt onto one of the chairs, her voice still hard. "What happened to your leg? I saw you limping."

Vince wouldn't meet her level gaze as he handed her the

glass. Instead he turned to stare at the fragments of colored glass littered across the floor next to the bed.

"Something happened, didn't it?" she prodded, popping four of the white pills in her mouth and washing them down with several long swallows of cold water.

"Yes . . . no . . . shit, I don't now, Mary," he said helplessly, turning to look at her. "I'm not sure. I mean, we drank a couple of bottles of wine and I wasn't exactly as sober as a judge. You know what the doctor told me; low blood pressure can cause hallucinations. Hell, I was running around a cemetery in the middle of the stinking night chasing shadows . . ."

He stopped and shook his head.

"What happened?" she asked more gently, her voice low and concerned.

Quietly and carefully Vince told her about the open crypt door, the piercing red eyes and his panicked flight. He was embarrassed to hear his own voice describing what now seemed to be nothing more than a case of nerves and an overactive imagination.

"Why don't we get some sleep?" he finished. "Maybe we'll be able to put it all in perspective in the morning."

"I've got to take a shower," she sighed, feeling light headed, even though the pain was subsiding as the aspirin took effect.

Vince sat in a chair, slowly tugging off his muddy shoes, his mind retracing his bizarre experience in the cemetery. Had he seen something in the crypt? Had there *really* been two gleaming crimson eyes, cold and hard, staring at him from within that fetid tomb? Did something really chase him back to the cottage?

God, it was maddening.

It's crazy, Cassidy. Crazy.

He heard the shower start and imagined Mary, naked and statuesque, stepping under the warm spray of water. He could see her skin beading with moisture, the cascade flowing over her breasts . . .

Despite all that had happened, he felt a familiar stirring in his groin.

Remembering their early morning meeting with Bedlow, Vince picked up the small travel clock he had taken from his luggage and setting it to the time on his wrist watch—was it only ten o'clock?—he placed it on the nightstand.

Finished undressing, he studied his skinned leg. There was a nasty, puffy bruise on his skin and a small cut, but no real damage. He sat and applied the peroxide to it and then covered it with a Band-Aid.

"Great," he mumbled to himself. "At this rate, we'll have to buy bandages by the case."

Mary returned, a large bath towel wrapped around her. She looked pale, but appeared not to be suffering too many side effects from her fall.

Actually, she was feeling perfectly fine and it bothered her. She had had less serious bumps and bruises which had caused her much more trouble. She felt as if she hadn't even banged her head at all, let alone been knocked unconscious.

Vince smiled at her. "You look wonderful. You feel alright?"

She nodded, dropping the towel from around her and stepped naked to the bed. She slid between the sheets and smiled at him.

"I think I need to be comforted."

Vince turned off the overhead light and walked carefully back to the bed, climbing in next to Mary to avoid the broken glass on the opposite side.

Wordlessly, they clung together in the dark, their passions rising. He slid his hand between her legs, seeking the damp warmth of her femininity. Her eager tongue touched his neck, caressed his chest as her hands manipulated his erection.

He rolled atop her. She moaned as he entered her. They began moving together in the ancient ritual of loving and sharing.

It had been a long time since they had really "made love." His apprehensions and frustrations about work and her anxieties about him and her school, had smothered and blunted their passions. When they did attempt to find solace in each other's arms it had more often than not ended in apologies muttered in the dark and even greater frustrations. Tonight, however, their passions were strong, their lusts an almost unquenchable hunger.

They reached orgasm as one, writhing and crying out as their bodies exploded with long-suppressed ardor. When the spasms had passed, when normally they would have disengaged, they both felt the need and desire sweep over them again. Almost immediately, they began again. If anything, they coupled with even more energy and vigor than the first time. Again they peaked simultaneously, gasping and grasping . . .

. . and again, they were consumed with an undiminished fire and an unbridled lust.

"No more, Vince," Mary panted, after their third climax. She pushed him off her. "What's wrong with us?"

Vince lay next to her, gulping breaths. "Pretty amazing. My God, I could do it again." He could feel his erection, hard and swollen, throbbing between his legs.

"Vince," Mary said, still panting, an edge of alarm in her voice, "I still want you. I want you like crazy."

In spite of the irrationality of it and knowing it was insane, impossible, they could not control their carnal needs and, like mating beasts, they coupled for a fourth time.

Wrapped in the throes of passion, their bodies overriding their intellects, they were unaware of the dark shadow spreading over their tangled bed, shrouding them in an impenetrable blackness.

Nor were they aware of the two shiny red eyes that eagerly watched them copulate from outside the window which overlooked the still, night-silenced cemetery.

THREE

Her long bony fingers, porcelain white and wrinkled with age, rested lightly on the three-legged pointer as it glided smoothly over the polished surface of the Ouija board. It would stop first at one letter and then at another, spelling out words, answers really, to her questions.

Agnes Hardwick sat very still in the straightbacked chair and watched the pointer move. As it landed on each successive letter, she spoke it aloud so it could be captured by the small voice-activated tape recorder resting on the opposite side of the table.

As a rule, she could remember the content of messages without referring to the recording; however, Agnes was a practical, pragmatic woman and she knew at her age—almost 80—she could not always depend on her memory.

The pointer stopped and she removed her fingers form it, a curious expression on her face.

"What's all this about?" she asked aloud, her words echoing off the bare walls of the small, round room.

"There are those who need your aid," she said, repeating the message to herself and the still operating recorder. "Who could possibly need help from an old woman like me?"

Agnes was a retired school teacher. She had spent 45 years in the Denver Public School system trying to instill in her students some sense of history. By and large it had been a fruitless task, but every year, for all those years, there had always been one or two, and occasionally more, students who actually understood what she was attempting to impart. She had regretted none of her time spent with those children. Even if they didn't always grasp the significance of the Dark Ages or the Renaissance, they generally responded to her compassion, warmth and understanding. How many times had she counciled a boy whose girl had jilted him or a girl who had been ostracized by her "clique" because she was dating the wrong boy? How many times had one of those children come to her, crying over the death of a parent of classmate? How many pregnant girls had she comforted and how many frightened fathers-to-be had she advised?

And, besides, she had often thought, having had no children of my own, all of those boys and girls had become my extended family

Agnes had been married to Franklin Hardwick, an engineer, for 38 years. He had been more than a husband, he had been a soulmate and friend and had never despaired having wed her, even though she was unable to have children. He had been dead now for 20 years, but still the memory of him would often sweep her with bittersweet feelings and occasional tears.

It had actually been Franklin who had introduced her to the Ouija board and its spiritual guides. Naturally, Agnes had scoffed and thought him daft for dabbling with such an obviously ridiculous device. In fact, she had refused to even sit with him when he would stay up late at night and ask the board questions. She believed it was a waste of time.

When he had finally convinced her at least try it, she had offered every possible explanation for the shrewdly accurate responses the board gave her husband's questions.

It was just his subconscious mind answering; it was like a horoscope, so general it could be interpreted a dozen different ways; it was only a cheap parlor game and unworthy of serious attention.

Then there came a night when the board told a doubting Agnes Hardwick that there was a great evil looming in her future. Naturally she dismissed it as the fabrication of an overactive imagination. In fact, when the gunman entered her classroom the next day waving a pistol, telling her he would kill her and all of the students if his demands weren't met, the Ouija board's prediction was the furthest thing from her mind.

Only after the man had been coaxed out of the building by patient police officers and carted away to the psychiatric ward at Denver General Hospital, and anxious parents had gathered their frightened children, did Agnes remember the Ouija's prophecy.

And when she had remembered it, she had almost collapsed. From that point on, she was a believer.

She never became obsessed with the Ouija. Franklin had cautioned her that it could become obsessive and consequently dangerous. Neither of them being particularly religious, although neither were atheists, they did not suffer from the accute guilt church-goers experienced when confronted with the wonders of the Ouija. They were prudent in the use of their board and only consulted it once or twice a week. Sometimes a month or more would pass when neither of them chose to sit down to question its spirits.

They had never mentioned their interest in the Ouija to anyone. Both were respected members of the community, active in local politics and well thought of by their friends and neighbors. It was not that either of them was ashamed of their pursuit, but people are often frightened of things they cannot understand or explain. Neither Franklin nor Agnes saw any reason to mention their interest to anyone and stir up sentiments best left undisturbed. The Ouija board was often cast into that vague, nebulous realm of mysticism, New Age religion or even Satanism. Why open a can of worms needlessly?

Since her husband's death, Agnes had shared her interest with one other person, Joshua Ortega. Like her, he was well into his seventies and a former teacher. They had met a few years after Franklin's death at a regular meeting of the neighborhood's elderly. Normally Agnes had avoided such get-togethers, believing a person was only as old as they felt and had not wanted to be around a lot of doting old fools recounting their ailments and lamenting their faded lives.

However, much to her surprise, the group was a lively, active bunch who enjoyed discussing politics and current affairs and liked playing bridge. It was at the bridge table that she had met Joshua. By chance they had been partnered and, through his shrewd bidding, they had taken the evening's prize, a dinner for two at a local restaurant.

Naturally, he had insisted that she accompany him to the restaurant and over plates of pasta they had become fast friends.

Besides, he was a dapper, well-educated man who could discuss complex subjects with insight and understanding. He was tolerant and kind and even-tempered.

Joshua had only recently returned to Denver after having taught high school in Los Angeles for the better part of four decades, he had explained. His five children were all in California and his wife was dead. His retirement was secure and, against his children's wishes, he had decided to return to his old neighborhood.

Over the ensuing months, Joshua and Agnes had become close, accompanying each other to dinner once or twice a week and regularly entering bridge tournaments at the Senior Center.

On one evening, when Joshua had asked Agnes if they could simply sit and talk—it turned out to be the anniversary of his wife's death—she invited him over for dinner.

She let him talk at length about his wife and their happy years together. At some point the conversation turned to her relationship with Franklin and quite accidently she mentioned the Ouija board.

Joshua had studied her for several minutes.

"Do you really believe in it?" he had asked.

Never one to be glib, she looked at him evenly and nodded. "Yes." She expected him to express some concern for her soul or some other such dogma, but much to her surprise, his response was quite unexpected.

"So do I, more or less," he said, smiling over the rim of his coffee cup. "In fact, I have used one on a few occasions. I don't particularly care to spend much time with them, though. There are too many other interesting phenomenon to explore. But I'm glad you aren't the stuffy, narrow-minded school teacher of the popular stereotype."

"What do you mean by 'other interesting phenomenon?' " she had wanted to know, curious about this new facet to Joshua's character.

He had smiled. "While I was in college, lo those many years ago, I took a course in ancient beliefs. The professor, quite an eccentric fellow, discussed the various religious beliefs not directly affliated with Christianity, Judaism, Moslem, Hindu or Buddist religions. It was quite fascinating and it led me to do a lot of reading and research into all manner of arcane religions and beliefs."

"Did your wife share your interest?" Agnes had asked.

A frown had crossed Joshua's face and Agnes feared she had asked an embarrassing question.

"No," he responded flatly. "She was a good Catholic and thought I was being disrespectful of the Church. I never mentioned my research to her after one very nasty argument. In time, she thought I had forgotten all about it and it was never a problem between us again."

When he had finished speaking, Agnes sensed relief in her friend, as if telling her his secret had had the same effect as entering the confessional.

"Do you still study and research?"

He again smiled. "Oh, yes. I have many books and papers on the subject. It is now a hobby. I enjoy researching the mania and myths to which people have succumbed."

They had talked well past midnight and this new wrinkle in their relationship had drawn them closer together. Joshua never asked to see her Ouija board and she never offered. It was enough that they shared one another's secret.

Franklin had explained to Agnes when she first became serious about the board, that each one was supposedly governed by a group of select guides or spirits, whatever a person chose to call them. Long before Agnes had joined Franklin in his interest in the spiritualism of the Ouija, he had constructed his own board in their basement. It was finely crafted table, with each individual letter and number made of light, golden oak, inlaid into a dark oak surface.

It was at this table, housed in the small turret room of the house she and Franklin had purchased years before, that Agnes now sat, puzzling over tonight's message.

"What do you think, Solomon," she asked the gray and white Persian cat curled up on a pillow near her feet. "Who would need my help? Shall we try it again?"

Solomon looked at her with disinterest and turned away to clean his paws.

"You're a big help, you furry cretin," she gently scolded.

Agnes studied the board for several more minutes. She was tired and it was late, very near midnight; however, she knew she would never sleep if she did not at least attempt to discover the meaning of the message. Besides, it was the best time of the night to run the board. It was quiet and there would be no distractions to drag her away.

Again, she positioned the planchet and rested her fingers lightly on its smooth surface.

"Tell me more about this aid I am asked to render. To whom can I be of assistance?" Her question hung in the air for several seconds and then the pointer trembled and began to move.

"T-H-E-Y A-R-E I-N D-A-N-G-E-R," she spoke, as the planchet darted about the board. "T-H-E-Y A-R-E S-T-R-A-N-G-E-R-S T-O Y-O-U. T-H-E-Y N-E-E-D Y-O-U."

"How can *I* help them?" she asked, a little impatiently. It sometimes irritated her when the board played cryptic games.

Again, the pointer darted over the table's surface. "E-V-I-L I-S A-L-L A-R-O-U-N-D T-H-E-M. Y-O-U H-A-V-E T-H-E W-A-Y T-O A-I-D T-H-E-M. T-H-R-O-U-G-H U-S."

"Who are they?"

"T-H-E-Y W-I-L-L B-E-C-O-M-E K-N-O-W-N T-O Y-O-U."

The planchet then dropped to the bottom of the board, where "Goodbye" was skillfully inlaid in the wood and Agnes knew the session was over. She reached across the table and turned off the recorder.

"Very mysterious, Solomon," she said getting slowly to her feet, her arthritis flaring painfully through her knees. "And very curious. Who on earth could an old woman with bad joints and a delicate stomach help? Goodness, it's all very odd. Come on, Solomon. I suppose everything will be explained in due course. It always is. Still, I don't like messages like that. They worry me."

She moved slowly to the door and, opening it, called to Solomon, who immediately leaped off the pillow and pranced airily out of the room and down the steep staircase. Agnes, turning off the light and closing the door, followed the cat, at a somewhat slower pace.

When she reached the kitchen at the base of the stairs, Agnes stepped over to the counter and opened a bottle of Bufferin. Taking three of the pills, she filled a glass with water and sat down at the small kitchen table. Solomon wandered aimlessly around the room, unusually restless.

"You feel it, too, don't you?" Agnes said to the cat. "Something unsettling is happening and, like it or not, I'm being drawn into it. I think I'll call Joshua in the morning, maybe he'll tell me I'm just a foolish old lady and I can be shed of this bad feeling."

As Agnes left the kitchen intent on going to bed and attempting to sleep, Solomon suddenly hissed and spit. Agnes whirled and looked at the cat. He was in the middle of the kitchen, his back arched, fur standing on end and his teeth bared. He glared at the window overlooking her small backyard.

Agnes followed his gaze, but the two red, hungry eyes, which had watched so closely, had already vanished into the darkness.

FOUR

The jangling of the alarm brought Vince Cassidy instantly out of a shallow, restless sleep. He reached across Mary's form, slapping at the clock twice before hitting the plunger and turning it off.

Five o'clock in the morning. There was just a trace of faint light from the east leaking into the bedroom. It was too damned early to get up, he decided. Of course, Oscar Bedlow would be there at six and he certainly wouldn't be pleased to find his new caretaker grabbing an extra forty winks.

He threw back the covers and swung his legs off the bed, groaning from the painful ache in his groin. Gingerly, his fingers probed the raw flesh and he winced, shaking his head.

Images of the previous night flooded back. How many times had they done it. Five? Six? For Vince it had become something other than love-making and something more akin to the mindless rutting of a sex-starved beast.

It had frightened both of them.

"Come on, kiddo," he said to Mary, shaking her lightly. "Time to get out of the rack." She murmured something unintelligible and rolled away from him. He shook her a second time and her eyes came slowly open.

"Already?" she whined.

"Yeah, 'fraid so."

Mary hoisted herself up on her elbows and looked around the room, trying to place her surroundings. Her eyes were puffy and her lips bruised. She rolled on her side and gingerly touched her breasts.

"What happened to us last night, Vince?" she asked.

"That's a very big question, Babe. I don't know. I suppose there's some Freudian explanation. I sure wish I knew what it was." He got to his feet, expecting to feel at least some stiffness in his barked skin. It felt fine. He bent over and peeled off the bandage.

"I'll be damned," he breathed.

"What?" Mary asked, sliding out of the bed.

"Look at my leg. Not a damned mark." She bent over and looked at the spot on his shin still outlined by the adhesive from the bandage. There was no bruise nor any trace of a cut.

"That's amazing, Vince."

"Hell, that's frightening. I've never been a fast healer. You remember when I cut my hand on that piece of glass last year? It took weeks to heal. This is weird."

"Well, I don't know what to tell you," she said, straightening.

"Let me see your forehead," he said, reaching for the bandage just below her hairline.

She brushed his hand aside. "I'll do it. You're liable to take off my hide." Carefully Mary peeled off the Band-Aid. "Well?"

Vince's eyes opened wide. "Gone. Not a mark."

Mary stepped stiffly across to the vanity mirror and studied her reflected face. "I don't believe it. How could we both heal so quickly?"

"Beats the hell out of me. We'll have to think about it.

Right now we've got to get dressed and ready for the arrival of the infamous Mr. Bedlow."

They trooped into the bathroom, shared a quick shower and returned to the bedroom to dress. Vince pulled on a flannel shirt and a pair of blue jeans, wincing as he tugged the fly closed and felt a twinge of pain in his groin. Mary sat naked before the vanity mirror applying her make-up.

"I'll go start some breakfast," he told her, leaving the room.

When he was gone, she set aside the soft brush and looked at herself in the mirror.

"Mary, you are one scared broad. If you can't admit it to him, you'd better admit it to yourself." She didn't want to tell Vince how frightened she felt, for fear he would simply walk out on the job.

Maybe they both *had* hallucinated the night before. She glanced at the undamaged bedroom door. It certainly didn't show any signs of having been ripped apart by some clawed monster. Maybe it was just being around a cemetery. All their childhood fears and terrors were suddenly being dragged out of the dark, secret corners of their minds. How many movies had she watched while growing up, which featured spectral creatures emerging from graves? How many video massacres had she screamed her way through? How many nights had she awakened screaming after a particularly grisly horror film had planted dark seeds in her mind?

"So how come we boffed like bunnies?" she asked her reflection. That had been no hallucination. Her legs felt sprung and her vagina was sore and raw. Sex with Vince was always good, but last night had turned just a little ugly.

Mary shivered. The room was cool and there she was sitting around in the buff. She pushed the confusing thoughts out of her mind, hastily finished applying her make-up and raced around the room gathering her clothes.

When she entered the kitchen, wearing a pair of soft

gray corduroy pants and a bulky knit sweater, Vince smiled at her.

"Coffee?"

"Please."

They ate at the small table, sipping their coffee and eating scrambled eggs and toast. Neither of them had much of an appetite.

"I imagine Bedlow will be pissed when I tell him about the vandalism at that crypt. I should have called him right away," Vince said, pushing aside his half-empty plate.

"Maybe not. After all you don't have to tell him you were out there. You can just 'discover' it this morning when we make the rounds," Mary suggested.

He frowned and nodded. "True. Although I hate to lie to him on my first day . . ."

The claxon blare of a horn cut Vince off. He glanced at this wrist watch. "Six on the nose. I'll go open the gates."

Bedlow's slate gray Cadillac sat in the driveway, its gaunt driver watching Vince closely as he unlocked and pushed open the gates. Bedlow drove through and parked near the cottage. Vince walked over to his employer as the man climbed out of the big car.

"Aren't you forgetting something?" Bedlow called as Vince approached.

"What?"

"The gates," the man said impatiently. "You didn't lock the gates."

Feeling like a chastised child, Vince returned to the entrance, pushed the gates together and secured them with the chain and lock.

"That's very important to remember, Vince," Bedlow told him as he walked back toward the cottage. "Always keep the gates locked."

"I won't forget again," Vince promised, hiding his irritation.

"Is Ms. Renata joining us?"

"I'm coming," Marry called from the door, pulling on a light jacket as she hurried out of the cottage.

"Good," Bedlow smiled, showing those too-perfect, oversized teeth. "Shall we start?"

Vince nodded.

"Let's begin by walking the fence all the way around the grounds." Without a further word, Bedlow started off at a brisk pace, following a well worn path along the inside of the stone-based iron fence. He pointed out things to watch for; bent bars, tracks in the dirt, or mud on this occasion, crushed shrubbery.

"Anything suspicious," he concluded. He turned to Mary. "And how was your first night with us?"

She blushed. "Oh, interesting. A little unsettling."

"Yes, I imagine it is. A new house, strange surroundings. You'll get used to it. Really, there isn't any place more restful than a cemetery, don't you agree?" He looked at her expectantly.

"Ah, sure. Yeah, absolutely." Mary felt like a fool, but if Bedlow thought she was, he gave no indication. He simply smiled approvingly and kept marching along the fence line.

It was two miles around the park and the walk gave Vince a chance to really see the cemetery for the first time. There was row upon row of headstones, uniformly laid out neatly and geometrically. Mixed in among the usual graves was what he thought to be an inordinate number of mausoleums and crypts, ranging in size from small, only large enough for a single casket, to huge, amply suited for holding several generations of a family.

A number of the headstones were unusual in design and ornamentation. Several had elaborately carved stone figures atop them and others sported meticulously chiseled scrolls and designs decorating the granite or marble. Some were in odd shapes for tombstones. Vince spied a pyramid over one grave and a round, black granite stone ball over another. There were several grave markers which were more like modern art than headstones.

One thing became very clear to him as he studied the cemetery. The people buried or entombed here seemed all to have had both enormous egos, a need to be remembered, and the money to translate their egotism into unique, ostentacious and expensive resting places for their mouldering bones.

He found it quite unsettling.

"How many graves are there?" Mary asked, as they neared the cottage, almost finished with the circuit of the grounds.

"Six thousand, eight hundred and twenty-nine," Bedlow replied without pausing to consider. "Filled to capacity. In fact, there hasn't been a burial here for almost twenty years."

Vince whistled softly. "If you don't mind my asking, where does the money come from to maintain the grounds?"

Bedlow smiled again, seemingly enjoying the opportunity to answer their questions and display his knowledge. "When the cemetery was founded in 1887, it was determined that no one would be buried here without providing funds for the upkeep of their grave. As a result, there is no potter's field, but there is a large endowment in the bank which generates more than enough interest to maintain Mansfield quite nicely."

They had reached the cottage and paused by Bedlow's Cadillac.

"Would you like some coffee, Mr. Bedlow?" Mary asked.

His gaunt face frowned briefly and then he politely declined. "No. No time. Now we must walk the various roads cutting through the cemetery and inspect the graves."

Vince felt his stomach tighten. They'd soon be at the vandalized crypt. He dreaded Bedlow's reaction when he saw the open door and, God only knew, what kind of damage to the occupants.

"Shall we go?" Bedlow asked impatiently. Not waiting for their answer, he marched briskly off down the gravelled road which passed the crypt Vince had visited the previous night.

Bedlow glanced constantly from side to side, his emotionless eyes scanning the graves and tombs. As they neared the crypt, Vince stared at it. The iron-banded door was closed and, from where he was, the lock appeared to be in place. When they reached it, he veered off the road and approached it, his heart pounding.

"Is something wrong, Mr. Cassidy?" Bedlow asked, stopping.

Vince stood before the door. The weathered old lock was unmarked and undamaged. Swallowing a lump in his throat, he looked through the small barred window. Inside there were two dust covered, stone vaults, their heavy lids firmly in place. A thick layer of undisturbed dust covered everything inside.

"I say, Mr. Cassidy," Bedlow called again, his voice edged with impatience. "Is there something wrong?"

Vince turned. "Uh, no . . . no. Everything seems fine. Sorry, I just wanted to make sure."

"Yes, well, that's very good, but there's a lot of ground to cover and we haven't a lot of time. Shall we be off?"

Vince nodded and started back toward the road. He stopped and looked at the two stone figures sitting at either corner of the crypt's roof. He could feel the blood drain from his face when he saw, not toothsome gargoyles, but small, serene angels, one holding a harp and the other a flute. Not believing his eyes, he dashed along the side of the crypt and studied the two figures on the back of the roof. They were identical to the ones on the front.

Vince stared at the effigies for several moments. A chill passed down his spine and his flesh suddenly felt icy.

Where is that fucking little demon?

"Vince," Mary yelled nervously. "Come on."

He shook his head in confusion and hurried back to the

road where Mary stood waiting for him. Bedlow was already twenty yards ahead.

"You look like you've just seen your own ghost, Vince. What's wrong?"

He quickly told her about the undamaged lock and the missing gargoyle.

"Vince," she whispered, grabbing his arm. "Whatever happened to us last night was just . . . some kind of mass hallucination. Maybe your blood pressure was wierding out on you and maybe I *was* dreaming, like you said. Maybe I tripped, banged my head and dreamed everything."

She didn't sound too convincing and look on her face told Vince that she knew it, too.

"Come on," he said, moving faster. "We'd better catch up with Bedlow before he has a fit."

"Yeah," Mary muttered. "He parades around this place like a goosestepping Nazi general."

They caught up with Bedlow in another few minutes. He said nothing, but continued to glance to his left and right, looking for anything unusual.

As they topped a rise at about the center of the cemetery grounds, Mary caught sight of something half way down one of the even rows of headstones.

"Look," she cried, pointing. Bedlow and Vince stopped and stared to where her extended finger indicated.

"Vandals!" Bedlow snapped, much too hastily Vince thought. He couldn't even tell exactly what was out of order.

Bedlow turned and moved quickly down the row, Vince and Mary close behind. When they caught up with him, Mary gasped and Vince groaned.

A grave was opened, the freshly turned dirt flung several yards in every direction. An old, rotting casket jutted out of the hole, its lid fairly ripped off its rusty hinges and the mouldy, stained interior empty.

"*This* is what we guard against, Mr. Cassidy." Bedlow's voice was filled with recrimination and accusation.

"Who would do something like this?" Mary asked, studying the headstone over the defiled grave.

"I have no idea, Ms. Renata. It is enough that they do it!"

"Boris Wainwright," Mary read the chiseled words on the stone. "Born, 1841. Died 1898. He's been buried nearly a century . . ."

"Yes. Yes. Yes," Bedlow snarled. "Mr. Wainwright was one of the founders of Mansfield. Not a rich man, but well off enough to afford a place here.

"Mr. Cassidy. Return to the cottage and bring a shovel. We must rebury the casket immediately."

"Empty?" Vince could not fathom the man's logic.

"Yes! Now hurry."

Realizing Bedlow was not to be quibbled with, Vince wheeled and raced quickly back to the cottage. A storage area built next to the cottage contained an assortment of shovels and spades. He grabbed one and returned to the open grave.

"Now, Mr. Cassidy," Bedlow ordered sternly. "Please place the casket back in the hole properly, close the lid and cover it."

Reluctantly, Vince dropped into the hole and wrestled the oblong box into position. The wood was soggy and pieces of it crumbled at his touch. As he bent to close the lid, he could smell the cloying, foul odor permeating the rotted material lining the casket. It made him nauseous and he fought to keep from vomiting.

The lid closed, Vince stood carefully on the box and hoisted himself out of the hole. He picked up the shovel and, as Bedlow watched him with those cold, expressionless eyes, he began scooping and scraping dirt into the hole. It quickly became apparent that the grave robbers had scattered the dirt too far and wide for enough to be easily retrieved to refill the hole.

"It will be necessary for you to use your truck to haul a load of dirt up here to finish filling the hole. You will find an ample supply of earth piled behind the cottage. Please proceed quickly.'' Bedlow spoke to him with the arrogant, patronizing tone of someone instructing a child.

''You want it done right now?'' Vince asked, already knowing the answer.

''Yes. I will wait here for you to return. I believe you will find a wheelbarrow in the storage shed.'' With that Bedlow leaned against a tombstone, crossed his arms and began his wait.

''I'll help you load the dirt, Vince,'' Mary offered, only too glad to be away from Bedlow.

''He's a real charmer,'' Vince groaned, as they walked back to the cottage.

''Yeah, a truly delightful guy. Have you noticed anything odd about this cemetery?''

He stopped and turned to look at her. ''Are you kidding? I haven't noticed anything that isn't odd.''

Mary blushed. ''Okay, you're right. But, when we were walking around the fence, I didn't see one cross. Not one. There were angels, cherubs and all that sort of thing, but no crosses, no stars of David, nothing.''

Vince thought about that for a few seconds. ''You're right, I haven't seen any either.''

They resumed walking. ''And something else,'' he said. ''That grave back there. Whoever dug it up didn't use a shovel. There were no signs of a shovel blade in the ground. None.'' He considered his next statement carefully, before he spoke. ''In fact, it doesn't look like Wainwright's grave was dug up at all. It looks like it exploded. Like the ground just blew open.''

Mary paled and fell silent.

FIVE

Vince emptied the wheelbarrow for the last time and, using the blade of the shovel, tamped down the dirt on the grave.He was sweating under the warming morning sun and was filthy from loading and unloading the dirt. He had toiled under the watchful eye of Oscar Bedlow, who made no attempt to help nor spoke to him while he worked. Mary sat quietly in the cab of the truck, avoiding conversation with Bedlow.

Burying, or rather reburying, the ancient, and now empty casket gave Vince time to mull over the bizarre and inexplicable events of the last 24 hours. He couldn't rationalize any satisfactory answers and there appeared to be no logical reasons for what he and Mary had experienced. And what exactly *had* they experienced? Hallucinations? Hysteria? Delusions?

Was his nightmare confrontation at the crypt only a manifestation of his body's chemical imbalance? A side effect of his medical problem? It was almost comforting to believe that; certainly better than accepting his sensory memories. The crypt door had been opened, hadn't it? There had been something inside that foul, silent tomb, hadn't there? And something had pursued him, hadn't it?

Did Mary only hallucinate the thing at the bedroom door? Were the claws slashing the wood, trying to get at her, only a product of a feverish mind? Where the muddy marks on her leg just the result of unpacking rain and dirt splattered boxes and not evidence of probing, lusting fingers?

And what about the cuts on Mary's head and his leg? They'd been real enough last night. He'd touched the blood, felt its oily stickiness between his fingers, smelled its coppery scent. Was that too only an illusion?

Was their fevered sexual frenzy just an explosive response to the tension and stress of the last few months? Had they simply let their animal needs overpower their humanity?

Or was it the cemetery? Was their spark of life amid the lifeless mouldering aftermath of death somehow affecting their behavior at some primitive, sub-conscious level?

Shit, Cassidy, you're an archaeologist, not a psychiatrist. Give it a rest.

Now he was covering an act of sick vandalism that wasn't vandalism. The more he thought about it, the more convinced Vince became that no *one* had dug up the grave. While he was throwing dirt back into the hole, he had reconfirmed his earlier suspicions: There were no shovel marks on the walls of the grave, no footprints in the clumps of freshly turned earth, in fact, no signs of anyone having been around the grave at all.

Forget it, Sherlock. Do the work, take the money and keep your mouth shut.

He did welcome the exertion. It had been a long time since he had done any real physical labor, not since the dig six months ago. The feel of his muscles flexing and stretching invigorated him. Even the salty sweat covering his face and body gave him a sense of having done something worthwhile.

He almost laughed. Was reburying an empty casket a worthwhile pursuit?

"Very good, Mr. Cassidy," commented Bedlow, leaning nonchalantly against a tombstone, as Vince finished. "Shall we complete our rounds?"

Vince sighed, but nodded. "Sure."

May climbed out of the truck and joined them as they continued walking up and down the graveled lanes cutting through the acres of cold stone and the many eerie and silent mausoleums. Vince was relieved when they had finished the tour without finding more desecrated graves or violated crypts.

At the cottage, Mary bid Bedlow goodbye and went inside.

"That, Mr. Cassidy," Bedlow told him when they had reached the Cadillac, "constitutes your primary responsibilities. Of course, you must be vigilant at all times. There are always those who seek to destroy and vandalize. However, the morning tour is the most important facet of your work."

"Should I tell you if I find another grave like Wainwright's?"

Bedlow nodded. "Absolutely. And then proceed just as you did this morning. Reburial of the casket is crucial."

Vince thought about it for a minute. "Who would want those old bones, Mr. Bedlow?"

The gaunt, skull-faced man shrugged. "I have no idea." His tone didn't convince Vince.

"Does this happen often? I get the impression it's a common occurance. I mean, you weren't exactly surprised this morning." Vince tried hard to keep from sounding confrontational or challenging.

"It happens occasionally, Mr. Cassidy. It is unfortunate, but it happens."

"What should I do if I catch one of these sick bastards digging up a grave?" Vince asked.

Bedlow smiled humorlessly. "I doubt you will. No one ever has."

"But if I do?"

"Follow procedures," was all the older man would tell him, something dark crossing his already stark contenance.

Bedlow started to climb into his car and then paused and fished his billfold out of his pants pocket. He pulled out two crisp hundred dollar bills and thrust them at Vince.

"Your bonus for this morning's work. You weren't hired for physical labor and you should be compensated for your efforts."

Vince accepted the bills with unabashed surprise. Before he could thank his generous benefactor, the man was in his car, firing up the engine. Vince shoved the money into his pocket and hurried quickly to unlock the gates.

As Bedlow started driving the Cadillac out of the cemetery, he stopped and motioned to Vince.

"Don't forget, Mr. Cassidy," the man said, as his window lowered. "The full moon is very near. There will be a tour arriving the night of the full moon. Be sure to open the gates."

"I won't forget," Vince answered, an odd chill creeping down his spine.

After Bedlow left and the twin iron barriers were once again secured against the outside world, he joined Mary in the cottage kitchen where she sat quietly sipping a cup of coffee.

"Sucker's pretty free with his money," Vince said pouring himself a cup of the rich brew and plopping down in the chair opposite Mary. He pulled the money out of his pocket and handed it to her.

"Vince," she said, frowning, her eyes studying the coffee in her cup, ignoring the money. "Doesn't *everything* around here strike you as pretty weird? All the shit last night, which may have just been an anomaly, and that grave this morning?"

He reached across the table and covered her hand with one of his, not surprised to feel it tremble. "It's a hell of a lot more than weird."

Mary looked up at him, her dark eyes round and frightened. "Vince, I'm scared. I'm afraid to . . . spend another night with you, here . . I . . ."

"I know, Babe. It's spooky. I just feel like . . . Well, hell, what else have we got right now? If we can stick it out a month or two, we'll have enough of a stake to move on." He was torn between his concern for Mary and his sense of desperation. He loved her, wanted to spend the rest of his life with her, but he'd never been able to cope with being broke, unemployed, unproductive. At least here, at Mansfield, there was something.

Mary smiled. "You're right. Anyway, this afternoon, I want to take the truck and go open a savings account with the three grand and then I'd like to go down to the university campus and get set up for classes."

"Good idea," Vince said, meaning it. If she got away from the cemetery for awhile, maybe she'd feel better. "I'll go get the truck and bring it back down here. I want to clean out the bed."

They talked for a time about Mary's courses and her excitement about attending a new school, with new professors and the possibilities for meeting new friends. It brightened Mary's flagging spirits.

Vince sauntered up the lane to retrieve his truck and cast a suspicious eye on the freshly covered grave. Why the hell did Bedlow insist on reburying the casket? The man had been more concerned about getting that rotting box back into the ground than the missing bones. It was very curious and not just a little disconcerting.

He drove the Toyota to the back of the cottage and scooped the unneeded dirt back onto the mound piled discreetly behind a huge lilac bush. After sweeping out the bed, he found a garden hose in the storage shed and attached it to a faucet at the back of the house, intent on washing the truck's bed. As he dragged the hose to the truck he heard a voice calling to him. Startled he looked around.

"Hey, buddy, over here," the voice said. Vince looked

at the fence, spying a grizzled old man in a ratty, threadbare sports jacket and a pair of baggy, grease-stained pants. The man had an unkempt salt and pepper beard and wispy, uncombed gray hair.

Assuming the man was a panhandler, Vince tried to ignore him and continued to maneuver the hose around the back of the truck.

"Hey, asshole," snapped the old man impatiently. "I'm talkin' to ya."

"What do you want," Vince asked, just as impatiently, trying not to look at the man.

"A couple of minutes of your time." The old man was leaning against the iron spikes of the fence, his hands thrust into the pockets of his soiled jacket.

Reluctantly, Vince dropped the hose and walked slowly over to the fence, expecting to get hit for loose change. He dug into his pocket and fished out a few coins.

"Look, I've got a little over a buck in change. That's all," he told the old man.

"I don't want your stinkin' money," the man snapped indignantly. "I can provide okay for myself. I got somethin' fer you though."

Slipping the coins back in his pocket, Vince eyed the man closely. "Yeah? And what would that be?"

"A warnin', pal."

Vince almost laughed. "What are you talking about?"

"You the new caretaker?" The old man squinted in the bright sunlight.

"Yeah."

"Then you'd better know this place is bad. Real bad."

"What place? The cemetery?" Vince sounded much more cavalier than he felt. Little alarm bells were going off in his head and they made him uneasy.

" 'Course the cemetery. What the hell ya think I'm talkin' about? Jesus, boy, don't play dumb with me." The old man glared at Vince, his mouth screwed up into a hard line. "Ya think I'd hang around a place like this fer my goddamn health?"

"So what about this place?" Vince asked, in spite of himself.

"It's *evil,* boy. If ya don't know that, then ya're dumber than ya look. What'd they give ya to take the job? Money? Probably a bundle of it." The man spat the words in disgust.

"What the hell do you care? Look, I don't have time to waste bullshitting with you . . ."

"You're scared," the old man said flatly. "You've already seen somethin', haven't you? You've already been touched by that bitch!"

"Don't talk in riddles . . ."

"Can I take the truck now?" Mary's voice caused Vince to turn. She stood at the corner of the cottage, looking lovely in the light blue skirt and white blouse, the sun framing her, setting her black hair ablaze.

"Uh, yeah, sure," he answered.

"What are you doing over there?" she asked, walking toward him.

"Just talking to this guy."

"What guy?"

Vince looked around. The old man was gone. He strained to look up and down the sidewalk. It was empty.

He was genuinely confused. "There was a guy here just a second ago. Strange old man," he told her.

She frowned. "I didn't see anyone. Where'd he go?"

"I don't know."

"What'd he want?" she asked, opening the truck's door.

Vince thought a second. "Just a panhandler," he lied. Why upset her? She was already nervous enough about this place without giving her something else to worry about.

Mary smiled and tossed her hair in the warm sunlight. "Well, if you'll unlock the gates, I'll go get our financial affairs in order and see about getting set up at school. I'll probably be gone all afternoon. Will that be okay?''

''Sure. I think I'll relax and mellow out.'' Vince gave her a kiss and then walked around to the drive and proceeded to the gates.

After Mary left, he returned to the cottage, showered again and changed into fresh clothes. After a light lunch consisting of a ham sandwich and a couple of bottles of beer, he decided to go have another look at the crypt he had visited the night before.

Walking up the gravel lane, he was aware of the silence of the cemetery. It was perfectly still. There wasn't so much as a squirrel dashing about searching for food. No birds hopped about seeking fat worms or juicy seeds. It was perfectly still. Abnormally so, Vince thought.

He reached the crypt and again inspected the angel-that-should-have-been-a-gargoyle and then again peered into the cold, bleak interior. The two vaults inside looked as if they hadn't been touched in a century. He glanced at the date carved above the sealed door. The finely chisled numerals read *1909. Jonathan and Eva Cleary*.

Had they died the same year? Vince wondered.

He stood, staring into the tomb, watching dust motes drift in the soft light and suddenly decided he *had* been hallucinating the night before. Nothing, not a dog nor a rodent nor a human had been inside there for a very long time.

Actually feeling better, he ambled around the cemetery for another hour before deciding to head back to the cottage. He opened the door to hear the telephone ringing. Reaching it, he expected to hear Mary's voice. But the caller was not his girlfriend.

''Mr. Vincent Cassidy?'' asked a no nonsense woman in a crisp, business-like voice.

''Yes,'' he said, a pang of anxiety straining his voice.

''Mr. Cassidy, I have been asked to call you on behalf of a Ms. Mary Renata . . .''

"What's wrong?"

"She's going to be fine . . ."

"What happened?" Vince asked tensely.

"Mr. Cassidy," the woman continued in the same emotional tones. "Ms. Renata was in an automobile accident. She is at Denver General Hospital and is fine. She asked me to call you to let you know that she will be arriving by taxi cab shortly."

"She's okay?" Vince blurted.

"Yes. Some cuts and bruises," the woman said, her voice softening. "She's fine. A few days of rest and she'll be as good as new."

Vince thanked the woman and hung up. A sense of terrible dread was gripping his stomach and he was afraid he was going to be sick. Mary was an excellent driver. She might be unfamiliar with Denver, but she knew how to handle herself in heavy traffic.

What the hell is going on? It's like everything is suddenly going nuts.

The blare of a horn set Vince scurrying out to the gates. A Yellow Cab sat in the driveway. As he fumbled to open the lock, Mary, pale and drawn, climbed out of the back seat. The blue skirt was now wrinkled and looked limp. He noticed a dark stain on her white blouse. She leaned toward the window and paid the driver and then walked slowly to Vince. He pushed one of the gates open and rushed to her.

"They just called me. Are you okay?" He studied her face.

She smiled wanly and nodded. "Yes. Just shaken. I have a few cuts, but nothing major. I'm sorry about the truck . . ."

"Screw the truck," he said quickly. "It's you I'm worried about."

"I'm okay, really," she said, slipping her arm around his waist. "Just a little shocky and tired."

They slipped through the gates and, after Vince had secured them once again, walked to the cottage.

"What happened?" he asked her after she was seated at the kitchen table.

Mary studied her hands, folded on the table in front of her. "It's so strange, Vince. I'm not sure. I left here and went to a savings and loan down the street and opened a savings account. Then I drove on to I-25 and started north for the downtown area where the Auraria campus is. I was about halfway there and all of a sudden this big black four-wheel drive pickup started to weave in front of me. It cut me off and then hit its brakes. I tried to pull around it, but the turkey won't let me by. He kept cutting me off. Finally, he pulled into the center lane and I started to pass and that's when he hit me."

"On purpose?" Vince asked, suddenly angry at the anonymous truck driver.

Mary nodded, fighting back tears threatening to flood her eyes. "Yes. He just turned the truck into the side of the Toy. He hit it so hard, I couldn't control it. Oh, Vince . . ." she sobbed.

He hurried to her and kneeling, encircled her in his arms. "It's okay, Babe. It's okay." he soothed.

"Th . . . the truck went off the highway and hit a light pole. I . . . I think it's totaled." The threatening storm of tears suddenly burst and she clutched at Vince desperately. "I . . . I was so scared . . ."

He held her close, smothering her trembling body in his arms. "You're okay now."

She pulled away, staring at him, her dark, moist eyes flashing. "I'm *not* okay, Vince. I'm scared. What's going on?"

He shook his head and gently brought her back into his arms. "I wish I knew, Babe."

After a time, he convinced Mary to go upstairs and lay down. Emotionally and physically exhausted, she complied without protest.

After he heard her pad quietly up the staircase, Vince sat at the kitchen table, sipping on a bottle of Corona and, for the hundredth time, tried to make sense of the last 24 hours. Coincidences were coincidences; they happen to everybody. There are cycles to everyone's life. Ups and downs.

He could remember his childhood when his father was out of work, bills were unpaid and his mother had been in a terrible auto accident—*thank God, Mary's wasn't as bad*—and everything seemed to be crumbling around them. He and his sister, terrified for their mother and sensing their father's depression and desperation, thought their world was coming to an end. Just when it looked the worst, when their father's temperament was swinging like a pendulum between raging anger and abject self-pity, their mother came out of her coma, a telephone call summoned their father to a new job and suddenly their world slipped back into an orderly, normal routine.

"Cycles," their mother had told them when she came home from the hospital. "Life is filled with endless cycles."

Vince could hear his mother's words echoing in his mind.

Cycles.

So maybe that's what all this was about. Just another in those constant, changing cycles.

"Maybe my fucking moon is in the wrong house or my sign is hanging on a bad cusp," he mumbled to himself, laughing without humor at his inane joke.

If only it *was* funny.

Restless and frustrated, Vincent drained the bottle of beer and slipped quietly up the stairs to the bedroom. Mary was lying on the bed, still dressed, sound asleep. She was breathing in deep, measured sighs. He pulled the bedspread across her from the opposite corner and left her to rest.

Downstairs, he found himself standing at the living room window, staring out over the expanse of the cemetery. It was peaceful and oddly restful, a silent, unmoving sea of carved stone and polished marble.

Who had they been, all those people tossed out of the living world and now turning to dust under their massive monuments? What kind of people had they been, what had they accomplished in their lives?

It's very peaceful.

Had their lives been filled with the same joys and pains and triumphs and tragedies that others experienced? Had they been good or bad?

Go walk among the dead. Feel their tranquility.

Vince turned from the window and tugged another bottle of beer from the refrigerator. After opening it, he stepped out of the front door and, without even considering it, began walking along the lane leading into the heart of the grounds.

Like moving into another world.

Oblivious to his course, Vince wandered up one lane and down another, looking at the mausoleums and headstones with a new appreciation. Since he and Mary had arrived, the cemetery had seemed frightening, even forboding. Now, however, he was seeing it differently. What could be so frightening about a resting place for the dead?

His mind became consumed with the intricately cut stones, the craftsmanship and variety of the carved names and dates gracing the smooth polished surfaces. He marveled at the greens and rosy reds and browns of the marble and the simple beauty of the dark granite. He became consumed by the symmetry of the even, aligned rows and at the variety and architectural elegance of the mausoleums, realizing that no two were alike. He became fascinated by the statuary, the cherubs and angels, which looked as if they would spring into life at any moment.

Vince found his former dread and unease washed away in a flood of wellbeing and harmony. There was an order and purpose in this place he had not considered before.

Why was it frightening last night? Why would anyone be frightened of the dead?

"Hey, buddy," called a vaguely familiar voice which dragged Vince out of the almost hypnotic trance. He shook his head, trying to clear it and then glanced around, amazed that the sun was already slipping behind the distant mountains. How long had he been walking the grounds? Surely not hours. Yet, the sun was going down.

"Hey," came the voice again. "Over here."

He looked toward the fence, realizing he was at the far southeast corner of the cemetery, the furtherest point inside the grounds from the cottage. The weather-beaten, grubby old man he had spoken with that morning stood on the sidewalk outside the iron fence.

"What . . . ?" Vince asked, feeling as if he was awakening from a long, deep sleep.

"Don't let it get ya. Don't let this place suck ya in. If ya do, yer lost. That bitch, she's a cunnin' one. She'll grind yer bones 'neath her feet, ya don't watch yer ass." The old man's clipped, cryptic words chilled Vince.

"I don't know what you're talking about," Vince snapped defensively.

"Yes, ya do," the old man barked. "Ya know, but ya don't wantta believe it. Ya don't wantta let yerself believe it. But ya still *know!*"

"Who's goin' to grind my bones?" Vince asked, despite his better judgement. The man was obviously a lunatic, turned out to some asylum like a thousand other unfortunates that no one cared to protect anymore.

"The Black Bitch, ya damn fool! Who the hell ya think I mean?"

"Listen," Vince fairly snarled, taking a step closer to where the man stood. "There's no one here except my girlfriend and me. No one else. What the hell are you babbling about? Why don't you go find a place for the night? Get some food? And leave me the hell alone!"

The old man's rheumy, bloodshot eyes studied Vince for a long moment and then his chapped, cracked lips pulled away from his yellowed, uneven teeth and his mouth became a twisted grimace.

"Yer a fool. A damned fool. Ya listen ta me, boy. Ya go get that woman and ya get outta there. Ain't no place fer ya and that sweet thing ya brung with ya. Ain't right, ya draggin' her into a place like this. Ya hear me, boy? Get out!" As the old man spoke, his wrinkled, dirty hands clutched the bars so hard, his fingers turned white.

Vince started to say something when an odd, unidentifiable cry from the middle of the cemetery caused him to whirl around. His nerves tingling, he stared into the spreading twilight, trying to discover the source of the strange, unnatural sound. Nothing moved.

He turned back, intent on probing the crazy old man with another question, but the man was gone. He had vanished, just as he had that morning.

Mystified and as unsettled as he had been before his strange walk among the tombstones, Vince suddenly felt a desperate need to be back at the cottage with Mary.

It was almost two-thirds of a mile from where he stood to the house. A long walk and already the sun's afterglow was starting to fade. Feeling at once foolish and not a little frightened, he started off at a trot, intent on reaching the cottage as quickly as possible.

The trees lining the lane suddenly seemed menacing and Vince veered to the middle of the graveled road, constant jerking his head to the right and then the left trying to catch sight of shadows which flitted in the perifery of his vision.

Did something move near that headstone?

Vince kept trotting down the lane, even as his side began to ache and his calf muscles tightened in protest. A cold sweat covered his face and salty drops ran into his eyes and down his cheeks.

Was that a figure crouching at the base of the big pine?

His breath was coming in great gulps and his mouth and throat were as dry as the dust inside those looming mausoleums. His feet, now heavy, as if weights had been attached to them, slapped hard against the gravel, echoing off the surrounding, night-blackened stones.

Were those cold unhuman eyes watching him from the corner of the bulking crypt?

He was halfway to the cottage. Without any lights to warm its dark windows, it was more a cold, black ediface than a welcoming warm home. But Mary was there, probably still sleeping, dreaming . . .

Was that the sound of muffled footsteps pacing him?

Vince wiped his jacket sleeve across his face as he continued to jog along the lane. He was afraid he was going to vomit, the pain in his side seemed to be spreading into his stomach. The beer he'd drank earlier—*did I finish the one I'd taken with me?*— felt heavy and sour in his roiling guts. The movement of his legs was inflaming his groin.

Was that a black shape moving near the cottage?

He emerged from the lane, crossed the driveway and fell heavily against the front door. He cursed as he turned the knob and the door refused to open. Not having a lock on it and knowing it fit the opening perfectly, Vince was suddenly seized with panic. Still fighting for breath and crenching his teeth against the pain in his abdomen, he banged his shoulder against the thick wood three times before the door yielded and banged open.

Not pausing, he moved through the dark foyer, turned on the living room lights and raced up the stairs. In the hallway, he was assailed by that odd odor of mould and decay that came and went in the house like an evil wind.

Mary!

Reaching the bedroom door, he pushed it open and stumbled in. Not pausing, he hurried to the prone figure on the bed.

"Mary?" he said softly, not wanting to frighten her.

The figure stirred.

As he reached the bed, he looked down and cried out in horror.

Looking back at him, framed in a peaked hood, just visible in the gloom, was a hideous skull-face, its blackened, cracked flesh stretched tight over the bone. Teeth—*fangs!*—huge and hooked, curled out of its mouth and a wet, dripping tongue darted over them. Twin eyes, pupilless, like molten pools of swirling red and yellow fire, glared at him.

The Thing's terrible lips spread into a smile and a hiss poured from its black mouth.

Vince sprang back. His heel caught on the edge of the carpet and, unable to catch his balance, he crashed to the floor, rolling onto his back . . .

The Thing rose slowly on the bed. It sat upright, its body enfolded in a ragged, ebony black cloak.

Swept with dizziness, Vince scrambled on his hands and knees, groping for the door, a strangled cry bubbling from his throat.

The Thing's lower body shifted and its enfolded legs swung off the bed. Its swirling, glistening orbs shone in the darkening room like the fanned embers of a rekindling fire. They glared at Vince, piercing him with unholy power and unbridled hate.

Vince grabbed the doorknob and pulled himself to his feet. He was gasping, sobbing, his throat constricted by terror. Tears streamed down his cheeks.

The Thing sat on the edge of the bed, extending its rag shrouded arm toward Vince, a bony black skeletal finger beckoning to him to come to it . . .

. . . come to *Her*.

Vince took an unwilling step forward, feeling as if his body was no longer his own to command. His mind was clouded, entrapped by a force he could not comprehend.

He took a second shaky step toward *Her*, his mind entranced and entrapped by those shifting, swirling eyes . . .

PART TWO
THE GATHERINGS

Evasive, fleeting, blown like a chaff
    Across the chill and pallid dawn;
A touch, a sigh, a breath, a laugh,
    Then once again the Curtain's drawn:
Yet Memory, roused from ruined days,
    Turns comforted, and goes her ways.

—J.C. Powys

SIX

The old man crept through the dark, litter-strewn alley, keeping to the shadows, hugging the rough brick walls of the old apartment houses. He carefully sidestepped the occasional pools of light streaming from kitchen windows and mindfully negotiated the jumble of battered garbage cans and assorted junk haphazardly scattered over the oily, potholed asphalt.

Red-eyed rats glared at him from among the debris, refusing to flee as he approached, preferring to guard their scavenged rot than risk losing it to one of their bolder fellows.

A hollow-eyed mongrel dog, its flanks slack and sunken, growled at him from behind a dumpster. The old man waved his hand and hissed and the dog withdrew with one last, half-hearted bark.

Tobias Rathbone was used to taking this unsavory route to his home. He'd been living—hiding really—in this derelict section of the city for months now. It was a place where a man could lose himself among the faceless and forgotten; the living dead outcast by the subtle, vague forces that lurk in the shadows of all cities, all nations, all civilizations. Here in this crumbling, decaying ruin were men and women who never found the means to exist among their fellows, simply clung to life and survived. For as many reasons as there were unwashed and unwanted, they clustered together seeking only to endure until the next meal at the Mission, the next welfare check, the next bottle of cheap, poisonous wine. Their world, which Rathbone now shared, was an endless series of struggles against pain and hunger and death. It was, unlike the larger world surrounding it, a place where life was a series of sharp contrasts; black and white, life and death.

It was, Rathbone thought ruefully, as he stepped into a dark doorway and fitted a key into a heavy, sturdy lock, much like the world of the cemetery; black and white, good and evil.

Glancing quickly up and down the alley to make certain he was unobserved, Rathbone ducked into the door, closed it and snapped the deadbolt in place. He stood at the top of a flight of old and worn wooden stairs. Gripping the railing, he descended the steps to the concrete floor below. A dim, bare lightbulb hung from the raftered ceiling. Its weak light shown dully off rusted pipes and tarnished copper tubing that ran from the boiler dominating the room. It was uncomfortably hot in the room and Rathbone hastened past the boiler to a door hidden by its bulky shape.

Again producing a key, he let himself into the room beyond, turning on the light as he entered.

In contrast to the surrounding world, the apartment was elegant and sumptuous, an oasis of refinement amid a desert of disintegration and deterioration. The bookcases lining the teakwood-paneled walls were filled with handsomely bound, well-worn volumes. The furnishings were all well preserved antiques from a variety of eras. A Victorian setee, covered in dark red velvet, sat near one wall. A pair of 70-year-old fan-backed chairs sat opposite the setee, a low, claw-footed table in front of them. A

Phyfe side table with an acanthus-leaf design cut skillfully into its legs, an art deco lamp on its shiny top, sat opposite the door. The floor was covered with a rich Persian carpet.

Rathbone moved through the room and entered his bedroom. Sitting on the edge of the brass bed, he stripped off the ragged, dirty clothing. Carrying them to the closet, he stuffed them into a plastic bag. He then stepped into the bathroom and took a long, hot shower, letting the water wash away the filth he had used to cover his face and hands and mat his beard.

When he finally returned to the living room, it was as a dapper, neatly groomed gentleman, wearing a brocade smoking jacket over a silk shirt and finely tailored wool slacks. A Meerschaum pipe, the yellowed bowl a clawed hand holding a skull, was clamped between his teeth.

Rathbone had purchased the pipe years before, the design amusing him, playing on his sense of the ironic.

He sat in one of the fan-backed chairs and studied the smoke swirling from the pipe.

The young fool at Mansfield had no idea what he had done by going to the cemetery. Didn't he realize his presence there was a catalyst? Couldn't he sense the malevolent aura of that unnatural, unholy place? Didn't he know that by accepting their cursed money he was like Judas taking the bag of silver for his betrayal?

Rathbone wished he knew who was the betrayed.

And that young woman. Did she know what was happening around her, perhaps to her? Couldn't she convince her young man to flee from there?

Or had both of them already been touched by the cemetery's powers?

It had been a long time since those two miscreants Bedlow and Terrance had employed a "caretaker." What were they up to now? How did the young man and woman fit into their evil games?

Rathbone pushed himself out of the chair and stepped to a section of books apart from the others on the crammed shelves. His finger traced the titles until he found the one he sought and tugged it from the shelf. Returning to his seat, he opened the dusty, yellowed pages and began leafing through them. The printing was in a tight, delicate script, written by a hand long dead. He would read the passage and then move on, attempting to find something he dimly remembered.

He read for nearly an hour, pausing only once to refill and light his pipe. Finally he paused, his finger scanning a paragraph as he reread it a second and then a third time.

''*And be ye warned,*'' Rathbone read aloud. ''*The Beastly Creature comes to those She casts her evil eye upon and does seduce them with her power and her evil. She bestows life upon those beneath the mattock and it is a life devoid of the true spark of living. She loathes that spark. Her's is a gift of illusion and evil, for She is Death's enemy and Apollyon's bedmate and origin. Tis said She despairs for the dead and gives them comfort. Be ye warned, tis a sham and a dark enchantment. She serves only the fires of Hades.*''

Rathbone rested the heavy volume on his lap.

It could be that *She* has returned . . . or been summoned, he thought. He knew the history of Mansfield and the thought of the dark, spectral creature roaming that unholy place chilled him.

Was that, perhaps, the design behind the cemetery's creation? Was that the rationale for its incorporation over a century ago by those terrible men? Men like Bedlow and Terrance.

Those two had been watching over that place for a long time. They had only recently realized that Rathbone was watching over them. How they learned of his presence was unknown, certainly not through their own talents and powers. They had gone, except for the dark rituals they performed and that, Rathbone knew, was not a talent, but a learned ability.

And Bedlow and Terrance had developed that ability to

an art. They were accomplished at weaving evil incantations which, in turn, gave *other* beings power. It made the pair very dangerous.

Rathbone carried the book back to its place on the shelf and wandered into the apartment's small kitchen.

"Now to have to hide like a common thief," he mumbled to himself as he searched the cupboards for something to eat. "It's damn humiliating."

Yet, he knew that Henry Terrance had dispatched a legion of his minions to search for him. In this derelict building, in this carefully designed room, he was temporarily safe, but for how long? His sojourn at the cemetery in the guise of an old bum had been risky and, he knew, even the bright light of day could not keep him from being detected by the forces of the Black Bitch. If she was lurking among the long dead, then she was everywhere in that place and whether it was dark or light, she would know he had been there.

As he was taking a large can of Chun King pepper steak out of the cupboard, he heard the shuffling and scratching outside his door. The sound of claws scraping on the wood-veneered metal caused him to drop the can to the floor.

He had been followed. Or at least traced. He had no doubt that his sanctuary was discovered and he would have to move quickly to keep it from being breeched.

Rathbone hurried to the door. The scratching and clawing was growing louder and the sound of something foul and loathsome snuffling outside the door sent cold shivers through his aged body.

"I cast you away," he breathed through clenched teeth. "Out and down! Back to the Pit!" As he spoke, the index finger of his right hand traced mystic, ancient runes on the surface of the door. Where his finger moved, incandescent sparks erupted, setting the thin wood smoking and burning.

The sounds outside the door withdrew. The clawing and

scraping ceased and the snuffling turned to a low, angry growling and then an agonizing cry.

Still he marked the door with the antiquated, archaic signs until the entire surface was scarred with them and the smoke they emitted filled the room.

"Be gone demons!" Rathbone hissed. "By the Elements of the Earth and Arcane Powers, *Be Gone!*"

He could sense the departure of the things beyond his door. Sighing, he stumbled to his chair and dropped into it, his energy drained and his mind numbed.

"Tobias," he said, rubbing his old eyes. "You're growing weak and old. Such a simple spell would not have phased you a few centuries back. Now it exhausts you." He knew it would not exhaust those who dispatched whatever had lurked beyond his door.

He sat for awhile, regaining his strength, lamenting the absence of other Druids to aid him combat the rising tide of the Occult Madonna.

SEVEN

Agnes Hardwick handed Joshua Ortega a cup of steaming tea. His dark brown, wrinkled face, framed by the mane of bright silver hair, was screwed up in a frown. His shaggy mustache drooped forlornly around his mouth. He took the cup and absently stared at the brew within.

"It's an interesting tale, Aggie," he finally said. Sitting at her kitchen table, she had related the messages from the Ouija board. Joshua had listened intently, letting her explain the subtle feelings she had experienced as well as the words themselves.

Solomon, the Persian cat, was curled up on his pillow in a corner of the kitchen. He had been flighty all through the previous night and still would jump frequently from his bed to stare at the windows, occasionally hissing and spitting. Agnes found his behavior particularly worrisome and thought it most peculiar.

"More than a tale, Josh," she said, pouring herself a cup of hot water from the kettle and dropping in a tea bag. "After I went to bed last night, I had the oddest . . . feeling . . . of being watched. I can't explain it, but I could sense something watching me . . ."

"Aggie," Joshua said firmly ."You're letting yourself get frightened. Just because your Ouija board tells you something, it doesn't mean it's going to happen. You know the board can be very cryptic, if not downright wrong."

His patronizing attitude annoyed her. She was only too aware of the vagaries of the Ouija board.

"I know you're a student of such things, Josh, but you're not a practitioner. Don't discredit what *I* know. I may be old, but I'm neither a fool nor a senile old crone. I've learned to respect what the board tells me." Her indignation edged her words and the irritation she had hoped to keep in check spilled out.

Joshua looked at her, his eyes a mixture of hurt and concern. "I didn't mean to insinuate that I thought you were . . . senile, Aggie. I just don't want you to become enmeshed in anything out of your realm of . . . experience."

She smiled at him. "I know. I'm sorry if I snapped. It's just that whatever is happening, I think I can help." She looked at her watch. It was eleven-thirty, time to climb to the turret room and try to learn more from the board.

"Will you join me, Josh?" she asked, getting slowly to her feet.

He looked away and stared at the darkness beyond the window. "I . . . I don't know if I can, Aggie. It . . . the prospect is a bit frightening."

"Using the board?" she asked evenly.

He smiled and shook his head. "No, of course not. It's this request you've received. I'm more than just a little concerned about it. Are you sure it's not a trick?"

Her lips set in a hard line and she squinted her eyes at him. "Joshua, I've used that board for years. I know when I'm receiving messages from *my* spirits and when I'm receiving from others or darker ones."

He sighed and closed his eyes, nodding. "Yes, Aggie, I know you do, but . . ."

"But nothing, Josh," she said firmly, without anger.

"Some people play with Ouija boards, like they were playing Scrabble or Monopoly. Well, I don't. It's not a toy or a game. It's a serous business and it can be dangerous if you don't know what you're doing. *I* know what I'm doing."

He looked up at her and smiled, his dark eyes looking almost sad. "Alright then. Let's retire to your tower, Madam."

She laughed and turned to the door leading to the stairs. "With two of us," she said as they ascended the steep steps, "we should receive tonight's messages very clearly."

Seated on either side of the board, the tape recorder on, ready to be activated by the first sound, they placed their fingers lightly on the planchette.

Solomon was curled on an old pillow, carefully watching the humans with his big, luminous eyes, as if knowing what they were about to do and not liking it.

"Can you tell us more," Agnes asked the board. Immediately the planchette began gliding over the table top.

"T-H-E E-V-I-L I-S A-C-T-I-V-E. I-T G-R-O-W-S." Her voice spoke each letter clearly and crisply. There was no other sound in the room save the soft hum of the recorder as it captured Agnes's voice.

"How can I help?"

"F-I-N-D T-H-E O-N-E W-I-T-H T-H-E P-O-W-E-R."

"What power?"

"A-N-C-I-E-N-T P-O-W-E-R. A F-O-R-C-E O-F G-O-O-D."

"Where is this powerful one?"

"H-E I-S N-E-A-R Y-O-U."

They stopped, removing their fingers. Agnes shifted, her back feeling stiff and uncomfortable and her arms tired.

"It still hasn't told you how you're going to find this . . . this powerful person," Joshua pointed out. "Or for that matter, who he or she is."

"Patience, Josh," she answered. "It'll tell me in good

time. Did you notice how quickly the pointer was moving? You're an excellent channel for the spirits. Very strong."

He smiled. "For someone so inexperienced you mean."

"That too," she laughed, deciding not to mention the incredible rush of energy she had felt when his fingers joined hers on the planchette. He was nervous enough as it was.

They sat quietly for several moments. With no sounds to activate it, the recorder's red light winked out. Agnes, eyes half closed, focused on an imagined point in her mind, drawing her energy to it; Joshua stared absently at Solomon, waiting for Agnes to resume.

Then, although the room was silent, the red light on the recorder flashed on and the tape began to whir softly. Agnes glanced at it, alarmed. She looked at Josh, putting a finger to her lips.

The recorder ran for over a minute and then the light winked out again.

With trembling fingers, Agnes reached over and turned it off. Punching the rewind button, she let the tape whirl back until it stopped at the beginning.

"What did that?" Joshua breathed softly.

She shook her head. "I'm not sure. I think, perhaps, someone just left us a message."

Joshua rubbed a nervous hand across his stubbled chin and absently stroked his bushy moustache. His eyes were locked on the tape recorder in Agnes's hands.

When she started the tape, they listened to her voice reading out the litany of letters. Then there was a click marking the spot where the machine had shut itself off. After a second of blank tape, there came a series of crackling and hissing sounds, alien and disquieting. Finally, amid the cacophony, they heard a voice, deep, rumbling and slow, sounding like a 45 RPM record played at 33.

"Be gone, least you die, old woman. I will crush you beneath my cloven hooves and scatter your stripped flesh

and bloody bones to the carrion. Be gone. Or I will lead my brethren into your bed and let them pleasure themselves between your hoary old thighs. Be gone! I will inflict a thousands tortures on your body and laugh as you writhe in terror. Be gone, old woman.''

The awful voice faded as did the terrible sounds. Agnes and Joshua stared at the machine as if it were some vile apparition.

''Mother of God,'' Joshua said, his eyes wide. He got shakily to his feet and backed away from the table. ''Leave it be, Aggie.'' His eyes stilled stared at the machine.

''I . . . I can't, Josh,'' she said. ''Don't you see? Like it or not I'm a part of whatever madness is being played out. Why else would I receive such . . . such an evil message. Why else would I be warned?'' Her voice pleaded with him to understand.

He shifted his eyes, looking at her with horror. ''Didn't you hear? Don't you understand?''

She nodded and forced a weak smile. ''Yes, Josh, I heard. But tell me. Why was I warned? Why not simply destroy me?''

He could only stare at her.

''I'll tell you,'' she continued, her voice rising with defiance and a new awareness. ''I was warned because they *can't* get me. For whatever reason, I'm protected. If they could get me, don't you think they would have gotten me out of their way already?'' She thought about the unseen eyes she had felt watching her the previous night. A chill passed over her.

Joshua slumped against the curved wall. ''Aggie, don't talk crazy. This is . . . is something of *pure evil.* What do you know about the *real* powers that rule this world? The real evil?''

''I know enough to realize I might actually be an obstacle to it.'' She felt an unaccustomed anger toward her friend. Why was he so frightened? She knew—and how, she wasn't sure—that he was under her protection. "And I think I like that; being in their way."

"Aggie . . . I . . ." He could not articulate the terror worming its way into his heart, chilling his very soul. All the years he had spent studying ancient religions, mystic arts, superstitions and legends, he had viewed them as an abstraction, something to be looked upon with scholarly eyes. He had long ago admitted to himself that there were things beyond people's comprehension; arcane forces and powers shifting and working mysteriously beyond the veil of human understanding.

Now he was confronted by the reality of Evil. That veil had been lifted and what lay beyond was terrifying. Something mortal man was not meant to see; not meant to endure. His comfortable sense of the abstract had suddenly become a very horrifying, very real truth.

"Come, Josh," Agnes said softly, her voice low and prosaic. "Let's continue."

He looked into her kindly eyes. He could detect a change in them, as if something old and primitive had welled up in her soul and filled her with new power. They penetrated him, soothed and calmed his inner turmoil.

He stepped quietly to the table and slipped back into his seat. Without a word, he placed his fingers opposite the old woman's on the planchette. This time Agnes asked nothing. The small, heart-shaped device simply began scurrying over the board. When it landed on letters, Agnes did not enunciate them, she had not bothered to turn on the recorder again. The pointer moved for some time and then finally stopped.

"What did it say, Aggie? I couldn't keep up."

She smiled across the table at Joshua. "It told me much. The evil is in a place of the dead. A cemetery, I assume. Somewhere in or near Denver. The force of evil is very powerful there and it will take a combination of our power and the Druid's to help contain it."

"Our power? What powers do I have?" Joshua asked,

again feeling a dread clutching at him, dispelling his sense of calm.

She patted his hand. "You have a power. Believe me, when it is necessary, you will know how to use it."

"Well, what's all this about a Druid? There aren't any Druids. They're gone! Isn't that a hint that maybe, just maybe all of this is a lot of nonsense?"

"Was that message on the recorder nonsense?" Agnes asked.

Joshua grunted and shook his head.

"According to the board," she went on. "There's one near us. He's the powerful ally we're supposed to find. We'll do that in the morning." Her matter-of-fact tone caused Joshua to peer closely at her. There was, indeed, a change in her; a new strength and a strong resolve.

"Still, Druids haven't been around for seven or eight hundred years, Aggie," he explained patiently, secretly beginning to question her sanity and his own. "They're all gone. Don't you understand?"

"What happened to them?" she asked curiously, ignoring his plea.

Joshua frowned and shook his head. Agnes was patronizing him and he knew it. Well, fine, he decided. I'll humor her. Besides, this is my strong suit.

"Okay, a quick history lesson. The Druids were a strong religious force among the Celtic inhabitants of Gaul," he began, his voice sounding professorial and knowing. "Largely in what is known today as France and the British Isles. Their religion is thought to have been very similar to Christianity, although they apparently had no Savior. They were very adept at astrology and, some believe, magic. They apparently understood the secret and mystic powers held by animals and plants. They especially revered trees, primarily the oak. I suppose that's why many now believe them to have been heathens and evil. But really, they were very civilized."

"What happened to them, Josh?" Agnes prompted. She

was genuinely interested and, at the same time, wanted to keep him from dwelling on the messages they had received.

"The Romans invaded what is now France. They managed to stamp out the Druids," he continued. "However, the Romans didn't reach Britain until later, so Druidism survived there for a while. It was largely ignored by the coming of Christianity. Actually, they believed in life after death, just as Christians do. Only they believed the soul entered the body of a new-born baby. Sort of an endless recycling."

That made Agnes laugh.

"But, Aggie, the Druids have been gone for centuries," he reinterated.

"Well, there's one around now," she said flatly. Her tone told him she would not argue the point.

"And just how are we going to find him?" Joshua demanded, his frustration with her evident.

"He's not far from here. We'll drive down there in the morning. He may even be expecting us."

Joshua was suspicious. "Drive down where?"

"Somewhere around old Market and Larimer Streets."

"That's a pretty bad neighborhood for a couple of old folks to go poking around in, don't you think?" His concern was real. He knew the area she referred to was filled with cheap bars, grimy pawn shops and sleazy pool halls.

"Don't worry, Josh. We'll be fine."

He sighed in fatigue and defeat. "Well, if we're going exploring in the morning, I've got to go home, Aggie. It's late and I need some sleep." He started to rise and she touched his hand.

"You'll stay here tonight, Josh," Agnes told him, as though it was a foregone conclusion.

"Here?" He eyed her curiously.

She detected something in his look and blushed. "Don't be silly, Joshua Ortega. I'm far to old and tired to try to seduce you. I just want you to stay here tonight. You can sleep on the couch.''

''But my house is close. I can meet you here in the morning and we can go looking for this mysterious stranger . . .''

''No,'' she said firmly. ''You will not leave here tonight. I . . . I'd feel better if you were here, with me.''

''But . . .''

''No ifs, ands or buts.''

He nodded. ''Alright, if it'll make you feel better. But I expect a hearty breakfast. And you know there'll be talk,'' he teased, winking at her.

''Good,'' she said, getting out of her chair. ''I haven't been the subject of any good gossip for a long time. Now come on, let's get some sleep.''

They laughed, the humor a thin disguise for their unspoken worries, and left the room. Solomon followed them silently down the staircase to the kitchen.

Later, alone in her bedroom, Joshua already comfortably asleep on the big couch in the living room, Agnes sat on the edge of her bed petting Solomon.

''I had to lie to him,'' she whispered to the cat. ''How could I tell him I couldn't protect him if he went home?''

Solomon purred and meowed in reply.

''He does have powers, but they're not strong enough yet and may never be. He could never thwart an attack. I know now that I can defend us both.'' She thought about that for a moment. ''Of course, I'm not sure how. I just know it.''

She could not explain her new knowledge and self-awareness. It was as if something buried deep within her had been awakened tonight. Agnes did not understand all of it, but she knew it was a force that embued her with a power that was almost palpable. And it seemed to have beneficial side effects. Her body, usually stiff and sore after a long, full day, felt healthier and stronger than it had in thirty years. There were none of the minor aches and pains that seemed to constantly plague her. Her mild arthritis was certainly supressed, if not completely eradicated from her old joints.

Suddenly Solomon hissed, sinking his claws through Agnes's flannel nightgown into her flesh. She moaned and lifted the cat off her lap, as he squirmed and spat.

She glanced at the window and cried out at the apparition staring back at her. The gaping, fang-filled mouth was open, its serpentine tongue flicking, smearing the glass with dark slime. The snout, not unlike a pig's, blew a cloud of hot steam and the eyes gleamed a crimson evil, their tiny black pupils fixing Agnes with a withering, hate-filled gaze.

She stared at it for a long moment, still holding the struggling cat firmly in her hands.

"By the Elemental Forces, begone demon!" she said, wondering where the words had come from. They had simply sprung from her without thought.

The creature at the window backed away from the glass and she could just make out leathery, bat-like wings beating the air.

"Be gone!" she hissed again.

With one last flick of its forked tongue, the creature wheeled and vanished from her sight. She could visualize it, soaring high into the night sky, flapping its way back to its master . . . or mistress . . . not unlike a falcon returning to the arm of the hunter.

Something came over Agnes. Unmoving, her eyes staring sightlessly at the bedroom window. A dark vision filled her mind. She could see the demon gabbering to a black enshrouded figure. The thing was covered by a flowing, tattered cape with a peaked cowl which kept its visage in darkness.

When the flying demon finished its gibberish, a black, bony hand darted out and caught the thing's head in a vise-like grip. Agnes could see the long, twisted fingers applying more and more pressure on the demon's misshapen skull. It writhed and shrieked and tried desperately to flutter away. Then, in spray of dark, noxious liquid, the head burst and the demon's body, flopping in a grotesque parody, dropped to the wet, worm-infested ground. Suddenly other things fell upon its lifeless body, ripping it to shreds.

Agnes shook off the horrible vision and slumped back on the bed, shivering and exhausted.

Solomon moved closer to her, nuzzled her cheek and, getting no response, curled up on the pillow near his mistress's face and slept.

EIGHT

Mary lay awake long after Vince slipped into a fitful sleep. When he would toss or turn, she would rest her hand on his brow or lightly touch his arm to soothe him.

She stared into the dark, attempting to sort out the confusing images and thoughts colliding in her mind. So much had happened. Last night's sexual frenzy; the disintered, empty casket; that maniac on the highway and the resulting wreck . . .

The images flashed and tumbled through her head, making her restless. A sense of dread settled over her like a heavy shroud. She felt depressed. Over and over again, Mary tried to make sense out of all that had happened. There were no rational answers; only more questions.

What is happening?

After returning from the hospital and talking with Vince, she had fallen into a deep, restful sleep. Although she could not remember the details, she knew she had dreamed. There had been unsettling visions which left uneasy sensations flitting around the corners of her mind.

While she was still deep beneath that sea of unconsciousness, something had stolen over her; a presence, she now thought. Some *thing* that had shared her space and her body as she slumbered. It was at once a terrible thing which fought her for control of her mind and soul and at the same time calmed and comforted her.

Vaguely she could recall a voice whispering to her, telling her things she could not now recall, but which touched a part of her that was both terribly ugly and darkly pleasurable.

Still asleep and not alone, Mary had felt herself rising from the bed. Shifting to sit on its edge . . .

Mary had been suddenly jolted awake. The bedroom lights flashed on and, squinting in the glare, she saw Vince crouched at the open door. His mouth was opened and his eyes were wide. He was screaming at her.

Startled and confused, clutching the bedspread to her breasts, she too had let out a scream.

Vince continued to gape at her after his screams turned to choking sobs. His face was bloodless. His eyes were huge and filled with unreasoning terror. He had looked at her as if he did not know her; as if she was something wholly evil and grotesque.

Finally, he slumped against the wall, eyes squeezed shut, and called her name over and over again. He had dropped to the floor, his hands covering his face as great, wrenching sobs shook his body.

Mary had rushed from the bed and knelt beside him. She tried to take him in her arms, but he pushed her away, pressing himself against the wall.

"Get away from me!" he had cried. "Get away!"

"Vince?" she said softly, hurt and frightened. "It's Mary, Vince."

His eyes, again round and wild, stared at her. There was a look of total bewilderment in them. After a few seconds, he blinked away the tears and then his contorted face softened.

"Mary?"

"Yes."

"Oh God, Mary," he sobbed, reaching for her. She took him in her arms and he clung to her, crying, unable to speak. Her heart broke for him. She desperately wanted to know what had frightened him so, but she dared not ask.

In time he sighed, wiped his eyes with his hands, and struggled to his feet.

"Vince," she said, standing near him, her arm around his waist. "What happened?"

He looked at her and flushed. "Nothing."

"Nothing?" she echoed. "You don't act like that over nothing."

He summoned up a weak, half-hearted smile. "Just tired, I guess. The light played a trick on me is all. Really, it was nothing." He shifted uncomfortably and was clearly embarrassed.

Macho bullshit, she had thought, although she kept the thought to herself.

"I'm bushed, babe," he said. "I think my blood pressure is jacked up again. I'm going to bed."

"Did you take your medicine?" Mary had asked.

"Yeah," he answered, half-heartedly. She didn't believe him, but decided not to make an issue of it.

"You're sure you're okay?" She touched his brow, relieved to find it cool.

"I'm okay, just tired. Now, come on, let's go to bed."

"You want anything to eat?"

"No."

"Me neither," she agreed.

"How do *you* feel? You had a pretty bad day." Vince took her shoulders in his hands and looked into her eyes.

Mary made a face. "I've had worse," she lied.

"Well, I just don't want you to get upset," he told her, pulling her close, hugging her.

Hell, she thought, how much more upset can I get?

While Vince undressed and crawled wearily under the

covers, she had gone to the bathroom to take off her wrinkled, soiled clothes and take a hot shower. When she returned, Vince was sound asleep, snoring so loudly, she had to make him roll over.

She was glad he wasn't awake. It was a little disconcerting climbing into the large bed next to him. She was still sore and bruised from the previous night's excesses.

She had lain there for hours now, unable to sleep and too afraid to leave the bed—leave Vince—and go downstairs to read or fix coffee. She simply lay there under the covers, her mind filled with those cascading images and confused thoughts.

Had they only been there a little over a day? she wondered, amazed at how long a time it seemed.

Something dark passed over the window opposite the bed.

Mary refused to look, terrified by what she might see.

Something rustled at the window, sounding like a breeze-shifted branch lightly scraping the glass.

Still, she would not look.

She knew there was no tree there. It was her imagination, she told herself. There was nothing out there. This is the second floor, there's no place for any*one* or any*thing* to stand.

There's nothing out there! Nothing . . .

Mary, came a whisper from across the room, from inside her head. From the window. It was a dream-voice, real and not real. Soft and tender, full of honey and warmth.

Don't look, she told herself. Don't look . . .

Mary, come join me.

Oh, so soft, so gentle. An angelic voice, filled with beautiful promises.

NO! she cried to herself, I won't look.

Mary, come join me. Come be with me.

It was pleading now, but still tender and laced with such sad longing.

OH GOD, NO!

Mary, come join me. Come be with me. Come lie with me.

The desire and the yearning pervaded her mind, touched her body, stirring warm sensations.

NOOOOO . . . It was a voiceless protest; a terrified plea.

Mary, lie with me. I will set your soul aflame. I will fill the void in your body with my flesh.

The voice was growing more urgent now, hinting of impatience. The desire was turning to need and the need was great.

Mary was suddenly very uncomfortable. A shudder, not from cold, but from anticipation, passed over her. She was starting to sweat under the weight of the covers. Her light nightgown was suddenly soaked and sticky. She was stricken with dread and disgust as she felt the growing wetness between her thighs as her flesh stirred in response to the cajoling voice. Her heart was racing and her mind was suddenly, unwillingly, focusing on her body's needs.

You want me, Mary. You want me to take you. To have you.

Solicitious and demanding, the dream voice was edged with lustful hunger.

She was starting to breathe heavily and she could not remain still. Her legs worked under the covers, thrashing at them, kicking them from her.

Lurid, graphic images flashed through her mind: A golden bodied man caressing her, his tongue flicking over her breasts, his hands massaging her buttocks, probing between her thighs. His powerful, beautiful body on hers, in her . . .

Come, Mary. Join me. Feel my hardness inside you.

The honeyed tone was gone. It was commanding her

now, a voice reserved for dark rooms where sweating bodies sprawled on tangled sheets.

She was panting. Her breath coming in deep gulps. Her breasts grew hard and she unconsciously began massaging her hard, erect nipples, moaning at the sensual, erotic pressure of her stroking fingers. She felt flushed and feverish and her blood was rushing wildly through her veins as her body grew rigid.

Those images, lustful and enticing, danced behind her eyes, exciting and pleasuring her.

Mary. Mary! MARY! You know you want me! You know you need me. Come to me! Give me your body!

An order, filled with obsession and lascivious carnal want.

Her loins were on fire. She could feel herself slipping into a consuming trance, her conscious mind unable to control the moist heat burning between her legs. The need for release was growing stronger with each passing second. Her ardor was causing her body to seethe and pitch on the now sodden sheets. Her hips thrust in the age-old rhythm of passion and lust. Her light gown was a damp mass, clinging and knotted uncomfortably around her, binding her.

Come to me!

Dominating, commanding, the dream voice was now filled with anger and frustration. It reflected a sexual appetite which could not be left long unquenched.

Mary could hardly control her passion now. Her body ached with a desire so deep and so accute, it was almost painful. She was slick with sweat, brought forth by the feverish heat of her intense need. She continued to touch herself, caressing her breasts, stroking her belly, probing the wetness between her legs.

She looked at the window.

A face, disembodied, hovered there, glowing and smiling, but without warmth. It was the beautiful, handsome face of an Adonis. Curly locks falling over a smooth, unlined forehead; inviting, golden eyes dancing like rippling pools of passion; gleaming, perfect teeth framed by full, sensual lips.

A golden, sun-bronzed hand, beckoned to her from the darkness. It motioned for her to rise from the bed.

Be with me, Mary. Share my body. Let me impale you on my staff of pleasure, my rod of sensual iron. Come, Mary. Come!

No longer demanding, the voice was sensual, persuasive; a masculine, yet melodious voice to match the Adonis countenance.

She started to climb out of the bed, unable to control herself. The visions, the fantasies, were growing clearer, more inviting. She could almost feel the golden man moving on her, in her, his muscles tensing with each thrust.

And she could see herself writhing in pleasure, clawing, crying and trying to match his every move . . .

Yet a small part of her knew if she went with this vision—this god-like thing at the window—she would be lost. She knew it and was still powerless to control her burning need and fierce desires.

She paused, half out of the bed, staring longingly at the face in the window.

MARY! COME TO ME! NOW! YOU KNOW YOU WANT ME!

Still she hesitated. Mary forced herself to look at Vince. Wake up, Vince, she tried to say, but her mouth was too dry to form the words.

Please, Vince, wake up. Please, Vince . . .

MARY! HE CAN NEVER PLEASURE YOU AS I CAN! HE IS NOTHING! LOOK AT HIM, MARY. SEE HOW HE SLEEPS WHILE YOU BURN? SEE HOW HE TREATS YOU? HE CAN NOT QUELL YOUR DESIRES, MARY. BUT I CAN. I CAN. COME WITH ME NOW.

The words held no promise except for the certainty of unbridled lust . . .

. . . and it was enticing, inviting.

Her will was slipping away. Her body, hot and tension with passion, craved the Adonis at the window.

NO!

Mary's mind was again filled with images. They were dark and perverse, the sexual act reduced to bestial brutality and cruel lechery. She was horrified as the images aroused pleasurable, seductive aches in her.

Vince.

I can't betray Vince. I can't lose him or myself. I can't! The words screamed in her mind, but she could not find the means to articulate them aloud.

The voice spoke in her mind with an air of superiority. It was supremely confident and arrogant. It knew Mary could not long resist the desperation and fire burning in her soul and ingoring her flesh.

MARY, YOU MUST COME TO ME NOW! YOU BURN FOR ME, MARY. FOR ME! NOT FOR HIM. COME TO ME.

Again the urgency. All the tenderness and seductive entreaties were gone, replaced by a fierce, dark need.

With an effort of will, the sensual ardor prickling her body and her breath coming in panting gasps, she flung herself toward Vince. He stirred, but did not wake. She touched him desperately, groping under the blankets.

IT IS USELESS MARY. YOU CAN NOT DENY ME. YOU ARE MINE!

She clung to Vince, her hand manipulating his flesh, feeling it begin to harden. She was frantic. There was no tenderness in her touch, no gentle attempts to arouse him. While he did not wake, he began to moan softly and threw a caressing arm over her back. Mary was crying now. The crawling need in her body suddenly bringing forth a clutching, terrible fear.

MARY! STOP IT. YOU ARE MINE! YOU WILL BE MINE!

The possibility of defeat tinged the words, bringing forth a raging sense of betrayal.

Vince, still asleep, but now aroused, shifted toward Mary. She, in turn, still fought the terrible urge to leave the bed, to go to the face—the thing—at the window, to give herself to it totally and completely.

MARY! MARY! MARY! MARY! YOU NEED ME, NOT HIM. ONLY I CAN QUENCH YOUR FLAME! ONLY I CAN SATISFY THE HUNGER AND THE NEED!

The dream voice made its last, final plea; a frantic entreaty.

Mary's terror was beginning to give way to hope. She knew she was winning. Even though the desire and passion churning in her almost unbearable, she knew she could defeat the thing at the window. It was attempting to possess her through her flesh and if she could smother the fire torturing her body before she lost her will to resist, Mary knew she could win.

With a little effort, she pulled Vince atop her. He was vaguely aware of his motions, but still bound by sleep, either natural or unnatural.

She guided him and he entered her . . .

MARY, YOU FILTHY WHORING BITCH! YOU SLUT!

The voice hissed and crackled with complete betrayal and angry defeat. The thing had lost, if not its war, certainly this battle.

Vince thrust into her and Mary matched him, her hips rising and writhing beneath his weight. Her passion and desire intensifying, she knew she would at least defeat the thing at the window. They rocked and bucked on the bed until Mary erupted and Vince followed suit, exploding in her an instant later.

The unholy hunger died.

There was a scream of rage at the window and Mary peered over Vince's shoulder and immediately squeezed her eyes shut.

Gone was the golden god-face. Now, a leering skull, wisps of stringy hair clinging to its pate and tatters of dried, brittle flesh hanging from its cheeks and chin glared at her with two flashing wells of swirling crimson and orange. Enormous, hooked fangs glistened in the faint moonlight.

I beat you, you son of a bitch! I beat you! She wanted to sob and laugh at the same time. She knew she had won and in doing so had saved herself from a fate . . .

. . . worse than death she wondered?

Vince rolled off her damp body, muttered softly, but still did not waken. She reached down and pulled the covers over both of them and trembling, snuggled next to him. His warm flesh and his nearness comforted her.

Mary did not look at the window again. If whatever had been there was still near, she did not want to see it. She sensed that, for now, she was safe.

Soon she drifted into a natural, deep and dreamless sleep.

They both awoke when the alarm blared at five-thirty. Groggily they climbed out of bed.

Vince looked at Mary sheepishly. "Did what I think happened last night, happen?"

She blushed and smiled, looking away. "Yeah."

He shook his head as he tugged on his robe. "I didn't even wake up. Sorry . . ." He gave her a hug and kissed her gently.

"Don't be. It was . . . good." She hurried to the bathroom, not wanting to tell him *why* they had made love nor why it was so very good. As he had done for her the night before, she now wanted to spare him more anxiety. There was no need for Vince to be alarmed further. Enough had occurred already to drive most people mad. Why burden him with yet another bizarre . . .

. . . what?

What is happening?

She had tried—and failed—to understand all that had taken place since she arrived. The clawed thing at the door; their unnatural sexual appetites; the face at the window; Vince's terror in the cemetery and his hysteria last night. It was all an unfathomable mystery, an enigmatic nightmare.

Mary was equally mystified by her own reactions. Yes, she was terrified, frightened. Yet why was she reacting so rationally? Her fears were very real, but she felt ever so slightly detached from them, as if all of this was happening to someone else.

I should be ready for the straight jacket and rubber room boys by now, she mused. Instead, I'm taking too much of this in stride.

She decided to talk to him about leaving the cemetery and their jobs as soon as possible; no sane person could live in this kind of nightmare environment. She broached the subject a little later over coffee and toast.

"Leave?" he said, looking at her over the rim of his cup. "Where to?"

She shook her head and sighed. "I don't know. Away from here. Th . . . this place is . . . is bad, Vince." Her eyes were imploring and she searched his face for support.

"I couldn't leave and keep their money. I mean, they paid us in advance. If we bolt now without giving the money back, it'd be like stealing."

"Then we'll give it back!" Mary was close to hysteria and Vince looked genuinely surprised.

"Just like that?" he demanded. "We just hand back the money and toss ourselves out on the streets? What the hell are we going to do then? Panhandle? No money. No car. Shit, that's crazy!" He was on his feet, leaning over the table shouting in her face.

Mary blinked but refused to back down. "This . . . this place is trying to . . . to destroy us. Can't you see that?"

Vince pushed away from the table, moving about the kitchen in agitation. He looked out the window, studying the quiet, misty tombstones in the early morning light, then he whirled and leveled a finger at Mary. "I see what you're doing. You're trying to break up the first good thing that's happened to us.'' He gestured wildly toward the window. ''What I see out there is a fucking cemetery. It's filled with old bones from a lot of egotistical jerks who poured good money into monuments so they'd be remembered. And that is *all* I see!''

Mary looked at him. She felt hurt and betrayed. Couldn't he see what this place was doing to them? ''Vince it's . . .''

''It's what, goddamn it?'' he exploded, grabbing a jar of coffee from the counter top and hurling it to the floor. It exploded in a shower of glass fragments and scattered grounds.

She looked at him with huge, frightened eyes. She felt so afraid. For him and herself. This place had somehow changed them and still changing them, influencing them. Mary wanted to reach out and take Vince in her arms. She wanted to convince him to leave.

But one look at his angry, red face told her it would be useless.

''What the hell do you want from me?'' he screamed, lashing out at one of the cabinets with his foot, cracking the door with his heavy boot.

Mary had never seen him like this and it terrified her.

''Nothing,'' she whispered, not looking at him. She did not want to do anything to provoke him further. This violent mood was so alien to his nature, that she knew instinctively he was very dangerous right now.

''Yeah, right,'' he snarled sarcastically, storming out of the kitchen and crashing out the front door.

She sat quietly for a moment and then covered her face with her hands. The tears came in a flood.

Oh, dear God. What's going on? What is this place doing to Vince? To me? God help us!

Mary felt such a sense of despair and sadness she thought she could never again smile or know happiness. All she and Vince had asked was an opportunity to work, to survive and to make a better life.

Instead they walked out of a relatively comfortable, if frustrating reality, and into an endless nightmare.

Vince started walking along the path next to the fence. He was uncharacteristically angry and there was a tight ball of fury in his gut, burning and growing.

What the hell *does* she expect from me, he thought. What a bitch! I get a decent job and she pisses and moans about it.

He stomped along the path, eying the fence, but concentrating on that little knot of anger growing in his middle. It was spreading through him, rushing through his veins and filling him with a consuming rage.

A part of him found it pleasurable, exhilerating.

He'd show her. When he finished here, he'd go back to the cottage and show her. What the hell did she want anyway? What was so bad about this place? What the hell was wrong with working here?

The raging anger was expanding. Vince felt it clutch at him like a powerful hand, gripping him, holding him. He was sweating in spite of the early morning chill. He touched his face. It felt hot and feverish.

Mist shifted and creeped among the stones and around the trees and bushes. Its wispy tendrils snaked across the wet grass and entwined around Vince's legs. With it came a heightening of his rage and anger; a mindless and raw emotional fury.

Vince stopped.

"I'm going back and kick her cheap ass!" he yelled at the stillness.

But he couldn't. Not just yet. He had to make his rounds. He had to inspect the cemetery. No telling what some filthy vandal had done during the night . . .

. . . he had to make his rounds.

He turned and continued on the path, cursing and mumbling to himself.

"Get the rounds done," he hissed. "Then I can stomp some sense into Mary."

Mary rose from the table and stumbled up the stairs. The coffee was churning in her stomach and a wave of nausea swept over her. Bitter acid burned her throat and she barely reached the bathroom before she retched and vomited.

She sat on her knees in front of the toilet for a long time, her hand on the edge of the sink to steady her against the vertigo. Her vision was blurred with tears and dizziness.

After a time, she got slowly to her feet and moved shakily to the bedroom. Lying on the big, canopied bed, she waited for her stomach to settle and her head to stop spinning.

What is happening?

NINE

Joshua Ortega parked his Buick next to the curb near a sleezy pawn shop. He glanced, first at Agnes, who sat quietly, her handbag clutched in her old hands, and then at the ragged assortment of derelicts leaning or sitting against the wall of the building.

"Are you sure you want to do this?" he asked her.

"Yes," she answered firmly. "I have to."

He turned and fixed her with a hard stare. "This is *not* a good idea. Look at these people. They're down-and-outers. They'd as soon knock us in the head for loose change as look at us."

"Are you frightened, Josh?" she asked quietly, not trying to provoke or insult him.

He looked away from her and nodded. "Yes. I'm not a young man. There was a time I'd have walked anywhere in this city without a worry. Now . . ." He shook his head.

Agnes reached over and patted his brown, wrinkled hand with hers. "We'll be fine. I promise."

"How can you promise that? We're just a couple of old geezers lining up to get our heads bashed in like lambs being led to the slaughter.'' He was agitated and upset. In the cool morning light, the thought of demons and creatures and Ouija boards and ominous messages from another dimension paled against the prospect of walking in this decayed, desolate neighborhood where violence was a matter of survival.

Agnes sighed. ''They stay here, Josh. I'll go alone.'' She pushed open the door and stepped stiffly out into the warming morning air, already fouled by the stench of auto exhaust and diesel fumes. Cars, trucks and motorcycles roared up and down the street, pumping more noxious poison into the air and adding to the general roar of the city coming to life. Sirens and horns wailed and bleated in the distance. She glanced up and saw the bluish clouds of pollution moving around the tops of the towering buildings dotting the Denver skyline.

''Damnit, Aggie,'' Joshua snapped, getting out of the car. ''You make me feel like the coward I'm not.''

She glanced over the car's roof at him and smiled. ''I'm sorry. I don't mean to make you feel that way. I know you're not a coward. But will you trust me. Please?''

He grimaced and nodded. ''Alright. But lock the car. I don't trust any of these folks.''

The dozen or so men surrounding the pawn shop made no move toward them, but to a man, they eyed them with suspicion and curiosity as the pair stepped to the sidewalk and made for a nearby alleyway.

Joshua held Agnes's arm firmly in his massive wrinkled hand, keeping a careful eye out for gaping holes and dangerous cracks in the sidewalk. He glanced around occasionally to make certain no one was stalking them.

Agnes walked with poise and grace, her head held high and her back erect. She felt very good, better than she had in years. The gnawing arthritic pain was gone and other than some minor stiffness in her knees and elbows, she could not remember feeling this vigorous and unhampered by aches and pains for many years.

She knew Joshua was nervous and intimidated by this seamy, dangerous neighborhood. Normally, she would have been just as fearful, but she *knew* they were safe. How could she explain it to him? What could she say to make him understand the sense of well being, purpose and power that was flooding through her? There were no words she could find to express it. He would simply have to trust her.

After the departure of the grisly night visitor, an event she had not mentioned to Joshua, she had slept well. She awoke early, feeling refreshed and alert. While she drank her first cup of tea, Agnes considered her calm and undisturbed state of mind. She knew she should be cowering in her bed, dreading to leave it for fear another nightmare creature was waiting for her, ready to pounce. Instead, she was relaxed and filled with a sense of power and a calm resolve.

Agnes had waited for a time before rousing Joshua from the couch. As he had awakened, she could see his eyes change as the memories of the previous night filled his mind. He had pleaded with her to abandon her plan to go downtown, but she had only shooed him off to the bathroom to shower while she fixed them a quick breakfast.

Now, moving carefully along the sidewalk, she followed the instructions the Ouija board had given her. When they reached the alley, she turned to move down it.

"Aggie," Josh whispered, looking down the narrow, trash-strewn passage. "This is definitely not a good idea."

"Come on, Josh," she said, stepping into the dim, ominous tunnel between the tall, delapidated buildings.

He glanced back, expecting to see a horde of club-wielding, ragged men about to fall upon them. Instead, he saw only the endless stream of cars moving up and down the avenue and the down-and-outers shuffling on the sidewalk across the street.

As they stepped into the alley, the street noises were suddenly muffled by the brick and concrete surrounding them.

Agnes led the way, deftly moving around the mounds of garbage, piles of rags and heaps of papers and junk. Her eyes were fixed on a doorway halfway down the alley. When they reached it, she unhesitatingly twisted the knob and pushed it open

They stared into the gloomy interior, the sunlight filtering in, catching the dust motes dancing in the musty, warm air.

"Here?" Josh asked, peering suspiciously into the opening, stroking his moustache nervously.

"Yes," she said, pulling her arm free of his hand and stepping inside. A naked, low-wattage bulb dimly illuminated the opening. Without pausing, Agnes gripped the railing of the old staircase and began descending. Pushing the door shut, Joshua reluctantly followed her.

When they reached the room at the bottom of the stairs, an old boiler squatted in the middle of the concrete floor. Agnes did not pause, but moved beyond it to the door hidden by its bulk and knocked.

"I hope you're sure . . ." Joshua said, his words dying on his lips as the door was pulled open.

They both stared at the handsome, white-haired man who flashed them a warm smile, stood aside and, with a wave of his hand, motioned for them to enter.

"I've been expecting you," he said in greeting.

Joshua cleared his throat as they moved into the opulently appointed room. "You knew we were coming?"

Their host nodded and smiled gravely. "Yes. Please come in. Can I offer you some coffee or tea?"

"Tea, please," Agnes said, marveling at the walls of books and the finely preserved furnishings.

The man asked them to sit and then vanished into the kitchen, returning almost immediately with a tray holding a pot of hot water, three cups and an assortment of teabags.

"Tobias Rathbone," their host said, as he poured the steaming water into the cups.

Joshua glanced at Agnes and then introduced himself.

Agnes smiled and looked at Rathbone knowingly. "I believe you already know my name," she said.

Rathbone nodded. "Indeed, I do. Agnes Hardwick." He glanced over her shoulder and smiled. "And quite an array of spirits. Your guides have summoned an extraordinary group to lend you aid and support."

Joshua looked around, seeing only the wall of books and the fine pieces of furniture.

"You can see them?" Agnes asked, moving the string on the teabag up and down in the cup, the saucer poised on her lap.

"Oh, yes. I can see a great many things." Rathbone's eyes darkened. "Sometimes, too much."

"What do you know about . . . everything that is going on around us?" Agnes asked, eyeing Rathbone curiously.

Rathbone heaved a heavy sigh. "I know more than I wish to know and yet not enough. There's a disturbance near us. A very ominous disturbance. It's a coming together of powerful forces and great disorder."

"Oh, Christ," Joshua exploded. "Let's cut all this cryptic bullshit and get down to brass tacks. I'm tired of hearing all this mystic mumbo-jumbo. What in the hell is going on?"

Agnes looked at him, surprised and amazed, a hint of a smile playing on her lips. Rathbone, too, studied the aging Hispanic with something close to amusement.

"You're right, Joshua," Rathbone said. "You're absolutely right. I have a penchant for speaking in riddles. I'll try to be more explicit."

Joshua nodded, his eyes locked on Rathbone's. "I, for one, would appreciate that."

"I assume you have both heard of Mansfield Memorial Cemetery," he said, looking at them.

"South of town?" Agnes asked. "Very private, if I recall. I haven't heard anything about it for years."

"It's still there," Rathbone went on. "It's filled now. I don't believe there has been a burial there recently. Not for a couple of decades, at least. Anyway, it appears to be the center of all this activity we've been experiencing.''

Joshua, still mistrustful of Rathbone, fixed him with a leveled gaze. ''Why?''

''It's complex. The cemetery is a . . . focal point of . . . evil, for lack of a better word. A place where forces have gathered.

''Now, before you ask,'' he rushed on, motioning quickly with his hand to keep them from interrupting. ''Mansfield has an odd history, which makes it the ideal gathering point for these malignant powers. In fact, I believe it was designed and built for exactly that purpose.''

''A place created specifically for this evil power to gather?'' Joshua asked, unconvinced.

''Yes.''

''What makes it different than any of the other cemeteries around the city?'' Agnes wanted to know.

Rathbone placed his empty teacup on the tray and leaned back in his chair, staring into the middle distance.

''The cemetery was begun over a century ago by some very distasteful men. They were enchanted . . . or more properly, entranced by dark, evil forces. These weren't men who sat around their parlors holding hands in a seance or fiddling with Tarot cards. Not at all. These were men who tapped into satanic powers, conducted damning ceremonies in dark places, practiced human sacrifice and committed acts of debauchery that rivaled some of the most disgusting atrocities in history.''

Agnes and Joshua listened intently, their forgotten cups of tea growing cold on their laps, as Rathbone's deep voice rumbled on.

''These men unleashed forces that they could not come anywhere near close to understanding. Still, they tried to control them, manipulate them and ultimately use them for their own greeds and lusts.

''They attracted quite a following and it was all kept very quiet. If one of them mentioned his association with the others, he would simply be found dead or would have a terrible accident. They were a very serious, very dangerous lot."

"Why hasn't any of this ever been publicized?" Joshua asked, warming to Rathbone's tale despite his skepticism.

Rathbone laughed without a trace of humor. "Quite simple. None of the group wanted to end up under the wheels of a train or crushed by a piece of machinery or dropped down an elevator shaft or worse. In short, the others knew every move each individual made."

"So they were Devil worshipers?" Joshua pressed.

"In a way. Your religion would call it the Devil. It has been called by many names over the centuries, but it has always been Evil.

"They didn't simply worship the Devil. They became . . . tangibly evil themselves. They were devils, of a sort, I suppose. Oh, they weren't out trying to capture souls or lure innocent people into what you would call Hell. They used their attachment to the dark forces for their own ends. Money. Power. Sex. Whatever they wanted, they could obtain." Rathbone paused and stared absently at the ceiling, his mind pondering his own words.

"How does the cemetery figure into all of this?" Agnes asked after a time.

Rathbone blinked, pulling himself out of deep thought. He smiled at the old woman. "Ah, yes. The cemetery. It was designed as a . . . temporary resting place for these people. Conventionally, many people believe that when they are dead they either simply cease to be or they pass on to another plane of existence. The burial of their body, as ritualistic as it is, is simply a place to deposit their earthly remains for eternity. A final resting place.

"But these men and, I should add, women—there were a few in this evil fellowship—wanted a place to rest until they were resurrected . . ."

"Resurrected? As in: Brought back from the dead?" Joshua asked, his tone blatantly mocking.

Rathbone bobbed his head, his mane of white hair floating about it like a halo. "Absolutely. However, not exactly as you would believe. Basically, you probably believe in a Judgement Day of one sort or another. Either everyone rising at the end of the world or each soul facing *his* or *her* own judgement day upon death."

He studied Joshua for confirmation. The other man shrugged noncommittally and nodded.

"These men thought they were seeking basically the same thing. Only they tapped into a force that doesn't concern itself with rising souls. Not hardly.

"Through some ritual or another, I don't really know which, they aligned themselves with the Dark Mistress . . ."

"Who?" Agnes interrupted.

"Oh, She's known by many names. The Dark Mistress, the Woman of the Blackness, the Ebon Whore, the Occult Madonna. I personally prefer to think of her as the Black Bitch," Rathbone glanced at Agnes. "Pardon the expression."

"None of us are children," she said.

"Indeed, we are not."

"So what is this . . . this Occult Madonna?" Joshua wanted to know.

Rathbone did no answer immediately. Instead, he poured another cup of hot water and dropped a tea bag into it. Then he fixed his questioner with a hard stare. "Some say She is the mother of Satan; the mother of all Evil. Actually, I don't know. Nor, frankly, do I care. It is not my role to determine her origins. It is my role to defeat her, if I can and, most certainly, nullify her threat at all costs."

Joshua stood up, placing his cup carefully on the tray. "I'm sorry, Aggie," he said. "I can't sit here and listen to this nonsense. I've read a lot of occult literature and more than my share of mysticism and I've never run across references to a Black Bitch or the Devil's Mother or whatever you want to call her. I think we're wasting our time . . ."

"Sit down, Josh," Agnes said sternly, her eyes flashing.

"Aggie," Joshua said, his face darkening. "It's rubbish. It's some great scheme . . ."

"Yes, Mr. Ortega," said Rathbone, not moving from his chair, a frown twisting his mouth. "It *is* a great scheme. A great, evil scheme. And like it or not, you're a part of it."

Joshua paled slightly, his resolve crumbling. "A part of a delusion, I think . . ."

"No," snapped Rathbone. "You don't think. You may have read and studied all the books and monographs and articles on the mystic and the ancient forces, but you're still trapped by your own disbelief. Well, let me assure you. It is not an abstract. It is a reality. Out there, at that cemetery, there is a force of infinite evil. It's real. A dark power that's becoming a physical presence."

Joshua stared at Rathbone. He was a proud man, not used to being spoken to in such a rough manner nor used to having his beliefs questioned.

"Josh," said Agnes, her voice quiet and gentle. "Please. For me. Won't you sit down and hear what Mr. Rathbone has to tell us?"

He looked at her and nodded ever so slightly. "For you," he said, dropping back into the chair.

"Please, Mr. Rathbone. Continue," she said, still very subdued.

"Indeed, there are very few references to the Black Bitch in literature. But, She exists, none the less. She is, in fact, the enemy of Death. Death is transformation. Not an evil thing, but a benign power, relieving the sick, the old, the tired of their maladies . . ."

"And taking life from the young, the healthy, the innocent," Joshua added bitterly.

"Yes," agreed Rathbone without elaboration, refusing to rise to the other man's bait. "The Black One gives the dead the promise of renewed life or more precisely, the parody of life. She can raise the bones, animate them, instill a spark of consciousness, but there is no real life."

Agnes found herself shuddering. "It's dreadful to think about."

Rathbone agreed. "It has consumed my thoughts for far too long, I fear. My powers are growing weak and I am tired. It has been a very, very long road."

'Who, or should I say what, exactly are you?" Joshua asked, a bit too harshly. His pride was still smarting.

Rathbone laughed, a deep, booming bass drum sound which rumbled from someplace deep within him. "I am, like you, flesh and blood. My flesh is older and my blood a little thinner, but I am human, mortal."

Joshua squinted and studied the other man suspiciously. "How much older?"

"Oh, some years . . ."

"How many?"

Rathbone sighed and shook his head. "You're very persistent, Mr. Ortega. All I will tell you is that I have seen and experienced much. My people were of an ancient order. I will say no more."

Joshua and Agnes exchanged glances. Perhaps, this strange man *was* crazy, the victim of his own madness.

Agnes thought about the message from the board. If this was indeed the Druid, then he could be the old, ancient entity she was instructed to seek out. If he wasn't, his madness was remarkable, if not darkly fascinating.

Rathbone waved his hand in dismissal. "Believe me or not. Just know that I am *not* mad. I've lived too long to grow angry when others choose to think me a liar. Or insane."

"I know you're not insane, Tobias," Agnes said. "May I call you that?"

"Of course," he smiled. "Let me add that I truly have lived in this worn out old body too long. I am growing very fatigued and I grow tired of the fight." Rathbone spoke wearily, his voice holding the accumulative lassitude of a score of lives lived.

They were all silent for several minutes. Agnes studied

the titles on the spines of the books arranged on the shelves near where she sat, Joshua gazed absently into his tea cup and Rathbone, eyes closed, leaned back in his chair.

"There is much to do," he said at last, eyes still shut.

"I'm still not sure where we should begin," said Agnes quietly. "In fact, I don't understand my role in this at all."

Rathbone straightened in his chair. "Of course not. Let me prepare another pot of water and then we'll talk." He got stiffly out of his chair and picked up the tray.

After he moved into the kitchen, Joshua leaned toward Agnes, his voice a whisper.

"This is . . crazy, Aggie. Let's get out of here."

She looked at him, again the fire burning in her eyes. "Josh, will you just relax? This is so unlike you to be so . . . so damned closed minded."

Joshua was taken aback. Agnes seldom swore and her icy, angry tone startled him.

"Alright," he sighed. "We'll hear him out. But if he puts you into any danger . . . I'll . . " He did not finish his vow, interrupted by Rathbone's return.

Agnes touched Joshua's face and smiled. "You're a sweet man, Josh. I appreciate your concern."

Rathbone placed the tray on the table and offered them both a cryptic, knowing smile. Joshua had the uncomfortable sensation that his mysterious host had heard his every word.

"I've been to the cemetery," said Rathbone, as he refilled their cups. "Yesterday I went there. It was very dangerous for me. As I said, my resources have grown weak recently and a short time ago I had a brush with two very evil blackguards who are still hunting me. As it happens, and by no small coincidence, they are the overseers of the cemetery."

Blackguards, Agnes thought. What an odd and archaic word to use. But she let it pass and instead asked, "What did you learn at the cemetery?"

Rathbone shook his head sadly. "They—my two adversaries—have lured a young couple there. They no doubt came willingly and innocently to be caretakers. I tried to warn the young man, but to no avail. Whether or not he realizes it yet, the cemetery and the entity which now roams there has trapped him and the woman."

"And how do you know these two people are in danger?" Joshua prodded.

Rathbone looked at him and smiled. "I know. But what I don't know is why they were chosen. These overseers don't do anything without a purpose."

"What kind of danger are they in?" Agnes asked.

"I'm not sure. If that Black Bitch *is* involved—and I believe She is—the danger is terrible. Already, I know they have been victimized."

"Then why don't they simply escape?" Joshua's skepticism was still forcing him to spar verbally with Rathbone.

"I doubt they can. The girl left the cemetery yesterday and returned in a taxi. Their vehicle was wrecked. I think the forces there want them to stay."

"You mean they *can't* leave?" Joshua snorted, ignoring Agnes's disapproving glance.

Rathbone fixed him with a hard stare. "Exactly. They move around within the confines of the cemetery, but they can't leave. Oh, they might consider it, but they can't. Something will always stop them."

"And what can we do to help them?" Agnes's voice was firm and controlled. She had now resolved to do whatever was needed, regardless of Joshua's doubts and objections.

Rathbone fished a pipe from one of the pockets of his jacket and a worn leather tobacco pouch from the other. He filled the pipe, tamped the tobacco down and lit it with a kitchen match taken from a small holder on the table. With a cloud of smoke drifting around him, he looked at Agnes and smiled warmly.

"You're a remarkable woman, Aggie, to be gifted with

the ability to contact other planes. Many try, but most can only reach the perimeters of the other dimensions. You can reach their hearts.''

''Through the board you mean?'' she asked.

He nodded. ''You have great energy which allows the spirits an effective channel through which they can contact our world.'' Rathbone glanced around the room again and turned back to Agnes. ''Judging by the array of spirits accompanying you, you are safe from those spirits which can enter your head and possess your mind.''

''Such a thing can happen?'' she wanted to know. She had never experienced such a phenomenon, although she usually *heard* the voices of the spirits in her mind even as the pointer darted over the board.

''Oh yes,'' Rathbone told her emphatically. ''Then can enter your body and hold it. It is very bad and can be very dangerous. However, your guides are very strong.''

''You still haven't answered her question, Mr. Rathbone,'' Joshua said, his voice edged with impatience.

Rathbone laughed softly. ''Always the pragmatist, eh, Mr. Ortega? Very well. I'll tell you exactly what we have to do.

''We have to go to the cemetery together. Getting inside will not be easy, but I have enough power left to get us through a few simple metal bars. Then we will use your board, Aggie, to make contact with one of the spirits that walk that place . . .''

''You want me to contact this . . . this evil *thing?*'' Agnes blurted, her hand at her throat.

''No,'' Rathbone snapped. ''Absolutely not! That could prove disasterous. You'll contact one of the dead buried there. It will not be hard.''

''This is beginning to sound more insane by the second,'' Joshua cried in disgust. ''Do you think I'll allow Aggie to break into a cemetery and . . and commit an act of . . .''

"Of what?" challenged Rathbone, his voice level, his eyes blazing with an unnatural fire.

Joshua looked at the woman, his eyes beseeching. "Aggie, for God's sake. This is nuts! You're too old to be running around a cemetery. Can't you see that?"

"Josh," she answered in a steel-hard voice which he could not believe came from her, even though he sat across from her. "Enough! either you listen and be quiet or you leave. Tobias and I have things to discuss. I can't believe you're being such an old fart!"

Joshua stared at her, his mouth working, but no words came out. A vein in his temple throbbed and his face grew dark. He started to rise and then slumped back into his chair with a muttered curse.

"Don't be too harsh, Aggie," said Rathbone, much to the woman's surprise and causing Joshua to look at him curiously. "He is not trying to discourage you because he thinks I'm a madman; he's trying to dissuade you because he knows I'm right. Isn't that correct, Joshua?"

The other man was quiet for a long time and then he nodded, but said nothing. He stared at the carpeting, his hands clasped together between his knees.

"You see, Aggie," Rathbone continued. "Joshua is filled with raw psychic energy, although he denies it. He may have told you that his interest in what your world so mistakenly calls the occult, was purely academic. It isn't. Joshua is a man filled with a gift which he tries to shun, but can not."

"Is that true, Josh?" Agnes spoke softly, feeling ashamed for her earlier harshness.

Joshua drew in a deep breath, lifted his head and looked first at Rathbone and then Agnes.

"It's true," he said in a low, toneless voice. "I've always recognized an . . . ability in myself. I've felt it all my life. I suppose thats why I read and studied all that material for all those years; I hoped to discover what it meant, what it was for. I learned a lot, but not about my . . . gift.''

Joshua's eyes strayed to one of Rathbone's bookcases, scanning the titles to avoid looking at the other two.

''Because your books can't tell you,'' interjected Rathbone. ''The power is developed by training and use, not by sticking your nose in a book.''

Joshua glared at his host. ''Then *you* tell me what it is. I've spent a lifetime trying to figure it out.''

Rathbone's voice was calm and patient, but not patronizing. ''Your energy is raw. I supose at some point it could have been developed and focused, but that time is past. You've denied it too long and now it will have to be channeled through Aggie. That's why you're part of all this. Think of yourself as a battery; an energy transmitter and Aggie as the receiver. If you consciously link up to her, she'll be incredibly potent.''

Rathbone looked curiously at the old woman. ''Have you two ever worked the Ouija board together?''

''Only once. Last night.''

''Anything unusual happen?''

Agnes nodded and told Rathbone about the strange tape recorded message and her new sense of strength and resolve.

''You see, Josh,'' Rathbone said. ''When you both linked up, you opened a portal of sorts for that entity. It was your combined powers that did it. Aggie was drawing on your vast resources and has revitalized herself both physically and mentally. You have an awesome reserve.''

Joshua was speechless. After years of fruitless searching, a stranger offered the answer to the puzzle of his life. It sounded unbelievable, yet he knew Rathbone was close to the truth.

He just wasn't sure he could, or wanted to the force harbored within him.

''So,'' Rathbone said. ''Do we proceed together or not?''

"We do," Agnes replied immediately, looking questioningly at her friend.

Joshua thought for a moment and then slowly nodded. "Yes. Like it or not, I can't let Aggie down." Frankly, he could not allow her to face something as monstrous as this *thing* Rathbone described alone.

"Good. We have much to plan and prepare for. Shall we begin?"

Rathbone sounded much more confident than he felt. There was a malignant force stalking all of them and to deal with it, they had to confront it on its own ground. He had no romantic delusions about such a confrontation nor about his own abilities. Evil was evil and its malevolence was never to be assumed to be anything but the combined power of *all* Evil.

Chaos was near and he had doubts about his own skills, let alone the untrained and unchanneled capabilities of Agnes Hardwick and Joshua Ortega.

TEN

The guttering candle struggled against the Stygian darkness cloaking the subterranean room. Its feeble flame formed a small, dim circle of light which barely crept beyond the edge of the battered and stained top of the round table, illuminating only the two pairs of hands resting on the rough surface.

The fat, sausage fingers of one pair of hands were wet and sticky with gore which formed a spreading puddle on the dry wood. The others, in contrast, were long, ghostly white, and as unblemished as bleached bone.

The room was silent save for the shallow breathing of the two at the table and the faint creak of the heavy hemp rope, which supported the thing suspended in the corner. It slowly turned in the blackness as blood softly and steady dripped to the wooden floor. Occasionally, small feet would scurry across the stone floor and fierce, tiny eyes would momentarily glisten in the candle's weak light.

The coppery stench of blood and the noxious stink of burned and scorched meat and singed hair permeated the room, mingled with the heavy smells of mold and rot. A smokey pall, trapped by the damp, moss-slickened stone walls, shifted around the flame like spectral fingers, weaving cloudy patterns in its dim light.

"The rite is done," Henry Terrance rumbled, his fat face emerging from the shadows, allowing the fluttering flame to highlight his expressionless features. He kept his blood-drenched hands on the table, ignoring the dark, wet blotch they formed on the wood.

"Is it sufficient?" Oscar Bedlow asked in a flat voice. His skeletal features and gaunt body were still shrouded in the darkness.

Terrance nodded slowly. "Yes. The sacrifice and blood rite are simple enough." The corpulent face twisted into a frown. "Are you sure no one saw you take the kid?"

"Henry," Bedlow answered, irritation lacing his words. "You know I'm no amateur. The child will simply be listed as a runaway. One of thousands. His body can join the bones of the others at the bottom of the pit. It's not as if it was the first time I've done it. Don't worry about it."

"Ordinarily I wouldn't Oscar. But I don't like it when we have to snatch kids. It's very risky . . ."

"And worth the risk," snapped Bedlow. "The boy was wandering alone along that bike path by the canal. No one saw me." He rubbed his hands together anxiously. "The time of the Rising is almost at hand. That's what's really important."

The rope continued to creak and groan in the darkness as the eviscerated corpse slowly turned.

"So it is, Oscar. And that's why we can't take any chances. Have you any idea what they would do to us if we were to be caught?" Terrance was being uncharacteristically worrisome, much to his companion's annoyance.

"We won't be caught, Henry."

"And what about Cassidy? His influence on the girl is stronger than we anticipated. Why don't we simply rid ourselves of him?"

Bedlow leaned forward, his gaunt face grotesquely illuminated in the yellow glow, his lips pulled back in a sneer, exposing his large ivory teeth.

"Not yet. You're damned well beginning to wear on my nerves. Patience, Henry, patience. We'll be rid of him soon enough. Already his influence is weakening and his will is being sapped. Don't be so damned contrite. Everything is going just as planned."

"Except for Rathbone," Terrance pointed out, spitting the name as if it were a curse. "No one planned on his arrival."

"True," Bedlow nodded. "Nor the old woman. Still, we have to expect some stumbling blocks. The forces that are assembling at Mansfield naturally attract opposing forces. We'll eliminate both of them soon enough."

"If they should join together . . ."

"Undoubtedly they will. It'll make the slaughter that much easier. Two for the price of one." Bedlow's mouth split into a sardonic grin, his oversized teeth again gleaming in the candle light.

"We almost had Rathbone, Oscar. We almost had him."

"It was our own fault he escaped us. We underestimated his abilities."

Terrance nodded. "Yes. He's powerful, but not unstoppable. He *does* command some awesome elemental forces, but they are weakening and he can't affect a sustained assault. Still, he worries me . . ."

"Bah!" Bedlow roared. "You're ranting like an old hag." He leaned closer, his chair creaking, and glared at his fat companion. His eyes were quizzical as they studied Terrance. "Are you afraid?"

Terrance frowned. "No. Of course not. It's just that now, with everything set into motion, we're suddenly confronted with opponents we hadn't anticipated."

"The Rising will solve that, Henry. When our fathers, grandfathers and their comrades walk again, all our efforts will have been worth it." Bedlow's eyes shifted and clouded as his mind turned to thoughts of the Rising. A century in the planning and soon the fruits of those plans would be fulfilled.

That was the promise *She* made to Mansfield's founders over a century ago. They would be granted life on earth after their deaths; they would rise from under the ground and out of their stone sarcophaguses and be given new life. Again, they would walk among the men and women of the world.

She would give them the opportunity to defeat Death.

Neither Bedlow nor Terrance had any idea exactly how those long-dead men had first reached Her. No doubt some incantation performed in this very room had brought Her forth. Both their grandfathers had been there. What an experience it must have been; what an accomplishment to tap into such a primal force. To have watched as She took form and shape before their very eyes, stepping forward from some mystic dimension to offer them an eternity of life and omnipotence over their individual worlds.

Bedlow could remember his father telling him that some of those with his grandfather that fateful night had actually gone mad from sheer ecstacy. They had raved and cried out until the others were forced to kill them, fearing that in a state of mental collapse, they would babble their success to others outside the Circle.

"Think of it, Henry," Bedlow said to Terrance, who sat sullenly, his gore-splattered hands still resting on the table. "Think of what it will mean when our fathers and grandfathers again join the living. Our power will be unbelievable. Anything we want—absolutely *anything*—will be ours for the taking. The combined strength of our ancestors and their comrades . . ."

He suddenly stood, his hands braced against the table, his face luminescent in the flickering flame. His eyes sparked with the mania of his dark destiny. The pupils, surrounded by the red-veined milkiness, fixed Terrance with a gaze so intense and mad, even the obese man shivered.

"Nothing can stop us," Bedlow hissed, his clenched fists poised on the table top. "Nothing."

"We've still got to stop Rathbone . . ."

A fist slammed to the table top. "Will you stop whining about that old fuck?"

In spite of himself, Terrance flinched as his companion's voice echoed off the stone walls. He was only too aware of Oscar's temper, his uncontrollable rages and his penchant for violence.

In fact, although he would never admit it, Bedlow scared him. Terrance had watched him kill at the slightest provocation, literally tearing victims limb from limb with his bare hands and unnatural strength. He had witnessed the unbridled sexual lusts, unleashed on women and children, not to abate until the object of his brutal appetite lay dead or had been reduced to a quivering mass of bloodied, torn flesh. He had watched in fascination as the gaunt, skeletal man inflicted such torment on man and beast that life seeped away only after days of unrelenting pain and unfathomed agony.

Even today, when the need for haste to complete the blood rite was paramount, Bedlow had milked the child's terror and torment for all it would yield. It was always left up to Terrance to handle the rituals and rites. Bedlow simply enjoyed the slaughter.

In the silence, Terrance was reminded of that so recently completed ritual, by the groan of the rope as the dead, blood-drained corpse continued to rotate in the darkness. Below it, in the pit covered by the wooden cover, were the remains of countless other victims, sacrificed for their blood and the accompanying power its proper use could bring the skilled practitioner.

A century of blood and bones and stolen life was heaped in the black recesses of that pit. Soon the fruits of all that suffering and death would come to pass.

"You're right, Oscar. I'll turn my energies to better things," Terrance said quietly, not looking at Bedlow.

"Good," the other man said, dropping back into his chair, his face receding into the darkness.

"Today's ceremony will insure the success of our rituals on the night of the full moon," he continued. "Two more days, Henry. Just today and tomorrow and the Rising will commence."

"You didn't hear from Cassidy this morning?" Terrance asked.

"No."

"Good. Then there were no more open graves. There have been enough as it is, Oscar. I'd hate for our fathers to . . . to reemerge like Wainwright and the others."

Bedlow's voice hissed from the darkness. "It's *Her* way! *Her* choice! It's not for us to second guess Her decisions. Perhaps Wainwright and the others deserved to be brought back incomplete."

"Perhaps . . ." Terrance sounded unconvinced. "Still. It was such a . . . a mockery."

"Mockery? Be careful you don't mock Her," Bedlow warned.

"I'm not, Oscar. But what are we to do with *them*? We can't keep them locked up forever." The fat man frowned.

"She'll decide that, Henry. Don't worry about it. Besides, they may prove useful. There are other things to worry about."

"Of course," Terrance sighed.

"Now," Bedlow said calmly, his fingers steepled on the table. "What to do about Rathbone and that old woman."

"We've attempted to frighten the old woman off, but she has too much grit and nerve. It quite frankly surprises me," Terrance said.

"You would think she'd take our warnings more seriously. Only someone very bold or very naive continues in the face of such admonitions."

"Naive, I think," the fat man said. "Perhaps bold, but certainly naive."

"Once Rathbone is crushed beneath our feet, she'll be almost too easy to destroy. He's the one we have to stop."

Terrance thought for a few moments. "If we can lure him to the cemetery, it'll be no problem. If his powers are already fading, they'll be virtually useless at the cemetery, in the face of the Madonna."

"Don't underestimate him, Henry," Bedlow cautioned. "His kind have always been resourceful and tenacious."

The fat man nodded. "True. But once he's in the cemetery, he'll be defeated. He can't stand up to Her power for long. It's simply a matter of getting him there."

"It won't take much," Bedlow asserted. "In fact, he's already been there. Twice."

"Inside?" Terrance demanded excitedly, his face twisted into a mask of horror.

"No. Outside. But he made contact with Cassidy. Fortunately our new caretaker is too well rooted in the reality of the physical world to have paid him much attention." Bedlow laughed softly.

"Rathbone disguised himself as a bum," he continued. "It naturally fooled our people watching the cemetery, which was no doubt his intention. But She knew and that's all that matters. She is formidable."

"He must have known that She would detect his presence," Terrance said.

"He did. His concern for Cassidy and the woman took him there. That's his weakness and the bait we'll use to bring him *inside* the grounds," explained Bedlow.

Concern filled Terrance's eyes and marked furrows in his fat-swollen face. "We'll have to be careful. Nothing must happen to the woman . . ."

"Don't you think I know that?" snapped Bedlow. "It's not what happens to her that matters. It's what Rathbone assumes is happening to her that will bring him to us. The man is unimportant."

"Mary Renata," Terrance muttered the name in amazement. "I wonder if she has any idea who her ancestor was?"

"Not likely. She died almost two and a half centuries ago. But I've always wondered what went through the minds of those people accused of witchcraft and ultimately put to death? Did they curse their god? Did they disavow their faith when the flames started burning their flesh?" Bedlow's voice trailed away as he pondered the questions.

Terrance's frown evaporated and his plastic, artificial smile appeared. "Especially Maria Renata. A woman who devoted her entire life to that rabble, only to have them turn on her. It must have been . . . demoralizing."

Bedlow brayed in laughter. "A good word for it, Henry. Demoralizing. Yes, she must have been totally demoralized. She never knew the truth of her own birth."

"Now," he continued, again getting out of his chair. "Let's pull the cover off the pit and dispose of the body so we can get back to our work."

The fat man smiled in agreement, lifting one of his hands to his mouth so his tongue could lick at the sticky blood.

ELEVEN

Mary scrambled from the bed when she heard the front door bang open. Her stomach was still churning and as she stood, clutching one of the bedposts for balance, a fresh wave of nausea swept over her. She'd been lying on the bed for over an hour fighting the sickness, confused and frightened. She could make no sense of what was happening to her and to Vince. She desperately wanted to run away from Mansfield and yet she was afraid to step out of the gate; afraid for what would happen to her; afraid of what might happen to Vince.

What's happening to us? Why is it happening?

"Mary! Where the hell are you?" Vince yelled, thundering up the stairs. His boots slammed against the risers and thudded down the hall.

Mary could not answer. Her voice was constricted, her mouth dry. When Vince roared a second time, her knees were suddenly wobbly and for an instant she feared she was going to fall. Clinging to the canopy post, she watched the door, her eyes were wide, waiting for . . .

. . . what?

Vince burst into the room. His face, flushed and sweaty, was contorted and his eyes were wide and wild. Mary saw the madness in them and shrank away from it. His arms hung at his sides, his massive hands clenching and unclenching rhythmically, his fingernails digging bloody gouges into his palms.

"Slut," he hissed, not moving. "What do you want from me? What do you expect from me? Doesn't matter what I do for you, it ain't enough."

Vince stepped slowly into the room, kicking the door closed with his booted foot. He took another step towards Mary and she could only stare at him in naked terror.

She'd never seen him like this, never been afraid of him before.

"Well, it's time you learned a thing or two about ol' Vince," he continued, unfastening his belt and slowly pulling it free. "I'm going to beat your ass good . . ."

"Vince!" Mary screamed, stumbling away from the bed, judging her chances of reaching the door before he could grab her. They weren't good.

"Talk to me, Mary," he snarled, his lips curled back from his teeth as he continued to advance on her. "Tell ol' Vince how you been such a good woman."

She made a move for the door and Vince side stepped, effectively blocking the way.

"No way out," he snarled.

She edged away and then dashed to her right, Vince following like a shadow. Hoping to catch him off balance, Mary veered to her left and was almost past him when his hand shot out. The blow glanced off her shoulder and she staggered backward.

Stumbling into the wall, Mary fought the paralyzing panic welling in her. Her mind considered and dismissed a half dozen options in the space of a heartbeat. She was trapped. This was more than another of Vince's hallucinations. Something was holding sway over his reason, controlling his basic personality.

What's happening to us?

Mary could dash for the closet and lock herself inside, but where would that put her? Vince would either break down the door or simply wait her out. She could try to use something— anything—as a weapon with which to defend herself, but there was nothing close. Besides, Mary was afraid of truly hurting Vince. He was not in control of himself. If she managed to hurt him, she might do permanent damage or, worse, only manage to enrage him further.

Come on, Mary, she told herself. You kept your cool last night. You can do it now. Think! Think!

Her back to the wall, she drew a deep breath, squared her shoulders and stood erect. She could see only one viable option. With an effort, she forced herself to meet his hateful glare.

"Vince." Her voice was low and calm. It was taking all of her control to keep the hysteria tearing at her insides from gushing out of her mouth. "I love you."

"Slut! Whore! I'm going to beat you within a inch of your cheating life!" He snapped the belt like a whip, the tip popping like a rifle shot in the confined room. "I'm going to t . . teach y . . you."

"Put the belt down, honey." Mary spoke in soft, even tones filled with love and concern. There was no trace of the dread grasping at her heart in her voice.

Vince looked confused and his eyes fluttered as an odd expression crossed his face.

She sensed his inner conflict. He was struggling with whatever was controlling him. His eyes glazed for an instant, the madness replaced by fear.

"I love you," she said again, imploring him to believe her. She had to stay very calm. She knew her words would have an impact. She simply had to keep herself in control and keep working at breaking down whatever terrible force was blocking Vince's individuality from reemerging.

Vince's eyes were still locked on hers. He swayed. A look of pain passed over his face and his brow wrinkled in consternation. Mary could see the intense inner struggle he was waging etched on his face. For an instant his face relaxed, almost calm, but it passed and the anger returned. He began to advance again. The belt lashed out and its tip cracked, scant inches away from Mary's face.

"Vince," Mary entoned softly, edging very slowly along the wall, trying to position herself to make one last desperate dash for the door. "Honey, I love you. You don't want to hurt me, do you?"

"I . . . I . . ." He stammered and again paused, his eyes darting to his right hand holding the leather belt. He was suddenly breathing gulps, his chest heaving. His hand began to quiver and the fingers inched open. He stared at the belt in disbelief and dropped it as if was something alien and poisonous.

Mary watched. She could make it to the door now and flee, but she was rooted to the spot. Her heart was breaking for Vince as he again struggled with his inner demon. When he slumped to his knees, she rushed to him, all thought of escape forgotten.

Kneeling beside him, she circled her arms around his trembling body.

He gasped and shuddered with a great sob.

"Oh my God, Mary," he cried, pressing his head against her breast. "Wh . . what happened to me? To us?"

She shushed him, gently rocking him in her arms, her own tears now flooding her eyes. For a long time they sat there, Mary making comforting sounds and Vince clutching at her as if he was a frightened child.

Would Vince have beaten her; maybe killed her? she wondered.

Yes.

In the cold light of reason, the realization shocked her. Could she trust this wouldn't happen again? Could she be certain Vince wouldn't turn on her at any moment?

It's this damned place.

"What did happen, Vince?" she finally asked.

He drew a deep breath and shook his head. "I'm not sure. I was walking along the fence and I . . . I was so angry. Angry at you. Angry at everything. Everything but this fucking cemetery."

Mary shivered, holding Vince closer. As he continued to speak, she stared vacantly out one of the bedroom windows at the unmoving tops of the trees growing across Mansfield's grounds.

"I was *so* angry. I was enraged. I wanted to get back at you for . . . for something. I was jealous and bitter and . . ." Vince's voice broke and he pushed away from her. Head bowed, he sat in the middle of the floor. Finally he sighed and looked at her, his eyes wet and red. "It was . . . maybe like insanity. I was there, but not in control. Something *else* was inside of me. Jesus Christ, it was terrifying."

"Vince, we've got to leave."

"I know."

"Then let's get out. Now." Mary climbed to her feet, wiping her tears away with the back of her hand.

He looked up at her. "Will they let us?"

"We've got to try, Vince. We've got to! If we don't we'll end up killing each other, if this place doesn't kill us first."

He got up and took her in his arms. "Okay. Let's get the hell out of here."

Not wanting to waste time packing all of their things, they simply piled their clothes in a couple of battered suitcases. Vince grabbed the bags and they hurried down the stairs.

"Where should we go?" he asked when they reached the living room.

"It doesn't matter." Mary's voice reflected her tension. Now that they had decided to leave, she was suddenly terrified something would stop them. All she could concentrate on—all she *would* allow herself to think about—was getting out of this damned house and away from the cemetery.

"We'll have to call a cab," Vince told her, wishing he still had the pickup. "I want to get my tools. They're around the back."

Mary grabbed his arm.

"I'll go with you."

"Why?"

She gave him a hard look and he nodded. "Okay."

They stepped out the door and started along the front of the cottage. As Vince rounded the corner, Mary paused and looked at the acres of stone and marble interspersed among the towering pines, oaks and elms.

Under the morning sun, the cemetery was still and peaceful. For a moment, Mary wanted to laugh at her apprehensions. What was so wrong with this place? It was really quite lovely. Restful . . . safe and serene.

"Mary?" Vince looked around the corner, studying her. She continued to stand and stare vacantly over the cemetery grounds, a faint smile caressing her lips. He hurried to her.

"Mary!" The harshness of his voice broke the spell. She blinked and looked at him.

"Let's get out of here, Vince," she cried, almost panicky, realizing just what a tremendous influence the cemetery could exert on her.

He nodded, took her arm and led her to the back of the cottage. As Mary stood waiting, while Vince gathered his tools into the battered old metal box, a horn blared. They exchanged alarmed glances.

"Shit," Vince snarled. "Wait here." He walked to the side of the cottage and peered around the corner to get a view of the gate. Returning to Mary he shook his head. "Bedlow."

"Let's just go," Mary pleaded.

"Not yet. He'll stop us or have us stopped. Come on." He motioned for her to follow him.

"No. If we don't leave right now, we may never be able to."

"And if Bedlow suspects we're planning to cut out of here, you know damned good and well we'll never get away. All we have to do is see what he wants and wait until he's gone."

Vince was right and Mary knew it. Still, his logic did not quell the fear and frustration gnawing at her.

The horn blared again, sounding insistant and impatient.

"Go inside and hide the bags," Vince told her.

"Why?" she asked defiantly. "We're not prisoners."

"Aren't we? Just do it! Please."

Reluctantly, Mary walked back into the house while Vince trotted to the gate.

"What took you so long?" Bedlow asked after driving through the open gates and climbing out of the Cadillac.

Vince snapped the heavy lock and forced a smile as he looked up at Bedlow.

"Sorry. Were you waiting long?"

The tall, gaunt man shook his head. "No. How did your rounds go?"

"Fine," Vince lied. Actually, he could barely remember walking the fence and crisscrossing the grounds.

"Excellent. I'd like to have a look around. The full moon is almost on us, you know." Bedlow's sardonic smile was broad and Vince detected a quiver of excitement in the man's words.

In spite of the morning heat, Bedlow wore an overcoat, buttoned and belted.

"Right." Vince was momentarily mystified.

"The tour group." Bedlow reminded him.

Vince smiled and nodded. "Of course. I forgot. You know, we're still trying to get adjusted to everything."

"Naturally." Bedlow looked around. "Where is Ms. Renata? She'll join us on our walk, won't she?"

"Uh, sure. She just went inside for a minute. I'll get her." Vince started toward the cottage praying Bedlow wouldn't follow.

"Perhaps you have some coffee ready?"

Vince stopped and turned around. "I'm not sure. But we can make some if you'd like." He cursed himself silently, aware of the nervousness in his voice. He felt the sweat running down his sides as the older man fell into step with him. He opened the front door and held it for Bedlow.

Can't let him influence me, Vince thought. I've got to keep my presence of mind.

"Mary," Vince called. "We've got company. How about some coffee."

There was no answer.

"Mary?"

Still no answer.

"She must be upstairs," Vince told Bedlow. "Why don't you make yourself comfortable and I'll go find her."

"Fine," Bedlow answered, somewhat suspiciously, Vince thought.

Leaving Bedlow in the living room, Vince climbed the stairs. On the landing, he called for Mary again. There was no answer. Apprehensive, he hurried to their bedroom. It was empty. She was not in the bathroom nor the other bedrooms.

Where the hell has she gone? Vince wondered, refusing to let himself panic.

He returned to the stairs, mustering a smile for Bedlow's benefit. However, when he looked down from the landing, he could not see his employer.

Descending the stairs, he heard a shout from outside.

Taking the remaining steps two at a time, Vince raced out the front door just in time to see Mary pull away from Bedlow.

"Ms. Renata," the pale man was saying quietly. "I think you're overreacting."

"Overreacting?" she yelled back. "Bullshit! I just want out of here. Th . . . this place is . . . evil!"

"Ms. Renata," Bedlow said patiently, looking down at

her with an unreadable smile. "You're just not used to Mansfield yet. Give yourself some time . . ."

"Mary," Vince soothed, hurrying to her side and slipping an arm around her shoulders. "What's wrong?"

"Damnit, Vince," she snapped, jerking away from him. "Cut the crap. Why don't you tell him we want to leave?"

Bedlow turned slowly and fixed Vince with a questioning look. The smile was still playing on his mouth, but his eyes were as hard and cold as the bottom of an empty grave.

"You want to leave, Mr. Cassidy?"

Vince tried to meet his eyes, but couldn't. "Actually, yes we do."

"And why is that? Haven't we provided you with every amenity?"

"Yes," agreed Vince. "In fact, you've been very generous. But Mary and I are not cut out for this . . . place."

"What he's trying to tell you, Mr. Bedlow," Mary blurted, "is that we don't like being prisoners."

"Prisoners?" Bedlow said, sounding genuinely surprised and not a little amused.

"Right. Prisoners. Who are you trying to fool? We're trapped here . . ."

"That's nonsense," Bedlow soothed, cutting Mary off. "You're free to come and go as you please. I told you exactly what we expected when you were hired. There was nothing said about you not being able to come and go as you pleased."

"And when I tried, I was almost killed." She involuntarily shuddered as she remembered the wild scene on the Interstate.

"You're not seriously blaming *me* for your accident?"

"And how did you know I had an accident?" Mary demanded, sensing an opening.

Unflustered, Bedlow continued patiently, as if speaking to a child. "The hospital called Mr. Terrance. They wanted to verify that you worked for us. Insurance purposes."

His calm, logical explanation deflated Mary. She felt her fury waning. He was so damned reasonable. Too much so.

"Really, Ms. Renata, there's nothing sinister about it."

Vince met Bedlow's gaze. "A lot of strange things have been happening since we got here . . ."

"Strange is a pretty mild word for it," Mary cried, some of her fire returning. She looked from Vince to Bedlow. "It's been a nightmare!"

"Ah," said Bedlow, nodding his head. "I see." His arm swept around in an all-encompassing arc toward the sea of gravestones. "You've been victimized by them."

Both Mary and Vince looked at the man in disbelief. Was he actually going to admit that Mansfield was more than an ordinary graveyard?

"I will assume neither of you has ever been around a place such as Mansfield before. A cemetery, I mean. They are so steeped in mythology and superstition, it's no wonder you've been unnerved. Your imaginations have probably been running away with your reason . . ."

"That's ridiculous," Mary snapped. "What we've experienced hasn't been our imaginations."

"Then what was it?" Bedlow patronized.

She shook her head, glancing sideways at Vince. "I . . . we don't know and that's why we want out of here!"

Bedlow turned and gazed over the cemetery. A look of dismay traced lines over his skullish face. He stared for a long time before he finally spoke.

"Alright. I realize there is probably nothing I can say to convince you to stay. But, please, won't you just walk the grounds with me?"

"I don't think that's such a good idea . . ." Mary said, pausing when Vince laid a hand on her shoulder.

"Why?" he asked Bedlow.

Their employer turned and studied them for a moment. "To give me one last opportunity to convince you Mansfield is benign."

Vince glanced at Mary and shrugged.

"Vince, let's just go."

"It'll only take a few minutes," Bedlow prompted, smiling again, his huge teeth glistening in the brilliant sunlight. "Don't you at least owe me that much?"

"Okay," Vince agreed, avoiding the withering look Mary flashed at him.

"Just a leisurely walk," Bedlow said, starting toward one of the dirt roads cutting through the cemetery. Vince started to follow, only to be stopped by Mary.

"What's wrong with you?" she hissed, keeping her voice low.

"Nothing. I'm just trying to get us out of here with as little hassle as possible. So we humor the guy for a little while. What's wrong with that?"

"You want out of here without any hassle? Then let's go now. Forget him." Mary was obviously desperately afraid and made no attempt to hide it. She sensed their escape was about to be thwarted.

"We'll go. I just think we owe Bedlow more of an explanation . . ."

Mary shook her head. "Fine. You go kiss his ass if you want, but I'm getting out of here right now. Give me the key to the gate."

"I thought you had the other one. You were taking off when he stopped you, right?"

"I was going to climb the fence. I . . . I just couldn't face him. When you came in the front, I slipped out the back. He must have seen me when I passed the window." She glanced up the road where Bedlow was walking slowly away from them.

"What'd he say to you?" Vince asked.

"He was . . . I don't know. Odd. Wanted to know if I'd walk with him. When I said no, he put his hand on me and . . . and it felt like the touch of a dead man. Cold, you know. That's when I screamed." The words poured out in a torrent. "Now do you understand why I want to get away from here? Everything is too twisted."

"Look," Vince said patiently. "Why don't we just walk around the place with him and then take off?"

"Because there's no reason to, Vince. If you're not leaving with me now, then give me the key so I can leave. I'll lock up and toss the key in the driveway." She held out her hand, her face set.

Vince knew Mary well enough to know there was nothing he could say to change her mind. When she was determined to pursue a course of action, she was too stubborn to be dissuaded.

"Alright," he sighed, handing her his keys. "Where will I meet you?"

"I'll wait down the street. Away from here. When I see you come out, I'll meet you." She took the keyring and clutched his hand, making one final plea. "Come with me."

"I'll only be an hour or so," he answered, in exasperation, giving her a half-hearted kiss on the cheek.

"Bring the bags when you come," she told him, striding away. It took all her resolve to leave him there.

Vince watched until she had closed and locked the gate and tossed the keys inside. He was depressed when she did not turn around and wave. She simply hurried away. For a second, he was ready to dash after her, but something stopped him. For some unknown reason, he knew he had to talk to Bedlow.

There was something he had to tell him although he was not certain of exactly what it was.

He caught up with the other man as he was inspecting the heavy, weather-stained door of one of the crypts.

It was now late morning and the heat was building. Vince was sweating beneath his light shirt and marveled at Bedlow's cool demeanor. The man still wore his overcoat and yet showed no sign of discomfort from the heat.

There was no sweat on his brow and his face was as pale as ever.

"Ah, good," Bedlow said amiably. "You decided to join me." He looked around curiously. "Where is Ms. Renata?"

"Gone."

Something dark shifted in Bedlow's eyes. "Gone? Where?" Vince detected a note of alarm in the man's voice.

"Just gone. She won't be back. Even if I stay, she's out of the picture, Mr. Bedlow. And frankly, I can't blame her." Vince stood near Bedlow and could smell the man's stale, faintly noxious breath.

"I wish she had stayed," Bedlow sighed, his eyes darker than Vince had ever seen them. "It is such a big job trying to keep up with this place. She really didn't give it a chance."

"Maybe," muttered Vince. "Actually, I'm going to join her as soon as we've finished."

"That's not a very encouraging attitude, Mr. Cassidy. I feel as if I'll be wasting my time, no matter what I say." Bedlow straightened, apparently satisfied that the crypt door was secured and strolled away.

Vince looked at him for a minute and then followed. "It's not that I don't appreciate this job. I do. But, this place is, well, unsettling. I can't begin to explain to you all the things that have gone on since we arrived."

"What sort of things?" Bedlow asked, clasping his bony, white hands behind his back.

"Bizarre things."

"Tell me about them." Bedlow's voice was very enticing and encouraging. Before Vince realized it, he was telling Bedlow, in graphic detail, everything that had occurred to him since he and Mary had first arrived at the cemetery.

While he talked, Bedlow listened sympathetically, making no comment. Vince finished, detailing the inexplicable anger that had overwhelmed him that morning.

"Interesting, Mr. Cassidy," Bedlow commented matter-of-factly. "Most interesting."

"That's all . . . all you have to say?"

"Damn!" Bedlow suddenly snapped, staring at a crypt they had just reached. Its door hung open and the hasp was twisted. "I thought you said you checked the grounds this morning."

"I did," Vince answered.

"Apparently not very damned well." Bedlow rushed to the open door and looked inside. Another curse broke from his lips.

Vince looked past Bedlow to stare inside. The interior was layered with dust and smelled of decay and rot. The two sarcophaguses, carved from enormous blocks of stone, rested on either side of the small building. One was coated with decades of filth and grime, appearing to have been undisturbed since the day its occupant was placed within. The other, however, was open. The heavy slab which served as its top, leaned against the vault, one chipped corner on the floor. The lid looked as if it had been thrown off.

"You're telling me, you didn't see this when you made your rounds?" Bedlow stormed.

"No."

"You have no idea what this means, Mr. Cassidy." Bedlow stepped into the fetid room and looked into the violated vault. "It's empty. Damn. Another one . . ."

"Apparently I missed it . . ." Vince stared at the open stone vault. He could just make out the rotted, crumbling remains of an ancient casket. Its wood, once polished, was dull and the rich velvet interior was fouled with fungus and darkly stained from the decomposed corpse.

Bedlow whirled. "Yes, you missed it!" he snarled. "You fool! Now this creature is roaming around confused and dangerous. If it should be seen by anyone or get free of the grounds . . ." He paused, glaring at Vince with pure hate.

"What are you talking about?" Vince asked, completely mystified.

Bedlow sneered at him, his voice high and threatening. "You're so ignorant! So annoying. I'm sick of this charade. You are absolutely useless to me!"

In the face of the man's fury, Vince backed away, intent on bolting out the door and making a run for the gate, several hundred yards away. As his foot cleared the opening, the other man sprang at him.

Bedlow was as quick as a cat and unbelievably strong. In one move he had his hands around Vince's throat, the long powerful fingers burying themselves in his flesh, shutting off his air.

Vince struggled desperately. His fists flayed against Bedlow's head and glanced off his shoulders. His fingers sought the man's eyes, but he could not reach them. He tried repeatedly to kick his attacker in the groin and thighs, only to find he was being held at arms length.

Flashes of light began popping in the corners of his eyes. His vision was becoming fuzzy and blurred. His lungs felt as if they were about to explode. He could hear the pounding of his heart, the adrenalin racing through his blood making it thunder in his chest. There was a ringing in his ears like the staccato beat of a triphammer.

"You're done, Cassidy. It's time for you to get out of my hair once and for all!" Bedlow's huge teeth flashed as a malicious grin spread over his face. "You've served your purpose!"

The unrelenting pressure on Vince's throat continued. He was growing weak, blackness was creeping over his eyes. His lungs needed air. They strained with effort to draw in life-giving oxygen.

He's killing me!

Vaguely he felt his body being lifted off the floor. There was an explosion of sharp pain and the snap of bone as his left shoulder and arm were slammed against a hard, cold stone surface.

I'm dying!

The pressure at his throat continued. It was unrelenting . . .

Mary! Mary, I'm dying! Why didn't I go with you, Mary? I love you!

Blackness was enveloping him. He was drifting, floating . . .

Vince was vaguely aware of a horrible cloying stench and the grating of something heavy . . .

. . . and then an eternal blackness closed over him.

PART THREE
STRUGGLES

Unbound, unharbour'd, toss'd like scum
    Along wild shores and desolate seas,
A trail of weed—a track of foam—
    A murmur of the hurrying breeze;
Yet, clinging to the drowning mast,
Despair discerns her at the last.

—J. C. Powys

TWELVE

Mary walked away from the cemetery, tears rolling down her face. Why wouldn't Vince come with her? Why was he determined to have one last talk with Oscar Bedlow?

The thought of that ghoulish man sent a chill through her and despite the warm late morning air, she hugged herself. Couldn't Vince see that the man was not normal?

Unless . . .

. . . Vince was under the influence of *that place again*!

She couldn't let herself think such things. It was a mental trap she knew she had to ignore. Vince was fine. He simply wanted to make a clean break with Bedlow. He'd be out soon.

Away from the cemetery, Mary felt as if a great weight had been lifted from her. She desperately wished Vince was with her and yet, feeling selfish and hating herself for it, she was glad to be away from Mansfield.

Mary crossed the empty street and moved west along the sidewalk. She didn't slow her pace until she was a block away from the northwest corner of Mansfield's rusty spiked fence. Along the street was a series of old warehouses, looking forsaken and abandoned. To her right was a high wall of weed-covered earth. According to a battered sign, a water treatment plant lay beyond the earthen wall.

Two blocks ahead, on the corner of a busy intersection, Mary could see a Seven-Eleven Store. She decided to walk to it, buy a Coke and kill some time before Vince joined her.

If he joins me.

No! She couldn't allow herself to think such things. Vince just wanted to talk to Bedlow for a few minutes, to ease his guilty conscience about leaving so soon after they arrived. That was all. Then he'd be out of the cemetery and they'd be away from it forever.

After getting the soda and a small cellophane bag of dry, chewy donuts, she strolled back along the sidewalk, stopping a hundred yards from the western edge of the cemetery. The entrance was over three blocks away, but by climbing up the earthen embankment, she had a clear view of the driveway. She sat down on a patch of grass and waited for Vince.

The soda and donuts were long gone and the sun was already past its zenith when Mary began to worry. Bedlow's Cadillac had not yet emerged from the cemetery nor had Vince. Although she had left her watch in the bedroom, she knew she'd been sitting on the hard ground for at least two hours.

What's taking him so long?

A white car, bearing the familiar blue and silver shield of the Denver Police Department and sporting emergency lights across its roof, cruised slowly by. The officer eyed Mary suspiciously. She actually hoped he would stop. In fact, she had almost decided to jump to her feet and flag him down, when she was distracted by a white haired old man coming slowly up the embankment toward her.

The police car's siren suddenly split the air, its lights flashed and it rocketed away, no doubt summoned to another human disaster.

Mary watched the man approach, less apprehensive than

curious. He was too well dressed to be a vagrant and walked with an erect, purposeful carriage. He wore crisply pressed gray slacks, a white shirt, the sleeves rolled back from his wrists, and a pair of shiny black boots. Mary estimated he was in his late sixties or early seventies. His brown face was kindly and his intense black eyes were oddly soft. He wore a thick moustache which drooped around his mouth.

"Excuse me," he said. "Do you happen to be one of the caretakers from the cemetery?" He motioned towards Mansfield.

"Why?" Mary asked suspiciously, getting to her feet, her hand absently brushing away the grass and leaves clinging to the seat of her slacks.

The old gentleman smiled sheepishly. "Pardon me. I am Joshua Ortega. I'm here as a friend."

"Do I know you?"

"No."

"Do we have a common acquaintance?"

"I don't believe so."

Mary studied him. "Then what do you want?"

Apparently her tone was more harsh than she had realized. The man held his hands up, palms forward and smiled, flashing a row of even, white teeth.

"I mean no harm. May I sit down? I'm not as young as you and I need to catch my breath."

Mary shrugged. When Ortega was seated, she suddenly felt awkward and sat down again, watching the stranger closely.

"I still don't understand what you want," she said, vaguely distracted, again glancing down the street toward the cemetery gates.

"I'd just like to talk to you," he said calmly.

"About what?" she demanded.

"You. Actually, you and your fiancee."

Mary frowned, brushing back a strand of hair which had

fallen across her face. "What's Vince got to do with this. *What* are you talking about."

Joshua cleared his throat. "It's . . . involved."

"What did you mean about being here as a friend?" she asked, glancing toward the entrance to the cemetery, disappointed that Vince still had not come out.

"You are from Mansfield, correct?" Ortega said more as a statement of fact than a question.

Mary nodded agreement.

"May I ask why you are out here," he asked, again motioning toward the cemetery. "And not in there?"

"I . . . I'm waiting for my fiancee. He's going to join me here soon." Mary heard the hollowness of her own words and looked away from Ortega.

"You are leaving that place?"

"Yes."

"Bad things have happened to you there," Ortega said quietly. "Things that are . . . well, unnatural. Am I right?"

Mary was quiet, feeling suddenly confused. Bad things. That wasn't the half of it. But how could he know about them?

She looked at the elderly man. "Who are you?"

"I told you. I . . ."

"Yes. Your name is Ortega. But who *are* you really?"

The man stared into the distance for a moment and then looked at the young woman, his eyes slitted against the glare of the sun. "I am going to tell you about myself and my friends. Please, don't think me crazy. Hear me out. Then decide."

Mary listened intently, while he told her about Agnes Hardwick and Tobias Rathbone, about dark enchantments and ancient curses and a supernatural being who cheated Death and made a mockery of life. She could sense in his words and manners that Ortega was uncomfortable telling her these things; as if, when spoken aloud, in the light of day, they sounded as foolish to him as they should have to her.

Oddly, they did not sound foolish or surprising. And that frightened Mary even more.

When he finished, she looked at him for a long time. He returned her gaze, his face impassive. Then, for the hundredth time, she glanced toward the gate. There was still no sign of Vince . . .

. . . or Bedlow.

"It's a fantastic story," she said, still gazing at the cemetery.

"Yes, it is."

"And you believe it?"

"Yes."

"I'm not really surprised. But . . ." Mary turned toward Ortega, another frown twisting her mouth. She leveled a finger at his chest. "Y . . you're trying to tell me that the cemetery is . . . what? *Haunted*?"

Ortega shrugged. "Yes. I suppose that's about it. Maybe not quite as tame as that, though . . .

"Not as tame," she said ruefully. "No shit."

Ortega nodded, eying the young woman closely. "It's all true, isn't it?"

Mary was quiet for a long moment. Shading her eyes, she absently watched as a white city bus rumbled along the street, the inevitable cloud of diesel smoke trailing it. She was suddenly conscious of the sun bathing her in its relentless, searing heat. Her blouse was sticky, her hair damp and beads of sweat were rolling down her face. Gancing toward the west she saw the heavy, wet white clouds building into thunderheads. They promised relief from the heat.

Mary finally sucked in a deep breath and looked at Ortega.

"It's true. You wouldn't believe what's happened to us since we got here. It's been a nightmare. Something out of a fever dream." The words came in a rush. She was suddenly telling the elderly man everything, her voice pleading to be believed. When Mary paused, wiping away a few telltale tears, Ortega whistled softly.

"It's good you're out of there."

Mary got to her feet. "I have to go back."

"You can't! It's too dangerous. The influences inside there are . . . very powerful." Ortega struggled to stand.

"Look, Mr. Ortega . . ."

"Josh."

Mary was suddenly nervous, anxious to go back to find Vince, terrified at the prospect of returning to the cemetery. She looked from Mansfield's enclosed grounds to Ortega and back.

"I have to go. Vince should have been out by now. He was only going to talk to Bedlow for . . ."

"Bedlow? He's in there with *Bedlow*? Alone?" The old man's brown face twisted as he cursed silently to himself. "Rathbone told me about that guy. You *can't* go back in. I won't let you." He made reached for Mary's arm, but she jerked it away.

"I have to!" she cried, fighting back the storm of tears and the impending panic. "I can't just walk away and leave him there."

Ortega spread his hands in supplication. "Look, I know you don't know me from Adam. But you've got to trust me. If you go back in, there's no telling what will happen." He glanced over his shoulder, squinting into the sun to peer down the empty street. "If you'll just wait, my friends will be here."

"I . . I can't." Mary was verging on hysteria.

He gently touched her arm. "Please. Just wait here for a few minutes. I'm parked down the street. Let's go to my car and we'll drive to the Seven-Eleven to use the phone. I'll call Tobias and Aggie. They'll get over here right away. Tobias will know what to do."

"Why don't we just call the police?" Mary asked, hope flaring in her voice.

"And tell them what?" Joshua asked in return, trying not to sound patronizing. "That demons are haunting a cemetery? I'm afraid they'd lock me up for lunacy."

Ortega could see the fear welling up in the woman's eyes. He was reluctant to leave her, but he desperately wanted to talk to Agnes or Rathbone.

That morning, it had been decided, Joshua was the logical one to attempt to contact the young caretakers. Tobias and Aggie were known to Terrance and Bedlow and the forces they were allied with. Ortega was not.

It had taken considerable time convincing Joshua to drive to the cemetery. He had protested by pointing out he had absolutely no idea how to persuade the couple to leave Mansfield. Ultimately Aggie broke his resistance by reminding him of the terrifying message they had received on her tape recorder. Could he, or any one of them, leave those young people in the hands of such an evil force?

Ortega had agreed to talk to the caretakers, but he could mask neither his misgivings nor his dread. Their bizarre mission notwithstanding, cemeteries left Joshua cold. Since his childhood, he had found the burial rite more than a little disconcerting. Maybe it was the endless parade of funerals he had attended as a child or the countless coffins poised above dark, black holes in the cold ground into which his family and friends were to be sealed for eternity.

Or maybe he was the victim of his superstitious grandmother and her haunting tales of the dead, demons and devils. She could subdue the most disobedient of her grandchildren by conjuring up images of the firey-eyed *diablo* that stole naughty children out of their beds in the dark of night. Where this devil carried them to was left undescribed, but the children knew it was someplace horrible where an unimagined fate awaited them.

In retrospect, his grandmother may have been closer to the truth than he or even *she* realized . . .

Ortega had decided to avoid drawing attention to himself and had parked his car several blocks from the cemetery. As he approached the graveyard on foot, he had spotted Mary perched on the incline surrounding the water treatment plant. He had watched her for almost half an hour. She fit the sketchy description Rathbone had given him. He had chanced speaking to her.

After she had begun talking and he realized how truly frightened she was, his own apprehension had vaporized in a wave of compassion.

Now he was confused. He couldn't force her to do anything. Yet, based on Rathbone's warnings, he knew Mary's fate would be questionable, at best, if she returned to Mansfield.

"Why don't you come with me?" he asked.

"I *have* to wait for Vince. What if he comes out and I'm gone?"

What if he never comes out, Joshua thought bitterly.

"Then at least will you wait until I get back before you do anything?"

She nodded.

"Please," Ortega said earnestly. "Don't go back in until my friends and I get here."

Again, she nodded agreement. "I said I'd wait. I will. Now go call these friends of yours. I'll be here when you get back."

He studied her eyes, but couldn't read them.

"Really," Mary said emphatically, smiling weakly. "I'll wait."

"Good," he said. "We'll be back in less than an hour." He patted her arm and started down the embankment. Stepping to the sidewalk, he glanced back. The young woman was again staring intently at Mansfield. With a shake of his head, Ortega moved back toward his car.

Reaching it, he wheeled around in a broad U-turn and drove the short distance to the Seven-Eleven. He punched the numbers Rathbone had written down on a slip of paper and waited while the phone rang a half a dozen times before it was answered.

"Yes," Rathbone answered, in a flat and hollow voice.

"It's Joshua. I talked to the girl. She's already left Mansfield."

"Where is she now?"

"Waiting a few blocks from here."

"You left her?" Rathbone demanded in irritation.

"I couldn't force her to come with me," Ortega replied defensively. "She's waiting for her boyfriend. He's still inside."

There was a long pause. "Why did she leave, Josh?"

"It's a long story. Fear, basically. She's worried about the boyfriend. He stayed in the cemetery to talk to Bedlow. Neither one has come out."

"Alright," Rathbone sighed. "Aggie and I'll be there as soon as possible. You go back and stay with the girl. By the way, did you get her name?"

"Renata. Mary Renata. Guy's name is Cassidy . . ."

"Renata? Hell, Josh, get back over there right now!" Rathbone banged his phone down, severing the connection and leaving Joshua feeling more than a little unsettled. Why had he been so alarmed when he'd heard Mary's name?

The old man was a block away with his back to her when Mary saw Vince waving at her from the corner of the cemetery. He stood just inside the iron fence, motioning for her to come to him.

"Vince," she cried, waving and laughing with relief. She suddenly felt foolish, all her fears seeming very childish. Vince was fine. He was there, standing in the bright sunlight as fit as ever.

Mary hurried across the street and down the block. As she trotted toward Mansfield, Vince continued to motion to her until she was a dozen yards away and then he turned and vanished into the shrubbery.

Obviously he was planning to meet her at the entrance, she decided, breaking into a jog. She ran along the fence, looking repeatedly beyond it, trying to catch a glimpse of Vince through the bushes. He was not in sight.

She turned into the gravel driveway leading to the gates. Reaching them, she stopped and looked around.

Vince was nowhere in sight.

The gates, however, were unchained and she pushed one of them open. It swung wide into the empty drive. Mary stood staring into the graveyard.

Bedlow's Cadillac still stood near the cottage though the gaunt faced man was not to be seen.

An icy tendril of panic curled around Mary's heart. She stood just outside the cemetery; afraid to enter, afraid not to.

Where was Vince? Why had he summoned her back here and then disappeared? Where was he?

"Vince," she called out as loudly as she could.

No answer; only the faint rustle of the leaves on the nearby bushes as a hot breeze, carrying a hint of the coming storm on its breath, moved across the cemetery.

Mary caught a slight movement up one of the gravel roads cutting through the graveyard. Turning, she saw Vince standing by a towering oak, motioning for her to follow.

"Vince, what are you doing?" She still stood outside the gate and was reluctant to step through. Why was he playing this stupid game? Hadn't they agreed to leave?

Vince motioned to her again.

Why won't he talk to me?

Abruptly, Vince turned and walked away, disappearing beyond the crest of the small hill upon which he stood.

Mary had no idea what to do. She had no desire to reenter the disturbing world of Mansfield Cemetery, yet she couldn't simply leave Vince. In the time she had known him, she had learned that he was generally very purposeful and, perhaps because he was an archaeologist and therefore a scientist, very methodical. He did nothing without considering his actions first. Surely, if he wanted her to follow him, he had a damned good reason.

Or should have. This was, after all, a place where

nothing seemed to have a reason. He could be caught in the spell of the cemetery again.

And where was Bedlow? When she had walked out a few hours before, Mary had found herself relieved that she would never have to see the pale, emaciated man again. He was a part of everything that had happened to them. His very presence repulsed her, and his death's head smile turned her stomach and sent shivers running down her spine.

She stood at the gate for another several minutes. Her dilemma was maddening. Leave again and wait for Vince? Or follow him and chance yet another episode of terror within the damned cemetery?

The sun faded as rushing storm clouds passed over it, casting a gray pall over Mansfield. Thunder rumbled in the distance. Mary wanted to get away from there before the storm hit.

Should she go look for Vince?

What about the old man and his strange warnings? Hadn't his earnest appeal to her been enough to convince her that all she and Vince had experienced had been more than hysteria, illusion and nightmare? He was coming back. With help. If there was safety in numbers, then wasn't it smart to await their arrival?

A scream echoed across the cemetery. It was followed by another.

Vince was screaming her name.

Without another thought, Mary dashed through the gate and passed the cottage. She ran up the road where Vince had stood. Her heart was thundering in her chest and sweat was streaming over her body. She was gasping for breath, not from exertion, but from terror.

Mary stopped at the top of the small hill and scanned the sea of monuments and mausoleums spread out before her. Vince was nowhere in sight. Nothing moved except for the gentle flutter of bushes and branches in the now cool breeze.

Another peel of thunder echoed over the cemetery. A few drops of rain splattered on the ground at Mary's feet.

Catching her breath, she called Vince's name repeatedly, but the only reply was the faint echo of her voice.

Where the hell are you, Vince?

She was frightened now. She had heard him cry out her name; she had heard his terrified screams. Or thought she had. Now she wasn't so sure. Suddenly feeling very alone, Mary turned, intent on returning to the gates. She'd wait for the old man and his friends and together they could look for Vince.

When Vince's voice again broke the stillness, Mary whirled, her hand reflexively clutching her throat.

It was a high wail, somewhere between a pain-wracked scream and an hysterical plea. It came from near the large quarried stone mausoleum at the bottom of the hill.

The rain was starting to fall in big, wet drops, harbingers of a downpour.

Glancing from right to left, turning to insure she was not being followed, Mary moved down the slope. Her pounding heart seemed loud in her own ears. She walked on rubbery legs that threatened to collapse beneath her.

A small voice in her head kept telling her to turn and run. Save herself.

She couldn't, of course. To abandon Vince would be tantamount to abandoning herself.

Mary was suddenly running again, flying along the gravel road toward the crypt, oblivious to the steadily increasing rain. She had to find Vince and get him out of this place. If they could get away, they could go on with their lives.

She reached the door of the crypt. It was made of hammered brass and badly weathered. Its once bright, golden surface was now streaked with green and ocher by the years of exposure to the harsh elements. The heavy lock, which had kept the remains of the dead protected from the outside world for so long, now hung open.

Rain pelting her, Mary placed a tentative hand on the door and pulled. It grated open on rust-encrusted hinges. A dank, mouldy stench flooded out, assailing her nostrils and causing her to cough.

"Vince?"

She looked inside, but the interior of the mausoleum was inky and unnaturally dark. Her eyes could not penetrate that blackness.

There was a movement and Mary, unable to see what moved and unwilling to enter, started to move back. As she stepped away, something shot out of the darkness and clamped around her wrist.

She screamed and tried to jerk away. The grip on her arm was unyielding. As she struggled, she heard a jibbering, dry crackling sound, like the snarl of a dying animal.

Mary continued to pull frantically in an attempt to free herself. She tried to brace her shoulder against the wet, slippery doorframe while her fingers probed the rough exterior stones for something to hold on to. Her fingers slipped across the rain splattered stones. Inexorably she was being pulled into the black, rot infested interior.

She looked down, desperately trying to see what held her in its iron grasp. When she saw the fleshless fingers wrapped around her arm like yellow talons, she cried out in stark terror. The scream which tore from her lips came from deep within her soul; a primordial, animal cry of fear and loathing. It was the mindless cry of a living thing facing the inevitability of a horrible death.

Mary's fingernails scraped and broke along the rough surface of the mausoleum as she was dragged into the ebon darkness. Bloody trails marked the passage of her cut fingers.

Her screams became muffled and indistinct when the heavy brass door banged shut.

The driving rain soon washed all traces of her blood from the rough, hewed stones.

In seconds, the cemetery was again silent.

THIRTEEN

Agnes Hardwick watched Rathbone bang the telephone receiver into its cradle. She had listened while the strange old man spoke with Joshua, but had no idea what her friend had said that was so alarming.

"What'd he say?" she asked anxiously, setting her tea cup on the ornate table in front of her.

Rathbone looked at her, but his eyes were introspective and clouded.

"Tobias?"

"I've got to find something," he said absently, walking to one of his bookshelves and studying the titles.

"What did Josh tell you?" Agnes demanded.

"A name," he answered without stopping from his search. "A very familiar name . . . Ah, here it is." The old man pulled a thick, leather bound volume from the shelf and carried it back to his chair.

"What is it?" Agnes was growing impatient and not a little frustrated at the man's secretive behavior. "What did Josh say?"

Rathbone, much to her irritation, ignored her and started thumbing through the thick, brittle pages. She fell silent as he scanned first one page and then another, watching as tiny bits of dried and fragile paper drifted from the book to the floor.

"Here it is," Rathbone said excitedly after nearly ten minutes of searching and reading.

"Here's what?"

"Maria Renata," he answered, looking at her as if the name meant something to her.

"And who was Maria Renata and what's it got to do with Josh?" Rathbone caught the note of annoyance in the old woman's voice. He smiled apologetically.

"Sorry," he said. "I do get too involved sometimes. But this may be a key. Josh said he spoke to the young woman at the cemetery. Her name is Mary Renata. Now it may only be a coincidence, but I doubt it. Not with that Black Bitch involved."

"Who was this Maria Renata?"

Rathbone frowned now, a dark shadow moving through his eyes. He looked at Agnes and shook his head sadly. "A nun."

"A nun?"

"Yes," he answered, getting to his feet. "I'll tell you on the way to the cemetery. We've got to get over there right away. Things are coming to a head faster than I had expected. We have to talk to that girl."

"How are we going to get there?" Agnes asked as she stood, her old bones creaking in protest. "Josh took the car."

Rathbone smiled. "Oh, I have a car. You may find it a bit of an antique, but I've had it for so long, I hate to part with it now."

Locking the apartment securely, Rathbone led Agnes through a dark, litter-strewn hallway to the opposite end of the decaying basement in the old building. At another steel-clad door, he produced a key and opened it. They stepped inside a large garage area which held only a single vehicle.

Agnes, never an auto fanatic, believing cars were more often a curse than a blessing, nonetheless recognized the sweeping, classic lines of the Cord. The chrome on its "coffin nose" gleamed in the light and its huge, sweeping front fenders with their hidden headlights, were unblemished. The convertible top was already down, hidden from sight behind the seat.

"It's beautiful," she said. "You've had it all these years?"

"Since it was on the showroom floor in New York City in 1937. I lived there in the 30's." He ushered her to the car, held the "suicide" door open for her and then climbed in behind the wheel.

Using a remote control, he activitated a garage door opener. Starting the Cord's powerful V-8 engine, he wheeled it out into the alley, again pressing the remote control to close the portal. Carefully he drove into the street and then sped off through the afternoon traffic, heading south toward Mansfield Cemetery.

"Now tell me about this Maria Renata. How does a nun fit into all of this?" Agnes asked as Rathbone sent the car flying through traffic.

The old man glanced at her. "She was a sister in the Premonstratensian Convent of Unterzell. That was outside Wurzberg, Germany."

"When?"

"The early to mid-eighteenth century. She served the convent for 50 years."

"And then what happened?" Agnes prodded.

"And then they accused her of witchcraft."

"Witchcraft? That's terrible," Agnes said softly.

"She was beheaded and her body burned." Rathbone's voice caught and Agnes looked at him curiously.

"A witch? Was she?"

Rathbone shrugged. "Maybe. If my suspicions about the connection to Mansfield are correct, I'd be tempted to say yes. Of course, she may have been an unwitting tool of some dark force. It's always difficult to say for certain."

"Who accused her of witchcraft? As I recall, there was a lot of hysteria and witch hunting back then," Agnes said, trying to avoid watching the road as Rathbone sent the Cord flying through heavy, sluggish traffic.

Again he chanced taking his eyes off the road to glance at her. "She was accused by her fellow sisters."

"Other nuns?"

"Yes. It seems six of Renata's sisters were supposedly possessed by the Devil for several years. She was accused of witchcraft by one of them on her deathbed. Given the times, that was the equivalent of accusing someone of treason today."

Rathbone continued to power the Cord through the endless stream of cars and trucks. Its aerodynamic design and superior suspension allowed it to hug the road as it slipped among the other vehicles. He turned west on Colfax Avenue and headed toward Interstate 25.

"Using your words, it truly was a time of hysteria," Rathbone continued, sending the car around slower vehicles on the Colfax Viaduct. "It would be too simplistic to tell you it was a struggle between Good and Evil. It was much more than that. It was a political war between the Christians and the non-Christians."

"So how does this Renata person fit in, Tobias?" she asked, steering him back to the subject at hand, in an attempt to avoid a protracted discussion on the evils of the Dark Ages.

"A priest investigating Renata claimed one of the possessed nuns heard a demon speak from the old woman's mouth, saying it possessed her even before she was born. Naturally the priest assumed it was true, coming from one who had so recently been tortured, and decided Renata was cursed." An acidulous bitterness edged Rathbone's words and a dark frown etched his ancient features.

"What do you think, Tobias?" Agnes asked quietly, curious as to the man's obvious inner turmoil.

"It was a very bad time, Aggie," he said, not taking his eyes from the road as he turned onto the ramp leading to southbound I-25. "Remember, I was there. I saw innocent people bloodied and broken in the name of Greater Good. I had friends stretched on racks, whipped and burned at the stake. It was an atrocity committed by zealots who had little to do with serving their god and everything to do with gaining political power and holding sway over the masses."

"I'm confused, Tobias. You don't think these people were possessed by demons, yet . . ."

"Yet I'm willing to give credance to the Renata tale?" His voice was harsh.

"Yes."

Rathbone drew a deep breath and exhaled it slowly. He paid no attention to a man in a Mercedes who pulled up along the Cord, openly admiring it with an almost lecherous leer.

"The witchcraft hysteria was, by and large, just so much fear and superstition gripping frightened, ignorant people. But there were those who were truly possessed by evil. And others, like myself, who possessed special powers. In both cases the percentage was small. My people were virtually wiped out by Christian warriors bent on ridding the world of us and our religion, though we were far from the evil they sought.

"But for every truly possessed person that was slain, a thousand innocents were murdered." He stopped speaking to change lanes and move his old car to the center of the highway.

Agnes glanced to her right, staring towards the distant mountains. They were partially obscured by the dark rain clouds moving quickly and inexorably over the city.

Everything around her looked so normal. Her world was so distant and removed from the long past terrors of hysteria and witch hunts. There were no trials held in cramped church courts today. There were no smoke-filled chambers beneath castles and cathedrals where awful devices were employed to break bodies and spirits in the name of God Almighty.

Or were there?

This was the latter part of the Twentieth Century. Weren't such things as demonic possession and spectral apparitions only the fantasies of irrational minds? In actuality, wasn't the great horror now the mindless political gamesmanship and the threat of nuclear annihilation?

Agnes sighed to herself. She knew from experience—very recent experience—that it was not. She had been a part of too much to believe that the only evils on earth were Man-made. She looked at Tobias who was staring straight ahead, intently watching the highway.

"It must have been a time of great pain for you," she said sympathetically.

Rathbone nodded, a humorless smile on his mouth. "Yes. There was pain and fear and suffering. I was fortunate and never had to face the inquisitors."

"What's your theory about the connection between the nun and the young woman at the cemetery?"

He glanced at Agnes and smiled in genuine good humor. "You're bound and determined to keep me focused, aren't you Aggie?"

"Absolutely."

"It's only supposition on my part," he explained. "However given the whole circumstances of Mansfield and its heritage, I think I'm very close to the truth.

"Maria Renata, the nun, if she was indeed a possessed agent of the Devil, may have left a legacy . . ."

"What sort of legacy?" Agnes asked impatiently.

"It could be anything," Rathbone answered with a verbal shrug. "But I would be willing to bet that Mary Renata is a direct descendant of the nun. While this young woman may be a very decent person, inside her perhaps lying dormant, could be a seed which is very likely about to germinate."

"You think that's why Terrance and this Bedlow fellow recruited her to Mansfield?"

Rathbone nodded. "Maybe. I doubt they do much of anything without a purpose. Their ancestors founded the cemetery and set into motion a twisted plan. I don't believe for a minute that couple was picked at random. They wanted them, or at least the girl, there."

"Do you know what's going to happen?" Agnes asked in a small voice, her wrinkled hands clutching her small purse in a white knuckled grip.

"No. If the Madonna is involved—and I know She is—it's something very evil."

They were at the southern edge of the city now and Rathbone pulled the Cord into the exit lane and sent it down the ramp. He was forced to stop at a light at the bottom of the slope where a neighboring driver gazed longingly at the car and then nodded and smiled at Agnes. She smiled back, again feeling disconcerted. The driver probably thought she and Tobias were an old married couple out for a drive in their beloved car, talking nostalgically about times long gone.

What would you think if you knew the truth?

Rathbone pulled the car over to the curb. The low, bloated rain clouds were threatening to spill their contents at any second. He tugged the canvas top free and secured it over the interior.

"Does Josh have your Ouija board?" Tobias asked, climbing back into the Cord, bringing Agnes out of her reverie.

"Yes. It's in his trunk."

"Good. We'll need it."

"For what?" Agnes asked, mildly alarmed.

"We need to make contact with one of the people buried at Mansfield . . ."

"You mean you want us to *go inside*?"

Rathbone glanced at the woman and nodded. "Yes. We've got to make as clear a connection as possible between you and the other side."

"Isn't that going to be just a little dangerous?"

"Not a little dangerous. Very dangerous. But it's the only sure way to get at the truth."

"But if everyone buried in there is . . . was part of the scheme—whatever it is—won't any information we get be useless?" Agnes had not considered the possibility of actually entering the cemetery grounds and the idea was troubling.

"That's another risk. You know better than I the chances you take depending on messages from the other side. Sometimes you can link up with a spirit that's absolutely accurate and at other times . . ."

"You get a lot of crap," Agnes finished for him, blushing at her use of the mild expletive.

"Exactly," Rathbone chortled, trying not to out and out laugh at the woman. "It's still the best chance we have to find a way how to defeat the Bitch."

Rain splashed over the windshield and Rathbone flipped on the wipers. They labored against the fat, wet drops, just able to keep pace with the torrent.

"How are we going to get inside Mansfield and have enough time to run the board without running into Her or some of Her friends?"

Rathbone slowed for a traffic light and waited until the Cord sat idling with a low rumbling purr before answering. "I'm not without some resources, Aggie. I should be able to protect you and Josh while the two of you run the board."

"Josh isn't going to like this any more than I do, Tobias," Agnes pointed out, running a hand over her mussed and windblown hair.

"It'll be his choice, Aggie. But he'll have to know that we need him."

The light changed and Rathbone stomped the gas pedal,

sending the super-charged V-8 roaring away from the light. Agnes cried out, terrified they would crash on the rain-slick street, as the Cord maneuvered around a creeping Toyota.

"I've always loved this car," Rathbone whooped.

"I've always loved my hide," Agnes replied sardonically. "Will you slow down please?"

"Yes, of course. We're almost there. Isn't that Josh's car parked up ahead?" Rathbone motioned to the sedan sitting against the curb, the only car parked on the long, empty street.

"It is," Agnes replied, peering through the water streaked windshield.

Joshua Ortega climbed out of his car as Rathbone glided the Cord to a stop behind his Buick.

"Where's the girl?" Rathbone demanded, opening his door, oblivious to the rain.

"Gone," Joshua answered sheepishly.

"Where? Not back inside?" Rathbone made no attempt to hide his annoyance.

"I don't know. She was gone when I got back from phoning you."

"Damnit," snapped Rathbone. "I knew you shouldn't leave her."

"Tobias," Agnes said sternly from the opposite side of the car, ignoring the rain soaking her dress. "That's enough. There's no reason to be rude to Josh. We have to deal with the situation as we find it."

Joshua looked at Agnes. "I can handle it, Aggie."

Rathbone started to say something and then stopped and looked toward Mansfield. "We still have to go in tonight," he told them after several moments.

"Why not right now?" Joshua asked, surprising both Agnes and Rathbone.

"Too early for the board to do us any good," Agnes explained. "The best contacts are always made at night."

"Well we can't just not investigate the girl's disappearance."

Rathbone looked oddly at the Hispanic. "You've certainly changed your tune . . ."

"Hey, asshole," Joshua barked, thumping Rathbone's chest with his hand. "I'm not a coward. All this supernatural stuff is a maybe a little frightening, but I'm no more afraid than you."

Rathbone sighed. "Then you're scared enough. I'm sorry if you thought I was questioning your courage."

Joshua looked through the rain at the iron fence surrounding the graveyard. "She was a nice girl. I liked her. I felt for her."

Rathbone and Agnes exchanged knowing glances.

Agnes cleared her throat. "What now, Tobias?"

"We wait until dark." He looked at his watch. "That's four or five hours from now. Let's get out of here and find a place to wait until then."

"Wait a minute," roared Joshua. "Are you telling me you're just going to wait until dark and then proceed as if nothing's happened? Goddamnit, there's a girl in there and she may be in trouble!"

"Or she may be on a bus out of town," Rathbone retorted. "You don't know she's in there. You want us to go prowling around because the Renata girl *might* be there?"

"Rathbone," Joshua snarled. "It's broad daylight. What the hell can bother us?"

"Assuming they're in the cemetery, the same thing that got the girl and her boyfriend."

"Will you two stop it?" Agnes demanded, coming around the front of the Cord and pushing between the pair. "Josh, Tobias is right. We can't do much of anything right now. We'll just have to wait. If something's happened to those young people, there's not much we're going to be able to do about it right now. We have to consider the greater implications of all the recent activity."

Her brittle, harsh tone quieted both men.

"Now," she continued, not giving either a chance to continue their verbal sparring. "Why don't we go back to the Interstate, check into a hotel and try to sleep for a few hours. There's no reason to drive back downtown and then have to turn around and come back here. This could be a very long night, so let's quit the bickering and get ready for it."

Agnes rode with Joshua, who remained silent and morose. Rathbone followed in the Cord. She was chilled in her wet clothes and desperately wanted to get into a warm room.

They checked into a hotel near the Interstate, booking two rooms. Agnes retired to one and Rathbone and Joshua to the other. The desk clerk, mildly amused, agreed to call both rooms at eight that evening.

Agnes, feeling very tired and suffering from the effects of summer rain, slipped out of her sodden clothing and crawled under the covers searching for warmth. It came more quickly than she had anticipated and in scant minutes she drifted into a deep, sound sleep.

Rathbone and Joshua, on the other hand, were both restless with anticipation and anxiety. The knowledge of the coming confrontation weighed heavily on both men. They had shed their shirts and toweled themselves dry.

"I'm sorry about the girl," Rathbone said, as he stared out through the sliding glass door opening onto the small concrete balcony. He watched the cars on the interstate rush past in an endless, monotonous stream. They reminded him of mindless automatons trapped eternally on a ceaseless treadmill. Plumes of water in the wake of their passing created a hazy fog over the highway.

"Yeah," breathed Joshua. "So am I. I wish I'd been able to make her stay put. I feel . . ."

"Don't blame yourself, Josh. She told you she'd wait. Maybe she was lying and maybe she wasn't. It's a moot point now. There's a good chance she meant to wait for us and was either forceably taken back to Mansfield or was lured back.'' Rathbone's voice was flat and noncommital.

''Or maybe she simply took off,'' Josh offered hopefully.

''Yes, there's always that possibility,'' replied Rathbone with no enthusiasm.

''Tell me something, Tobias.''

''If I can.''

''Have you ever faced this . . . Madonna creature before?''

Rathbone was silent for a very long time, still staring out the window. ''No. Not personally. I've known one who did.''

''When?''

''A very long time ago,'' Rathbone answered in a distant, far away voice. ''Long before Mansfield was conceived. It was . . . well a very long time ago.''

''Where?''

''Europe. In some backwater village where a group of crazy men unlocked the secret of bringing Her forth. I had a friend named Timothy. He was very powerful and very astute. He learned She was holding sway in this village and travelled there to confront Her.''

''Was he successful?'' Joshua asked, his scholar's curiosity piqued.

''In a manner of speaking. He managed to send Her back to the hell from which She came and thereby thwarted Her conquest in this village.''

Joshua caught the sad note in Rathbone's voice. ''What happened to him?''

''He died.''

''Oh.''

Rathbone turned from the window as a flash of lightning split the western sky. He stepped to one of the straight backed chairs flanking a small, round writing table. Slumping into it, he looked at Joshua with eyes that were at once sad and oddly fierce.

''I followed him to the village. I was perhaps three days

behind him. When I reached that motley collection of huts and hovels, I was too late for the battle. Timothy was dying in one of the huts. The villagers had laid him on a bed and tried to comfort him as best they could, but they had nothing in their meager medical folklore to deal with his wounds."

Thunder, distant and muffled, rumbled.

"It must have been terrible . . ."

"I wept when I saw him. I wept when I plunged my dagger through his heart," Rathbone said, meeting Joshua's startled gaze.

"You . . . you killed him?"

"Yes. He begged me to. And if I'd been in Timothy's place, I'd have done the same and have prayed he would slay me."

Joshua was silent for a long time, contemplating Rathbone's harsh, painful admission.

"I suppose there was nothing you could have done for him," he finally said.

"Nothing," Rathbone answered. "You see, Josh. Timothy's flesh had been flayed from his body. The exposed musculature was burned and gashed. Gangrene had already infected the wounds. Killing him was the most decent thing I could have done."

Joshua nodded agreement. "It must have been an ordeal for you as well as for him."

The other man snorted. "It was. But it haunted me for more years than you and your children will ever see pass. To slay a friend, even in compassion, is among the most terrible burdens one can carry. I put it all to rest and found peace with myself only after a very long time. Now it's just a vague memory."

Rathbone rose from the chair and walked to one of the two double beds in the room. He stretched out on it and closed his eyes with a deep, heavy sigh.

Joshua, doubting he would be able to sleep, followed Rathbone's lead and stretched out on the other bed. His companion had drifted into sleep long before it crept over him. When he had slipped into slumber, he was haunted by images of his own body lying broken and twisted, the flesh peeled away, a breeding ground for all manner of loathsome insects that burrowed into his raw flesh as if he was already a corpse.

FOURTEEN

Agnes Hardwick awoke with a start. She was momentarily confused in the strange, unfamiliar surroundings. Only when the telephone screeched for the second time, did her memory flood back. She fumbled the phone off the hook and heard the recorded, metallic voice inform her it was eight o'clock. She eased the receiver back in place and rubbed a hand over her blurry eyes.

The vanishing sun, filtering in through the sheer curtains covering the balcony doors, cast a pale glow over the hotel room. The rain storm had passed, the clouds scurrying out over the plains to plague the small towns dotting its expanse.

Agnes sat on the edge of the bed for several moments blinking away sleep-spawned fog and orienting herself to the hotel room. Walking stiffly to the bathroom, she washed her face and combed her thinning hair. She studied the lined, wrinkled face in the mirror. It was pale and a little drawn. The eyes were clear, if a little lackluster, and there was the hint of dark circles under them.

"Aggie, you're looking pretty ragged," she muttered. Retrieving her purse from beside the bed, she fished out her small compact. Lightly powdering her cheeks, she put on lipstick and stood back to inspect herself.

"Better," she decided.

Gathering her purse, Agnes left the room. Rathbone and Joshua were just coming out of their door when she stepped into the hall.

"Did you sleep?" Joshua asked quietly.

"Yes, thank you. I feel very refreshed."

Rathbone grunted. "We'll all need to be as alert as possible tonight."

"Don't be so gloomy," Agnes said testily. "We know it won't be easy."

"Easy?" Rathbone snorted. "It's going to be like nothing you've ever experienced."

Agnes looked at Joshua, her eyebrows raised in question. Ortega shrugged and shook his head in reply.

They checked out of the hotel and, again taking both cars, headed back to Mansfield through the gathering twilight. Agnes again rode with Joshua, who followed the Cord.

"What put him on edge?" Agnes asked as they drove.

Josh frowned. "I think I did. I asked him about this thing . . . this Madonna creature. He told me a grim little tale about what She did to a friend of his. He got pretty moody. When the phone woke me, he was just sitting on the edge of his bed, staring out the window. First thing he did when I opened my eyes was tell me how rough he thinks it'll be tonight and how he depends on me. Grumpy as an old bear."

"What'd he tell you?"

Joshua relayed Rathbone's story about the death of his friend Timothy.

"He's frightened," Agnes muttered, staring at the Cord's taillights.

Joshua thought about that for a moment, trying to decide if a man like Tobias Rathbone *could* feel fear. He concluded it was possible. "Can't blame him I guess. So am I."

Agnes touched Joshua's arm. "We all are. Not only are we facing something totally alien, we're improvising our strategy as we go along."

He mumbled agreement and then lapsed into a sullen silence, concentrating on the road.

Agnes, her hands clasped on her lap, leaned back in the seat and closed her eyes. She willed herself to relax, attempting to quiet the tension jangling her already frayed nerves.

Everything was moving too fast. A few days ago she was just another old woman tending her flowers, reading her newspaper and coping—quite well, she thought—with the discomforts and mild infirmities of old age.

Now I'm going to creep around a cemetery chasing some . . . demon. It's ludicrous.

Of course she had to admit, somewhat ruefully, few of her contemporaries dabbled with Ouija boards.

She didn't open her eyes until Joshua stopped his car behind Rathbone's two blocks from the cemetery. It was almost completely dark now and the sky was a deep, velvety blue. An orange glow spread over the eastern horizon as the nearly full moon crept above the expanse of the Great Plains.

Joshua retrieved the small tape recorder and the Ouija board from the trunk of his car. He handed the board to Agnes and pocketed the tape recorder. Heaving a heavy sigh, he slammed the trunk lid and turned to Agnes.

"Ready?"

She smiled. "Stick with me, kid. Everything's going to be okay."

Joshua laughed softly. "You watch too much late night TV."

Rathbone, already out of the Cord, was watching the moonrise as Agnes and Joshua joined him.

"Tomorrow night's the full moon," he said, more to

himself than to them. "I can feel the gathering forces. I hope we're successful tonight . . ."

He left the thought unfinished and began walking toward Mansfield. Silently, Joshua and Agnes fell into step behind him. They moved slowly. To any curious, unknowing eyes, they were merely three elderly folks out for a late evening walk.

Rathbone scrutinized the ghostly, abandoned industrial building as they walked past it. The dark windows stared back like black, empty eye sockets.

"We're being watched," he whispered.

"By whom?" Agnes hissed.

Rathbone shook his head. "More likely, by what. I wish I knew. I can sense a presence, but I can't identify it."

Joshua looked around nervously, peering closely into the black shadows. Nothing stirred, but at one of the windows, for a brief instant, he was sure two red pinpoints peered back. He turned away shivering, trying not to believe they had been eyes.

He was frightened. In fact, he couldn't remember any experience in his life which so terrified him. There was nothing with which to compare this venture. His had been a life of scholarly pursuits. Oh, he had been in World War II, but the closest he'd ever come to real danger was when his unit was ambushed outside a small French village. Even then, he never did fire his weapon.

This was different. The enemy was nothing like Nazi troopers; it was like nothing human.

And there was that nagging doubt—or hope—that all of this was so much malarky; some stupid, sick joke perpetrated, not by the supernatural, but by deranged, misguided people with twisted, sick minds.

Actually, of course, he knew that wasn't the case.

When they reached the gravel drive leading to the cemetery gates, Agnes grabbed Rathbone's arm, halting him.

"Are we just going to waltz right in there?" she asked, her voice a low hiss.

He looked at her. "Of course. That Black Bitch knows we're here. She's probably known since we left the hotel."

Joshua pushed his face close to Rathbone. "Shit, Tobias, if She already knows, aren't we committing suicide?"

"Maybe. Maybe not."

"Maybe? What the hell do you mean: Maybe?"

Rathbone spoke patiently, but firmly, his voice rumbling up from some deep place in his gut. "Josh, this isn't some scientific expedition. You were a serviceman, think of it as a mission into unknown enemy territory. Just do what you're supposed to do and *I'll* do what *I'm* supposed to do. We win by working as a team, not by planting bad seeds in our minds about self destruction."

Joshua looked away, shaking his head. "Okay. Okay. Lead on."

Rathbone turned and started up the driveway. Joshua leaned close to Agnes, hissing in her ear.

"This is wonderful, Aggie. We're on a damned mission from God."

She laughed softly and then abruptly frowned. "You may be closer to the truth than you know."

"Swell."

They caught up with Rathbone at the gates. The heavy chain was firmly in place and the lock secured.

"Now what?" Joshua wondered.

"Stand back," Rathbone warned, placing his large right hand around the padlock. He clutched it so hard his arm began to quiver. At first there was an almost indistinct buzz and then, with a flash, his hand was consumed in a luminescent blue light. The light grew more intense with each passing second, until it flared into a heatless fire.

Agnes and Joshua watched in awe as white-hot chunks of molten metal fell from Rathbone's hand to splatter and hiss on the gravel. In seconds, the chain fell free and Rathbone withdrew his hand.

He looked at his wide-eyed friends, now standing several feet behind him. "An old, and I might say, useful talent."

"No shit," Joshua mumbled. "Sorry, Agnes."

"Oh, I agree," she said, still staring at the smoking, red and orange metal puddled at Rathbone's feet.

It was the first time either had witnessed the ancient man's powers and the display embued both with renewed courage.

"Now," Rathbone said, ignoring their gaping stares. "Once we go inside, stay very close to me. I'm honestly not sure what will happen, but you can be certain something will. If things get too difficult, we'll have to leave. Is that understood?"

Agnes and Joshua nodded.

"Good. Then let's go in."

Agnes clutched the Ouija board close to her as she followed Rathbone into the cemetery. The caretaker's cottage, off to their right, stood silent, its dark windows radiating a cold emptiness.

Joshua glanced at the house and turned immediately away. This time he was certain he had seen two red, pupil-less eyes watching them from one of the upper windows.

The moon was now clear of the horizon. Bloated and all but full, it cast an icy silver glow over the acres of dark tombstones and squatting crypts covering Mansfield's huge expanse. Its light gleamed off polished stone and created deep unfathomable shadows under trees and behind mausoleums. The towering pines, oaks and elms, black against the sky, stood silent and undisturbed, sentinels guarding the long-dead bones concealed by earth and stone. Their knotted branches, shrouded in motionless leaves, thrust toward the sky like the broken and misshapen limbs of grotesque, tormented beasts. Even the carved statuary perched on the monuments, were washed by the cold light, casting twisted and distorted shadows over the ground.

Somewhere in the distance, beyond the rusty iron fence surrounding the cemetery, an animal howled and was answered by the mournful bay of a moonstruck dog.

The trio proceeded cautiously, their feet crunching on the gravel as they made their way into the shadowed graveyard.

They stopped abruptly when the first scream shattered the night's stillness. It came from deep within the heart of the cemetery.

"Jesus," Joshua breathed. "What was that?"

"Ignore it," Rathbone commanded sternly, continuing along the road. He moved slowly and steadily, his eyes constantly shifting from side to side.

A second scream echoed through the grounds. It carried an unforgettable note of pain and terror and unthinkable torment; a human-animal cry ripped from the throat of someone unable to endure further agonies.

Joshua gasped and Agnes clasped her free hand to her breast, her heart suddenly pounding with such ferocity, she feared it would burst. Rathbone seemed oblivious to the hopeless wail and continued to walk forward. He kept them moving until they reached a thick stand of trees surrounding several headstones.

"Here," Rathbone said, pointing at one of the headstones.

"How do you know?" Agnes asked, bending in an attempt to read the name chiseled in the old, weathered marker.

"I just know. This is the grave of one we need to contact. Only one of a very few in this place, I think."

Again that horrible scream undulated through the night. It was even more intense and terrible than before and echoed for a long moment before finally fading.

"Do . . . do you think it's one of those . . . those young people?" Agnes stammered, a tremor in her delicate voice.

"Don't think about it," Rathbone snapped.

"We can't just ignore it," Joshua shot back.

"Yes, we can."

Agnes looked at the Rathbone's moon paled face. "Tobias, we can't just let them suffer . . ."

"It's a trick, Aggie," he replied.

"And if it's not?" she wondered.

"Then it's not. There's nothing we can do for them now."

Joshua cursed softly to himself as he patted Agnes on her thin, fragile shoulder.

"Begin," Rathbone instructed. "I'll protect you."

"Begin how?" the old woman asked harshly.

Rathbone pointed to grave. "Kneel by the grave, place the board over it and the two of you begin your communication."

Joshua and Agnes, angry at Rathbone for his seeming callousness and indifference, did as instructed. Kneeling opposite one another, the board between them, they centered it over the long-interred bones. The moon fell across the board, making the dark wood letters stand out in sharp relief against the lighter background. Agnes placed the three-footed pointer on the board and rested her hands lightly on it.

"Wait," whispered Joshua, fishing a hand into his jacket pocket. "I almost forgot this." He brought out the small tape recorder and turned it on. The tiny green light sparkled, indicating the machine was functioning and ready. After gently nestling it into the soft grass, he placed his fingers near Agnes's on the planchette.

For a long moment the pointer was motionless. It finally quivered and began to move in slow, erratic circles, never stopping on any of the letters or numerals. Agnes groaned, tripping the activator in the recorder. The tiny red light flowered next to the green one.

"Aggie?" Joshua said earnestly. "You okay?"

"Yes. I can feel her pain."

"Whose?"

"The woman we're trying to contact."

Joshua stole a quick glance at the headstone. He could just make out the name MARTHA grooved in the marble.

Agnes's breathing was now labored, a raspy sound coming from her throat. Joshua could see her eyes rolling upward in their sockets and he was about to pull away from the pointer when she exhaled a long, relieved breath and offered him a weak smile.

"I'm okay."

The planchette slowed and paused on one of the letters.

"H," Agnes entoned.

The pointer waivered as if confused and then stopped again.

"I."

Again it moved, hesitated and then stopped.

"S."

"His," breathed Joshua.

"H-A-N-D-S." The old woman entoned each letter softly as the planchette moved with greater speed and assurance over the smooth surface of the Ouija board.

"C-R-U-S-H-E-D T-H-E L-I-F-E F-R-O-M M-Y B-O-D-Y."

Agnes suddenly pulled her hands away as if they'd been stunned with an electric shock. She gently massaged her throat, looking at Joshua with frightened eyes.

"He strangled her," she gasped. "I saw it all. She was so young and pretty. She was trying to leave, to get away from him and he . . . he caught her at the door." She stared down at her own hands, starkly white in the moonlight.

"His hands were so large," she continued, speaking very slowly, her voice distant and hollow. "They completely encirled her neck. He squeezed and squeezed, burying his thumbs into her throat. She fought and struggled, but it was useless. She died in his grasp."

"You saw it?" Joshua asked incredulously, knowing Agnes had often been swept by emotions and feelings, but had never actually visualized a scene from the past.

"Clearly. As clearly as I see you now. And I . . . I could *feel* it. I could feel his hands . . ."

"Who killed her, Aggie?"

The old woman was silent for a moment. When she spoke, her voice was just above a whisper. "Her lover. Her father."

"Her father was her lover? And he killed her? His own daughter?" Joshua shivered, thinking of his daughter in California.

"I saw it. I felt it. It was . . . was terrible."

"It's Josh's power boosting yours," rumbled Rathbone, causing the two kneeling on the ground to look up in surprise. He had been standing stock still near them, listening to them while watching the surrounding area. "Continue. There is much we must learn and very little time."

Agnes took a deep breath and gingerly placed her fingers back on the planchette. Joshua did the same. Again the pointer began gliding over the board.

"P-L-E-A-S-E H-E-L-P M-E," she spelled out. "I A-M I-N C-O-L-D B-L-A-C-K-N-E-S-S. I A-M L-O-S-T."

"I'll help you," Agnes said aloud. "You must help me. Tell me about this cemetery."

"E-V-I-L. A-L-L H-E-R-E I-S E-V-I-L. B-E-W-A-R-E T-H-E D-A-R-K O-N-E. B-E-W-A-R-E T-H-E R-I-S-I-N-G."

"Martha," Agnes said gently. "What is the rising?"

"E-V-I-L. T-H-E D-E-A-D W-I-L-L W-A-L-K A-G-A-I-N."

Again Agnes lifted her hands from the planchette.

"That poor creature," she said sadly. "She was buried here by her father. He believed they would be together in the flesh again. He lusted for her even in death. She's filled with fear and hate. And she is so sad."

Joshua sucked in his breath. "Jesus, this is unbelievably sick."

"It's what I was afraid of," Rathbone hissed. "That Bitch is up to Her old tricks. I can sense the restlessness beneath the mattock. This hellish rising will come soon. Aggie, find out when it will occur."

"She may be getting tired, Tobias," Joshua said defensively.

"No, Josh, I'm fine. I'm feeding on your energy."

All three turned as the screaming wail, much closer now, burst over the cemetery. It was no longer human, but a bestial cry of savage rage.

Rathbone saw a movement near one of the crypts. A black shape swelled from behind a tombstone, rising high above it. An ebon cloak, like spreading wings, billowed around the thing as it rose higher into the warm, heavy air. It hung there motionless, a dark blotch against the deep blue night sky.

"Hurry," Rathbone prompted, not taking his eyes from the apparition.

Agnes and Joshua, having seen the thing manifest, stared at it in undisguised horror. Both were trembling. Joshua held a hand over his mouth, willing himself not to scream; afraid, however, he might vomit. He was vaguely aware of the spreading warmth between his legs.

"You've got to continue," Rathbone barked, a trace of desperation edging his words.

Agnes turned away from the creature and placed her fingers on the planchette.

"Josh," she called sternly. "I need your help."

He looked at her, his eyes wide and frightened.

"You've got to help me."

He blinked and nodded. "Yes. Yes, of course." He, too, returned his quaking fingers to the planchette.

"Martha," Agnes began. "When is the rising?"

As the planchette moved, the hovering thing let out an unearthly, blood chilling screech. It reverberated across the graveyard, echoing from polished marble and rough-hewed stone before fading.

Rathbone raised his hands before him. They began to shimmer with the dancing blue light.

"Go on!" he cried.

"The rising, Martha. When is the rising?" Agnes asked again, her words coming in short, ragged gasps.

"S-O-O-N. W-H-E-N T-H-E M-O-O-N I-S F-U-L-L."

"Tomorrow night," Joshua mumbled, sounding frightened and exhausted. He could feel his energy flowing into Agnes, draining him.

The black shape descended to the earth, its ragged cloak settling around it like folded wings. Soundlessly, it began to glide toward the trio.

As it neared, Agnes cried out and was suddenly toppled over. Joshua, too, tottered, clutching at the headstone to keep from sprawling. The ground beneath them trembled and then shook. Clods of moist earth and sod leaped and spewed into the air.

"Get up," Rathbone ordered. "Get up and stand behind me!"

The ground covering the murdered woman's grave was erupting in a fountain of dark loam and torn roots. It geysered into the air like a slow motion explosion, threatening to bury both Joshua and Agnes. They struggled, desperately attempting to get to their feet. Agnes grasped her Ouija board and looked around for the recorder. It had already been hurled into the darkness.

"Wh . . What's happening?" Joshua cried, spitting dirt from his mouth and wiping the sticky clay from his face. Stumbling, he took Agnes's arm and guided her to Rathbone.

"Start backing toward the gate," Rathbone yelled. "But stay behind me." His hands were now engulfed in the enigmatic blue flames. They sparked and flared, casting eerie, dancing shadows.

The black thing continued to float toward them. Its features were invisible beneath the peaked hood and it bore only the vaguest outline of a human shape. It was only an ominous, dark vestige stalking them.

Earth and fine sand still sprayed from the grave. The

hole deepened, nearing the rotting, worm infested casket holding the bones of the long-dead girl.

Rathbone backed slowly and Joshua and Agnes remained behind him, both glancing nervously from the dark shape pursuing them to the graveled road at their backs. More than once, Agnes's foot caught on a rock and she would have fallen except for Joshua's steadying hand firmly gripping her arm.

"Be ready," Rathbone said, lifting his hands higher, aiming them at the black thing. There was a blinding flash and a crystaline blue bolt of energy shot from his fists. It hammered into the dark shape, piercing it.

The black thing screamed in pain and fury. The hood flew back to reveal the dark skull-face partially covered by the cracked and tattered shreds of dried flesh. The twin tusk-like fangs, with their hooked points, shone brightly in the icy glow of the moon. The swirling pools of red and yellow of its pupil-less eyes now flashed at them.

From the exploding grave there came a mournful cry and with a gush of foul air and cracking wood, the coffin burst from the ground, toppling out onto its corrupted, decayed side.

"Sweet Jesus!" Joshua cried, oddly wondering if his sanity was going to slip away.

Rathbone collided with Agnes, who had stopped dead in her tracks, transfixed by the nightmare scene.

"Keep moving back!" he screamed.

Joshua fairly dragged her on.

The lid of the coffin fell open. There was a rustling within, followed by a tortured, raspy cry. Something emerged from the long sealed oblong box. It writhed and twisted on the ground and then slowly stood erect.

"Martha," Agnes sobbed.

The skeletal creature from the coffin, draped in darkly stained rags, twisted and turned, clawing at its fleshless skull. Light burned in the recesses of its eye sockets and its jaw worked frantically. A dry grating sound issued from it.

Agnes knew if it could produce speech, it would be screaming.

"That's the filthy Black Bitch's gift!" screamed Rathbone. "That's Her promise of life after death! Soulless animation and consciousness without reason!"

Joshua cried out as something darted from behind a crypt and slammed into him. He fell hard to the ground, his hand wrenched free of Agnes's arm. Before he could recover, something pounced on him. He started to yell as sharp, dry claws dug into the soft flesh of his neck, attempting to crush his throat and end his life. From his attacker came a jibbering nonsense.

Agnes was nearly dragged down when Joshua fell. She turned and screamed when she saw the rag-covered skeleton straddled her friend, its bony fingers encircling his throat.

Instinctively, she lashed out with her foot, catching the thing in its fleshless side. Brittle ribs crunched and snapped under her blow. The thing clicked its teeth together and with a creak of brittle bone, the skull turned. Black eye sockets, holding tiny pinpoints of orange fire, glared at her. The unintelligible jibberish continued, a haunting sound from an impossible source.

Keeping one bony claw around Joshua's throat, it reached for Agnes with the other, trying to slash her with ragged, mud-caked nails.

"Monster!" she screamed, swinging the Ouija board at the leering skull. The impact jarred her hands and caved in the thing's forehead. Before it could grasp at her again, she brought the board around in a sweeping arc. There was a brittle snap as the edge of the hard wood crashed into the fragile neck bones. The skull tumbled to the gravel drive and rolled down the gentle slope, finally coming to rest upright.

The orange light still burned in the black pits which had once been eyes.

With a dry rattle, the skeletal body crumpled into a heap atop Joshua.

"Get him up," Rathbone hissed at Agnes, as he unleashed another of the brilliant energy bolts.

Joshua was wheezing and gasping for breath. Agnes bent over him, calling his name frantically. His eyes fluttered open and he tried to focus them on the old woman. His lips moved, but only a hoarse, gagging cough came out.

Agnes tugged at his arm, trying desperately to drag him to his feet, but she hadn't the strength.

"Josh get up! You have to get up!" She yanked again, terrified he was too badly injured to move.

He nodded in understanding and pushed himself up slowly, one hand holding his bruised and bloodied throat. The jumble of bones and rotted shroud tumbled to the ground as he stood erect. Balancing himself with Agnes's help, he started to move.

Again, they backed toward the distant gates.

Something flashed out of the moon-bright sky on leathery wings, and raking talons tore across Rathbone's head. He cried out and thrust an arm toward the receding form. An energy bolt seared it in a silent explosion of blue fire. It spiraled out of the sky, thudded to the ground and vanished in a smoky burst of flame.

The Black Bitch, wary of Rathbone's power, paced them, but did not draw closer. Instead, hissing and spitting, she thrust back the folds of Her fouled and ragged cloak and motioned skyward with one of her gnarled and twisted arms. Her huge, clawed fingers clutched at the moon.

There was a thunderous clap in the cloudless sky and a score of deformed, shadowy shapes, with hungry red eyes, materialized from behind gravestones, atop hulking crypts and around the trunks of massive trees.

"Run!" Rathbone screamed at his companions. "Run as fast as you can!"

FIFTEEN

Agnes Hardwick heard herself screaming.

She felt disembodied and detached, as if she was watching from some distant vantage point as she ran for her life, her old, tired legs throbbing painfully as they carried her down the rutted road. Her heart beat frantically in her chest and thundered in her ears. A muscle cramped and clutched at her side and she panicked when she thought she would have to stop until the pain subsided.

But you can't stop! They'll kill you!

Agnes was hardly aware of her fingers buried in Joshua's arm or of her other arm clutching the Ouija board. The old man, still wheezing and coughing, stumbled beside her, moving at a listless, loose-jointed jog, propelled along as much by Agnes's strength as his own.

Rathbone remained behind, launching energy bolts in a frantic attempt to hold back the advancing horde of hissing and spitting creatures summoned by the Black Bitch.

She stood amid Her gathering minions, snarling and snapping at them. Cowering in Her presence, perhaps terrified of Her power and anger, the loathsome things rushed Rathbone again and again. They tried to overwhelm the old Druid and breach his defenses. Some circled wide, attempting to flank him, while others kept pursuing Agnes and Joshua.

The air was filled with the dry beat of leathery wings as yet more monstrosities began attacking Rathbone from the cold, moonlit sky. They jabbed at his eyes and face with razor sharp tridents and flashing scythes.

Blood flowed freely from a dozen tiny gashes in the Druid's face and hands. Yet for every successful foray the creatures made against him, half a score were felled by his awesome energy bolts. However, with each sucessive burst from his fiery hands, the blasts grew noticibly weaker.

He was bathed in sweat. Salty streams mingled with his blood, turning his face into a dark, grim mask. He brushed the sticky mess from his eyes while continuing to hold back the Madonna and Her demons with his rapidly diminishing powers.

The skeletal thing which had once been a young, vital girl, continued to writhe and twist near the desecrated grave. It flung its arms beseechingly toward heaven as if begging God for peace, an end to the torment.

The Madonna, a blotch of darkness against the night sky, floated closer to Rathbone. Her long bony arms were extended toward him, the sharp taloned fingers curled, ready to grip and rip his flesh. Her obscene visage shone in the silvery light, the hooked fangs glistening and those twin orbs of swirling fire piercing the Druid with hate and loathing.

She was kept at a distance by Rathbone's energy bolts, but as they weakened, She gradually closed on him. And, he, in turn, was showing signs of his fatigue and his waning power. His breath was coming in great gulps and as he moved backward, his feet were dragging on the gravel, as if lifting them was too burdensome.

Agnes glanced over her shoulder, a cry escaping her lips as she saw the horde of demons nearing Joshua and herself. They loped after them like hell-spawned hounds, their terribly twisted limbs propelling them over the grass and gravel at a frightening pace. They sprang over tombstones and pranced around crypts, jabbering and slobbering, their clawed hands clutching awful weapons which flashed menacingly in the moonlight.

"I . . . I can't go on," Joshua groaned, his feet stumbling. His voice was hoarse and raspy.

"You *have* to, Josh. You have to!" Agnes cried desperately in reply. "If you stop, they'll kill you."

The gates were near now. Agnes saw them looming ahead. But they were closed, which worried her, knowing full well they had left them open when they entered Mansfield.

As the two exhausted old people drew closer to the gates, Agnes's old heart, pounding with exertion and panic, sank. The heavy chain was wound through the bars and she could see a massive padlock binding the ends of chain securely together.

Trapped!

Agnes felt a weight settle over her, crushing her remaining hope. Even if they reached the gates, the creatures following would have them snared like wild animals driven from the bush. There was no place to turn; no place to hide.

They would have to turn and fight.

Fight with what? she wondered.

She and Joshua, who was sucking in breath in great, greedy swallows, reached the iron portals. They all but crashed into them, grasping the bars to keep from falling. Agnes released her hold on Joshua's arm as she slumped against the hard, cold iron. Joshua looked around and groaned. He suddenly realized they were trapped.

Agnes choked back a sob and turned. "Josh," she screamed. "We have to defend ourselves. Do you hear me? We have to keep these . . . these things away!"

The creatures were now forming an ever-tightening semicircle around them. Their slashed mouths, filled with sharp, wicked teeth, opened in what must have been smiles. They brandished and waved their weapons as they bobbed and loped closer and closer.

Rathbone was wearing down. His clothing was shredded and in tatters and blood flowed freely from tiny, painful wounds everywhere on his body. He stumbled once, almost falling, and as he was recovering his balance, a half dozen of the Madonna's monstrosities leaped at him. It was only a well-aimed—or lucky—energy blast which cut them down and saved him.

He chanced to take his eyes off his attackers for an instant and cursed softly when he saw Agnes and Joshua, their backs pressed against the gates, encircled by the snarling hell-spawned monsters. There was nothing he could do for them. If he turned his back to the Madonna to defend his friends, he would be cut down before he could unleash a single energy burst.

He looked away and continued to defend himself.

The reanimated bones of the murdered girl, contorting in supplication and horror, suddenly froze. The spark of life burning in the empty sockets glimmered and fixed on the black shape of the Madonna. After a moment, the creature was suddenly shambling across the grass, a dry, rustling sound coming from its fleshless form. It stumbled and staggered on spindly, brittle bones.

Rathbone saw this, neither knowing nor caring what it meant. The cemetery was filled with terrors out of a Dante-esque nightmare. He was so fatigued and drained, he knew he could not survive much longer. He was now battling, not to save his own life or the lives of Agnes and Joshua, but to do as much damage as possible to the Madonna before he collapsed under the weight of Her forces.

He knew, too, what would befall his soul when he was eventually killed. The death of his body and flesh were nothing in comparison to the eternal torment and suffering which would be his once the Bitch snared his spirit.

It had been one of the reasons he had, unwillingly and yet in love and friendship, slain Timothy so long ago. While the Madonna had infested his comrade with mortal wounds and torments, She had not yet claimed his soul. By driving his dagger through his friend's heart, he had freed Timothy from the Bitch's hellish grasp and assured him of rebirth without the taint of evil.

Who would free *his* spirit when he lay at Death's door? There was no one who could do for him what he had done for Timothy. Hence, Rathbone fought on, compelled to fend off his attackers to the bitter, but seemingly inevitable end.

The skeletal thing, its once crisp, white burial shroud now a mass of soiled, rotted rags flapping wildly about its bones, neared the Madonna. None of the snarling, hissing creatures paid it any attention, their efforts remained directed against the Druid. It staggered toward the cloaked entity, an odd, feverish determination in its unsteady gait.

Agnes and Joshua watched helplessly as their assailants continued to draw the circle tighter. Agnes knew it was only a matter of moments before those demonic creatures pounced upon them, bludgeoning and stabbing the life from their old bodies.

"My God," Joshua breathed. "Isn't there anything we can do?" He had regained his awareness, although he was still breathing in raspy gulps and his strength was sapped.

"Fight," Agnes hissed through clenched teeth. "There's nothing else we can do."

Rathbone, unleashing yet another blast of blue energy, watched the disinterred skeleton near the Madonna. He expected the Bitch to smite the thing down without hesitation. Instead, when the thing lunged on wobbly legs and collided with the source of all its agonies, the Madonna turned away from the Druid to face Her new attacker.

The grotesque animation lashed out at the ebon form with clawed fingers, tearing at the dark cloak and whatever lay beneath it.

The night filled with a high, piercing wail, not of pain, but anger. It was a cry of outrage and carried with it an accusatory scream of betrayal.

The Madonna's horde of malformed demons, obviously linked to their mistress by some psychic force, paused as one. Their misshapen heads all turned to stare at Her dark shape as She screamed at the offending, audacious thing striking Her.

Rathbone, suddenly free of the attack, turned and ran down the road. He knew this respite would be brief and could very possibly be his only chance at escape.

Agnes and Joshua, their backs still pressed against the gates, watched the Druid run toward them. They gazed in fascinated horror as the skeleton of the murdered girl attacked the Madonna. It was yet another in a series of blasphemous atrocities on this night of dark and evil abominations against all they had ever held sacred.

Rathbone, still running, using the gentle slope of the hill to gain momentum, motioned wildly at Agnes and Joshua.

"Move! Get away from the lock!"

As if his cry was a signal, the creatures were suddenly in motion again. They turned to face the Druid as he charged toward them, their weapons held ready to strike him down.

Rathbone raised one arm and leveled it at the assemblage of creatures and let loose an energy bolt. It was pale and weak, its faded, washed-out light reflected his waning powers. The bolt struck several of the creatures and while it did not destroy them, as a more powerful blast would have, it sent them tumbling and flying, clearing a path to Agnes and Joshua.

Behind Rathbone, the Madonna suddenly lashed out at the skeleton with one of Her huge, clawed hands. The blow shattered the hapless creature's head and it crumpled to the ground in a heap.

Turning away from the pile of bones, the dark entity let out another wail when She saw Rathbone dashing to the gates. Like a giant bat, She rose from the ground and fluttered toward Her three nemesises.

Rathbone reached the gate and grabbed the padlock in trembling, tired fingers. His face, streaked and caked with blood and sweat, twisted in a grimace as he mustered the last of his reserves to destroy the lock. A faint blue glow emanated from his fist.

"Hurry, Tobias," Joshua cried, watching the Madonna and Her horde storm down the hill toward them. "Please hurry."

The Druid made no response. If he heard the plea, he gave no sign, but kept his mind focused on the lock.

The creatures scattered about the gate, stunned by the energy bolt, began to stir, some climbing unsteadily to their feet. They snarled and spat at the three humans and one made a dash at them, a barbed trident raised.

Instinctively, Joshua lashed out with his foot as the thing neared Agnes. Much to his surprise, he struck the creature full in the face. His stomach turned, as his foot buried itself in soft, gelatinous tissue and the demon spun away, a geyser of dark, foul fluid spraying into the air from its crushed head.

The Madonna was very near, Her horrid, fanged death's head leering in the brilliant moonlight. The mad swirl of red and orange of Her eyes were even more frantic, sparking with unbridled fury.

Rathbone was shaking with effort. His hands continued to glow, but he could not generate enough power to destroy the lock. He swung his right arm around, his hand extended.

"Josh, take my hand!" Rathbone yelled.

"What?" Ortega stammered.

"Just do it!"

Mystified, Joshua stumbled to the Druid's side and clasped Rathbone's hand in his own. He immediately felt a surge of energy flow through his body.

There was a sudden burst of power, Rathbone's left

hand glowed and flashed with sapphirine fire. The padlock fell away in a burning mass of molten metal.

"Move!" Rathbone cried, his voice weak. He shouldered his way through the gates and stumbled into the driveway. Exhausted, his energies depleted, he sprawled to the gravel.

Agnes and Joshua followed the Druid out the gate. The horde of demons in pursuit.

"Help him," Agnes said to Joshua, grabbing one of Rathbone's arms. Her Ouija board tucked firmly under one of her own arms, she tried to pull the man to his feet. Joshua took hold of Tobias and together they dragged the man away from the gates.

Agnes looked back, surprised to see their pursuers stop abruptly at the entrance to the cemetery.

"They've stopped," she breathed, laboring with Rathbone's heavy, inert body.

"Is he dead?" Joshua asked, stooping to get under one of the Druid's arms.

"I hope not," she replied, wondering if her old heart and body were up to further exertion.

Again the shrieking, keening wail sounded and they both turned to watch the black, cloaked form of the Madonna rise above the ground. There was frustration in the scream and both Agnes and Joshua were filled with an odd mixture of satisfaction and horror.

Thwarting that evil Bitch and surviving was cause for elation. Yet the realization that they had barely escaped with their lives was sobering.

And still the denizen of Mansfield was free and unscathed.

When they reached the sidewalk, they stopped, carefully lowering Rathbone to the cool concrete. Agnes bent over him, lifting his head gently in her hands.

"Tobias," she said softly. No response. She felt his pulse. It was weak and his breathing was shallow.

"Josh, get your car. We've got to get him to a hospital. I think he's dying." The urgency in her voice sent Joshua, feeling ready for a hospital himself, hurrying down the street to where the cars were parked.

After Joshua left, Agnes looked at the cemetery again. The scores of demons were gone now, but a dark shape still hovered above the crypts and tombstones.

"You can watch us all you want, you monster," Agnes said softly. "But I don't think you can hurt us out here; outside your damned graveyard."

As if it heard her, black-enshrouded arms thrashed furiously at the air.

Rathbone moaned softly and Agnes looked at his drawn, lined face.

"Tobias."

"Aggie? We must have made it out." His voice was low, forcing Agnes to place her ear close to his mouth to hear his words.

"Yes. We made it," she said. "Josh and I are going to take you to a hospital. You need medical . . ."

"No!" Rathbone snapped, his voice suddenly loud and harsh. "No hospital. It's a waste of time. And we haven't much to spare."

"But you need attention . . ."

"No physician can help with what I need. It's not a problem a medical man can cure." His eyes fluttered and Agnes thought he had blacked out. She glanced around, looking for Joshua's car. She could see it pulling away from the curb down the street.

"Take me to your house," Rathbone beseeched, clutching at Agnes, who studied him in surprise. "Please. Just take me there. I'd rather not go to a . . . a hospital." His head slumped and for an instant she feared he had died. Pressing her ear to his chest, she was relieved to hear the steady thud of his heart.

Joshua brought the Buick sliding to a stop next to them. He climbed out, leaving the engine idling, and helped Agnes half carry and half drag Rathbone into the backseat.

"What about the Cord?" he asked, once the Druid was safely lying on the seat.

"I'll drive it," Agnes said nonchalantly.

"You? You haven't driven a car in years."

"True," she agreed. "Time I got back in practice."

"Why don't we just leave it?" Joshua wanted to know.

Agnes sighed, looking through the window at Rathbone. "It'd get stolen if we left it and he does love that car."

Joshua nodded, too tired to argue. "Which hospital?"

"None. We're going to my house."

"I thought . . ."

"Forget what I said and what you thought. Let's just get Tobias to my house and into a warm bed." The edge in her voice was plain and Joshua, shoulders slumped, nodded his assent.

"Get in," he said quietly. "I'll drive you to Tobias's car."

After turning around, Joshua drove back to where the other vehicle was parked. He found the Cord's keys in Rathbone's pocket and handed them to Agnes.

"Are you sure you can drive it?"

"Would you quit being such a doubting Thomas?" she said stiffly. "Just get Tobias to my house. And hurry."

Joshua waited until Agnes had the Cord running and then headed for north Denver and Agnes's home. She followed and they arrived without incident.

It was near eleven by the time they had Rathbone safely ensconced on the couch, covered with a blanket.

Agnes and Joshua retired to the kitchen. After she opened a can of cat food and fed Solomon, who had danced and rubbed around her legs, Agnes made them both steaming cups of tea. They sat quietly at the table.

"I don't want you to go home tonight, Josh," she said after some time had passed.

"Tobias has the couch," he commented flatly, without any humor, his fatigue evident.

"There's a bed in the back bedroom. You can use that."

"Why didn't I get to use it last night?" he asked, feigning hurt.

Agnes smiled. "It's not made up."

"Oh."

She cleared her throat and looked at Joshua closely. "How are you? Really?"

He studied his tea and then reached down to stroke Solomon. The cat sat contentedly near his leg.

"I don't know," he answered without looking at her. "I don't know how I am. I don't feel like I know much of anything right now."

"Josh?"

He looked up, his eyes hollow and heavy-lidded. "I just don't know. Tonight everything I've ever believed in was blown to hell and gone. Do you know what I mean? Our experience at that damned cemetery . . . Well, hell it . . ." He was unable to find words to articulate the emotions and feelings roiling in his mind, tearing at his heart.

"You know, Josh," Agnes said after a time. "I understand how you feel. I thought my world was pretty self-contained. I mean, after all those years of teaching school and being a . . . a sort of happy-go-lucky eccentric, all wrapped up in my secure beliefs and certainties . . . I just don't know. It's all topsy-turvy now."

"Yeah, right," Joshua said, brushing his moustache with his hand. He took a sip of tea and then yawned. "Regardless, I need sleep."

Agnes agreed and after they finished their tea, she led Joshua to the back bedroom which was filled with boxes of forgotten memorabilia and the assorted accumulation of years of living in one place. She found a clean pair of sheets and, with Joshua's help, made the bed.

"Josh," she said as she was leaving the room. He looked at her, catching the odd note in her voice. "Thank you for being there tonight. I'm sorry I got you caught up in all this . . ."

"Don't," he said quickly, motioning to her with his hand. "It wasn't pleasant, but at the same time . . . well, it was somehow important that I was there."

Agnes smiled. "Yes, Josh, it was very important that you were there. Now get some sleep." She left, closing the door softly behind her.

In her own bed, Solomon curled up on the other pillow next to her head, Agnes had the sensation of being watched. Repeatedly she glanced at the window, but saw nothing there.

In time she drifted into a deep, undisturbed sleep.

The rich smell of cooking bacon awakened her. Early morning light streamed in her bedroom window and the cat was gone. Investigating in the kitchen, Agnes decided. She pulled on her robe and padded down the hall. As tired as he had been last night, she couldn't imagine how or why Joshua would be up so early cooking.

She walked into the kitchen and paused. It was not Joshua standing at the stove, spatula in hand, but Tobias.

"Good morning," he said cheerfully when she stepped to the table. There were numerous tiny red scars on his face; cuts already healing. The look on Agnes's face must have said much about her confusion. He smiled. "I feel fine. Thanks for putting me up last night."

She continued to stare at him in unabashed amazement. "I thought after last night you'd be flat on your back for at least a week," she finally said.

"I've a strong constitution," he quipped cryptically.

"But you were . . ."

"Near death?" he finished for her.

"Well, we thought so."

Rathbone lifted several pieces of crisp bacon out of the frying pan and placed them on a paper towel to drain. "My body shut down to allow itself to regain its strength."

"I'll be damned," said Joshua, stepping into the kitchen. "I thought I heard voices, but I had no idea . . ."

"Oh, for heaven's sake," Rathbone cried, a smile playing on his mouth. "Will you two sit down and let me finish fixing breakfast?"

They both sat. Rathbone gave them steaming cups of hot water and let them fix their own tea. Meantime, he finished cooking the bacon and then scrambled eggs, acting at home in Agnes's kitchen as if it were his own. She felt a little disconcerted. No one else had cooked in here in a very long time.

When all three were finally seated at the table, plates of food in front of them, Joshua looked at Rathbone, his hand touching the dark bruises circling his throat.

"You made a remarkable recovery, I say."

Rathbone, his fork heaped with eggs poised before his mouth, nodded. "Yes, I suppose so." He poked the food in his mouth.

"But not as remarkable as you assume," he continued after swallowing. "Part of the reason I've lived such a long life is the blessing—or curse, depending on your view—of my very existence. I'm older than any human being on the face of the earth. Now think about that."

While they mulled it over, Rathbone continued to eat. After another few minutes, he continued.

"You see, I have powers that are, admittedly, not natural nor inherent in normal humans. They endow me with unusual abilities, as you have seen, and enable my body to store a great deal of energy. Last night I expended most of it. What was left was just enough to keep my physical body alive. I wouldn't have been able to continue much longer. Had Josh not helped me . . ." he shrugged.

"You'd have died," Agnes finished.

Rathbone looked at her. "Indeed. I would have."

"Amazing," Joshua entoned. "You were . . . in bad shape."

The Druid dismissed it with a wave of his big hand.

"It's unimportant. What *is* important is the fact that we escaped and learned valuable information."

"What information?" Joshua asked, voicing Agnes's thoughts.

"We learned a lot," Rathbone said enthusiastically.

Agnes stared at him. "We learned that tonight's the . . . what was it called?"

"The Rising," said Rathbone. "Tonight is the full moon. In fact, if I were a betting man, I'd say it has been exactly a century since all this madness began. A century since the wheels were set in motion for tonight's corruption."

Joshua thought for a moment and then drew in a heavy breath. "Last night, when . . . that thing came out of the grave . . . what happened?"

Rathbone's smile was humorless. "We contacted the soul, the essense, of a dead girl murdured by her own father. Obviously her body was placed in Mansfield because her father wanted her to be reborn with him. But she wasn't a part of the sickness that drove the people who created the cemetery. Maybe her soul had been trapped, I'm not sure. When she communicated with Aggie, she incurred the Madonna's wrath and was . . . summoned forth."

"Was she . . . that is . . . was her soul, her consciousness, aware of what an abomination she had become?" Agnes asked hesitantly, sadly.

Rathbone studied the old woman for a moment. "I think you already know."

Agnes lowered her eyes and nodded. "Yes."

"But," protested Joshua. "I thought you said the Madonna gave them the illusion of life. You mean that thing, that skeleton, held a soul?"

"Yes. For one like her, a betrayer of the Madonna's schemes, she was called forth with conscious thought. She knew who and what she was. It was a horrible punishment."

"God, that's awful," Agnes gasped, brushing away a tear. She had been deeply moved by the murdered girl's anguished plea through the Ouija board.

"It's done now," Rathbone soothed. "Her soul is free."

"So," Joshua said, trying to break the tension of the moment. "We found out that tonight is this Rising. What can we do about it?"

Rathbone stood, gathered the now empty plates and stacked them in the sink. "We learned more than that, Josh. We learned something of the extent of the Madonna's power."

Joshua raised a questioning eyebrow and Agnes looked up, wiping the last of her tears away.

"Look," the Druid continued, settling back in his chair. "We found She can direct Her little fiendish horde, but did you notice? She didn't really do anything to any of us. It was through Her allies that all the damage was done."

Agnes asked, "What are you getting at?"

"Simply that She can't hurt us directly. She can torment us and send things against us, but She can't touch us."

"You never knew that?" Joshua was surprised, assuming Rathbone knew everything about the Madonna.

"No. I assumed She could physically harm us, but I no longer believe that."

"What about your friend Timothy? She got him," Joshua pointed out.

Rathbone's eyes clouded and he nodded solemnly. "Yes. She did 'get' Timothy. I wasn't there, so I'm not sure how it happened. I do know, from what he told me before he . . . died, that She inflicted the wounds. Still, She didn't harm us directly last night."

"So you're really not sure?" Agnes said pointedly.

"I'm sure She didn't attack me or either of you. That means something."

"So now what?" Joshua asked, deciding further debate over what the Madonna could or couldn't do was useless.

"We go back tonight."

Joshua's mouth literally fell open. "You can't be serious? Jesus Christ! We barely got out of there alive last night and you want us to go back? That's crazy!'' He got up and stood behind Agnes's chair. ''I won't allow you to endanger Aggie any more.''

Agnes reached back and took Joshua's hand in hers. ''I appreciate that, Josh, I really do. But Tobias is right. We have to go back. We haven't a choice.''

He looked down at her and then at Rathbone. ''You're both out of your minds. We got our asses kicked last night. What can we possibly do by going back except get killed?''

Rathbone leaned back in his chair and crossed his arms. He fixed Joshua with a hard stare.

''You don't have to go,'' the Druid reminded him. ''We need you, but it has to be your choice. Aggie and I already know we don't have a choice. There are forces there that have to be stopped or at least checked. Not to mention the two young people who may still be in there somewhere.''

Joshua snorted, pulled his hand away from Agnes and began pacing the room. ''After what I saw last night, I doubt they're still alive.''

''I think for sure the girl is,'' Rathbone went on calmly.

''How can you know that?''

''I can't, Josh. It's pure instinct on my part. She and the man were lured to Mansfield for a reason. Judging from what I've learned, I'd say she's an integral ingredient to the Madonna's plan.''

Joshua was obviously confused. Agnes explained what Rathbone had deduced based on the girl's name.

''That's pretty thin reasoning,'' Joshua said, still pacing the floor.

Rathbone, much to both Agnes and Joshua's surprise, laughed heartily. ''It is. It's very thin, but it all makes sense. There are things we don't understand and maybe Terrance and Bedlow lured the girl there *thinking* she was a descendant of Maria Renata and have been fooled. We just don't know. But can we turn our backs now?''

Joshua was quiet for a long time. He was wrestling with

his fears and his desires. He was terrified of returning to the cemetery, but the thought of Mary—a woman he had met only yesterday and knew nothing about—in the hands of that thing, turned his stomach.

"Okay," he finally said, sounding beaten and dispirited. "We go back. But we damned well better come up with a plan that will do us some good."

"That's exactly what I intend for us to do," Rathbone answered.

Joshua looked at the clock. It was almost eight. Twelve hours, give or take a little, until they would go back to Mansfield. The thought sent a shudder through his body.

He suddenly felt very tired and the weight of all his years settled over him like a heavy mantle.

SIXTEEN

The air was foul, heavy with the cloying, bitter-sweet stench of decay. Candles, set in iron holders mounted on the slime encrusted walls, guttered and flickered, filling the claustrophobic room with a thick, smokey pall and formed dancing pools of yellow light on the rough stone, casting weird, distorted shadows across the floor.

For the hundredth time Mary tested the iron manacle encircling her leg. A heavy chain ran from it to an eye bolt screwed deeply into the wall. She had long ago given up attempting to pull or twist the eyebolt free; it was set hard and fast.

Dried blood flecked the manacle and streaked Mary's once-white shoes. In her struggles to free herself, she had only managed to rub her ankle raw on the rough, sharp-edged metal. Now, each movement of her foot sent waves of numbing pain rocketing up her calf.

Sitting in one of two old wooden chairs flanking a rough, crudely built table, she absently wondered if she would get blood poisoning and considered when she had last had a tetanus shot. She couldn't remember, probably not since she was a kid.

Mary had awakened, sprawled on the cold floor in the windowless, stone room. It took several moments to jar her memory and when it came flooding back, her stomach was swept with a churning nausea.

With one hand, she gently massaged the welt encircling her throat. The pain jolted her memory.

Everything appeared as flashing, disjointed images in her mind's eye. Lured back to Mansfield by Vince; dragged into the crypt by the unbelievably powerful . . . thing; the blackness inside the mausoleum; the two burning pits of fire and the unintelligible gibberish; her own screams; the second bony hand, stinking of mold and rot, suddenly clamped over her mouth, stifling her wails.

Stricken with terror, gagging from the reeking stench of the crypt and unable to free herself from the thing clutching her, Mary's mind had been thankfully engulfed in a sea of darkness.

When she had first awakened, she was lying on her bed in the cottage. The room was hot and stuffy and dark. At first she thought she was alone, but then she had seen a movement at the moonlit window. Involuntarily she gasped, thinking the thing from the crypt was there. The sound she made was muffled by the tight, thick gag in her mouth. When Mary had attempted to move, she realized she was bound hand and foot to the bed.

"Ah," said an almost jovial, thick voice. "You're awake. That's very good. There's something I want you to see."

Mary peered into the darkness and could just make out a huge shape moving toward her. A shiver ran through her and, had she not been gagged, she'd have cried out.

The bloated figure stopped and she felt the ropes binding her legs loosen and fall away.

"You're a fine looking woman." A massive, fleshy hand caressed Mary's thigh and she flinched, trying to jerk her leg away from the unwanted touch. "Now, now. Is that any way to treat the man who saved you from the creature in the tomb?"

Mary mumbled a bitter curse through the gag.

"You have spirit," the figure had said, his hand still probing the inside of her thigh. "I like that."

Mary closed her eyes and tensed as the hot, sweaty hand moved over her stomach and slipped beneath her blouse, edging toward her breasts. Her skin prickled and tightened as the moist flesh cupped and fondled her. His other hand then began moving up her thigh, touching and probing the softness between her legs. She squirmed.

"You're very nice . . ."

"Stop it!" snarled a voice Mary recognized as Bedlow's. She turned to look toward the door as the groping fingers were hastily withdrawn. The fat man moved away from the bed, to stand in the pool of moonlight.

"We haven't time for you to exercise your libido, Henry," Bedlow had growled, moving to the bed. His tall, lean form was only a dark silhouette.

"I . . . I barely touched her . . ."

"Don't explain," Bedlow had responded, cutting Terrance off. "Just untie her and bring her to the window. I want to make sure she sees this."

The fat man had moved back to Mary and began untying her hands, tugging and pulling on the rope unnecessarily hard, forcing the hemp to bite into her soft skin.

Sadistic bastard, she had decided, wincing.

"Get up," Terrance ordered. "And keep the gag in your mouth."

Rubbing her wrists to restore circulation, her body shaking badly, Mary had obeyed. She edged along the bed attempting to stay away from her obese tormenter. He had, however, grabbed her roughly and yanked her toward the window.

Bedlow joined them and Mary stood sandwiched between the pair. The tall, thin man pointed toward the moonlit cemetery.

His voice was thick with sarcasm. "There are your champions."

Mary looked out the window. In the cool, silver glow of the moonlight, she could see three figures moving up one of the gravel roads. Although she had not been able to recognize them, she was sure one of them was the old man she'd met that afternoon.

The trio made their way cautiously. Mary watched in horror as fleeting, flitting shapes scurried among the stones and crypts, silently pursuing the threesome.

After the three had stopped at a grave shrouded in the shadow of one of the great trees, she moved her face closer to the glass, watching in fascination as two of the three knelt over the grave.

"What the hell are they doing, Oscar?" Terrance demanded.

Bedlow shook his head. "I don't know. It doesn't matter."

"Don't be so sure," the fat man muttered.

"What?" Bedlow growled. "Do I detect a note of doubt?"

Terrance turned from the window. His voice was low and strained. "It's like you said, Oscar: Opposing forces have gathered."

Bedlow snorted. "Nothing can match Her power. Watch." He had again pointed toward the window.

Mary watched in awe as the three figures performed some unexplained rite over a grave. The gag had muffled her cry as the black figure of the Madonna rose above the intruders and the legion of misshapen creatures attacked the trio. Inwardly she had cheered when one of the three had unleashed a torrent of blazing blue energy.

And tears flooded her eyes when the three had been routed and forced from the cemetery.

"You see," Bedlow had hissed. "Nothing can stop Her! She's too powerful for the likes of the Druid and his motley collection of allies."

The fat man had snorted a laugh, his hand gripping Mary's arm painfully. His breath was hot and his voice husky with an excited passion, whether from the scene unfolding before them or his closeness to her, Mary did not know. "Yes. Oh, yes. And you, my dear, will get to meet our Mistress soon. Very soon . . ."

"Silence," ordered Bedlow, causing the fat man to flinch and release his hold on Mary's arm. "Her fate will be revealed to her soon enough. For now let's get her out of here . . ."

Unrestrained, Mary had whirled and dashed for the open bedroom door.

"Stop her!" Bedlow had yelled, running after her.

She had cleared the door and was running down the dark hallway toward the staircase, pulling the gag from her mouth. Behind her she could hear Bedlow and Terrance in pursuit. Something was knocked over and crashed to the floor in a cascade of smashing glass.

Mary's hand had found the railing and she dashed along it until she reached the stairs. Below, the living room was illuminated by an incandescent glow. The dark walls shimmered. Flying down the steps two at a time, Mary had been vaguely aware of movement all around the walls, as if the bizarre patterns on the wallpaper were suddenly alive, writhing like serpentine shapes.

As she neared the bottom step, the room grew more brilliant, bathed in the eerie, pulsating light. The maddening shapes on the walls coiled and undulated. Something flitted at the corner of her eye and as she had turned, a thin, slimy tendril lashed itself around her arm. She screamed, struggling uselessly against it.

Bedlow and the fat man had come thundering down the stairs, stopping halfway to watch as other rope-like tentacles shot out of the pulsing wall to circle Mary's other arm and both of her legs. She screamed as she was drawn against the hard surface. The bonds were as tough as catgut and reeked of rot and decay.

One tendril had drawn tightly across Mary's throat. She gasped, unable to free either hand to pull the choking thing away. Starbursts erupted before her eyes as she attempted to suck air into her tortured lungs. The room was spinning in front of her. She saw a dark shape rise before her . . .

. . . swirling pits of orange and red fire had filled her mind as Bedlow's mirthless laugh echoed, distant, hollow . . .

Now in the stone room, sick from fright and fatigue, Mary struggled to calm herself. Her head felt light and there was a gnawing ache in her stomach. She couldn't remember when she'd last eaten. The Coke and donuts? When was that? Yesterday? Last week?

It felt like an eternity, she decided.

She again studied her prison and felt the panic-driven hysteria plucking at the edges of her reason. The walls were close and appeared to be closing. The heavy, smokey air caused Mary to gag.

This is insane!

She squeezed her eyes shut and forced herself to slow her breathing. Mindless panic would yield nothing; not to remain calm, not to fight her fears, would mean a long slide into a well of dark madness.

Then, chilled, Mary wondered if she hadn't already taken that long, awful tumble.

She glanced around the room, trying to refocus her thoughts, dragging them away from that dangerous precipice. She studied the gray stones of her prison. A mossy slime coated much of their surface where tendrils of moisture oozed from above. The stones forming the ceiling were black with soot, evidence that the room had been in use for years. Mary had already noted the floor, worn smooth by the tread of countless feet over equally countless years.

Set in the floor in the corner near the door was a round, wooden cover. Its thick planks were stained dark, worn smooth and grimy from use.

Mary wondered what lay beneath it. A way out? A

passage into an ancient cistern or, even better, a sewage pipe?

"What good would it do?" she wondered aloud, contemptuously jerking the chain. "Even if I can open it, I can't get out of here." Still, her curiosity was aroused.

What did lay beneath that cover?

She moved toward it. The chain brought her to a stop a scant yard from it, but by kneeling, she was easily able to reach it. Gripping either side of the cracked and dried wood, she tried to move it. It was heavy and solid, difficult to shift, especially from her awkward position. Her arms began aching as she struggled with the wood.

Then, with a cry of triumph, she managed to shove it a fraction of an inch. The wood grated over the stone floor, exposing a crack of darkness. Instantly she was assailed by the powerful stench of rotted meat and ancient decay; a noxious smell of death and blood and putrescence.

Mary recoiled in horror, her hand covering her mouth. Coughing and choking she yanked on the cover until it creaked back into place and then returned quickly to the chair. Bitter bile was burning the back of her throat and for a moment she thought she was going to be sick.

She waited for her churning stomach to settle and the powerful odor to dissipate as much as it could in the confines of the small room.

Mary no longer had any desire to discover what was hidden beneath the floor.

As her coughing eased and the bittersweet fetor dispersed into the smokey air, Mary tensed as voices murmured from beyond the room's door. Instinctively, she clutched her arms around her body, her back arching against the hard wood of the chair.

There was a rattle and jingle of keys followed by the snap of the massive lock securing the door. It slowly swung open and the bloated figure of Henry Terrance, clad in a dark suit, stepped into the room. Oscar Bedlow followed him.

Terrance flashed Mary a humorless, insincere smile as he placed a paper bag on the table in front of her. "I hope these accommodations have not been too discomforting."

Mary glared at the pair. When she spoke, her voice was sharp and indignant. "Why the hell am I here? What did I ever do to either of you?"

Bedlow, his gaunt, pasty face split by a death's head grin, exposing his large teeth which shone in the candle light, snorted. "It is not what you've done *to* us, Miss Renata. It's what you will do *for* us."

Mary leaped to her feet, sending the chair tumbling over. "Why don't you cut out the cryptic bullshit? You . . . you've kidnapped me! Do you think you can get away with it?"

Terrance nodded. "Yes, my dear. Without a doubt, we can."

"You're both crazy!" Mary, arms crossed, clutched herself and stared at the two men. Her terror and dread were threatening to spill over in a flood of tears and a torrent of hysteria. She battled the horror-driven wellspring, unwilling to give Terrance and Bedlow the satisfaction of watching her become reduced to an emotional basketcase.

Bedlow's toothy smile remained in place, but something dark and sinister shifted behind his dark eyes.

"Perhaps, in your eyes, we are," he said slowly, softly. "But you know none of the realities behind your, shall we say, abduction."

"And if I did, I suppose I'd be all aquiver with excitement and anticipation."

"No," Bedlow said matter-of-factly. "I doubt you would be. But at least you'd understand why you're here."

"No doubt it's some grand scheme, some divine mission," Mary sneered, her voice mocking and bitter.

"It's important to us," Terrance agreed.

"So what is it? Pornography? Dirty pictures? You guys a couple of smut peddlers?" She said the words with disgust, although she knew, based upon what had happened to her and Vince—*where is he?*—that it was nothing so mundane.

Bedlow laughed. "That's very quaint." He looked at Terrance. "Pornographers, Henry. Miss Renata thinks we sell nasty pictures."

Mary, pale and drawn, sucked in a deep breath. "What do you want from me? Why am I here?"

Terrance smiled. "You'll know that very soon."

"Where's Vince?" she blurted. "What have you done with him?"

The two men again exchanged glances.

"He's gone," Bedlow said flatly.

"Gone where?"

"He left you, Miss Renata."

"No. He wouldn't do that. You did something to him!"

Bedlow sighed. "I didn't want to tell you . . ."

"Tell me what?" A tight ball of anxiety and fear formed in Mary's stomach.

Bedlow's voice lowered and an expression of sympathy settled on his emaciated features. "He's dead."

"You're lying!" Mary shot back.

"No," Terrance said somberly. "Oscar's telling the truth . . ."

"Neither of you would know the truth if it bit you on the ass!" she yelled.

"He's dead," Bedlow repeated, his tone carrying a note of finality. "You might as well accept it."

"He can't be," she said, as much to herself as to them.

"He is and that's all there is to it." Bedlow was obviously impatient and disinterested with the conversation.

Mary, eyes wet, glared at Bedlow. "Fuck you!"

He leveled a finger at her as he took a step forward. "Don't push us, Miss Renata," he hissed through clenched teeth. A dark fire burned in his eyes.

Terrance glanced from Bedlow to Mary, a curious look on his face. He said nothing.

Mary, defiant and realizing she had struck some nerve in Bedlow, started to taunt him further and then paused. Something warm moved over her. Around her. Through her. She felt as if some*thing* had touched her soul, soothing and comforting it. The odd sense of detachment she had experienced before settled over her. She felt distant from the cold, smokey stone room and her two captors. It was as if she were watching herself on film, involved vicariously, but not intimately.

Bedlow frowned as he watched Mary's face grow suddenly tranquil and becalmed. The dark circles beneath her eyes faded, the weariness etching her face evaporated. A flush of color blossomed in her cheeks and a hint of a smile played at the corners of her mouth.

He glanced at Terrance who was staring at the woman.

"What happened to her?" the fat man whispered.

Bedlow shook his head. "I don't know. Maybe something snapped."

Calmly, moving slowly and deliberately, Mary bent over, righted the chair and sat. Her hands folded in her lap, she cocked her head to the side and studied the men the way a person will peer at a spot on a wall while pondering something playing through their mind. It was as if she were seeing through them, beyond them.

"Miss Renata?" Terrance said hesitantly. If Mary heard him, she made no movement to show it. Her eyes remained fixed and blank and the almost-amused look on her face was unchanged.

Bedlow took two long steps and stood beside the woman. He waved a hand in front of her face, but Mary's eyes remained unfocused and unblinking.

"What the hell is going on?" Terrance asked anxiously. "Has she lost her reason?"

"I don't know!" Bedlow snarled.

"What'll we do?"

"I don't know! Damn it, Henry, will you shut up?" Bedlow lifted the woman's arm. When he released it, it flopped back in her lap. He bent and peered closely at her eyes. They were vacant and empty, as if she was in a trance.

"Should we . . ."

"Shut up, Henry!" Bedlow growled, cutting his companion off. "Let me think."

Mary heard them and understood the words. She could see them, yet the presence which had settled over her kept her from reacting.

It was a tranquilizing presence, totally unlike her experience in the bedroom when the golden face at the window had stirred her body and grasped at her mind. She felt oddly safe and disconnected. A warmth had spread to her mind and calmed it. The cold terror and bitter darkness she had known were driven back, replaced by wave upon wave of soothing, caressing light.

Be strong, Mary. The voice spoke in her mind. It was soft and sweet. *I will be with you always.*

And then the presence slipped from her.

She blinked and shook her head. When she saw Bedlow standing next to her, a troubled look etching his face, she automatically shifted away from him.

He breathed a sigh of relief.

"Are you alright?" he asked, surprising her with genuine concern.

"Why would you care?" she asked without vehemence or anger.

"I would care," he shot back.

Bedlow turned and looked at Terrance, shrugging his shoulders. "She's alright, Henry. Let's go. There's still much to do."

"You're just going to leave me here?" Mary asked in a flat, unperturbed voice.

"We'll be back," Terrance said as he followed Bedlow through the door. "There's food in the bag for you," he added before banging the heavy door shut. The lock snapped and Mary was again alone.

Yet, she did not feel alone. Her nerves were calmed, her anxieties quelled.

She thought about Vince. They said he was dead. The idea was disquieting now, but not heart-rending. If he was dead, there was nothing she could do to bring him back. And, too, if he was dead there would be a better time to mourn. That time was not now, not here.

The presence which had entered her had not only tranquilized her, it had filled her with courage and hope. There was a new found peace flowing through her which she had never felt before, yet it had not blunted the awareness of her situation. She knew where she was. She remembered much of what had transpired since she'd come to Mansfield.

It was important, she now realized, to maintain her emotional and mental equilibrium. She could not allow Bedlow and Terrance to send her mind tumbling off into some chasm of madness. She had to remain strong.

She had to trust The Presence.

And Mary knew, too, that the other times she had been in trouble or had been threatened, it had been the presence which had given her the odd sense of detachment. The unseen entity was a part of her and had been with her since her birth. It was there to protect and guard her. It even had a name, she realized.

Smiling, Mary reached for the paper bag and looked inside. There were two deli sandwiches, a hunk of cheese and a bottle of lemon lime New York Seltzer.

She unwrapped a sandwich and began eating, suddenly ravenous with hunger. Opening the seltzer, she lifted it and offered a toast.

"Thank you, Maria. Here's hoping we can get me out of this."

A draft of air stirred around Mary, embracing her in warmth.

In return, Mary smiled and drank deeply from the bottle.

SEVENTEEN

Tobias Rathbone had a very bad feeling about the impending journey back to the cemetery. It was nothing he could identify; nothing he could put his finger on. Just a feeling, vague and unsettled. It flitted at the corners of his mind, plucked at his conscience.

Sitting on the couch in Agnes Hardwick's bright, cheery living room, the events of the previous night seemed distant and very far away. Rays of sun streamed through the sheer white curtains, casting soft, diffused light through the room, delicately highlighting the old furniture. A soft breeze fluttered through the windows, stirring the curtains, carrying the clean scents of roses and freshly mown grass.

In one corner a 50-year-old Philco radio sat, its dial glowing as quiet music floated from its speaker. Agnes had somehow found a station that did not pander to those feverish for the cry and scratch of rock and roll, the whine of country and western or the self-conscious idiocy of talk shows.

Yet Rathbone knew the tranquility and mood in the room were illusionary and no more than a momentary distraction. Something gnawed at the edges of his mind.

He had napped briefly and had again seen the nightmare thing which had been his long dead companion and friend Timothy lying on a filthy straw mat. The dream vision had reached out for him, beckoned him to come closer, but he had drawn back, revolted and shocked. As dream-light fell over the flayed face it was not Timothy who stared back at him, but the cold, inhuman eyes of the Madonna . . .

He had awakened with a start.

Normally, such a dream would be merely a twisted reflection of the horror and terror he had faced and must face again. But to the ancient Druid, it was an omen. He was not dwelling on that centuries-old episode simply because he had related the tale to Ortega. He had lived far too long and had spent too many years dealing with that tragedy to let it now return to haunt his emotions. He couldn't even recall Timothy's face anymore nor summon up the sound of his voice. Time had robbed him of those good memories.

All he could remember was his friend's flayed body lying on a straw mat in a dank, dingy cottage in a village long forgotten. All his mind's eye could see was an unrecognizable lump of bloody flesh, infested with maggots and ridden with disease, which begged him for death.

And even that memory held no real pain anymore, only a small pang of regret and a faint hint of sorrow.

No. His feelings about Timothy and his first encounter with the Black Madonna—The Bitch—were surfacing as an omen. He was a gifted man and understood his talents well. These memories did not haunt him simply because he had verbalized them. There was a message in them, enigmatic and troublesome.

"Tobias?" Agnes Hardwick roused him out of his introspection. The Druid looked up with a start.

She walked into the room carrying a tray holding a tea pot, cups and fresh, hot muffins. The rich fragrances filled the sunny room with a homey warmth the Druid had experienced all too infrequently in his centuries as vigilant guardian.

"Sorry," he muttered, taking one of the two cups from the tray. "I'm afraid I was daydreaming."

Agnes studied him, raising one eyebrow ever so slightly. "You look pale. Are you sure you're alright? You had quite a workout last night. Your recovery was . . . well, remarkable."

Rathbone forced a smile. "Oh, not so remarkable. As I told you, my powers are rather unique. Besides, I've been through worse."

Agnes knew he was lying to spare her but she said nothing more about it. Placing the tray on the coffee table, she sat in one of the two wing-back chairs opposite the couch and lifted her cup. Sipping the steaming brew, she peered surreptitiously over the rim. The old man did look pale and worn. Not really well at all.

"Are you convinced we should go back there tonight?" she asked, already knowing the answer.

"Yes. We've been over that, Agnes." He too slowly sipped his tea.

"Josh is asleep in my room. The dear man is exhausted."

Rathbone set his cup down and looked at her. "He's frightened, Aggie. He's an old man and he's very frightened."

She frowned. "He's not a coward, Tobias." She sounded defensive.

"I know. He's very brave. But bravery and fear are good allies. They balance one another. I respect him. He did well last night."

Agnes's smile was wan and without humor. "I truly wish I hadn't dragged him into this mess."

Rathbone smiled and shook his head. "Dear Aggie. You didn't drag him into it. It was fated. You and Josh and I were fated to come together."

She made no comment, only continued to study him.

Rathbone set the cup and saucer down. "We are like a

trident. A three-pronged pitchfork, out of balance and not as effective if one tine is missing."

The metaphor brought a smile to the old woman's lips. "That's poetic, Tobias, if a little crude."

"I'm serious, Aggie. Together our individual powers are amplified and enhanced. If one of us is missing, the others' powers will be lacking."

"Not yours," she said.

Rathbone nodded. "Yes, even mine. While you draw energy from Josh and me, I draw from both of you. It is almost mathematical in its simplicity, Aggie. Think of it this way. One to the power of one is just one. But three to the power of three squares itself. In our case, it forms a power block of awesome proportions."

"Then why, with this *awesome* power, were we driven out of the cemetery last night?" Agnes asked, refilling her cup.

"Power alone is often not enough. It has to be coupled with knowledge. And strategy. Last night we had the power, but no real plan and only a vague awareness of what we were up against."

"But can we win?"

The Druid leaned back against the cushions of the couch and closed his eyes. "We *have* to."

Joshua Ortega wanted to open his eyes.

He knew he was dreaming. He knew the black shape pursuing him, grasping at him, was a subconscious phantom, a figment of his overwrought mind.

He was running, feeling his heart thundering in his chest and his leg muscles knotting in protest. He could feel sharp talons sinking into his leg as the clawed hands tried to trip him. Hot, foul breath washed over him as teeth snapped at the back of his neck.

Run.

It's going to get you.

Run.

It wants to strip away your flesh.

Run.

It wants to see you writhe in mortal pain and agony.

Run.

His heart was pounding so hard he knew it was going to explode in a splash of dark blood and ruptured muscle. His temples throbbed and splinters of pain shot through his head. A tight cramp formed in his left side, threatening to double him over.

And still he ran and still the black shape followed, trying to drag him down.

It's only a dream!

Joshua knew that. He knew he was trapped in the twilight world of his own mind. If only he could wake himself.

But he couldn't. It was as if a barrier had been erected between this realm of illusion and the real world.

The black shape was right behind him now. A step back. So close he could feel its rotted, ragged garment brush at his heels. Fangs snapped and claws raked and still he kept running.

And then he fell.

With a cry—a scream he knew echoed beyond his dream—he went sprawling head first onto wet, dank earth. Mud splattered his face and filled his mouth and eyes. Choking and blinded, Joshua tried to scramble up, but was smashed into the mud and ooze as a massive weight crashed down on him.

As he struggled and fought, his lungs aching for air, two moist, leathery hands encircled his face, hooking themselves on either side of his jaw. A sharp, bony knee dug into his spine and his head was suddenly yanked backward until the nape of his neck was pressed toward a spot between his shoulder blades.

Another bit of pressure, another few ounces of force and Joshua knew his neck would snap. He was gagging, as he tried in vain to bring his head forward. Blood was running down his neck, staining his chest, as the sharp, jagged claws furrowed into his flesh.

His spine creaked as he was arched backward. His body from the waist up hung suspended above the black mud. He tried to strike at the thing holding him, but his arms were leaden, impossible to lift.

Another fraction of an inch and he would die . . .

There was a blinding blue flash. Joshua knew it was not a part of the nightmare. It was alien. It was from outside his mind, as was, he suddenly realized, the black shape trying to kill him.

A second flash illuminated the darkness, followed by a piercing, animal scream. Instantly, the pressure relaxed and he was released to flop back into the mud. Slowly he rolled over.

All around him, swirling like a vortex, were flashes of blue and bursts of red and orange. The black shape was slumped in a low crouch, retreating away from a figure standing erect, blue fire dancing from its fingertips.

Joshua peered into the dream mist and tried to make out the features of his rescuer. Very slowly, as if a veil was lifted, he could see the figure more clearly: tall and powerful with wide shoulders, a broad chest and legs planted like tree trunks. From his angle, he could not make out the man's face.

Another burst of blue, electric and searing, shot from the man's hands. It slashed through the black enshrouded body and another howl of rage and pain filled his mind. The black thing—The Black Madonna, Joshua realized—twisted and contorted and was gone.

Joshua watched the figure turn and step toward him. In the dream light he could see the features now. He knew them. They were younger, handsome and unlined, but it was unmistakeably Tobias Rathbone.

"Wake up, Josh," the figure said, bending over and shaking him. "You can wake up now."

Joshua felt himself rising from the deep well of sleep

toward consciousness. He opened his eyes, blinking against the afternoon light.

"Josh? Are you alright?" asked Agnes, leaning over, peering at him, her hands on his shoulders.

He groaned as he moved, his back sore and stiff. He touched his jaw, wincing when his fingers probed the bruised flesh.

"Yeah," he croaked. "I think I'm okay. What happened?"

Agnes shook her head. "I'm not sure. You had a bad dream . . . a nightmare. We heard you yell and found you . . . all twisted on the bed." She looked away, gazing out the window into the bright afternoon, biting her lip and blinking back tears of relief. "Josh, I thought . . . I thought you were dying."

As her words rushed out, he reached up and touched her cheek with the back of his hand.

"I'm okay."

Joshua turned and for the first time saw Rathbone seated in the bedroom chair, his eyes closed, his face pale.

"What happened to him?" he asked, concerned, starting to get up. His movement caused his sore back to flare with pain.

"He . . . he saved you, I think," Agnes answered, looking at Rathbone as the Druid's eyes fluttered and finally opened.

"Was it really you?" Joshua asked the other man.

Rathbone nodded, breathing deeply. "Yes."

"But how . . . ?"

The Druid shook his head. "One of my many talents, Josh. Don't worry about it. Just be thankful you cried out in your sleep."

"Was it that . . . that creature?" Agnes asked, looking from Joshua to Rathbone.

"It was," the Druid acknowledged. "At least a part of Her."

"Was She trying to kill Josh?" The old woman could not hide the quiver in her voice.

"Oh, yes," Rathbone said. "She knows he's your power source. If She had slain him, you'd be weaker and by extension, so would I. Remember, Aggie, the trident. She wanted to break off a tine."

"Two to the second power?" Agnes asked rhetorically.

Rathbone snorted and smiled. "Exactly."

"What in the hell are you two talking about?" Joshua demanded, swinging his legs off the bed. He winced as he stood, finding it difficult to straighten.

"Never mind, Josh," Agnes said, studying him gravely. "Are you sure you're alright?"

"Yes," he said impatiently. "I'm fine. Just a little stiff." He looked at Rathbone, still sitting in his chair. "What about you, Tobias? You used a lot of energy."

Rathbone pinched the bridge of his nose between his thumb and forefinger. "I'm okay. It doesn't take as much power when I'm on that plane."

"You were so . . . so young."

Rathbone laughed. "Only there. Astral bodies don't age, only physical ones." He grinned at Joshua. "I cut quite a figure a few hundred years ago, huh?"

In spite of himself, the Ortega laughed. "You did. And I'm glad." He drew a deep breath, his hand absently brushing his thick moustache. "Thanks."

"Forget it."

"Come on, you two old fools," Agnes said as cheerily as she could. "You both can use a cup of coffee." She walked out of the room, trying not to let either man see how badly she was shaking.

After Agnes vanished into the kitchen, Joshua stepped to where Tobias still sat.

"Can we *really* do it?"

"Tonight?" Rathbone made a face and shrugged. "Maybe. If we don't, there will literally be Hell to pay." He fixed Joshua with a dark, steely stare. "And even if we do find a way to win, we still may have to pay a heavy price."

Joshua looked at the Druid for another few seconds, then nodded and walked stiffly out of the room.

Rathbone continued to sit in the chair.

Why did he keep thinking about Timothy? Why was his dead friend's ravaged body haunting his mind?

What portent was hidden in that grim memory?

EIGHTEEN

Mary was asleep when the monsters came for her.

Her head rested on her folded arms atop the rough table, strands of mussed hair tumbling over her face. After Bedlow and the fat man left, she had been overcome by a wave of exhaustion. As the vision blurring weariness settled over her, Mary willingly allowed it to engulf her like a comforting, warm blanket.

She drifted into a heavy, pleasant sleep, laced with vague, soothing dreams. She felt The Presence still with her, filling her with an odd, yet welcome tranquility. For a time, a sweet voice filled her mind, whispering quieting words. Words she would not remember, yet which planted seeds of strength and knowledge and power in Mary's subconscious.

And then The Presence slipped away, flowing out of her gently and easily, like warm honey from an earthen ewer. She settled into a natural, undisturbed slumber.

It ended as a massive weight exploded against the heavy planks of the locked door. The thick wood groaned and splintered in protest.

Gasping in confusion, Mary bolted awake. The blow echoed off the stone walls as the ancient door trembled.

For an instant she thought she was still asleep, caught in a nightmare's web. But a second blow, more fierce than the first, brought her completely, totally awake, the nightmare a sudden reality. Mary knew someone—some*thing*—was trying to break in; trying to reach her.

She scrambled out of the chair and stood with her back pressed against the wall, cursing the chain binding her leg.

Again, the door shuddered from a jarring blow.

Old images flashed through Mary's mind. Lurid, stark images of scantily clad women chained or tied to tables or walls in dark, smokey rooms. Those hapless, wide-eyed maidens screaming as menacing men and hideous monsters brandished hot pokers or wicked knives, threatening unspeakable acts. She had viewed a thousand such crude, disquieting scenes on the covers of the old pulp magazines her father had so lovingly collected and saved.

Mary now felt like one of those dehumanized, terrorized women thrashing and struggling and begging on the cover of *Weird Tales* and *Black Book Detective* or *Dime Mystery Magazine*. She was now one of those women, chained in a dim, smokey room, helplessly awaiting an unknown fate.

In those stories, of course, the hero always rushed to the rescue. Her father had frequently had to explain that to her. And on more than one occasion, he had come to her rescue in the blackness of her bedroom while she struggled in the clutches of a nightmare.

But this wasn't a fantasy tale nor a nightmare which could be dispelled with a gentle touch and a few softly whispered words. This was real. There would be no hero rushing to her defense.

Her father was dead.

And Vince was dead, too.

How can he be dead?

The thought of those old magazines was somehow disquieting. With a sinking heart she realized the calm detachment she had felt earlier was gone, evaporated into nothingness with the intangible entity which had filled her with such comfort.

Another blow hammered the door and one of the planks bowed inward with a sharp crack.

By God, I'm not going to die like some simpering wimp.

Desperately, Mary glanced around for something to use to defend herself. There was nothing in the room except the table and two chairs. Swearing softly, cold sweat beading her brow, streaking her face, she grabbed the table and pitched it over on its edge. As it banged to the floor, another heavy, rending blow hit the door and a second plank groaned in protest.

Mary wrapped her hands around one of the table's legs and tried to break it free. While the table was old and battered, it was solidly built. The leg barely moved.

Again, something massive and heavy slammed into the door. More wood broke and bits of rock and mortar settled to the floor as the old, rusted hinges, mounted into the stone, loosened.

Mary knew the portal would soon collapse under the barrage. In panic, she lifted her foot high and brought it down again and again on the stout leg. After the fifth blow she was rewarded with a sharp crack as the metal and glue holding the leg in place gave way. The next time she kicked it, the thick wooden shaft broke free.

The door all but shattered with the next blow. The top hinge ripped out of the stone amid a shower of dust and tiny bits of rock.

Mary, her eyes wide and staring, her teeth clenched, gripped the table leg with both hands. Holding it out and back from her body, she felt like the child she had been, waiting for the next ball from that silly Murdock kid who had always tried to bean her with a wild pitch.

The door crashed to the floor, sending up a cloud of dust and dirt and chips of wood and bits of stone. She peered at the blackness beyond the opening trying to discern who, or what, had battered down the door. In the dim, guttering light of the candles, now melted down to stubs, she could only make out dim shapes . . .

. . . and three pairs of burning, unblinking scarlet pinpoints of light.

Mary tensed, her hands moist and slick on the dry, cracked wood. She watched as the first of the things shambled into the room. No longer detached and distant, she found herself stifling a scream.

Daddy! Daddy! Come stop the nightmare!

But Daddy was dead.

Vince was dead.

Soon, she would be dead, too.

The thing was little more than a skeleton. Tall and angular beneath its foul rags—once a man's suit but now rotted and ragged—it was covered with mould and dirt. From its yellowed skull hung wisps of hair and shreds of dried, tattered flesh. Its jaw opened and closed rhythmically, the large, stained teeth clicking a grim and grisly tattoo. Like its mouth, the thing's bony hands, sporting long, yellowed nails caked with grime, opened and closed methodically.

Mary flinched when she realized the small pits of scarlet fire were burning in the thing's black eye sockets.

Vince! I need you, Vince!

Vince is dead.

As it stepped into the weak candle light, a second skeletal creature stumbled into the room behind it. The second creature wore a mud-caked, grave-stained dress. Tiny pieces of the corrupted fabric fluttered to the stone floor as the thing trudged behind its mate.

A third skeleton followed the other two.

Between them they carried a heavy, rough cut timber; a beam or support taken from a ceiling or wall. Its forward end was broken and smashed from having been repeatedly rammed into the door.

As if on cue, the three released the timber and let it fall unnoticed to the floor.

Mary kept the table leg poised, watching the three things in horror. They moved with a somnambulistic, mindless shuffle. Each step was halting as if it had to be planned before it could be taken. Their ancient, dried bones grated and rattled and their feet scraped the stone flooring as they shambled toward her.

No heroes. No father. No Vince.

She shivered, feeling the cold sweat trickle down her back and over her face. The one in the rotting dress and the other in the fouled suit, flanked her while the third, wrapped in unrecognizable rags, plodded straight toward her. Their jaws moved, their yellow, broken teeth clicking. A discordant chattering began issuing from their throatless bodies, filling the room with a grim, hellish gibberish.

"Get away from me!" she screamed desperately.

The woman-thing paused and then, as if propelled by an unseen force, lunged at Mary with amazing quickness, the talonlike fingers trying to clutch the table leg. She dodged and swung at the same moment. The heavy staff caught the creature across its left temple, smashing a gaping hole in the brittle, dried cranium. The blow sent the skeletal figure spinning to the floor where it fell with a clattering of bones. A high pitched cry came from its carcass as it struggled to regain its footing.

The other two creatures, equally animated and unexpectedly quick, leaped at Mary even before their companion hit the floor. One grasped the table leg, trying to jerk it out of Mary's hand. She clung to it desperately, her knuckles white from the strain of holding her nearly ineffectual weapon. The thing yanked on it repeatedly, forcing needle-sharp splinters to lance into Mary's soft palms.

The other still-standing creature brought a balled, bony hand around in an arc, catching Mary across the side of her face. She staggered painfully against the cool stones of the wall, still clutching the rough wood in her bleeding hands.

As the one thing continued to pull and tug at the leg, the second launched another blow toward her head. Mary moved and the hard bone hand glanced off the side of her neck. It was a numbing blow but hardly stopped her frantic struggle.

She cried out as the table leg was ripped from her hands and cast across the room where it banged against the far wall.

Both the monsters made to grab her, but Mary rolled along the hard stones just managing to avoid them. As she moved, the chain rattled. Standing so near the eye bolt, several feet of it was looped at Mary's feet. Without considering, she stooped quickly and clutched as much of the excess linked metal as she could. She bit her lip as the manacle again bit into the torn, cut flesh around her ankle.

"Bastards!" Mary screamed, her voice high-pitched and hysterical. Her fear and the accompanying adrenaline rush allowed her to clutch the chain and ignore the blood oozing from between her fingers and down her arms.

The two things were again striking at her as she swung the iron links. It smashed hard against the arm of one of the creatures, cleaving the bone and sending its grasping hand and forearm spinning to the floor. An unearthly howl, not of pain, but rage, filled the room.

The second skeleton attempted to clutch her throat with its sharp fingers while she was bringing the chain around for another swing. Mary ducked back and swung the chain again. Like an axe, it slashed into mold-encrusted ribs, splintering them. The thing banged into the wall and Mary hit it again while it was off balance. More of the ancient ribs shattered as the iron wrapped around the monster's spine.

The one-armed thing turned and grabbed at her, its fiery eyes burning with blazing scarlet. Mary pulled on the chain, trying to free it. Tightly wound around the creature's yellowed spine, it was effectively lodged.

She was able to dodge two more vicious swipes while continuing to pull on the chain. The ensnared creature struck at the metal, splintering its hard nails.

Finally, with a desperate yank, the chain came loose accompanied by the snap of breaking bone. The torso of the creature waivered and wobbled and then stumbled to the floor, the leering skull cracking hard against the stones.

In that instant, Mary's attention diverted, the other creature's fist caught her on the chin and she was sent sprawling heavily to the floor. Tiny lights exploded behind Mary's eyes and her peripheral vision danced with blurry, rough-edged shadows. The left side of her face throbbed and her mouth held the coppery taste of blood. A dark trickle oozed from between her lips and down her chin.

She threw herself to her right as the clawed hand came slashing at her face. The long, hooked nails shattered and ripped on the stones where her head had been only a second before.

She screamed and kicked as a hard, bony hand clamped around her unfettered ankle. She almost screamed as she saw the creature she'd cut in half holding her ankle in both its undead hands. The grip was as firm as the iron encircling her other leg. Sharp talons sank into her flesh, cutting deep and unleashing a fresh flow of blood.

The woman-thing joined the other two, its eyes glowing with inhuman ferocity, seemingly undaunted by its smashed and battered skull.

Thrashing, striking out blindly, her reason overridden by the instinct to survive, Mary battled against the abominations tearing at her. Her clothing ripped and tore in a score of places. Her arms and legs were scratched and bleeding in a dozen more. She scrambled away from the creatures until the heavy chain brought her up short, sending another burst of pain searing up her calf.

She was on her back, her manacled leg extended straight

out, the chain unforgivingly taut. There was no place to go, no further room in which to maneuver. The creatures, including the one with the gaping hole in its smashed skull, gathered around her, their impossibly powerful hands holding her to the floor. Their crimson eyes shone and glistened in the smokey room.

One of the things bent toward her, its jaws working and snapping. A clawed hand poised far above its head, ready to scythe down and rip out Mary's throat.

Mary's eyes, large and round, were locked on the unwaivering, hooked hand. Already the yellow nails were streaked with blood.

My blood!

She sucked in shallow gulps of the bitter, acrid air, burning her lungs. The smoke in the room seemed somehow denser, thicker. Or maybe it was only her blurred, dimmed vision which made the room seem darker.

Still the bony hand hovered over her, ready to deliver the death blow. In one brief microsecond, Mary could see herself writhing on the stone floor, geysering blood from the severed arteries.

She squeezed her eyes shut against the vision and waited for it to end.

Our Father which are in Heaven . . .

The air within the room suddenly stirred.

Hallowed be Thy name . . .

Those candles still burning, flickered and danced before being extinguished by a powerful gust. It seemed to have issued from the very walls. The last candle was blown out and the room was enveloped in an intense darkness.

Thy Kingdom come . . .

All Mary could see were the six pinpoints of hellish fire staring down at her.

Thy will be done . . .

And then abruptly they were gone. The room erupted in a maelstrom of swirling wind. She could hear the chairs and table tumbling and banging across the floor. The chattering and clanking of the three creatures grew loud, almost frantic.

On earth as it is in Heaven . . .

Confused and frightened, Mary rolled to the wall and pressed herself against its coolness. She moved to lay on her stomach and buried her face in her hands.

The wind grew stronger, cyclonic in its force. It rushed over her, tugging at her clothing and lashing her hair. For a terrifying second, Mary feared it would carry her into its vortex, slamming and smashing her to death against the stone walls. She continued to pray.

Objects bounced off the walls, crashed to the floor. Mary was sure she heard a high-pitched, inhuman whine, but in the roar of the wind, she could not be certain. It rose briefly and was abruptly silenced.

As suddenly as it had risen, the whirlwind stopped. It did not die down or abate slowly. It simply ceased. One instant the room was alive with it, the next it was calm and deathly silent.

Mary lay huddled against the wall for a long time before she finally dared to move. She could see nothing in the darkness. And for that she was grateful. The unnatural maelstrom had apparently saved her from those three *things*. She looked around, but could not locate their glistening scarlet orbs.

Pieces of wood, little more than sawdust, and brittle fragments of what must have been bone, settled on her face and bloodied hands.

Mary?

The voice filled her head. It was soft and beautiful, and carried with it the familiar sense of peace and detachment.

"Y . . . yes?" She found herself mouthing the word before she realized it.

I am sorry I left you.

"Who . . . who are you?"

All will be revealed in time, Mary. For now, you must be strong. Much depends on your strength.

"But I . . ."

Do not speak. Do not worry. Just be strong.

"I . . ."

Shhh . . .

The voice of The Presence faded from her mind, but the tranquility it had brought remained with her. She did not move from her place on the floor until she heard an angry curse.

"What the hell?" Henry Terrance bellowed. Mary looked up to see the fat man framed in the doorway. He held a tall, tapered candle in one hand and something large and bulky was draped over his other arm.

"Where are you?" he shouted, moving across the room. As he walked there was a pop and crackle, like breaking glass, under his feet. He stopped near Mary and thrust the taper toward her face.

"You're alright? That's good." He extended a puffy hand to help her to her feet. She brushed it aside and slowly stood on her own.

In the yellow flickering light, Mary could see a deep, disturbed frown lining Terrance's face and darkening his eyes.

"What happened?" he hissed.

"I . . . I don't know . . ."

He thrust his face close to hers. "Don't give me that! I want to know what happened in here!" Mary was assailed by the pungent scent of garlic and onions on his breath.

"I don't know," she roared back defiantly. "Ask those . . . those monsters . . ."

"What monsters?" Even in the dim light, she could see the fear come into his piggish eyes. He chewed at his lower lip and stared at her.

"'They were in *here*?" he demanded.

"Yes."

"How . . ."

"How should I know," she answered, stepping away from him and out of the circle of light. The chain she dragged rattled and grated on the floor. Her cut hands ached and her bruised neck and shoulder throbbed. She was very tired.

Terrance snorted in disgust. "Damn it."

He moved away from her. Mary watched as he laid a bulky plastic bag on the floor and then fished several fresh candles out of his coat pocket. He moved around the room, fitting the new tapers into the wrought iron holders set in the wall and then lighting them from the candle he held in his hand. Within minutes, the room was again reasonably well lit.

Both Mary and the fat man stared around them in total surprise and bafflement. The two chairs, the table and the wooden planks of the massive door had been reduced to chips and splinters. Nothing was left which was recognizable as ever having been crafted furniture. The floor was littered with dirty white bone fragments, none of them larger than a quarter. That explained the crunching sound Terrance had made as he crossed the room.

Terrance stooped and examined one of the pieces of bone. He studied it closely for several long moments, turning it over and over in his fat fingers. He finally looked up and glowered at Mary.

His voice was low and menacing. "What happened?"

"I don't know."

He straightened slowly, almost painfully and stepped toward her. "Don't tell me that. You were here. Now what in the hell happened here?" His voice boomed in the small room, echoing like a hollow, flat thunder.

Involuntarily, Mary winced. She could see a threatening rage darkening the fat man's eyes. She drew a deep breath and ran a hand over her mussed, tangled hair. "Three . . . *things* battered down the door," she began, her voice low, but level and steady.

"Yes. And?" Terrance demanded impatiently.

"And they came after me, you son of a bitch! They

tried to kill me!'' Mary roared, her eyes flashing fire. A knot of anger was now twisting at her stomach.

The fat man's eyes were slits. ''Impossible.''

''Bullshit. That's exactly what happened . . .''

''And I suppose *you* did this to them?'' He held up the bone fragment in his hand. ''I suppose *you* ground them into so much dust.''

''No. I don't know what did that,'' she lied, praying she would not betray herself. There was no way in the world she would tell this pig-of-a-man about The Presence. ''The candles went out and . . . and I don't know what happened!''

Terrance stared at her for several more seconds before tossing the bone chip away and again surveying the room.

''They got out somehow,'' he said quietly, more to himself than to Mary. ''They got out and came after you. They shouldn't have, but they did. Somehow they broke Her hold on them.''

''What . . . who are you talking about?'' A tremor passed through Mary, chilling her.

He turned, his face smiling without humor. ''That's something you'll discover soon enough.'' He looked one more time at the mess littering the room. ''She must have done this. To save you.'' For some reason, that amused Terrance and he belched a ringing laugh.

The fat man waddled over to pick up the bag he'd brought in with him. He carried it to Mary and shoved it at her.

''What do you want now?'' she asked him, not taking the bag. She looked down at her bloody, injured hands.

''What the hell happened to your hands?'' Terrance demanded, his alarm genuine.

''I was defending myself . . .''

''We must bind them. Take off your blouse.''

''What?''

''Take it off. I'll use it for bandages. To stop the bleeding.'' As he spoke, he never took his eyes off the dark blood streaking Mary's palms and fingers. For just an instant, Mary saw the tip of his tongue as it flicked over his fat lips; moistening them.

"They'll be alright . . ."

"Do what I tell you!" he roared. "Now!"

Something in his voice warned Mary not to protest further.

"Is that how you get your jollies? Watching women undress?" Mary asked, turning her back and tugging off her blouse. When Terrance made as if to move around her for a better view, she held the blouse over her breasts.

Terrance's eyes were again narrow slits and his mouth a hard, angry line.

"Do it! Don't make me hurt you," he warned. Streaks of crimson were creeping up from under the collar of his shirt. "You won't like it."

Be strong, Mary. The soft voice floated into her head.

"Alright" she said, sighing. She handed him the blouse and as he took it, he stole a glance at her breasts, cradled in a sheer bra.

Terrance laid the garment bag on the floor and ripped the arms from the torn and soiled blouse. He then took Mary's hands in his and studied them. His touch was surprisingly gentle. He peered at the bloody flesh closely, his face inches away from the raw wounds. Again his tongue darted from his mouth and Mary thought he was going to lick them clean.

She pulled her hands away. "Just wrap them, please."

He looked up at her, something dark and mad dancing in his eyes. He blinked and nodded.

"Yes. Yes, of course."

Madness. Madness.

It took Terrance only a moment to wind the sleeves of the blouse around her hands, leaving the fingers exposed.

"I'll clean them and remove those splinters later," he told her as he finished. He retrieved the bag from the floor, found its zipper and opened it. Reaching inside, he pulled out a soft, white gown of light, gossamer cotton.

"Now. Take off your clothes and put that on," Terrance growled, again wetting his fat lips.

Mary stared at him. "Why?"

"Just do it!"

Reluctantly, she reached out and took the gown from him.

"Come on, come on, get on with it," he ordered, his tongue again flicking over his thick, puffy lips.

"Not until you get away from me." It was her turn to stare, her eyes dark and flashing.

"What's modesty among friends?" he asked sarcastically.

"Nothing," she said, glaring at him. "But then we're not friends."

Again Terrance's face grew red with anger and frustration. "I ought to . . ."

"What?" she yelled back at him. "Knock me around? Get off a little of that *macho* puss pocket you call manhood? Don't make me laugh."

Mary knew she was pushing him, perhaps too hard and too far. Yet she could not have cared less. He was a grotesque parody of a man; a slab of swollen, diseased fat flesh. Had he ever been truly human, she decided, the essence of it had been bled from him long ago.

For an instant, she thought Terrance was going to strike at her. He stood ready, his face scarlet, his eyes dancing with hate and rage and his hands balled into meaty fists.

But the moment passed. Softly, vehemently, he called her a string of filthy, vile names and walked away, pretending to examine the bits of crushed bone and splintered wood littering the floor.

Turning her back to him, Mary unfolded the voluminous gown. Only after she pulled it on over her head and used it to over her body did she pull off her slacks. She was forced to slide them over the manacle and down the length of chain.

The fabric of the gown fell around her body in great,

cascading folds and Mary felt vulnerable and defenseless beneath its thinness and insubstantial weight.

She decided she might as well be naked for all the good the gown did.

Just like in the pulps.

And, no doubt, this was exactly the psychological impact Terrance intended to have on her.

"Why do I have to wear this?" she asked Terrance, who now stood by the open doorway watching her.

"You'll find out soon enough," he replied, his earlier anger replaced by another of his ulcerous smiles.

Mary started to make another bitter, barbed reply, but paused as the warmth of The Presence again touched her and she was filled with a great sense of peace and quiet.

Be strong, Mary. Be strong.

"No nasty remarks? No bitter accusations?" Terrance sneered. "How refreshing." He moved away from the doorway and stepped toward her.

His face twisted into an awful grin and a crazed light filled his eyes. "It will soon be time, my dear. It will soon be time and you will learn all you will *ever* need to know."

He produced a key from his pants pocket and bent to unlock the manacle. While he fussed with the lock, Mary was tempted to lash out at his unguarded head with her foot, but thought better of it. Where would she go? Where, in fact, was she? Hurting him might only make matters worse.

And besides, the sense of peace and well-being from The Presence filled her with that odd, yet wonderful detachment.

Mary did yank her foot away when Terrance stroked it softly. He only chuckled and tugged open the manacle, ignoring the raw and bloody flesh circling Mary's ankle. Straightening, he took her arm.

"Now, my dear. The time of the Rising is close. Soon. Very soon, you will be witness to and a part of one of the greatest events in a thousand lifetimes. Can you appreciate such an event?''

He studied her face with true inquisitiveness. When he saw the disinterest and unconcern in her eyes, he shook his head sadly.

''No,'' he sighed. ''I suppose you cannot.''

Gently, like a father guiding a child, he led her out of the room. He carried one of the tapers in his free hand and paused at an open door across from the room they left.

He thrust the candle through the dark opening. ''As I thought. Wainwright and his friends got out. Tore a beam out of the ceiling. Amazing.''

He noted Mary's indifference and moved her toward a set of steep stone steps.

''You'll understand it soon, my dear. Oh, how you'll understand. And how your attitude will change.''

As Terrance and Mary stepped to the stairway, neither noticed the long black shadow spreading across the floor behind them.

PART FOUR
THE RISING

Inurn'd, enwrapt, seal'd with the mole
    And shrouded in the worm's embrace;
A mattock's heave, a coffin's roll,
    A shudder through the soundless place:
Yet from its everlasting bed
Death hears the Occult Madonna's tread.

—J.C. Powys

NINETEEN

The stench of decay and rot infested the narrow, cramped space. While the odor was overpowering, it was the pain which sickened him. Each movement of his left arm sent excruciating waves of fire surging up its length, numbing his shoulder. His head throbbed and his badly bruised throat was raw and sore. The air he sucked into his tortured lungs was dank, heavy and fetid. Brittle bones, all sharp points and jagged edges, were raking and stabbing at his back with his every move.

He was entombed. He could not straighten his legs, so short was his prison, and his calf muscles ached with knotted cramps. His arms, pressed against his sides, touched the cool, slimy walls. He had tried once to raise his head in the blackness, only to have his forehead knock hard against the massive stone slab scant inches above his face.

When he had first roused, a wave of panic set him to screaming in rage and despair until his voice grew hoarse, aggravating his already damaged throat muscles.

Had he lost his mind? And if not, how soon before he slipped into madness?

Perhaps it was the constant pain in his broken arm

which kept him sane. While the searing, tearing grind of bone on broken bone sent him spiraling in and out of lucidity, it also kept him firmly rooted in his wretched reality.

He tried to remember . . .

Mary had left.

Where had she gone? For help?

No. She had simply left Mansfield. And him. She had escaped.

Why hadn't he gone with her?

Something had happened.

What?

Bedlow.

Bedlow had tricked him, taken him deep into the cemetery and . . .

. . . and tried to kill him.

"The son of a bitch tried to kill me," Vince Cassidy mumbled to himself in the darkness, his voice hollow and gravelly, edged with bitterness.

He found the concept, the idea, so farfetched, so unbelievable, he momentarily wondered if it had not all been some feverish hallucination.

Yet here he was, sealed in a crypt, entombed in old marble and laying on a bed of smashed, shattered bones. His arm was broken, his throat was swollen and bruised and his lungs labored for clean, unpolluted air. It was no fever dream. No hallucination. This was real.

His right hand gently massaged his tender, mauled neck.

The thought of Oscar Bedlow enraged him. He had been such a fool to trust that scarecrow. But he knew it was more than Bedlow's influence. It was the cemetery's. The damned place had affected him, trapped him.

"What the hell kind of place is this?" he wondered aloud, strangely comforted by the sound of his own voice. Proof, he decided that he was still alive.

Thank God Mary is safe.

But is she?

He thought about that. She had left Mansfield: walked out, preferring to wait for him outside its iron fence, away from its strong, malignant power.

He was sure. When he didn't come out, she'd certainly have called the police and told them he had vanished in the cemetery.

They would search.

They were probably searching right now. It gave Vince hope.

But how would they know where he was? How would they know where to look? There was no way for them to know he was sealed in this stone sarcophagus; this *tiny* marble prison. They wouldn't open all of them. They couldn't.

Vince sucked in a breath and gritted his teeth against a bolt of pain lancing through his arm. Cold, clammy sweat drenched his cramped and sore body.

It he could only turn over, he might be able to brace his back against the stone lid and force it open. If he couldn't completely displace it, he could at least get fresh air to his burning lungs. He could get a wedge of light into this eternal blackness.

And he could make his cries for help be heard.

Attempting to turn his body over was easier said than done, in the tight, close space, with the old bones for a bed. They were serving as effective spikes to hold him in place. If he drove one of them into his side or back it would insure his death. He would die alone, unfound, sealed in another's grave.

An archeologist's nightmare. Any man's nightmare. His nightmare.

Besides, he wondered, would his damaged arm allow him to make such an effort? Still, he couldn't simply lay there, hoping someone would find him before the air turned poisonous.

You gotta do something, Vince old boy. You gotta do something.

He tried to move onto his right side, opposite his shattered arm. A sharp bone jabbed him in the back, ripped his shirt and scraped his skin. He groaned as he felt the warm trickle of blood ooze from the shallow wound. He cried out as yet another spasm jolted his left arm when the two ends of fractured bone grated together.

He waited for the red-hazed agony to ease. And tried again.

It seemed an eternity before Vince was able to maneuver himself enough to rest on his stomach. He was bleeding from a dozen small, stinging wounds. The myriad of bones—surely there was more than the remains of one body entombed with him—had stabbed and slashed him time and again. More often than he could recall, blinding pain had threatened to steal his consciousness.

He remained motionless, his face pressed against the smoothness of an ancient skull, and gulped the rancid air.

The easy part's over, Vince old boy.

His own rueful humor pleased him. If he could laugh, he could survive.

Or else he had already toppled into a pit of insanity.

Worry about it when you're out of this shithole.

Slowly, by inches, he brought his knees forward, feeling and hearing the bones beneath him crackle as his legs dragged over them. When he had positioned himself with his back braced against the slab, trying to ignore the agony that was his left arm, Vince lifted. His back arched and pushed. Slowly he straightened his good arm and brought his legs up. His head hung forward, his chin almost touching his chest.

It felt as if he was trying to lift a car. The slab was impossibly heavy. His knees ground into the hard stone and sharp bone. His back muscles tensed and knotted until he feared they would implode. His right hand ached and throbbed, while his toes, curled and bearing an inordinate amount of weight, went numb.

By millimeters, the slab shifted. It grated and groaned in

protest, but it moved. Its hard, massive weight bore into Vince's back with unforgiving force. More than once, he cried out as his spine ground against stone.

But it moved.

Rewarded for his effort, Vince made one final, desperate push. The marble slid to one side and a rush of fresher, although still fouled and corrupted, air flowed into the vault.

He slumped in exhaustion. The nerves in his damaged arm exploded with gut wrenching spasms. Gulping his breath, his mind fuzzy and clouded with dizziness, he faded into a darker oblivion for some minutes . . .

. . . or hours. He could not be sure.

When he had regained consciousness, Vince strained his neck to pour through the inch-wide crack he had opened between the slab and the rim of the vault.

It was dark beyond the opening. But it was a less all-consuming blackness than inside his tiny, narrow tomb. Somewhere, far out of his line of sight, a faint trace of light was filtering into the mausoleum. As feeble as it was, it offered Vince enormous hope.

And when there was a quick movement. A dark, fleeting shape passed across his line of sight. The movement was accompanied by the clop-clop of hooves, like a pony walking on cobblestones.

Tense, trying to control his ragged breathing, Vince strained to catch another glimpse of the figure.

Nothing moved now.

He gasped as something heavy leaped atop the marble cover of the vault. Its movement echoed and banged as it clattered above him.

Continuing to stare out through the narrow crack, trying desperately to discern something—anything—familiar, his eye was suddenly jabbed by something fleshy and blunt. It exploded in a blinding, agonizing red haze.

Vince cried out, his good hand covering the right side of his face. He rocked backward, his eye flooding with tears as needles of pain exploded in the soft tissues and lanced into his brain.

He heard the marble cover over his head grate and grind as it was shoved back into place. The narrow strip of faint light vanished and he was again sealed in impenetrable blackness.

The staccato clop-clop atop Vince's tomb continued. It drummed and thumped and clattered until it filled the tiny marble box with a constant, maddening thunder.

Vince wanted to cover his ears, but could only muffle one with his good hand. The hammering over his head coupled and merged with the throbbing, sickening agony in his left arm and injured eye. Cold sweat again bathed his body and soaked his clothing. He choked and gagged and an unseen spray of bile and vomit spewed into the dark. It splashed and splattered back into his face.

Vince began shaking violently. His body thrashed against the confining wall. His head thudded first on one side of the narrow tomb and then on the other. Back and forth, until blood clotted and matted his hair and sparks burst before his glazed eyes. Blood and spittle flecked his lips as his teeth chewed his tongue and cheeks.

Mercifully his mind was enveloped in darkness. His body relaxed and was still.

The hooves continued to pound and stomp for long minutes and then they, too, fell silent.

Vince slowly became aware of hovering above his body. He could see it, sealed and entombed in that narrow, fouled stone box. Although it was dark, he could see himself clearly, lying there inert and helpless.

What did this mean? Was he dreaming?

Confused, but not at all frightened, he felt himself rise every higher, passing through the marble covering his body. Now suspended within the musty, dank, gloomy interior of the crypt, he could see a second sarcophogus and the dirty stained glass window opposite the mausoleum's doors. Something, a twisted, deformed shape, crouched in the deep shadows near the vault containing his body. He wanted to see the thing more clearly, but could not. It remained in darkness as if aware he was watching from above.

Slowly Vince became aware of the light. It was brilliant, a glowing ball of inviting warmth ahead of him. It beckoned him, drew him to its promise of comfort and care and peace. He floated toward it, the crypt fading away as he passed effortlessly through the granite walls.

There was neither pain in his eye nor in his arm now. In fact, he felt no aches or pains of any kind. He was overwhelmed by a sense of tranquillity and renewal. All his cares, all the terrors he had so recently experienced, were miraculously washed away and almost forgotten.

He wanted to be part of the light.

A figure, a handsome young man, bathed in the warm illumination, materialized before him. The man was cloaked in flowing white which shimmered brilliantly in the light. His eyes shone with vigor and youth. His long, graceful hand beckoned to him.

Vincent, you must go back. The words touched his mind. They were sweet and warm and pure. The man's smile was tender and understanding.

No. I want to go to the light.

The spirit's head shook slowly, sadly.

It is not your time, Vincent. You must go back.

There's only pain back there. Why didn't he understand? Why couldn't he realize Vince was at peace now? He did not want to return to that black grave and dark madness.

Vincent. You are needed there. It's not time for you to be here. The words flowed into his mind like warm honey.

I died. He knew it was true. He was dead, yet felt no sadness, no regret. He never wanted to leave this warm place where there was only harmony and contentment.

Why would he go back to that tomb with its stench and decay surrounding his battered and broken body?

Yes, Vincent. You have passed over. But it is not your time. You are needed. There are others who need you. You must go back. The smile was unwavering as the spirit's eyes looked into him and touched his soul.

I . . . I can not.

You can, Vincent. You must. You can not stay here.

He felt the gentle pull and tried to fight it. The effort was useless. The figure was fading away, growing smaller. He was withdrawing from the light, moving backward, downward. The glow also faded, and he was once again in the crypt. He flowed through the stone above his body, returning to the fetid darkness inside the sarcophogus.

Gently, he slipped back into himself and slid into the quiet blackness.

TWENTY

Tobias Rathbone sat quietly at the small vanity in the old woman's spare bedroom. He had told Agnes and Joshua the truth. He needed to rest. But there was no time now to lie idle and inactive. The confrontation he had long sought was drawing near. He had known since the day he had cremated Timothy's ravaged body those many years ago, that he would have to face the Madonna. It was inevitable.

Rathbone had spent a score of lifetimes both dreading and anticipating the moment he would come face to face with that dark, evil Bitch.

The previous night's battle had only been a preliminary round. Like two pugilists, he and that unholy entity had sparred and tested one another. Tonight they would meet for the final time, both armed with new knowledge of their opponent.

The Druid had no illusions about the consequences of the impending battle. If the Bitch should win, the effect on the world would be devastating. He knew a victory for Her and Her minions would not suddenly alter the nature of the world. Not immediately. Her followers would subtly, but inexorably, assume power and control in a thousand ways. They would grasp for that power through money and position, striving to spread their influence until they held sway over a vast, dark empire.

It might take them a decade, a century or a millenium, but a victory tonight would set into motion a reign of terror unlike anything the world had ever witnessed.

A victory for the old Druid and his few allies would signal no great changes, no upheavals in politics or business. It would simply allow the world to continue on, fumbling and stumbling its way in search of the elusive balance and delicate equilibrium so long sought and so seldom found. A victory would not change the world, but it would insure that the world would not be changed for the worse because of the Madonna's vile alliance with Her bedmate: Satan.

Rathbone sighed and studied what he had written on the sheet of paper. His spidery handwriting, filled with the flourish and flair of the calligraphy of another age, covered the page in neat, even lines. When he had finished rereading what he had written, he carefully folded the sheet and tucked it into an envelope. Sealing it, he took up the pen and wrote Agnes's name on the front and then carefully propped it up against the vanity mirror.

That finished the last of his own preparations. He had already slipped out to Agnes's garage where Joshua's Buick was parked and prepared the vehicle for the journey to the cemetery.

Rising from the chair, Rathbone left the room to find the others. Agnes was sitting alone in the kitchen, a half completed crossword puzzle on the table in front of her. She wore a pair of worn and faded slacks and an old flannel shirt and looked remarkably fresh and relaxed after the long night. He marveled at her composure and stamina.

"Did you rest?" she asked, as he sat opposite from her.

"Enough," he answered.

She looked at him. "I'm curious about something, Tobias."

"Yes."

"Night before last," she said, staring into the old Druid's eyes. "A . . . a demon or whatever they are, came here, to the house. I drove it away with words that just . . . just sprang into my mouth. Words that were more yours than mine . . ."

The old man smiled. "They were mine. You know that I was aware of you long before you were aware me. I have certain influences and abilities which allow me to affect others when necessary.

"You banished the thing by calling on elemental forces. I command many of those forces. It was, indeed, I who put those words in your mouth." He laughed softly. "After all, I had to make certain we met."

Agnes nodded. "I thought as much."

"It bothers you?" He peered closely at her.

"Some. All of this bothers me. It's so . . . so alien." Agnes shoved the folded newspaper aside and reached across the table to take Rathbone's hand in her own.

"What are our chances tonight?" she asked, her voice very soft.

The Druid frowned. He could easily lie to her, but to what end? If she was willing to join him, she had the right to know the truth.

"I won't tell you our chances are good. We are few and our opposition is great. If I were an odds maker, I'd say we had a ten-to-one chance of coming out alive." He spoke evenly, his voice low, but unwaivering. "Are you having second thoughts?"

"No. Not really. I'm an old woman. I've had a remarkably enjoyable life. If I die tonight . . . well it's better to die struggling for something important than in a hospital bed with tubes and wires and who knows what all stuck in my body. If it's my time, then I want it to count for something."

"That's very noble . . ."

Agnes snorted. "Noble? Not at all. It's selfish. I want to be sure I'm remembered, even if it's by a bunch of nasty little monsters. I want *them* to know, that even if they beat me, it was one hell of a good fight."

Rathbone stood. "Fair enough. Now, I want you to get Josh. There is something I have to do to help us tonight."

Joshua was outside trying to read the sports section from the *Rocky Mountain News*. He was sitting in an aluminum folding chair placed in the cool shade beneath the spreading branches of a large maple in Agnes's backyard. He could not keep his mind on any of the stories. Drew Litton's sports cartoon had made him laugh, but he couldn't muster any interest in the countless tidbits from the Broncos training camp nor in the coverage of the previous day's baseball games.

His mind was on the cemetery. Like Rathbone, he was filled with bad feelings and dark premonitions. Joshua was certain—as certain as he was of anything in his life—that tonight would bring death to them. Maybe one of them, maybe all of them. But he felt certain there *would be* death.

He would never admit it to Rathbone or, God forbid, to Agnes, but he felt an icy clutch at his heart, like a giant hand squeezing out his life.

In his own mind, he knew he was the weakest link in the fragile chain the three of them forged. His was merely a support role. He hardly understood it and had only the vaguest clue as to his ability to supplement the others' powers with his raw energy.

If anyone was destined to die, it was he.

"Josh," Agnes called from the backdoor. "Tobias wants us." Welcoming the interruption, Joshua forced his bitter, unsettling thoughts away.

What the hell, he decided, entering the house. I can't live forever.

The sun was low in the west as the three gathered in the living room. Agnes and Joshua were seated on the couch and Rathbone sat in one of the chairs opposite the coffee table. There was an almost tangible electric tension between them. Each of their faces reflected their own inner turmoils and conflicts.

"So," Rathbone began, absently filling his pipe. "We are agreed? We all go?"

The others nodded mutely.

"Good. I will tell you this. There is no real plan we can follow, no elaborate strategy we can employ . . ."

"We're just going to march into the cemetery like lambs to the slaughter?" Josh interrupted, earning a stern look from Agnes. His fingers nervously stroked his moustache.

"No," the Druid answered somberly. "We're going in there ready to fight. But we'll have to stay together. If we get separated, our combined powers will be lost. Dividing us will be the chief tactic they'll use against us. That's the most important thing to remember: not to allow ourselves to become separated."

"And if we are?" asked Agnes.

"Then we'll each be on our own," he answered. "To die as best we can."

"Is that it?" Joshua said, sounding mildly amazed. "That's the plan?"

"Not all of it," the Druid replied, producing a felt marker from his shirt pocket and holding it up for them both to see. "This will help you, too." He got up and went to Joshua, motioning for the mystified man to move over so he could sit between them on the couch.

"Give me your arm," Rathbone said.

Ortega, giving Agnes a curious glance, extended his right arm toward Rathbone. The Druid, the uncapped marker in his right, took the other man's arm in his big, powerful left hand to hold it steady. He then began drawing ancient, arcaic designs on the brown flesh.

"What the hell . . . ?" Joshua mumbled, feeling the

wide felt tip slide over his skin. He forced his arm to remain steady as the marker tickled and glided its way from his elbow to his fingertips.

"Runes," Rathbone responded without pausing. "Powerful magic. I'm going to mark your arms and faces. It may strike you as bizarre, maybe crazy, but you'll have to trust me. This is a very strong defense."

Agnes watched as the Druid's hand skillfully and quickly drew patterns over her friend's forearms. She did not attempt to hide her amusement when Tobias finished Joshua's face. The markings covered his features, forming a disjointed, meaningless mask.

"I feel foolish," was all Joshua said as he rose from the couch and stepped to a mirror hanging on one wall. "I look even more foolish," he continued, after studying himself for a moment.

"You look fine," Agnes laughed as Rathbone moved closer to her and began tattooing her ivory skin as well.

By the time twilight forced them to turn on the overhead light in the living room, Rathbone had finished. Agnes and Joshua looked at one another and smiled.

"We look like a pair of scrimshaw statues," Agnes said.

"I'm glad my children aren't here to see this," Joshua said drily. "After all the grief I gave them about too much make-up and the evils of tattoos, they'd hoot me out of town."

Rathbone stood across the room and studied them. In his eyes he could see beyond the shapes and patterns lining their faces. He could see the aura of power around them created by the runes. It was a very brilliant blue in his eyes, although no other could see it, and when the pair stood close or touched, it flared an incandescent azure.

"You're as ready as you can be," he pronounced. "The rest is up to you. You have to strengthen your minds and hearts now. I can't do that for you. It is likely that tonight you will experience and witness things you've never imagined, never felt. Do what you can to make yourselves ready to face them. We'll leave shortly."

"Should I take my Ouija board?" Agnes asked.

"Yes."

She nodded and walked out of the living room and proceeded to the staircase leading to her turret room. She had, as was her habit, returned the board to its place in the special room.

Solomon the cat followed her as she climbed the steep steps. As if sensing something out of the ordinary, he rubbed against her legs and made meowing sounds, purring loudly when his mistress stooped to scratch his chin and rub his head.

"And what about you?" she asked the cat. "What will become of you if I don't return? Who'll take care of you?"

The cat purred in reply.

"I suppose I could call Mrs. Blake down the street. Ask her to take care of you . . . No. That would be foolish. I'll be back by morning and besides you wouldn't like her house. She's too fussy for the likes of you."

Agnes retrieved the Ouija board and started to leave the room. She paused to glance around. She had spent many hours here communicating with other dimensions. She wondered if she'd ever sit here again, her fingers lightly touching the planchette as it glided over the familiar board.

With a shake of her head, she turned off the light and closed the door, making certain she had not closed Solomon in the room.

If I never do come back here, she thought, I've a lot of good memories to take to my grave.

On the way down the stairs, she decided Solomon would be fine. She would leave a window open so he could get in and out. If she didn't return, he would undoubtedly find some other cat lover from whom he could charm a meal and wheedle a caress.

"Are we ready?" Rathbone asked as Agnes joined the men in the living room.

Joshua exhaled loudly. "As ready as we'll ever be."

"Then we go . . ."

Rathbone was cut off as the house suddenly shuddered with a violent jolt. Dishes rattled and pictures wobbled. Somewhere in another room, a heavy piece of furniture crashed to the floor amid the sounds of shattering glass.

The trio looked at one another as the front door banged shut and the window sashes slammed down.

"Earthquake?" Joshua asked, bracing himself against the wall. His voice told the others he no more believed that they were experiencing a natural tremor anymore than they did.

"She's trying to stop us," Rathbone yelled, attempting to make his way across the now heaving and pitching floor. Cursing, he stumbled and fell heavily to the carpeting.

As the old house continued to groan and sway, fissures spidered the walls, sending bits of plaster and paint flying across room. Agnes watched in horror as a gray-green slime, thick and dark, bubbled out of the ragged cracks and oozed down the walls.

Joshua, too, tumbled to the floor. Groaning as his old bones throbbed in protest, he pulled himself toward one of the windows. He fumbled with a brass table lamp, its shade crushed and bent, finally able to grasp it. Rolling on his back, Joshua cocked his arm and let the lamp fly at the glass, covering his face to protect it from the splintering shards. With a heavy thump, the lamp hit the window and rebounded to smash painfully into the old man's upraised arm.

Letting out a cry, his injured arm clasped in his other hand, he rolled back onto his stomach.

The floor was still pitching, the walls quaking, as he retrieved the lamp, rolled over and again hurled it at what should have been a sheet of eighth-inch tempered glass. Again the heavy metal failed to pierce the window pane and bounded harmlessly to the floor.

"Forget it, Josh!" Rathbone yelled. The Druid had made

his way to the door. Struggling futilely to open it, he discovered it was firmly sealed. With one hand gripping the knob for support, he placed the index finger of his right hand against the door and began to etch blue-flamed runes on its hardwood surface. As he traced the wavering patterns, he was repeated tossed and thrown from side to side. The runes smoked and crackled, leaving blackened scorch marks on the wood. As he continued to sear the arcane designs on the door, the disturbance began to lessen.

Agnes was braced in the doorway between the living room and kitchen, her back pressed against one jamb, her arms against the other. It took all her strength to maintain her balance. Her arm and leg muscles were already quivering and shaking from exertion.

"I need your help," Rathbone called to Ortega, letting go of the knob and extending his hand to the other man. Joshua, unable to stand, crawled as quickly as he could across the carpet. When he was close enough, he reached out and grabbed the Druid's fingers.

Instantly, there was a rush of power between the two, a bonding of flesh and energy. A burst of sapphire sparks sprang from their linked hands, showering harmlessly to the floor. The enormous potency of Ortega's psychic abilities energized Rathbone and the runes he was etching became more pronounced, appearing on the wood with greater definition.

There was a deep, reverberating rumble followed by the cacophony of snapping lumber, cracking walls, breaking dishes, shattering glass and tumbling furniture. The racket was deafening, abnormally heightened as if by giant, phantom amplifiers. Joshua, his right hand in Rathbone's, covered an ear with his left, trying to blot out as much of the terrible noise as possible.

The kitchen ceiling near Agnes split open like a rotten fruit, spilling out more of the noxious slime, along with mortar and lath. A heavy ceiling beam tore loose above her, long embedded nails screaming as they were ripped free. It tottered and creaked and then with a groan and in a cloud of fine dust, it swung toward her. As if by design, the end above Agnes remained in place while the opposite end came down like a hammer.

Agnes threw herself toward the couch. The beam grazed the back of her left leg as she jumped, the blow propelling her over the armrest to sprawl awkwardly on the soft cushions. Panting, she tumbled to the floor just as the beam crashed, unnaturally, through the doorway and thudded onto the couch.

"Aggie!" Joshua yelled. "Are you alright?"

Agnes, dazed but unhurt, nodded her head vigorously and started moving over the still pitching and rolling floor like a drunken sailor crawling across the deck of a storm-tossed ship.

Rathbone finished the last rune just as the living room ceiling caved in.

His magic, boosted by Joshua's enormous power reserve, had broken the dark enchantment barring the door. He yanked it open and, still clutching Ortega's hand, leaped through the opening, sending the screen door slamming back on screeching hinges. The ceiling shuddered and shook. Hunks of plaster crashed to the floor creating a thick, dirty white cloud. With an ear-ringing crescendo, it buckled in the middle and whooshed into the room below.

The two men lay on the porch as the room behind thundered an echoed. A billowing, choking fog of dust and dirt spilled out into the warm night air.

"Aggie!" Joshua yelled, his voice suddenly desperate. Ignoring his aches and pains, he scrambled to his feet. He stumbled to the door, repeatedly screaming the old woman's name.

Rathbone was right behind him. The Druid, reserved and cautious, peered into the room while restaining the other man with a firm hand.

"Let go of me," Joshua cried, struggling to pull free.

"Don't be a fool, Josh," Rathbone responded, stepping

in front of Ortega and carefully picking his way through the heaps of debris. ''Aggie?'' he called.

''H . . . here,'' the woman stammered. She lay huddled beneath the heavy coffee table, surrounded by lengths of two-by-four, chunks of crumbled plaster and pieces of fractured lath.

The men rushed to her. Joshua shoved the table over and gave her his hand.

''Are you hurt?'' he asked, his voice quavering.

''No.'' Her voice was muted and shaken. With Joshua's help, she got to her feet, running her free hand through her mussed hair. The arcaic designs on her face and hands blended with the fine powdery dirt giving her an aboriginal countenace.

''Thank God,'' Joshua breathed, putting a protective arm around her shoulders and guiding her to the door.

Rathbone stepped away from them and moved into the demolished kitchen. He soon joined them on the porch holding Agnes's Ouija board and its planchette.

''You'll need these,'' he said, handing them to the woman.

''Was it . . . the Madonna?'' Agnes asked, still wrapped in Joshua's arm.

''Of course,'' the Druid snapped. ''What'd you think it was? An earthquake?''

Agnes flinched at his harsh sarcasm.

''Ease off, Tobias,'' Joshua shot back, his marked face twisted in anger.

Rathbone started to make a reply and then turned and stalked away, stepping off the porch and vanishing around the side of the house.

''What the hell is eating him?'' Joshua asked bitterly, brushing dust and dirt from his moustache.

Agnes moved away from her companion and stared out into the quiet street, noting that none of her neighbors had come to investigate the uproar. She wondered if they had even been aware of it. It was, after all, the product of a black and evil bewitchment.

After a moment, she turned and looked at Joshua.

"He's frightened. Badly frightened. We were all caught completely by surprise just now. Do you think that's happened to him often? With his powers? To be taken off guard has to have shaken him."

"He doesn't have to take it out on us, does he?" Joshua mumbled, his anger fading.

Agnes took his hand. "That's just it. He's not angry at us. He's mad at himself and his failing powers. He's relied on his abilities for so long, it has to be very hard for him not to be able to trust them."

"Then why the hell are we following him back to that cemetery?"

Agnes's voice was soft and introspective. "Because we haven't a choice. We're all there is. We're all he has."

Joshua said nothing.

They both turned when Solomon meowed in aggravation. His fur streaked with dirt, the cat sat primly, studying them from the doorway as if seeking an explanation for the destruction of his home.

Agnes stooped to pick him up, stroking his dusty fur.

"We've got to go," she told the cat. "You watch what's left of the house." The cat nuzzled her and purred. She held him another minute and then set him down and shooed him back into the house.

Joshua kicked the scraps of wood away from the doorway and with some effort, pulled the heavy, rune-scarred door shut.

"Afraid I'll get burgled?" Agnes asked, a wry note in her voice.

"Solomon'll keep it all safe," the old man laughed. "I guess tomorrow I'd better get my tool box and do a little handiwork."

"You'd be better off bringing a bulldozer."

No longer able to postpone their departure, the two

walked arm in arm around the corner of the house. They found Rathbone standing outside the garage near his beloved Cord. Hands thrust in his pockets, he stood staring at the night sky.

"City lights always wash out the stars. Can't appreciate the night sky in the city," he told them gently as they walked up to him.

Agnes glanced skyward, trying to remember the last time she had seen the heavens in their full glory. "When my husband and I use to go into the mountains, I always insisted we not pitch a tent. I liked to watch the sky and wonder."

"About what?" Joshua asked.

"Everything."

There was a long, quiet pause while the three old people contemplated the few visible stars. They all tried to find some comfort in such a simple, common pleasure in order to avoid dwelling on the night's mission.

Finally Rathbone broke the silence. "We have to go. Josh, will you get your car?"

Oretga fished his keys out of his pants pocket and went into the garage. A moment later they heard him let out a cry of consternation. Agnes turned and started toward the garage, fearing yet another attack by the evil thing they sought to destroy. Rathbone held her back.

"He's fine. He just discovered some of my work." Agnes was surprised to hear Rathbone chuckle.

They waited while Joshua backed the car out of the garage. As it rolled onto the gravel driveway and into the faint light cast by a distant mercury light, Agnes saw the thick, black markings traced over the shiny paint.

"Not taking any chances?" Joshua asked, stepping out of the sedan.

"More runes?" she asked, looking from the car to the Druid.

"Protection while we're on our way," he explained flatly.

"At this point," Joshua sighed, "nothing you do surprises me."

They left moments later. At Tobias's insistance, all three sat in the front seat, Agnes in the middle, flanked by the two men.

Joshua drove south to Interstate 70 and then headed the car east in the moderately heavy traffic. He made the turn to southbound I-25 at the "Mousetrap," Denver's infamous interchange, and merged into the frenzied flow.

Only Tobias noticed the other car pull along side, pacing them. For a second he feared it was another of their enemies, but when the teenagers in the backseat pointed, staring at their oddly marked car, he smiled.

What a sight we must be, he mused to himself. Old codgers in Halloween make-up driving a car to match.

They were silent all the way to Mansfield. None of them had anything left to say. Their thoughts were turned inward: wondering, speculating, dreading.

Rathbone focused his thoughts on his faltering powers. Would they be enough? Was he leading these two trusting people to their deaths?

Agnes was less morose. She had made peace with herself and decided to do whatever had to be done. If they failed and if she died, then so be it. There were times when a person had to make a stand. To the old woman, this seemed to be as important a time as any in her life.

And Joshua, intently watching the highway, his eyes already tired and scratchy, could not shake the feeling that in addition to his friends, Death was riding with him.

TWENTY-ONE

Henry Terrance stood, naked from the waist up, in the living room of the caretaker's cottage, his enormous stomach sagging over the top of his pants. He held a tumbler of whiskey in one hand and a freshly opened bottle in the other. His corpulant face was split by an unusually sardonic grin.

"To us!" he toasted, lifting the glass high into the air.

Oscar Bedlow, as pale and gaunt as ever, sat quietly in one of the big chairs, frowning at his companion. He raised his own glass with a listless indifference.

"It's too early to celebrate, Henry," Bedlow said dourly, after sipping the whiskey. "But after tonight, we'll have cause to toast our success."

"You don't get it, Oscar," Terrance laughed. "We've already won. Those three old geezers barely got out of here with their lives last night. The girl is ours and her boy friend is dead. There's nothing to stand in our way."

Bedlow looked unconvinced. "I'll only feel good about it *after* tonight. After The Rising has been completed. Until then, I'll worry."

"Bah!" Terrance cried, refilling his glass. "The only

worry I had was that son of a bitch Rathbone. Hell, they had to carry that old fart out of here."

"That's just the problem, Henry," Bedlow grunted. "We saw them carry Rathbone out of here. But he wasn't dead."

"That bastard was as good as dead!"

Bedlow shook his head in disgust. "You amaze me. He's a Druid. You have to *kill* them to stop them and even then I'm not so sure it's enough."

Terrance turned and walked to one of the other chairs and sat heavily, his huge stomach quaking and sagging as he sank into its deep cushions. He took another gulp of liquor.

"It's really going to be something, Oscar," he said absently, his voice far away.

"What are you babbling about?" his companion demanded.

"Just thinking," Terrance muttered. "After tonight, my father and grandfather will be back. They'll use their Midas Touch to make us another fortune."

Bedlow harrumphed and glanced at his wristwatch. He was only too aware of the financial condition of the Terrance fortune under Henry's stewardship. While his grandfather and father had built an empire in banking, mining, and lumber—with no small amount of help from the dark powers granted them by their alliance with the Madonna—Henry had lost most of it on lavish living and poor business judgement. Not to mention his abnormal lust for young boys. More than once his indiscreet pederasty had cost him handsomely to avoid messy court appearances and probable lengthy prison sentences in Canon City.

It was not surprising he wanted to see his ancestors live again; perhaps they could undo the mess he had made of their efforts.

With the lights off, the room grew dark as night crept over the cemetery. Neither man bothered to turn on a lamp. They simply waited, tense and anxious, each wrapped in his own thoughts.

"It's time," Bedlow said when the room was almost completely shrouded in darkness. He stood and proceeded to take off his coat and unbutton his shirt.

Terrance stood, draining his glass, the ice cubes clinking against his teeth. He dropped the tumbler in the chair and bent over to retrieve a long, flowing robe from the floor. Donning it, he pulled up the peaked hood which concealed his large, bulbous head.

Bedlow, too, removed his jacket and shirt and slipped a similar robe over his head. He then moved through the darkness to the door. "I'll get the girl, Henry. You go open the gates. They'll be here soon."

"If things hadn't gone so badly," Henry carped, "that Cassidy punk would be here to do this scut work."

"Well, he's not here," snapped Bedlow. "So just do it."

"Are *all* the survivors coming?" Terrance asked.

"Of course. No one would dare miss The Rising."

The fat man followed Bedlow out into the warm, heavy night. He pondered the century of blood rites performed under each full moon. All the families buried in Mansfield would be represented tonight. And even though the cemetery was filled, there were less than three hundred attending The Rising.

The founders of Mansfield discovered, when their children grew to adulthood, that some would not accept the covenants of the Circle and the requirements of their legacy. Some had threatened to betray the Circle and it had been expedient to eliminate them. After a few unfortunate experiences, the group determined it would be necessary to keep their progeny to as small a number as possible. Marriage within the Circle was encouraged, many believing that a coupling of two from within the sphere of the Madonna's influence resulted in children innately qualified to serve as Mansfield's guardians. Rarely did these couples have more than one child; the fewer offspring, the tighter the Circle, reducing the risk of betrayal by one of their own.

Now the heirs of Mansfield were coming together to witness the return of their forebears. After a century's wait, there would be an awesome reunion.

With these thoughts in his mind, Terrance turned reluctantly toward the gates, while Bedlow moved to his Cadillac, parked out of sight behind the cottage.

Terrance fished beneath his robe for the key to the padlock securing the gate's chain. Pulling it out, he opened the lock and pushed one of the gates open. As he was crossing the gravel to move the other gate, his foot struck something heavy lying on the ground. Cursing, he picked it up and peered at it, unsure as to what he had discovered. When he realized it was the solidified remains of the padlock Rathbone had melted the previous night, he swore and dropped it as if it still held the magic fire.

''Fucking Druid!''

Suddenly paranoid, Terrance looked around suspiciously. The thought of Rathbone frightened him. He and Bedlow had tried to kill the wizard when they first learned he was in Denver. They had failed. The Madonna had sent Her army against him, but they too, had been defeated, although not before weakening the Druid enough to force him into hiding. He had been difficult to locate, protected. Terrance knew, by his powerful magic. It had only been a few nights ago that the Madonna's minions had located him. He had driven them off and then appeared at the cemetery with those other two old crocks.

''Damn, stinking Druid bastard,'' Terrance snarled.

While the fat man fumed in the darkness, Bedlow unlocked his Cadillac and dragged Mary Renata out of the back seat, her white gown oddly luminescent in the darkness. He loosened her bonds and pulled the gag from her mouth.

''Are you ready, my dear?'' he asked, as she studied his robe. His bony, skeletal face was obscured by his cowl.

"For what?" Her voice was flat and indifferent.

"The experience of your life," he answered quietly.

Mary hugged herself in the warm night. Although she still felt phlegmatic and apathetic, it could not keep her from knowing, understanding the dark promise in Bedlow's words.

A low rumble heralded the arrival of an unmarked bus. Its windows were tinted a smokey gray, making it impossible to see the occupants. Amid the squeal and sigh of brakes, it ground to a stop near the cottage. Immediately behind it, another bus appeared. Within minutes, seven of the monstrous vehicles were parked side by side, though none of the passengers disembarked. An eerie, unnatural silence hung over the area.

The edge of the swollen, bloated moon broke over the eastern horizon, penetrating the velvet blue sky with its cold, icy illuminescence.

After watching the buses line up one by one, Bedlow turned to Mary, his face still hidden by the peaked hood. "You'll understand everything very soon. It won't be long at all now, my dear. Not at all."

She remained silent.

Henry Terrance came waddling around the corner, excited and animated, swathed in the enormous black robe.

"They . . . they're here, Oscar," he panted. "It's almost time. It's like a dream. All these years and now, finally, it's going to happen!"

Mary's arm firmly in his grasp, Bedlow turned toward the fat man. "There is still much to do. Get everyone off the buses and lead them to the heart of the cemetery, to the vault. We must be ready when the moon is up."

Terrance nodded and moved to the buses. He said nothing, simply raised his arm over his head and motioned with his hand. Immediately, figures began filing off the buses. All wore black, hooded robes. With the fat man leading one column, they walked single file up the various driveways radiating from the cottage toward the center of Mansfield. None of them spoke. The only sound coming from the throng was the shuffle and crunch of their feet on the gravel.

"Are they all as sick as you?" Mary asked Bedlow as he forced her to join a line of marchers.

The man snorted a harsh laugh. "It's all a matter of definition, Miss Renata. What you call 'sick', we may consider normal."

She fell silent as they continued up the roadway. Plagued with an odd mixture of emotions, the indifference she felt blunted the terror, which should have rocked her with seizures of hysteria. Yet she knew, feeling the natural, instinctive fear welling up in her heart, that her end—death or worse—was near.

The jaundiced moon now hung like a leering eye above the Great Plains. Its radiance transformed the cemetery into a stone garden of light and shadow, tombstones and crypts standing out in sharp relief against the inky darkness of the towering trees.

The mass of darkly robed men and women moved steadily into the center of Mansfield, gradually flowing into a series of concentric circles around a huge, low vault holding the bones of a family of four. Its rose colored marble, veined with streaks of white, glistened and shimmered in the cool light.

Bedlow led Mary through the still, silent crowd to the vault. Wrapped in the flimsy white gown, she stood out in stark contrast to her black robed antagonists.

"Get up," Bedlow ordered, indicating the top of the crypt.

"Wh . . . what?"

"Get on top of the vault."

"Why?"

He turned toward her, the lower part of his face washed by the moonlight, his large teeth flashing. His voice was low, menacing. "Don't play games, Mary. Just do as you're told."

She hesitated.

"Do it!"

"And if I don't?" She sensed her role in this bizarre ceremony was important. Why else would they go to all this trouble? Maybe, by pushing all his buttons, she could stall for time and find a way to escape the madness.

"There are things that can happen to you that'll make you wish your worst nightmares would come true." Bedlow gestured and the cemetery was suddenly alive with an insane, terrible laughter. From around the silent, statue-like figures, red feral eyes peered and greedy, forked tongues flicked in the moonlight.

Mary heard and saw this and sighed. "*You're* my worst nightmare, fucker!" She turned and hoisted herself onto the vault.

"You know all this," Mary swept her hand in a broad, encompassing gesture, "won't go unnoticed by people passing the cemetery. There'll be police here to investigate . . ."

Bedlow laughed. "You underestimate the Madonna's power. To eyes beyond Mansfield's fence, all will appear normal and undisturbed." He pointed at the marble monument "Go to the middle of it and wait."

She followed his orders, standing erect and poised on the smooth stone which was still warm from the day's heat.

Mary scanned the sea of ebon figures. For a long moment they remained motionless and then they stirred, moving around headstones, closing in on the vault. As if one, they began a low, somber chant. The cadence was slow, but gradually became faster and the volume higher. The words, indistinguishable and unrecognizable, were intoned in a strange, long-forgotten tongue.

She could do nothing but watch. There was no place to run, no break in the ever-tightening circle of black mantled, chanting supplicants. She knew if she tried to flee, her tormentors would simply thrust her back onto the stone platform.

Or is it an altar?

Scurrying among the dark host, Mary could see small, misshapen creatures. They peered from behind their human counterparts and from atop gravestones. Their bright red eyes shone like blood-reddened crystals, cold and dispassionate.

The chanting reverberated across the cemetery now. Its pace grew faster, almost frenzied, building toward some unknown crescendo. The sing-song cadence held the sinister promise of lust and blood and violence.

Mary knew that if she was not under the spell of The Presence, she would be begging for it to end, pleading for a cessation of the noise and the madness. Instead, shielded from its total emotional impact, she stood statuesque in the center of the platform.

She closed her eyes and prayed.

TWENTY-TWO

Joshua Ortega parked the car near the industrial site across from the cemetery. He sighed audibly as he turned off the engine and stared toward Mansfield.

Rathbone anxiously studied the moon, now almost fully risen above the eastern horizon.

"We have to move quickly," he breathed. "They'll probably be starting their ritual soon and once it begins, the Bitch's power will magnify very quickly."

"What do we do?" Joshua asked, his tattooed face a grim mask in the silvery light.

Agnes looked at the Druid. "We can't just walk in the front gate, can we?"

"Why not?" Rathbone asked in return. "If we're careful we can waltz right in. With all the activity going on in there tonight, that Black Bitch may not even know we're there until it's too late."

Agnes thought about that. After what they had experienced last night and at her house this evening, how could She not know? What would She do to stop them? And, more importantly, what could they do to stop Her?

Questions without answers, she decided, keeping her thoughts to herself.

"Hey," Joshua hissed. "Take a look at that." He pointed down the street to where a string of buses was turning into the cemetery's driveway.

The Druid grunted. "The rest of the Madonna's followers, no doubt."

"That's strange," Agnes said, staring beyond the cemetery's fence as the first of the buses turned up the driveway.

Joshua followed her gaze. "What?"

"The bus went in and there isn't a sign of it. Where'd it go?"

"It's there," Rathbone answered knowingly. "The Bitch has created an illusion around the cemetery. From this side of the fence, everything appears absolutely normal. Just another quiet cemetery. It minimizes the possibility of discovery."

"She can do that?" Joshua whispered.

"Absolutely. Illusion is a part of Her power."

"But . . . there's so much to conceal." Joshua tried to comprehend the magnitude of the deception. "What is She?"

Rathbone studied the others in the fading light. "Evil."

"My God," breathed Agnes. "It's frightening. What *is* going on in there?"

"Nothing good," the Druid said, opening his door and stepping out of the car. "Let's go. I have an idea."

Mystified, the other two followed. Agnes took her Ouija board and planchette out of the backseat and joined Joshua. They had to move quickly to keep up with Rathbone, who was now trotting toward the gates.

"Tobias," Joshua hissed, as they ran along Mansfield's iron fence. "We'll be seen."

"I don't think so."

"But . . ."

Rathbone stopped and turned toward his companions. "If the Bitch has masked the cemetery, then whoever or whatever is in there can't see what's happening on the *outside*. It's sort of a principle of magic." He saw the skepticism in Joshua's eyes. "Don't worry about it. I know I'm right."

Without further discussion, he turned and resumed trotting toward the gates with Joshua and Agnes following. The last of the seven buses rolled off the street and up the drive.

-When they reached the low bushes flanking the gravel driveway, Rathbone halted again.

"Are you going to burn off the lock?" Agnes whispered.

"No," he responded, peering carefully around the shrubs. "It'd be waste of energy and I don't think it'll be necessary." He pointed toward the open driveway. They saw an enormously fat figure wrapped in a black, hooded robe, closing the two gates.

"That's Terrance," Rathbone said softly. "Come on." Without another word and much to the others' consternation, the Druid walked directly up the drive in full view of the fat man.

When Terrance saw him, he paused. Although his face was hidden beneath the cowl, they knew he was staring in amazement at the Druid. He started to turn, just as Rathbone raised his right hand. Something hissed in the air for a fraction of a second and the obese man walked away from the gate, leaving it unlocked.

Rathbone motioned for Agnes and Joshua to follow him. When they reached the gates, he drew the couple closer to him. his voice was low and raspy.

"We're going in now. Remember. We stay together."

"What'd you do to him?" Agnes wanted to know.

"An old trick," Rathbone replied. "I clouded his mind. He forgot about seeing me and he thinks he locked the gate." He had used the same trick when, disguised as the vagrant, he had visited Vince Cassidy and tried to convince him to leave the cemetery.

"If we go in, they'll see us," Joshua protested.

The Druid shook his head. "Not if we're careful. Just follow my lead and stay close." Although he tried to sound confident, inwardly he was worried. It was an assumption that the convergence of so many people in the cemetery would mask their presence. He had no way of knowing if it would actually be the case. After all, the Madonna knew they were coming.

Nodding to Agnes and Joshua, Rathbone ducked past the gates. They followed. The Druid slipped the chain through the iron bars and affixed the padlock, but did not snap it closed, in the likely event they would have to make a hasty exit.

The buses were parked side by side in front of the cottage. Black-robed figures began pouring out of them as the three infiltrators slipped behind a low hedge.

Agnes shivered as the mass moved in an eerie silence. They formed several lines and began walking deeper into the cemetery.

"Look," she whispered excitedly, pointing to her left. They could clearly make out the white gowned woman being led by a tall black form at the rear of one of the columns.

"It's her," Joshua said.

"Who?"

"The girl. The girl I talked to yesterday."

Rathbone nodded. "The Renata girl. I was right, she's important to whatever is supposed to transpire here tonight." He watched the Madonna's worshipers file up the driveways. They were radiating away from the cottage, but he knew they would all gather at one point, somewhere deep in Mansfield.

"Come on," he ordered. Keeping to the shelter of crypts and headstones, he took the lead as they hurried through the cemetery, following the black-robed horde.

Agnes winced as her legs cramped and her old heart began pounding. She wondered about the wisdom of three senior citizens—Tobias the senior of all citizens—racing through a cemetery in the middle of the night pursuing some supernatural phantasm.

She dismissed the thought as moot. They were here and there was no turning back now.

Agnes shuddered as they moved silently past the opened grave of the murdered girl. Faintly in the moonlight, she could see the heap of bones which had been torn from the ground. She looked away quickly, depressed and saddened by the sight.

Rathbone kept a careful watch for any sign of the Bitch's dark minions. He saw none of the little monsters and his psychic alarms could not detect any near them. At the same time he was hesitant to put too much trust in his powers. He was acutely aware of his failing abilities.

They slipped to the back of a large crypt as one procession of the Mansfield heirs marched past its front. Rathbone looked toward the end of the column and nodded.

"Stay here," he said, dropping low to move crab-like to a headstone bordering the gravel road. Keeping low behind the slab of stone, he watched as the end of the line neared. When the last three marchers were abreast of him, he stood and again thrust out his right hand. Without breaking stride, the three stepped from the back of the line and walked toward the Druid. He kept his hand leveled at them, guiding them. Like automatons, they walked directly toward the back of the crypt.

"Take their robes," Rathbone ordered Joshua and Agnes, still holding the three in his magical grasp.

Without a word, Agnes began tugging the black robe off a short, plump man, who, save for a pair of leather sandals, was naked beneath its concealing folds. Joshua, too, pulled one off a particularly attractive blond woman. Like her counterpart, she was naked and he marveled at her fine young body. Together they disrobed the third one, a middle aged man with the look of an accountant or banker.

The three captivated, entranced people stood stock still

through the whole process. Their eyes were glazed and blank, their backs rigid and their arms loose at their sides.

"Put the robes on," Rathbone snapped. "Hurry."

Agnes and Joshua slipped the stolen robes over their heads and adjusted each other's hood to make certain their faces were hidden. The old woman tucked the Ouija board under her arm beneath the flowing robe, praying no one would jostle her and discover it. When they had finished, they glanced at Rathbone.

"Okay," he said, keeping his voice low. "Catch up with the parade and join in. Don't do anything suspicious and don't say a word."

"What about you?" Agnes asked, concerned. "I thought we were supposed to stay together."

"I'll catch up. I have to take care of this bunch." He nodded at the three naked people. He still held his hand poised at them, holding them in his powerful grip.

Joshua frowned. "You're not going to *kill* them . . . ?"

"Of course not," the Druid snapped. "Now go on. I'll be with you in a minute."

After Agnes and Joshua were gone, Rathbone motioned with his hand and the naked trio stepped forward. He led them to a spot several yards away from the crypt, out of sight of the roadway, and motioned for them to halt. Communicating silently, he ordered them to sit and planted a suggestion deep in their minds.

Satisfied, he returned to the crypt, leaving the three leaning against a tree, all sleeping soundly. The spell and its accompanying mind control would last for at least two hours, three if the Druid was lucky.

Rathbone donned the remaining robe and hurried to catch up with the column. As he walked quickly up behind the silent marchers, he thought he saw a small, shadowy form dart behind a tombstone. He continued to watch the area, but nothing moved and he quickly fell into step behind Agnes, breathing a sigh of relief.

So far, so good.

Their group joined the others gathering around the marble vault. Standing next to Agnes, Rathbone felt the woman tense when the Renata girl was forced to climb atop it. He hoped she and Joshua would do nothing to give away their presence.

When the chanting began, he and his companions tried to join in, although the unfamiliar words were difficult to mimic and the cadence hard to anticipate. Still, they were able to make sounds which blended well enough with the general tonality of the dark requiem.

As the throng moved closer to the vault, the three imposters joined them. Following Rathbone, Joshua and Agnes slowly crowded their way through the press of people to the edge of the vault.

Standing there, the frantic and frenzied chant resounding across the graveyard, Agnes felt cold sweat trickle down her back. A chill quivered through her body and she fought the urge to clutch herself. Stepping closer to Joshua, she felt a tug at the hem of her robe. Looking down, she saw a tiny, leathery creature flitting away, its misshapen head bobbing and weaving among the black robes. She bit her lip, the pain and coppery taste of blood driving away her terror.

Rathbone, too, saw the tiny thing, another of the Bitch's servants. They were everywhere in the crowd, darting and dashing about like awful, demented children. For the time being, he knew they posed little threat. They were virtually mindless and craven and could only act on her command. Still, he and the others would have to be careful not to let any of the little cretins discover their charade. If one of them detected his presence, it was damn sure the Bitch would know about it immediately.

As suddenly as it had begun, the chanting stopped. The abrupt silence seemed louder and more disquieting to the three imposters than had the bedlam.

For a long moment there was no sound, no movement, only a gentle breeze stirring the trees. They watched Mary turn slowly on the polished stone, studying the crowd. The moonlight shimmered on her dark hair and illuminated the white gown to an impossible brilliance. The wind melded it against her body and stirred her shoulder length hair, but she appeared oblivious to everything. When she turned toward her three unknown allies, they were amazed at the vacuous, glassy look in her eyes.

Poor child. She's lost her mind.

Agnes shivered at the thought. What had they done to this woman? What were they planning? Clearly something dark and ugly.

And what the hell can we do?

The old woman felt a twinge of panic tear at her heart. She unexpectedly saw herself as singularly foolish. And she was very frightened. What was she doing in the middle of this madness? What possible good could she do? What difference could an eccentric old woman make in the midst of this horror?

You can't run now, Aggie, old girl.

Joshua, too, was battling a rising tide of terror and despair. He felt that of the three, he was the weakest. Agnes had the board and Tobias . . . well, Tobias had the *power*. All *he* had was an unknown supply of psychic energy. He was nothing but a damned storage battery.

Watching the girl slowly turn on the dais, his old heart broke. He was the one who had spoken with her, sensed her confusion and fear. And he was the one who had not been there when she had needed someone to keep her from returning, willingly or unwillingly, to this damned place.

He had to do what he could. If for no other reason than because he owed the girl something.

Unlike his mortal friends, the Druid did not allow himself to dwell on his fate nor question his reasons for being in the middle of this unholy ritual. He had spent centuries anticipating his chance to battle the Black Bitch, the Devil's bedmate. He had not looked forward to it with relish, but certainly with a sense of purpose and mission.

If he was the last of his race, his kind, and he thought he was, then it was more than personal revenge or some idealistic sense of thwarting Evil which brought him here.

It was his destiny and his duty. It was his birthright. And perhaps, he admitted, a question of his own ego and pride. A battle he could not avoid. He had to know if he was a match for that foul, monsterous creature from the lowest reaches of Hell.

All three were jolted out of their introspective reflections when one of the robed worshipers leaped onto the platform and took hold of Mary Renata's arm. The figure was tall and in the silvery light, his large teeth flashed in the shadows under his hood.

A second figure, the fat man whom Rathbone had mesmerized at the gate, struggled to heave his bulk onto the vault. No one moved to help him. After several aborted attempts, he finally managed to lift his fleshy body atop the cool stone. He stood and joined the other figure.

"The time has come," the fat man cried to the multitude. "We have waited all our lives for this moment. He have followed the tenants our ancestors gave us. We have kept the Circle unbroken; we have kept it untainted. We have sacrificed hundreds to insure the arrival of this night. We have kept the blood rites and performed the rituals. Tonight we reap our reward.

"A century ago our ancestors established this cemetery as a *temporary* resting place." He paused and looked out over the sea of black robed men and women. None stirred. There were no muffled coughs or cleared throats. Simply a deadly, attentive silence.

He continued. "Yes, a temporary resting place; a way station where they could await this night. *The night of their return!*"

Like a slow rolling wave, the chanting began again. It was low at first, but grew louder as it became more intense and insistent until it was a pounding cry breaking against the night stillness.

The fat man moved to the edge of the vault and motioned to one of the dark-clad individuals. Immediately the figure reached under his robe and produced a wickedly curved scimitar, its polished metal mirroring the moonlight. The fat man took the sword gingerly, wrapped his meaty fist around the ornately tooled hilt and raised it over his head.

The crowd, their combined voices still rocking the night with the ominous, monotonous rhythm of the chant, raised their heads as one to stare at the shimmering blade.

The fat man arced the scimitar once in the air and there was again silence over the cemetery.

"And now we are ready," the fat man cried. "The time has come. The Madonna is near us, with us. And we have our sacrifice."

Bedlow, still holding Mary Renata's arms, suddenly used his incredible strength to force her backward until she lay on the smooth marble. Terrance walked slowly across the dais to the pair, the curved blade still held high.

"With this woman," he continued, waving his free hand toward the prone girl, "we have fulfilled the final requirement. Before you lies Renata, heir to the legacy of the witch nun!"

A murmur of pleasure and assent ran through the gathering.

"In her veins flows the blood of the Madonna! And tonight we spill that blood in homage to Her presence, Her power and Her gift to us and our forefathers!" The fat man's voice was strong and resonant, the words pouring from his mouth with force and fervor. "It is her blood which will fulfill the promises and consummate the ritual to begin The Rising!"

Standing against the vault's hard, cold stone, the Ouija board slick with sweat beneath her arm, Agnes found herself horridly and grimly fascinated. The man's voice carried a dark and evil message, but its modulation and intonation was hypnotic and compelling.

Rathbone was unimpressed with Terrance's spiel. He was, however, gravely concerned and mildly confused. He realized the woman's life was about to be forfeited and he was perhaps the only one who could save her. Accomplishing that might be a greater challenge than he could meet. There were too many of the enemy around him and he had detected the presence of the Black Bitch although She had not yet manifested Herself. A rash move on his part now would surely jeopardize their mission.

The girl may have to die.

The thought sickened him, but it was a matter of the greater good. At least that was an acceptable rationalization. He wondered if he could live with it.

I wonder if I'll have a life to live after tonight?

The Druid's confusion came from Terrance's reference to the "witch nun." He knew, of course, it was Maria Renata, the nun put to death for witchcraft after serving her church for fifty years. But he could not understand how the Bitch's blood could flow in the woman's veins or within any mortal. Had that evil creature, at some time in the distant past, actually mated with a demon and given birth to a child? The thought unnerved Rathbone, whose life was a blur of terrible, grotesque memories. The implications of such a dark and monstrous union were staggering and not a little frightening.

"The Rising is upon us," the fat man orated. "The blood of this woman will mark the culmination of a century of hope and dedication and obedience!"

Terrance held the scimitar high above Mary Renata's throat. There was a palpable tension in the crowd, so electric the three imposters could virtually feel it crackle in the air.

All eyes were locked on that cruel blade.

Joshua Ortega held his breath. He wanted to leap atop the vault and do battle for the woman's life.

Why hasn't Rathbone done something? What is he waiting for?

Bedlow had the woman's arms pinned against the stone. Joshua saw her glazed, distant eyes suddenly open wide as if for the first time she realized her role in the sick and ugly ritual.

A scream tore from her lips as the fat man's arm cocked and his back arched, ready to bring all his strength into the killing blow.

Terrance let out a grunt of effort as he swung the blade.

TWENTY-THREE

Mary Renata was learning that some nightmares have no limits.

She lay on the marble dais—a vault for the dead—her arms firmly and painfully held against the hard surface by Bedlow's massive, powerful fists. She absently listened to Terrance's dark rhetoric, hardly able to concentrate on the words.

It was when he mentioned the Madonna—whoever or *what*ever She or It was—did Mary feel herself suddenly and inexplicably lifted out of her lethargy. It was as if the fog was burned from her mind in a blaze of understanding. And then fear.

Whatever power had been protecting her from fully comprehending her impending fate abruptly brought her back to total awareness. Her eyes locked on the shining blade poised above her throat.

Mary screamed in abject terror. Her voice wailed into the night with a banshee's shriek. Terrible images cascaded before her mind's eye. She saw the glistening steel slash down, biting into her soft flesh amid a geyser of dark blood. She saw the life fluid washing over the moonlit stone as her head rolled off the dais and into the crowd. She could see her headless corpse descrated and mutilated by a hundred tiny, jabbering creatures as they shredded the flesh from her bones.

She struggled and bucked, as much against the horrible visions as against Bedlow's powerful grasp. Fighting to hold her down, his hood slipped back, revealing his grinning death's head. His enormous teeth, flecked with spittle and gleaming in the silvery light, appeared razor sharp.

I can't die like this!

Mary watched the fat man suck in a deep breath as he bent backward, readying himself to drop the blade across her neck. For an eternity, the blade hovered there and then with grunt, Henry Terrance swung the curved steel of the scimitar.

All hell broke loose.

The blade arced down and was only scant inches from her throat when a flash of incandescent light split the night, sending the scimitar flying from his hand and into the crowd beyond. Spinning like a propeller blade, it decapitated three of the startled watchers before they could move.

A cry of anger and terror broke from the gathered crowd. Screams shattered the hush and silence. For a long moment, Mansfield's heirs stood stunned, shocked by the unexpected disruption, the sudden violence directed against their own. Then as one they cried out in bitter outrage and moved forward toward the vault.

Rathbone, unable to reconcile the need for the Renata woman's senseless death, had been ready to unleash a powerful energy blast at the fat man only to be beaten to the punch by some unseen and unknown force. The blast unnerved and confused him as much as it did the crowd.

Who else could wield such awesome power?

He might never know, he realized, making a decision. "Get away from here," he hissed in Agnes's ear as he moved.

Even as the blade was spinning away, Rathbone leaped onto the dais ready to destroy as many of the Bitch's followers as possible before he was overcome by the enraged mob.

This was not the time or place he would have chosen to make his stand. Yet he had told Agnes and Joshua that he had no plan and they would all have to improvise. It had to start somewhere. Here, he supposed, was as good a place as any.

Bedlow and Terrance were caught completely off guard. The fat man clutched his right hand in his left. The blast had jolted his arm, numbing it.

Agnes and Joshua were both confused by the swift turn of events. Joshua, pushed forward by the crowd, felt Agnes grab his arm and tug him away. They edged along the vault's face, completely ignored by the screaming, bellowing mob. When they reached its corner, they simply moved carefully and slowly to the back of the crowd, unchallenged and unnoticed. Within seconds they were free, moving into the sheltering darkness of the surrounding trees, crypts and tombstones.

Joshua was dazed. He had somehow thought their battle and confrontation would evolve naturally, like a well-fought military campaign.

"Now what?" he panted, as they stopped behind a crypt.

"I . . . I don't know for sure," Agnes answered, gulping air. "We've been separated. The one thing Tobias warned us against."

"Who saved the girl?" Joshua wondered.

Agnes shook her head. "I don't know. It wasn't Tobias."

Joshua thought for a second. "Could there be someone else here? An ally?"

"No. Tobias would have known."

"What can we do to help him now? Anything?"

Agnes reached beneath the robe and brought out her Ouija board. "Maybe." She dropped to her knees and rested the board on the long grass, motioning for Joshua to join her. He crouched opposite her.

"We might be able to link with an entity that can help us, maybe give us a plan," she said, producing the planchette from her shirt pocket.

With screams and cries of fury and dismay echoing in their ears, they began focusing on the planchette and board. Agnes closed her eyes and concentrated, blocking out the bedlam. Joshua could not bring himself to ignore the threat of the Madonna's horde which was so very close. But when his fingers touched the pointer, Agnes felt the electric shock as a powerful surge of energy flowed out of his body and into her own.

Bedlow, seething and raging, released his hold on Mary and jumped to his feet, ready to launch himself at Rathbone. Before he was able to move forward, the Druid lashed out with his foot, catching the gaunt man in the chest. Crying out in shock and indignation, Bedlow pitched backward off the vault and into the crowd.

As he sprawled onto the shocked group of followers, feeling their hands attempt to break his fall, Bedlow was consumed with a blinding fury. Rathbone, the meddlesome interloper, the enemy of the Madonna and all Her worshipers, was now threatening the work of a century. He had to be stopped. He had to be destroyed; eradicated and ground into Mansfield's dust.

Terrance, still holding his deadened arm, started to straighten, but was shoved from behind and went tumbling head first off the vault. His huge, bulky body plowed into the tightly packed mob, sending a score of people toppling like dominos, amid a barrage of curses and groans.

He, too, was filled with indignation, shock and not a little fear. The Madonna, yet to appear, would be wrathful and might just as easily unleash Her fury on him as on the treacherous Druid.

Rathbone kept his eyes on the crowd, constantly watching for the first of them to make a move. "Get up! Now! Hurry," he called to Mary.

Feeling dizzy and lightheaded, she struggled to stand. Her arms ached and tingled as circulation was restored. She was painfully aware of the raw scrapes and bruises covering her back and hips resulting from her struggle against Bedlow.

Mary had just staggered to the Druid's side when the mob surged forward. All around them, men and women, faces still shrouded by their black hoods, hands clawed and clawing, began scrambling onto the platform.

Rathbone, no plan in mind, began unleashing a series of energy bolts. They sparked against the marble, smashing the stone, and burst on fabric and flesh, setting the maddened attackers ablaze with eerie, sapphire flames.

Several of the would-be assailants, now writhing pillars of fire, jumped screaming and wailing into the mob. Flames from their blazing robes leaped and spewed over those watching in terror, igniting other heavy cloaks. In an instant, a score of shrieking, sobbing men and women rolled over the ground or ran into the night as the magic fire consumed and charred their flesh.

A woman, her robe discarded, ran naked and screaming among the tombstones as azure fire enveloped her body. Blinded by the druidic flames and her own horrible terror, she smashed headfirst into a crypt, her head cracking open like an over-ripe melon. She oozed down the stone while the magic fire continued to eat at her now dead flesh and bones until only the blackened outline of her body remained on the seared grass.

A hapless man, pleading for help, watched in terror as the magic fire turned his hands into torches before his wide, pain-maddened eyes. He clutched at a woman who was stumbling backward away from him. Grabbing her and encircling his arms around her body, he pounded his hands against the back of her robe. She, in turn screamed, pummeling him with her fists. With a whoosh, her robe blossomed into flame. As they fell to the ground, the man atop the cursing woman, she freed an arm and raked her nails across his face, gouging out an eye.

Their howls of pain faded as their bodies became a pyre of indigo flames.

A man, watching as his wife's body erupted in flames, stumbled over the gore-stained scimitar lying in the grass. In an attempt to fend off his shrieking, pleading wife, he picked up the heavy sword and swung it at her. The sharp blade cut through her neck and sent her blazing head tumbling through the air. Her body continued to struggle and shamble forward for another several feet before collapsing to the matted, burned grass.

Several of the energy bursts pierced the tiny, scurrying bodies of the Madonna's demons. They screamed with unholy wails as their leathery bodies flared like ancient parchment, instantly disintegrating in brillant flashes.

The stink of roasting flesh and burning hair filled the night air, mingling with the thick, noxious pallor of smoke hanging over the mob.

Joshua, taking his eyes off the planchette, glanced toward the hysterical mob. He could see darkly robed shapes scrambling atop the vault even as their brothers and sisters were seared and blasted by the constant barrage of electric blue bursts of raw energy. He shuddered as he watched first one and then another burst into flames.

He caught a fleeting glimpse of the white-clad woman standing behind Rathbone. They both were enveloped in an azure aura not unlike a giant bubble.

The Druid unleashed a steady onslaught of incendiary energy which stabbed into the crowd like vengeful lightning. Where he aimed, the magic-fire bloomed into death and destruction. Blue flames illuminated the area surrounding the vault in an eerie, cold light.

Joshua looked away. The scene was like something out of Dante's Hell and although the Druid's victims were evil, tainted by unbridled lusts and inhuman desires, their pain and suffering and torment were real and very terrible.

It sickened him.

The first wave driven back, the survivors stood at some distance watching in shock as their dying brothers and sisters writhed and screamed and pleaded. The unscathed offered neither aid nor help, having quickly learned that those touched by the Druid's hellish fire were beyond saving. The magic flames were like a horrible disease, spreading to any foolish enough to draw too near to those already stricken.

"We can make a run for it now!" Rathbone barked, clutching the woman's arm, pulling her to the edge of the vault. He let loose another burst to ward off a few of those bold enough to approach them. When four more robed figures burst into flames, the others fell back cursing and crying.

The Druid and Mary jumped to the ground and hurriedly began trotting away.

Agnes and Tobias let the planchette glide smoothly over the glossy surface of the Ouija board. He occasionally stole an anxious glance at the hysteria around the dais, but the old woman was entranced, seemingly oblivious to the choas. The power she was drawing from Tobias eliminated the necessity to watch the words being spelled out on the board. As the pointer moved swiftly from letter to letter, they were instantly translated into images and emotions in her mind.

After some time, Agnes lifted her hands from the pointer and ran them through her hair. Joshua could see her eyes glistening with tears and there was a sadness etching her face he had never seen before.

"What?" he asked anxiously, rubbing his own sweaty hands on his pants legs.

Agnes gave him a curious look. "I've learned a lot."

"What . . . who were you communicating with?"

Agnes glanced toward the oddly silent gathering spread around the dais. Her old eyes studied, without emotion, the still-burning forms lying on the ground.

"Someone long dead," she said, a note of despair in her voice.

Joshua said nothing.

"I've learned a great deal. Everything, I think. In fact, too much." She shook her head slowly, as if trying to clear away some dark, awful image. "I haven't time to explain it all, Josh."

She could not bring herself to tell Joshua the truth. It was a terrible reality and one she hoped she could spare him from learning.

"Right now we have to save that young man." She stood slowly.

"The caretaker? The man with the Renata woman?"

Agnes nodded. "He's alive. Follow me."

Before he could ask any further questions, she was quickly moving away.

"Aggie," he said, catching up with her. "Don't you want your board?"

"I don't need it now," she said over her shoulder, not breaking stride.

"Where are we going?"

"I'll show you soon enough."

They kept to the shadows, constantly watching for any of the Madonna's misshapen, demonic creatures. Still wearing their stolen black robes, they were unconcerned about being discovered by the Madonna's human followers.

"By now She has to know we're here," Agnes breathed as they moved into a pool of moonlight illuminating one of the stone mausoleums scattered throughout Mansfield.

"The Madonna?"

Agnes nodded. "We generated a lot of power with the board. She had to have detected it. I think the only reason She hasn't manifested herself yet, has something to do with Tobias. He's disrupted Her spectacle; taken Her by surprise. She'll make Herself known soon, which means we have very little time."

She stopped at the stained brass door of a crypt. Trying the handle, she muttered a curse when it refused to open.

"He's inside?" Joshua asked.

Agnes nodded. "You'll have to open this, Josh."

He moved beside her and grasped the door's heavy knob. It refused to turn. "It's locked, Aggie."

"You can open it, Josh," she said softly. "Concentrate."

He glanced at her, wondering if she had taken leave of her senses. How could he open this heavy, locked door with his bare hands?

"Just concentrate on it, Josh. Focus your energy on it," she urged.

Shaking his head, his left hand absently brushing his thick mustache, Joshua wrapped his right hand around the knob. He closed his eyes and twisted, trying to summon strength to his trembling muscles. Sweat broke out on his face and neck.

"Concentrate," Agnes whispered, her voice encouraging him to even greater effort.

Joshua placed his left hand over his right and continued to fight with the knob. Desperately he tried to focus his enormous, but untrained power on it.

For long seconds nothing happened and then an unexpected glare of pale blue energy danced over his clasped hands and the knob turned. The sudden flash startled Agnes and she stepped back in surprise.

The involuntary reaction saved her life.

The door exploded open and a leering, hideous shape leaped out. Slashing talons passed harmlessly through the air where Agnes had stood only a split second before. The door caught Joshua's left shoulder and he was knocked sprawling onto his back.

The creature, off balance, staggered on cloven hooves for several yards before righting itself. Snarling, it whirled to face the pair.

It was larger than most of the Madonna's demons, towering well over six feet. Its body was covered with matted, greasy hair which glistened in the moonlight. Long arms, powerful and simian, extended into massive clawed hands. Its legs were distinctly equine with powerful cannon bones below the bulbous hocks. Its head was round and large, with piercing cat's eyes, marked by twin nostril holes and a slash for a mouth which glistened with rows of long, sharp fangs.

"Josh?" Agnes cried, unable to take her eyes off the monster.

Ortega, stunned as much by his unexpected burst of power as by the blow, was struggling to his feet.

The monster moved quickly but warily, its luminescent eyes moving from Agnes to Joshua and back to Agnes.

"Wh . . . what do we do?" the woman asked.

"I don't know," Joshua answered, wishing he had a weapon. "Our robes may have it confused. It probably thinks we're part of the gathering."

Belying his hopes, the thing hissed at them, a dark, forked tongue flicking out of its grotesque mouth. It feigned a sudden rush at Joshua and then abruptly leaped at Agnes. Before she could move, it was on her, forcing her to the ground.

Only by blocking the thing with her arms did she avoid being killed instantly by those murderous talons. Holding it momentarily at bay, she screamed as the snapping jaws of needle-pointed teeth lunged at her throat. The thing's sudden move shook here hood back, exposing her marked face.

The creature cried out when it beheld the runes traced over her skin.

"Aggie!" Joshua yelled, dashing toward the pair. Terrified for her and unconcerned for his own safety, he grabbed one of the monster's arms and tried to pull it off her.

The creature was already moving away, hissing and howling as if the markings caused it real pain. Joshua's action gave it a reason to abandon the woman. It bounded to it feet, tossing Joshua aside effortlessly.

The old man staggered back. Before he could catch his balance, the thing was upon him. Snapping and snarling, it caught his arms in its powerful hands and forced him to his knees. He cried out has he felt his muscles and tendons explode with pain. His face was washed with the thing's fetic breath. The serpentine tongue flicked out, touched his face beneath the cowl and was instantly withdrawn. Again the beast howled and its jaws snapped.

Another second and Joshua feared he would be dead, unaware of the monster's revulsion to the ancient Druidic markings.

Agnes, sitting on the ground, watched in horror as they struggled. She knew the creature was suffering from exposure to the arcane and archaic designs, yet still it held Joshua's arms pressed back, trying break her friend's spine.

In one brief millisecond, Joshua decided he would not die like this. He would *not* let this filthy, Hell-spawned thing claim him.

There was a burst of azure fire. It consumed both Joshua and his hideous assailant.

A scream tore from Agnes's throat again as she watched her friend and the Madonna's monster vanish in a ball of raw energy. Her own cry was drowned out by a louder, more piercing cry of mortal pain and terror.

The blue fire abruptly dissipated.

Joshua sat crouched on the ground alone, untouched by the magic flames.

"Josh?"

"I'm okay," he muttered, breathing hard.

Agnes pushed herself up and rushed to him, throwing her arms around his neck. "I . . . I thought you . . . you were dead," she cried, her voice thick with concern.

He held her for an instant and then gently pushed her away. "I'm fine."

"What happened?"

"I wish I knew. I just . . . just felt a sudden rush of power and then . . . it was over." He shook his head, obviously as mystified as she. "We'll figure it out later. Let's find that young man. Right now." He climbed stiffly to his feet.

"Yes," she nodded, moving toward the crypt.

They hesitated at the door for only a second and then stepped into the dark, musty interior. It was faintly illuminated by the moonlight filtering through a grimy, small window opposite the door. The noxious animal stink in the room caused both of them to gasp and cough.

"Smells like a lair," Joshua commented.

"There," Agnes said, pointing to one of the two vaults. "He's in there."

Joshua, embued with a new confidence, stepped purposefully to the marble tomb, placed his hands on the edge of the lid and shoved. Blue sparks flared from his fingers and the massive cover slid away to bang against the crypt's wall.

"He's here," Joshua said, peering down into the vault. Vince Cassidy lay still and uncomfortably curled on a bed of sharp, jagged bones. A grinning skull rested near his head.

"Is he alive?"

Ortega placed his fingers on the man's neck and felt the strong pulse. "Yes."

"Thank God."

Vince stirred. Peering closely, Joshua could see the man's eyelids fluttering. There was a low groan followed by a raspy cough.

Joshua bent over and placed his mouth close to the other man's ear, wrinkling his nose at the smell of decay, rot and vomit. "Can you hear me?"

Agnes stepped to the head of the vault and looked inside. "He looks terrible." She studied the grime encrusted face, the swollen eye, the tiny cuts stitching his cheeks, and the dark splotches surrounding ragged tears in his shirt.

She jerked back when Vince's eye suddenly flew open and a hoarse, startled cry broke from his dry, chapped lips. He recoiled in terror from their strangely tattooed faces and black robes.

"It's okay," Joshua said hurriedly. "We're friends."

Vince blinked several times trying to focus his eye. In addition to his other aches and pains, his head was throbbing.

"Who . . . are you?" he croaked.

"Friends. Can you move?"

"Your . . . your faces . . ."

"Never mind that," Agnes soothed. "Can you move?"

"I . . . I don't know. My arm. It's broken." He gestured feebly with his right hand toward his oddly crooked left arm.

"We've got to get you out of here," Agnes said anxiously, looking toward the door. As if to punctuate her remark, a slight tremor ran beneath the mausoleum, loosening tiny puffs of dust from the walls and window ledges.

Vince tried to rise, yelping as yet another agonizing explosion of pain rocketed up his arm. He coughed and wretched, dry heaving. His stomach, already emptied of what little it had contained, ached as it spasmed. His rib muscles were knotted and stiff.

Joshua and Agnes moved quickly to help him. Careful not to touch his arm, they eased him out. He bit off a scream as the splintered ends of his fractured forearm ground together. He leaned against the vault, eyes shut, teeth clenched. Beads of sweat furrowed paths through the dirt and dried blood streaking his pale, haggard face.

Agnes winced when she saw the dark blood matting his hair and streaking his cheeks.

"He's not going to have it easy getting out of here with that arm," Joshua whispered.

"Can we bind it? Immobilize it, maybe?" Agnes wondered.

"Maybe . . ."

Joshua was cut off as another tremor shook the crypt. Its old stones creaked and groaned as they shifted ever so slightly against the crumbling mortar.

From within the vault came the clicking and the all-too-familiar jibberish. All three whirled to stare into the narrow, dark tomb Vince had just exited. The skull within rolled and tottered, its broken yellow teeth snapping together as red pinpoints of fire burned in the black eye sockets.

"Jesus!" Joshua, jumping back. "Let's get the hell out of here." He took Vince's good arm and led him to the door. He paused, scanning the surrounding area, and, satisfied no one—*no thing*—was watching, motioned the others to follow.

Once outside in the brilliant moonlight, Agnes bent and pulled up the hem of her robe. With a few quick, hard tugs, she ripped a seam. "Do you have a pocketknife?" she asked.

Joshua dug in his pocket. "No."

"I have," Vince wheezed. He slipped his right hand into his pants pocket, fished out a small knife and handed it to Agnes. She took it and quickly cut a long gash several inches from the split seam and then tore the strip free.

"This should do," she said, handing the knife back to Vince.

It took several more long minutes to get the broken arm strapped against Vince's chest. It had been excruiating to bend it, but once it was firmly in place, the pain subsided to a gnawing throb.

"We've got to find Rathbone and the woman," Joshua said as they began moving back into the shadow of the trees.

"What woman?" Vince asked anxiously, grabbing Joshua's arm with his right hand.

Joshua stopped and looked at him. The designs on his

skin, bathed in the icy silver light, stood out in sharp relief. He sighed. "Your girlfriend. Mary."

Something dark moved behind Vince's eyes. "She's here? In Mansfield? But she . . . she left . . . she . . ." His hold on Joshua's arm tightened, his voice grew low and deadly. "Where is she? What has that fucking Bedlow done to her?"

Joshua met the younger man's gaze and shook his head. "We don't know where she is right now. The last we saw of her, she was with a friend of ours. A very powerful friend."

Vince let go of his arm and began staggering forward. His cramped legs threatened to buckle as the circulation returned. He was stiff and sore and every effort sent a thousand tiny needles of pain shooting through his body. His voice was desperate. "We've got to find her! This place," he motioned with his good arm, "it seduced us. But I think it wanted her."

"It does," Agnes said flatly, taking Vince's arm, supporting him.

Both men looked at her expectantly.

"Is that what you learned from the spirit you contacted?" Joshua asked. He saw Vince give them a curious, puzzled look.

"Yes. The man in white," Agnes told him matter-of-factly. She turned to Vince. "I believe you've met him. He saved you in there, didn't he? He told you you'd be needed here."

Vince studied the old woman and then nodded mutely. Fleetingly, he wondered if he could trust these two and decided he had no other choice.

"Look," Joshua broke in impatiently. "We don't have time to discuss all the ins and outs of this thing right now. We've got to get out of here . . ."

He bit off his words as something darted at him from out of the darkness behind one of the mausoleums. He whirled just in time to fend off a small, sharp trident thrust at his face by a small, red-eyed creature. As the thing dashed past, Joshua kicked out with his foot, catching the little monster squarely in the face. It screamed as it rolled backward, the trident flying into the air.

"What is that?" Vince asked, staring at the thing on the ground.

Joshua moved quickly. The monster was trying to rise just as he sent his foot smashing into its head again. The leathery skin burst, and dark, vile gore splattered over the grass and up the front of Joshua's robe.

He turned quickly away from the twitching thing, swallowing the bile that burned the back of his throat.

"Let's get out of here," he called to Agnes and Vince.

Another tremor, more intense this time, shook the cemetery. It nearly knocked all three of them to the ground as it rolled and vibrated beneath them. Somewhere in the distance there were cries and screams and the sound of oddly muffled explosions.

They walked quickly, avoiding the moon-bright pools dabbling Mansfield's expanse and headed toward the northern edge of the graveyard. Several times they were forced to detour around clusters of black-robed worshipers. In every case, the knots of men and women were talking in low, excited tones.

They had reached the crypt near which Rathbone had left the three mesmerized worshipers who had been stripped of their cloaks. Joshua motioned to Agnes and Vince to crouch behind a crypt.

"From here on it's going to be touch and go," he whispered. "The place is crawling with black robes and those damned little monsters."

"Can you see Mary?" Vince asked hopefully.

"No."

The younger man hissed. "We can't leave without finding her."

Joshua turned and glared at Vince. "Listen, I don't

want to leave either her or Rathbone, but we don't have a clue as to where they are right now."

"Fine," Vince snapped back. "You two take off, but I'm not leaving until I find her."

Agnes laid her hand gently on his arm. "We're not unsympathetic. We just don't know where to look. There's nothing we'd like better than to find them. . . ." She stopped as a piercing scream split the night.

They all turned and stared into the tree shadows near where they hid. At first they could see nothing. Then, looming above the cemetery, a black blotch against the moonlit sky, they saw the unmistakable form of the Madonna. She hung in the still air, Her twin eyes glistened beneath the peaked hood, the only light in Her dark countenance.

Again the scream echoed in the darkness.

Something dropped from the folds of Her robe, tumbling to the hard ground. It lurched out of the shadows and into the moonlight. Agnes gasped and turned away. Joshua felt his stomach do a slow turn. Vince stared in sick fascination.

The thing had been a woman once, but now was a mass of bloody tissue, which shimmered wetly in the pale light. Her skin had been ripped away, exposing the musculature and in some areas, gleaming bone. Her lidless eyes were filled with stark terror and pain and utter horror. She collided with tombstones and trees, careening wildly, heedlessly; driven by madness and anguish.

"The reward for failure," Joshua mumbled.

"It's horrible," Agnes wept, unable to look at the desecrated human. It was as if the Madonna was mocking life with Her dark and twisted parody of birthing.

"That's what Rathbone said last night, Aggie. That's the kind of promise that filthy Bitch offers." Joshua turned away from the stricken woman.

"Mary," Vince breathed. "Where *is* she?" He forced

from his mind the terrible visions of her body rent and torn.

There was a whoosh above them and they were suddenly enveloped by the Madonna's evil, black shadow. Her dark form hovered over them for a long moment and then slowly settled to the earth. Her swirling eyes bore into them, transfixing them with an icy, demonic stare.

A long black arm materialized from the enfolding cloak and made a quick gesture. From behind headstones and crypts, scores of Her twisted, deformed minions appeared, rushing at the trio. They carried tridents and tiny swords and sported cruel, hooked claws and flashing teeth. In an instant, they had surrounded the three frightened, trapped humans.

A second gesture of the Bitch's hand sent Her horde of demons and monsters closer to Agnes, Joshua and Vince. Jabbering nonsense while prodding them with their tridents and swords, they forced the three to move away from the mausoleum and into the bright moonlight.

''Are they going to kill us?'' Vince whispered, receiving a painful stab in the back for his words.

''Eventually,'' Joshua replied, sounding sad and dejected.

At that moment they heard yet another cry and looked across the cemetery. Mary Renata, here legs pumping frantically, ran out of the concealing shadows of the trees. Barely a step behind, clawed hands grasping for her, dashed a huge, deformed thing, its gaping mouth split with a wide, evil grin.

''Mary!'' Vince screamed, just as her pursuer caught her and knocked her sprawling to the ground. As it shifted around, reaching for her, Vince and his companions could see the monster's engorged, abnormally large gentials. Rolling desperately onto her back, she lashed out with her bare feet, trying to ward off the creature. Effortlessly it grabbed both her legs in one of its massive, taloned hands and then in a quick, frightening move, fell upon her.

Vince, tears flooding his eyes and a bellow of outrage

and fury ripping from his throat, tried to break away from the creatures surrounding him. He lunged forward and then abruptly dropped to his knees as a barbed trident stabbed into his back. The sharp points tore his skin, inflicting intense, searing pain.

Agnes choked back a sob and Joshua cursed softly as they watched Mary, thrashing and kicking, pinned beneath the monster.

As she continued to scream, it spread her legs and arched above her.

The crowd surged and Mary and the demon were blocked from their view.

TWENTY-FOUR

Mary stumbled behind her mysterious rescuer, her hand firmly grasped in his. Running barefoot, it was difficult for her to keep up. More than once, she gritted her teeth and stifled a cry as sharp stones tore and bruised her flesh.

She was operating purely from instinct. Once the cloud of indifference had been lifted from her mind and she became fully cognizant of her ordeal, the shock had numbed her. Her mind was reeling with a kaleidoscope of disjointed images and half-remembered events.

Where is Vince?

Dead?

Dashing among the tombs and headstones, Mary felt her stomach lurch at the thought.

God, I love—loved—him.

Tears blurred her vision. Her heart felt heavy and for a fleeting second she wondered if surviving this ordeal without Vince was worth the effort.

Run! Just run!

Rathbone led her through the gauntlet of mumbling, cursing black robes. Some simply backed away from them as they dashed for safety, while others, terrified of his awesome powers, fled into the darkness. After several moments, the Druid suddenly turned, tugging at her to follow him into a dense stand of trees. He stopped and leaned against a looming elm.

"Are you alright?" he panted, sucking in deep gulps of air.

Staring at him, she nodded. "Who . . . who are you?"

"A friend. Rathbone." He began pulling off the confining black robe. There was no reason for it now. As camouflage it had served his purpose. It would deceive neither the Madonna nor her human and inhuman host any further. Mary helped him lift it over his head and shoulders.

"Do you know what is . . . is happening?" she asked hesitantly, still uncertain what to make of Rathbone. His awesome display of power, while saving her life, had frightened her. She wondered if she had simply been rescued by this strange, bearded old man only to become his pawn in whatever dark game was unfolding in this cursed cemetery.

Rathbone met her gaze. "I do. I haven't time to explain it all to you, but know this: *You* are the key. That's clear to me now." He left unspoken his concern for Mary's unknown benefactor who had saved her from Terrance. Who else, besides himself, had command of such awesome power?

It was a deeply disturbing puzzle.

"The key to what?" the girl asked hesitantly, obviously afraid of the answer.

"Something very dark and very evil," he responded cryptically.

"Damnit!" she snapped. "Don't play games with me. You don't know what I've been through. You . . . you can't imagine what has happened here. To me. To . . . Vince."

The Druid sighed and let her vent her anger and frustration. When she finished, he scanned the surrounding area, sure he had seen movement not far from where they stood.

"Yes, Mary," he breathed. "I can understand. Believe me, I know what you've experienced."

A sob choked her and tears filled her eyes. Clutching herself, she slipped to the ground. "Then . . . tell me. Tell me what's happening."

Rathbone retrieved the black cloak from the ground and slipped it around the trembling woman's shoulders. He squatted in front of her and spoke in calm, soothing tones.

"You're the unknowing heir to a horrible legacy. It's very complex, very involved. But, in short, you're the direct descendant of a German nun who was killed as a witch."

Mary's eyes grew large and frightened. "A nun?"

"Yes. Maria Renata. She had an illegitimate child which was given her name and was raised by her family and not in the convent. She kept that secret for most of her life.

"When she was an old woman, she was accused of witchcraft, of consorting with the Devil. In the records of her trial, there is no mention of the child. I suspect someone outside her family knew, and decided it must be a witch-child. Perhaps the spawn of the Beast."

Rathbone paused, allowing the girl to absorb the enormity of his words.

"*Was* . . . the child . . . the Devil's?" she asked meekly, feeling foolish at verbalizing such a question.

Rathbone averted his eyes. "Maybe. I don't know."

"You mean . . . ?"

He looked at Mary. She was pale and drawn, her fine features looking much older in the faint light. "I don't know, Mary. These fools here tonight believe it. It's a reality to them. And truth often has little to do with the perception of reality."

Rathbone jerked his head around and raised his right arm. Mary winced as a blaze of blue shot from his outstretched hand. There was a cry as the magic-fire ignited one of the

Madonna's creatures. It danced crazily for an instant, blue flames charring its leathery flesh, and then crumpled in a smoldering heap.

"Come on," he ordered, getting quickly to his feet. "We have to find the others."

"What others?" she asked, standing, her eyes riveted to the pile of smoking flesh and bone only yards away.

"Other friends." He took her hand and led her out of the stand of trees and into the bright moonlight. They were in the midst of a sea of crypts and tombs and headstones. Rathbone knew that an army could be concealed behind the stonework, waiting and watching.

The ground near them suddenly quaked, pitching them forward. They caught hold of a headstone, bracing themselves against the heaving, undulating earth beneath their feet.

"Damn," Rathbone snarled. "It's beginning."

"What?" Mary cried.

Near them a tall, weather-stained globe atop a tombstone tottered back and forth and then tumbled over. The ground began erupting over the grave the stone had marked. Dirt spewed and gushed into the sky and then, with a explosion, the earth erupted and the casket it had covered burst from the ground.

Mary gasped, even as the Druid took her arm and pulled her away from the disengorged coffin, its stained and rotting lid creaking open.

Another rumble shook the ground and two more graves vomited dirt and loam into the air. And two more caskets were heaved out of the earth.

Rathbone and Mary dodged among the tombstones. Dirt and dust and torn grass filled the air. Behind them they could hear ghastly shrieks and cries, gibberish wails of despair and horror.

Mary glanced back. She could see ragged, skeletal forms rising from the defiled, corrupted vaults. They shambled and staggered and howled, clawing at the sky, screaming at the cold moon.

More graves exploded around them. They were constantly forced to turn from one route to another. The night was alive with unintelligable wails and horrible cries.

"Why don't you destroy them?" Mary yelled over the rumble and muffled explosions.

"I can't waste the energy," Rathbone called back, not breaking his stride.

Again the earth shuddered. Directly in their path a score of graves erupted, their coffins crashing out of the holes. More of the long-dead abominations, reanimated by the Madonna's terrible powers, staggered forth.

"They're trying to surround us!" Rathbone yelled, turning sharply. His ancient heart was thundering in his chest and he was again gasping for air. He could feel his body, already fatigued from the previous confrontations, betraying him. His legs ached and his muscles cramped. He could not go much further. The healing his body had had to do after last night's battle had taken a greater toll on his resources than he had realized.

The heavy iron door of a mausoleum near them flew open and two grotesque things tottered out. They turned toward the running pair as Rathbone raised his arm and unleashed a destructive bolt of energy. The things exploded amid screeches of betrayal and terror.

"Inside," Rathbone cried, rushing past the heap of bones, till flickering and smoking with the magic-fire. He fairly dragged Mary into the empty mausoleum. Desperately, he pulled the iron door shut with a bang. Its lock was smashed.

The Druid slumped against the wall.

The interior was dark, but a shaft of moonlight illuminated the shattered marble littering the floor and the broken coffins inside the two vaults. A heavy, sick smell filled the air.

Mary glanced at the ruin for a second and then studied Rathbone. "Are you okay?"

He panted, eyes closed. "I will be," he finally said.

"We're trapped here," she whispered, looking at the door.

"We can defend this place until I get back some of my strength."

Outside the muffled explosions continued. The mausoleum occasionally quaked and groaned as fresh tremors shook Mansfield.

Something scraped at the door; hard nails dragging over the rusty metal. Mary retreated, a chill running through her body, as black, skeletal fingers were thrust through the door's barred window and the door was wrenched open.

Rathbone, still leaning against the stone wall, sent a feeble burst of energy smashing into the red-eyed monstrosity trying to enter the tomb. The blast all but disintegrated the thing in a shower of azure flames and flying bones.

The Druid slumped, sliding down the wall to sit on the rough stone floor. His eyes were closed and his breathing ragged.

"Don't die on me!" Mary cried.

She knelt beside the man and felt his pulse. It was rapid and strong. She touched his face, jerking her hand away as she felt his abnormally hot flesh.

She shook him gently. "Hey, are you awake."

The old man only groaned, his eyes remaining closed.

There was a gibberish cry from just outside, followed by a second and third. Then a cacophony of howling, indistinguishable jabbering and wailing echoed through the tomb. The door was again yanked open.

Mary leaped to her feet as another of the babbling things stepped into the room. She could see a score of them gathered behind the first. Their jaws snapped and their ancient, brittle teeth clicked.

"Wake up," she sobbed at Rathbone. "Oh God, wake up!"

The Druid didn't move. His breathing seemed to have stopped. Mary was sure he had died.

Backing away, remembering the incredible strength and agility of the three monsters in the dungeon, she picked up a piece of broken stone and threw it at the advancing creature. It smashed into the leering skull, breaking open a gaping hole above black pit of its left eye socket.

Still the thing moved toward her.

Stepping back, she gathered more chunks of the broken marble and hurled them at the creature. Although she hit it repeatedly, shattering another piece of its skull and splintering fragile ribs, it continued to shamble toward her. More of the things were now crowding into the small, cramped room.

Just as Mary's back pressed against the wall, two of the creatures sprang. Their hands clutched her arms as their long ragged fingernails dug into her soft flesh.

For a second they peered at her with their burning, red eyes and then they dragged her, screaming and kicking, out into the night.

All around the mausoleum, graves had been blown open, leaving a jumble of smashed and destroyed caskets. Clouds of dirt and dust billowed in the night sky, casting a haze across the staring face of the moon. Hundreds of the bizarre, reanimated things wandered closer, converging on the crypt.

She was roughly lifted from the ground, four of the things holding her arms and legs, carrying her away into the night. The others followed, forming a grotesque, ragged parody of a parade.

Mary wept. All thoughts of the old man swept from her numbed, terror-ridden mind.

After some minutes, she was released, dropped unceremoniously to the soft ground. Sprawling in the grass, surrounded by the skeletal creatures, she looked up and into the face a huge, fearsome demon.

It smiled at her, exposing sharp, gleeming fangs. Its lizard eyes flashed with dark menace as it reached for her. She scrambled back. The skeletal things moved away, allowing the demon to pursue her unaided.

It laughed at her.

She gasped when she saw its naked loins. Its unnaturally large phallus, swollen and engorged with blood, jutted from between its powerful legs.

Mary jumped to her feet and backed away. The demon continued to laugh as it stalked her. She whirled and ran through the leering crowd of skeletons. They let her pass unhampered.

As she dashed madly around trees and bushes and monuments, she could hear the demon's feet pounding against the ground behind her, its laughter filling her mind.

Mary burst out of the shadows and into the moonlight at the northern edge of the cemetery, not far from the cottage. Black robed women and men and scores of smaller creatures milled about, parting as she ran past them. The demon loped behind her, roaring and bellowing with racuous laughter.

Suddenly, she was caught in the thing's powerful hands and knocked to the ground. The demon, impatient now, grabbed both her wrists in one massive hand and spread her kicking legs with the other.

It loomed above her, its penis posied to stab into her body.

She screamed as it fell upon her . . .

Henry Terrance was stunned. After the debacle during the blood rites, he crouched near the base of the vault which had served as the dais, not moving until the Druid and the girl had raced into the night. Ignoring the smoldering remains of Rathbone's victims and paying little attention to the scattered cries of anguish and suffering, he hurried around the vault looking for Bedlow.

Terrance was afraid.

He now feared the blood rite would never happen; he feared for Mansfield's legacy; and most of all he feared the wrath of the Madonna. If the Renata woman's blood was not spilled on Mansfield's "sacred" ground, the Rising would turn into a terrible mockery of all he and the others had worked toward their entire lives.

He was also terrified to contemplate his own fate should he and Bedlow not complete the rite. If the Madonna should turn on him, unleash Her dark powers at his fleshy, fat body, he would learn the full measure of eternal torment.

Bedlow was standing, pale and gaunt in the moonlight, at the base of a spreading elm. His face was a mask of controlled fury and a bitter fire flared in his dark eyes.

"How'd he get in here, Henry?" Bedlow snarled as the fat man approached. "How the fuck did that son of a bitch get in here?"

"I . . . I don't know, Oscar. I . . ."

"You!" Bedlow cried, cuffing Terrance's fat cheek with the back of his hand. "You opened the gates. You were responsible! You let him in! You blew it, Henry!"

Terrance, staggered by the blow, stepped back, out of Bedlow's reach. "That's not true. No one got by me . . ."

"Save it, you fat toad! Tell it to Her!" Bedlow gestured over his shoulder. Terrance looked beyond his tall, gaunt companion, his mouth falling open when he saw the looming black shadow.

"Oscar," the fat man choked, desperation edging his voice. "You can't blame me for Rathbone. You're just as responsible . . ."

The shadow glided toward the pair. The dappled moonlight glinted on the two tusked fangs curving from the Madonna's mouth. The swirling pools of crimson and orange bore into him. Her clawed hands were extended, as if about to clutch Terrance's flabby throat.

"Henry," Bedlow hissed. "Find the girl! Get her back here." The ground shook. "Do you feel that? Can you hear those explosions. The Rising has started, you fool! Already our ancestors are learning of *your* betrayal! Spill Renata's blood before we lose everything!"

The Madonna ascended to hover above the two men. The vortex of Her eyes continued to transfix Terrance, holding him in an icy, merciless grip and pierced him with a cold, unforgiving stare. When She leveled a taloned, hooked finger at him, he knew fear.

"Find the woman, Terrance," Bedlow sneered, his voice low and menacing. "Find her and get her back here or we'll both pay the price."

The fat man blinked and turned away from the Madonna's hypnotic gaze and glared at Bedlow. He started to say something and, thinking better of it, whirled and ran away. He was frantic to find Mary Renata; frantic to save his own life.

"I'm going to kill Bedlow with my own hands," he promised himself. "The bastard's trying to use me as a scapegoat." His hatred and anger spurred him on. He rushed past clusters of black robed figures standing in silent, shocked fear. He shoved a tiny, hideous demon aside, sending it tumbling in the grass. It screamed at him, flashing its fangs, but made no move to attack.

In his single-mindedness and his terror, Terrance barely noticed the creature.

He had to find the woman.

Rathbone regained consciousness slowly, feeling like he was swimming up from the bottom of some black pool. His head ached and his mouth was as dry as cotton. While he could feel some regeneration of his powers, there was still a lingering languor in his body.

His first thoughts were of the girl.

Where was she?

Those monstrosities had carried her away. Certainly

they would kill her if they hadn't already. That was the one thing he could not allow to happen.

Slowly, wearily he got to his feet, wondering why he had not been slain. Perhaps it was fortunate they had been attacked by the resurrected creatures and not the Madonna's demons. The undead were single-minded and slow witted and probably not psychically connected to the Bitch as was Her demon horde. The newly-raised wanted Mary. Rathbone assumed he had merely been looked upon as a stumbling block. Once he was out of their way, they had lost interest in him.

Sucking in gulps of air, the Druid stepped outside. He had to find Mary. Should she be killed in this accursed place, that Black Bitch would win. The Rising would commence as it had been originally planned.

He could not allow it. He would not allow it.

Rathbone set off in search of the girl, praying he could summon enough power to affect her rescue.

Joshua and Agnes, their faces still concealed under the folds of the voluminous hoods, watched in horror as the demon pounced on Mary Renata. Partially pinned beneath its massive weight, the woman screamed and struggled, lashing out with her fists, repeatedly striking the monster's head. The blows were useless, she was no match for the demon. Inexerably it bore down on her.

"Jesus Christ," Joshua yelled frantically. "It's going to *rape* her." He started to move forward, but was forced back by a dozen of the hellish denizen, threatening him with their tridents and flashing swords.

Vince was slumped forward on the ground supporting himself on his right arm, his forehead resting on the matted grass. Three fresh spots of blood stained the back of his filthy, ragged shirt. Mary's terrified screams were fading in his mind, becoming distant, almost indistinct, as fresh spasms of pain tore through his broken arm and an agonizing paroxysm knotted his pierced, ripped muscles. His head thundered.

Several of the small, leathery demons prodded at Joshua, forcing him back. He cursed as the tip of one of the small swords bit into his left thigh.

"Bastards!" he spat, dropping to his knee, his hand clutching the wound.

Mary Renata was still screaming and fighting. The demon was spreading her legs. His smaller brethren and dozens of black robed humans were gathering around them, urging the monster on. The humans were frenzied. They wanted Mary dead, her blood spilled to complete the ritual.

"My God!" Agnes screamed. "Stop that . . . thing! My God, don't let him have her!" Frantic, she was terrified for Mary. She had learned the awful truth from the spirit and was now witnessing its dark reality.

Joshua ripped off his hood, exposing the arcane runes covering his face. Instantly, as if stunned by one of Rathbone's energy blasts, the knot of demons around him sprang back, crying out in terror. Their fierce, glowing eyes flashed and several of them hissed and spat like cornered cats.

Agnes too, pulled back her hood to reveal the Druid's marks. When she turned to the things surrounding her, they edged away in revulsion. They bared their teeth and thrust at her with their weapons, but it was all a half-hearted show. They knew their swords and tridents were not talismans against the Druidic runes.

Joshua stooped, hooking a hand under Vince's arm. The younger man groaned, mumbling inaudibly.

"Get up, boy!" Joshua roared. "You've got to get up!"

From where Agnes stood, her tormentors at bay, she could see the terrible struggle continuing between Mary and the demon. The young woman seemed to have now lost her battle, her screams had turned to pathetic, wimpering sobs. The demon was arched between her spread legs, holding her arms pinned to the ground. He was laughing hysterically in her face, his fanged mouth opened wide, his dark tongue flicking in and out like the head of a striking serpent.

The stricken onlookers' view was suddenly blocked as a seething mass of people crowded around the unholy couple.

Mary's tortured scream echoed in the night, silencing the crowd.

And then a blinding stream of light split the night. The shaft of cobalt blue energy exploded into the mob, so intense and brilliant that Joshua and Agnes had to turn away from it. Flames of magic-fire erupted amid the now screaming watchers. A second shot from the darkness burst against the demon, catapulting him off the woman. He tumbled and rolled, slamming hard against a headstone.

Screeching and bellowing, the demon staggered to its feet. Its head was seared and its features burned, virtually obliterated. Curls of smoke, rising from its scorched flesh, drifted into the moonlight.

The humans gathered around the demon and the woman scattered, shouting and yelling. The small cowardly creatures turned in fear, dashing to find shelter behind headstones and crypts.

The burned demon whipped its head from side to side trying to find its attacker in the shadows. He slapped madly at the burns, the resulting pain enraging him further. With a scream, he lurched toward Mary, still lying stunned and semiconscious on the ground. As he neared her, a second energy bolt lanced through the moon-brilliant night, this time bursting on his naked abdomen. The demon tottered and then keeled over, its torso blasted from its legs.

His death cry echoed over the cemetery.

With the second blast, the monsters surrounding Joshua, Agnes and Vince squealed and ran for cover. They cowered behind tombstones and dashed from sight around trees and bushes.

"Now," Joshua shouted. Agnes rushed to help him get Vince to his feet and the three stumbled toward Mary. As they neared her, Rathbone stepped out of shadows. He appeared drained, disoriented, his movements faltering and unsteady. Still, he moved toward the prone woman.

"Tobias," Agnes called. "Thank God."

The Druid said nothing. His face was blank and slack-jawed.

Vince, his senses regained, cried out as they reached Mary. He knelt and lifted her head in his good arm.

He looked into her terror-filled eyes and choked back a sob. "Oh, Mary, what have they done to you?"

"Save it," Joshua snapped. "We've got to get out of here!" He constantly glanced over his shoulder, scanning the area. Red eyes peered from behind markers and black-robed humans flitted around trees and shrubs. None made a move toward the five fugitives.

"Where *is* She?" the Druid cried, the dullness in his face suddenly washed away, replaced by an intense, dark anger. "Where the hell is that Black Bitch?"

"Tobias," Agnes said. "We've got to get out of here!"

Rathbone looked at her. "No. It's not finished."

"We can't keep fighting," she snapped. "There's too many of them. They want *her*!" She pointed at Mary. "If we get her out of here, they lose!"

"The only losers will be these fools who've been worshipping Her. She'll win! She always wins!"

"Rathbone," Joshua joined in, angry and frustrated. "We've done all we can. Aggie's right. We have to leave."

The Druid started to say something when he was unexpectedly slammed from behind by a hard blow which knocked him forward. He stumbled, barely avoided stepping on Mary, and fell to the ground.

The others gasped in surprise as Henry Terrance, his fat face streaked with sweat, his eyes wild, reached down and grabbed Mary's arm. While they argued, he had rushed from the shadows.

Vince made a move for the fat man, but Terrance lashed out with his foot and caught Vince's injured arm. Vince fell again and rolled back howling.

With amazing speed and agility for one his size, the fat man yanked Mary to her feet and began dragging her toward the trees. He kept the woman between himself and the others.

Rathbone, still on the ground, turned and raised his hand, ready to unleash a bolt of his awesome energy. He stopped. There was no way to hit Terrance without hitting the woman as well.

Mary staggered behind Terrance, the tattered white gown flapping about her bruised body. She was barely able to keep her balance and her bare feet were now scraped and bloody. Already out of breath and still dazed from her narrow escape, she was having difficulty comprehending the chaos whirling around her.

They plunged helter skelter into the dark shadows of the trees. Terrance was wheezing with effort, but kept his pace, dodging around the tombstones and crypts, leading Mary back to where Bedlow and the others waited.

Stop running, Mary.

The soft, familiar voice filled her head. The Presence. It was back with her.

Stop, Mary.

They were dashing out of the trees now, Terrance's grip on her arm like iron. She bucked at him, but he hardly seemed to notice.

Behind her, Mary was just conscious of a fresh outbreak of terrible screams and cries. They merged in the night with the constant explosive bursts of graves still spewing out the reanimated bones.

"I've got her!" the fat man screamed, as they broke into the moonlight. "I've got her, Oscar."

Stop running, Mary.

Mary dropped to the ground. She was dragged for several feet as Terrance continued to lumber toward Bedlow. Her dead weight finally brought him roaring to a stop.

"Get up you bitch! Get up!" His voice was panicked, frightened.

He started to tug at her arm, trying to yank her up, when he was suddenly and violently thrown backward. His feet came out from under him and he landed hard on his broad back. Air whooshed from his lungs and his grip on Mary's arm was broken.

Now you can run, Mary.

Confused, she sat for an instant staring at Terrance who flopped on his back like a turtle being tortured by cruel children. The sound of dozens of running feet pounding toward her forced her to move. Leaping to her feet, she turned and dashed back toward Vince and the others.

There was a collective cry of anger and rage as a mob of black robes pursued her. Their cries were frenzied, filled with hate and bloodlust. They screamed and cursed as they darted between trees and around tombstones, trying to surround her once again.

Mary knew if they caught her, she would be dead in seconds.

Reemerging from the trees, she let out a low, heartrenching moan. A score of humans and an equal number of the terrible little demons blocked her path. She could see Rathbone and Vince but there was no way through the surging mass of her human and inhuman tormentors. She could see the old woman on her knees, bent over Joshua Ortega's prone, unmoving body.

Several of the Madonna's minions were scattered over the ground, their robes and bodies flickering with azure flames. A smokey pall hung over the moonlit clearing and a noxious stench filled the air.

There had obviously been another attack after Terrance dragged her away.

Mary could hear her pursuers closing from behind, as the mob in front of her advanced.

"Help!" Mary cried, running along the edge of the trees. "For God's sake help me!"

Rathbone, drained and pale, his tangled, dirty mane of hair flying around his head like a halo, lifted his arm and unleashed yet another salvo of magic fire. The blue bolts were weak. When they struck their targets, they inflicted little damage and only sent their victims rolling in the grass, crying out in pain. Still, it was enough to clear a path through the horde and allow Mary the avenue she needed to make her escape.

The mob behind her broke through the trees as she sprinted past groaning humans and wailing monsters. Reaching the other four, she dropped to her knees. Vince grabbed her with his good arm and held her close.

"Thank God, Mary, you're safe."

She gulped air, staring wide-eyed at Agnes, stilling kneeling over Joshua. The old man's chest rose and fell, but his oddly decorated face was streaked with dark streamers of blood.

Vince's voice was low. "We were attacked after you and . . . and Terrance took off. He was hit in the head with something. A rock maybe."

"How is he?" Rathbone demanded, not taking his eyes off the gathering robed figures and their small hellish companions.

"I don't know, Tobias," Agnes answered, her voice thick.

"He's got to wake up," the Druid said. "I need his power. You've got to bring him around."

"He's hurt," she snapped, glaring at Rathbone. "He's not like you. He's mortal and he's old."

"If he doesn't come out of it, he'll be dead, Aggie. We'll all be dead." The tone of his voice sent a chill through Mary, who had listened to the exchange in abject silence.

Will this nightmare never end?

It was at that moment it truly began.

There was a thunderclap in the cloudless sky and the midnight dark vestige of the Madonna again appeared above Her seething mob of followers. Her ebon cloak spread, revealing the impossible blackness concealed in its folds.

Seeing Her, the mob screamed in delight. Bolstered by Her appearance, they spread out, circling their quarry.

"Joshua," Rathbone bellowed. "Wake up, man." He looked at Agnes. "Even unconscious, he should be able to use his powers to help himself. Why doesn't he?"

"He doesn't know," Agnes answered quietly, tears flowing freely down her wrinkled cheeks.

Rathbone thrust his left hand toward Mary. "Take it. Maybe I can draw some energy from you."

Hesitantly, she reached for his outstretched hand.

"Take it, damn you," the Druid snarled. "Vince, take her other hand. We'll form a circle. It may help."

Rathbone was grasping at straws and he knew it. It was Ortega he needed; the raw, raging energy in that old man could save them.

"Aggie," he called. "Leave him. Link with us."

Reluctantly, the old woman got to her feet. She felt resigned to her approaching death. There was no hope now and that fact depressed her. She was not afraid of dying, she had reconciled herself to her own mortality long ago, but damned if she wanted to die here. Not in this place of incarnate evil.

Absently she wondered if her soul would reach a happier, higher plane or be trapped forever in the dark limbo of the Madonna's Hell?

She stood on the Druid's right side and touched his shoulder, leaving his hand free to direct what energy he could summon. Standing behind Rathbone, she placed her other hand on the shoulder above Vince's shattered arm, forming the final link.

''Will this do any good?'' Vince asked no one in particular.

''Pray it does,'' Rathbone hissed in reply. Much to his own amazement, he could actually feel a slight surge of energy feeding into his body. It would not be enough, but it was something. It was more than he had had before.

Black robed humans were filtering in from all sides now, joining their other brothers and sisters. With all the fighting and killing, their numbers had been diminished, but still there were more than enough to overwhelm Rathbone's puny force. They formed an advancing wall of darkness beneath the floating Madonna.

With growing intensity and an increasingly terrible roar, graves continued to erupt, spewing forth the loathsome monstrosities.

''At least now there will be an ending,'' Rathbone mumbled to himself as he unleased a weak burst of energy toward the approaching sea of attackers. It burst on a knot of tiny demons and toppled them to the grass.

The Madonna made an awful sound, the primal scream of a thousand tormented voices, a wail of utter despair and hopelessness. It was an echoing, mind-piercing cry from the bowels of Hell.

As if in a spotlight, the moon suddenly illuminated Her face. The twin curved tusks gleamed in the silvery glow as the air stirred the scraps of mummified flesh clinging to her stained skull. Her swirling orbs of red and orange flashed in total fury. Her hatred was almost tangible to the four fragile humans preparing to meet Her onslaught . . .

. . . and their own deaths.

When the Black Bitch's banshee screech faded away, the sound of the exploding earth again swept over Mansfield.

The legion of Her followers slowly and warily circled Rathbone and his companions. Soon they would tighten the ring and by sheer weight of numbers overcome their quarry.

"Aggie . . . ?" Joshua Ortega's eyes fluttered as he reached out blindly, seeking the woman.

"Josh?" she said, not moving. "Josh, can you get up? Josh we need you!"

He sat up, wincing as his hand probed his bloody temple. Looking around, focusing his eyes, he swore softly.

"Josh, help us!" Rathbone cried.

"Yeah," he groaned, getting unsteadily to his feet. Without being told, he stepped between Agnes and Rathbone. He took the old woman's hand in his and squeezed it. "It's now or never."

When he placed his hand on the Druid's shoulder, everyone in the ragged pentagon felt the rushing, electric boost of energy flow through them. A shimmering aura of midnight blue suddenly encapsulated them in a shield of raw power.

The circling mob halted, a murmur of fear and confusion moving through it.

Again the Black Madonna gave tongue to the Her hellish cry.

Rathbone, invigorated by the incredible jolt of energy, fired a barrage of blue lightning bolts into the floating apparation. Unlike their previous encounter, this time his attack had an effect on the Madonna. Struck through her ebon body, She bellowed in pain and retreated.

"Alright!" Vince cheered. "Now we're ready to rock and roll with that Bitch."

"Don't celebrate yet," Rathbone cautioned. "We're a long way from getting out of here."

The black robed humans and the leathery demons retreated with their Mistress. Scores of the humans snarled and shrieked at their enemies as they moved back. The small, scurrying monsters glared at them, brandishing their swords and tridents. But they, too pulled back.

"What now?" Mary asked.

"I'm not sure," sighed Rathbone. "We've got to stop Her. We've got to stop this madness, this evil."

Agnes shook her head. "Isn't it enough that we've ruined Her ceremony? We've destroyed a century of preparation, isn't that sufficient?"

"No."

"Tobias," she said in irritation. "We've got a chance now. Let's not blow it."

"He's right, Aggie," Joshua said softly. "We can't just walk away now. We can't leave this half done."

The old woman exhaled audibly. "So what do we do?"

"I'm working on that," the Druid responded.

"Look," Mary cried. Her eyes opened wide as she watched the unsteady throng of skeletons shambling out of the darkness. There were hundreds of them, freshly unearthed, covered in their ragged and tattered shrouds. They were coming from all directions, stumbling and lumbering toward the tiny knot of defenders. The chattering jibberish issuing from their throatless bodies and the snapping and clicking of their jaws was unnerving, carrying the torment and anguish of their fettered souls. Their red eyes shone bright and evil.

"They've been cheated," Rathbone explained. "They were supposed to come back as human as they'd been when they were alive. And they would have, had Mary's blood been shed on this unholy ground. Now it's too late."

"I'll bet they're seriously pissed off," Vince quipped. His remark drew a humorless chuckle from the Druid.

"Exactly, my friend." Rathbone was about to again turn loose his power on the gathering things, when they all stopped as if on some silent command. Their glistening scarlet eyes were bright and piercing as they turned toward the Madonna's humans and Her demonic allies.

None of the five spoke and barely dared breathe. They watched the grim tableu unfolding before them in fascinated horror.

One of the darkly clad humans, sensing what was about to occur, screamed and started to flee, only to be impaled on the sharp barbs of a trident. The demon holding the wicked weapon yanked it free, letting the body slump to the ground.

Voicing their rage at the ghastly betrayal, the skeletal things were suddenly rushing forward. Their living heirs tried to flee, but the creatures were all around them. There was no place to turn, no place to run. Every attempt at escape was met with slashing taloned hands and snapping jaws.

Dark jets of blood shot into the air as throats were torn out and limbs were ripped from struggling bodies. The reverberation of the pain-maddened screams and terrible death cries echoed over the now empty mausoleums and the monuments marking voided graves.

A dark-haired woman, her hood back and her robe flying as she ran madly away from the carnage, was caught across the face by a sweeping, skeletal arm. Stunned, she whirled, attempting to escape the thing attacking her only to stumble into an open grave. Her hideous pursuer leaped in after her, emerging a moment later with her dripping, severed head held high in its clawed hand.

A half dozen beseiged men, unable to escape, stood back to back trying to fend off the monsters. They kicked and punched, fighting desperately, but the undead were impervious to the hard blows. More and still more of the creatures joined their unholy breathren until the humans were overwhelmed and crushed to the ground. They were instantly smothered under the mass of reanimated horror.

Above the nightmare scene, the Madonna hovered, a hideous grin splitting Her dark skull-face. She gestured with one of Her taloned hands and the horde of tiny demons, unmolested by the disintered monstrosities, detached themselves from the fray to dash toward the Druid's human pentagon.

TWENTY-FIVE

Linked, shrouded in the blue aura, the five watched as the demons scurried toward them. There was nothing to do but hold their ground; they had waited too long to make escape possible, even if they had decided to flee.

Like terribly deformed, hideous children, the Madonna's creatures loped toward them. Their numbers seemed endless. They howled and cried out, their mouths agape, revealing their sharp fangs which flashed in the moonlight. They waved their swords and tridents and slashed the midnight air with their clawed hands. Their winged brethren circled and swooped in the sky, wailing with bloodlust.

"Don't move," Rathbone ordered. "We'll be safe as long as we stay together."

His hands extended, the powerful energy channeling into his body dancing on his finger tips. He released a titanic burst. The beam of energy cut into the screaming mass. The nearest ranks were suddenly, terribly consumed in the hellish magic-fire. Writhing and twisting as their bodies burned, a score of the monsters tumbled to the grass.

Those behind stopped, seemed ready to turn and retreat, only to discover their Dark Mistress blocking their path. Having descended, She stood directly behind them.

For them, like their quarry, there was no escape.

They turned to fight.

The screaming and pleading from the black-robed worshipers continued to fill the night as the skeletal things chased them down and fell upon them in a terrible vengence-driven frenzy.

The blasts of Druidic fire burst again and again in the midst of the demon horde. As one wave was cut down, another replaced it. Rathbone's power burst upon several in the air, sending them spiraling to the ground where their flaming bodies smashed against marble and earth. Quickly those on the ground spread out, again attempting to circle the five humans.

"They're flanking us," Joshua warned Rathbone.

The Druid did not answer. He simply kept cutting down the advancing mob, focusing all his attention on the battle. Although he had an awesome power supply at his disposal, he was growing tired. His arms were weary and his body felt drained and used up. There was a debilitating fatigue weighing down his flesh and an unsettling lassitude permeating his soul.

Rathbone wanted to be done with this.

Still he kept slaughtering the misbegotten monsters and still they kept coming, spreading out around them.

"Why don't you try to stop Her?" Joshua yelled above the screams and cries.

"That's exactly what She's hoping I'll do. I can't destroy Her, but I don't think She can destroy us either," Rathbone cried, sounding exhausted.

"What do you mean She can't destroy us?" Vince demanded. "What the hell do you think is happening?"

"Not Her!" Agnes answered for Rathbone. "She's not attacking us directly. She never has. I don't think she can. It's always been through Her creatures."

"Right," the Druid agreed, unleashing another flurry of sapphire energy.

"We're almost surrounded," Vince cried, craning his neck to watch as the demons crept around them. His head and arm both were throbbing, making it difficult for him to concentrate on the battle.

Unexpectedly, the Madonna rose in the night sky and floated away. She dropped from sight in the trees. Simultaneously Her creatures stopped their attack and scurried to sanctuary behind tombstones and crypts.

Joshua sucked in a breath, "What the hell . . . ?"

Rathbone let his arms drop to his sides. "Don't break the circle," he said. "She's up to something."

Agnes studied Mary with sad and tired eyes. Her heart wept for the woman and for Vince, both so unsuspecting. She desperately needed to talk to Rathbone, but she had to do it alone. In this nightmarish chaos, there had been no opportunity. She needed to tell him the terrible truth . . .

Suddenly Mary's back went stiff. With a small cry, she pulled her hands away from Vince and Rathbone and slumped to the ground.

"Mary," Vince cried, moving to her.

"Don't break . . ." Rathbone was cut off as the scores of waiting monstrosities suddenly came running from their hiding places, and winging out of the sky.

Mary was lying on her back, her unseeing eyes opened wide. In the moonlight Vince saw something dark and sinister pass over her face.

"Help us," Rathbone yelled, again trying to keep the demons at bay. They were now spread too thin for him to take out more than one or two with each burst of energy. And with each successive blast, the bolts grew weaker, even though the Druid was still tapped into Joshua's power.

Vince started to leap to his feet but was bowled over as one of the demons dashed head-long into him. He fell heavily on his broken arm and was instantly riveted with an agonizing jolt of pain. Gasping, he lost consciousness.

Agnes was similarly caught by surprise. As she lost her grip of Joshua's hand, she caught a fleeting glimpse of the thing attacking her. She was revolted to see its eyes oozing sticky blood, blinded by its own hands in order not to be affected by the defensive symbols traced over her face.

She landed hard on a low tombstone, the air gushing out of her lungs as the stone hammered into her stomach.

Joshua and Rathbone continued to stand and fight. Both knew it was only a matter of time before they, too, would fall.

Henry Terrance was terrified. His heavy legs thudded on the gravel. His fat body quivered with each step and his face was streaked with sweat. He could feel his heart thundering in his chest and there was a tightness forming around it. Wide and wild, his eyes flicked from side to side as he tried to find sanctuary in the cemetery.

Behind him, loping and striding came a mob of the skeletal apparitions. Their firey eyes burned with hatred and Terrance knew they meant to kill him. He was the object of their vengence, the one they held responsible for the ghastly betrayal.

What had gone wrong? he wondered. What had turned a century of planning and preparation into this horrible—unthinkable—disaster?

The creatures were closing the gap. While their gait was steady and even, his own legs were growing tired and he was faltering. Tears of panic and terror flooded from his eyes merging with the sweat beading his fat face.

He screamed as ahead a half dozen abominations lumbered from the darkness of a mausoleum. He veered off the drive and started threading his way through the jumble of overturned and tilted tombstones. He moved slower now, forced to avoid the gaping holes and countless smashed, rotted coffins littering his path.

The creatures maintained their pace, dogging him like wolves pursuing a sick, tired animal.

"Bedlow!" Terrance screamed hysterically. "Oscar, help me." But, of course, Bedlow was far away.

He saw a crypt ahead, its iron door open. Turning, almost falling into an open grave, he ran toward it. Maybe, if he could get inside, he could bolt the door, find time to rest and plan his escape.

The skeletal creatures were only scant yards behind him now.

He reached the opening and dashed inside, yanking the door shut.

His scream was high and piercing like the scream of a woman.

The door banged open and Terrance was thrust back out into the moonlight, his feet dangling several inches above the ground. A sharp shaft of steel, dripping with his blood, jutted from his back. Screaming and crying, babbling insanely, perhaps pleading for his life or a less terrible death, he was carried out into the circle of leering skeletons. Their jaws clacked in approval.

The pike impaling him—a piece ripped from the iron fence surrounding Mansfield—was held by one of the things. It towered above him, its bone arms lifting the metal ever higher into the air until Terrance, like a totem, hung squirming and struggling above the leering skulls and burning eyes.

Writhing on the end of the spear like a fat, obese slug, his hands struggled futilely to dislodge the blood-slickened metal.

Suddenly and unceremoniously, he was dropped to the ground. Before death could forever spare him their wrath, his tormentors leaped on his corpulent body.

He finally died with a tiny wimpering gasp, his body ripped open, his limbs torn out of their sockets.

Henry Terrance would welcome Hell.

Mary felt The Presence settle over her again. She knew it was her protector, though this time it did not come to her offering peace and contentment, but instead lanced into her with an overwhelming sense of dark delight.

She could sense its evil.

The Presence shared her body, revelled in it. It spread a burning fury in her now, creeping through her like firey tendrils. It was a white-hot knot of hate and rage, a sense of disgust and loathing for all those she had so recently helped and who had helped her.

Vince . . . ?

She hated him so.

I love him.

Hate.

But the old man helped me. Saved me.

He is an enemy.

How can he be an enemy?

Enemy.

And the others . . . ?

Enemies.

Yes. Enemies.

And she knew, in a moment of dark revelation, that The Presence—her benefactor, her protector, her savior—was the Madonna. It had saved her from the monsters in the underground chamber. It had unleashed the powerful blast of energy which sent the fat man's scimitar spinning out of his hands. The Madonna did not want her to die, not on that dais. It had spared her for some other, more awful purpose. She understood these things even as the evil force was filling her body, clouding her mind and consuming her soul.

Vince! I love you!

While Mary struggled with the invader stealing her will, Rathbone and Joshua were barely able to keep the howling horde at bay.

"What's happened to our energy?" Joshua demanded, frightened.

"I'm . . . I'm not sure . . ." The Druid panted.

"You . . . you've been drained," gasped Agnes, getting slowly and painfully to her feet, her hands clutching her bruised stomach.

Rathbone sent a weak bolt of pale blue shooting into the face of one of the winged creatures circling above. "What are you saying?"

"Tricked. We've been tricked."

Agnes grabbed Joshua's outstretched hand and was pulled out of the path of a flashing sabre point. Still holding onto Rathbone, he lashed out with his foot, catching the demon-wielding monster on the side of the head, sending it sprawling.

"By the Madonna?" Joshua cried, watching the thing stagger away.

"Yes," Agnes shouted over the unholy din. "And, unwittingly, by the girl."

"Don't waste time, Aggie," the Druid ordered desperately. "What are you saying?"

"Mary Renata *is* a direct descendant of that nun . . ."

Rathbone drove back a knot of the tiny creatures with a series of bursts which stunned, but did not kill. "We've suspected as much."

"Yes. And we've known that the nun had an illegitimate child. What we didn't know was the father of the child." Agnes's voice broke for an instant.

"Aggie!" Joshua cried frantically.

"I contacted a spirit, a man in white. He told me."

"For God's sake, told you what?" Rathbone was too tired and frightened to be civil. The demon horde, now reduced to a very few moved among the grim, smoldering remains of their brethren. They kept back, watching and waiting.

"Damn it," Agnes snapped. "He told me the nun coupled with the Devil. The nun's child was . . . the Madonna!"

"Jesus," breathed Joshua.

"Now I understand," Rathbone sighed. He looked down at the prone form of Mary Renata and cursed violently.

The woman was changing, her flesh melting, sliding away from her gleaming white skull. Her once beautiful face was now replaced by the hideous, repulsive countenance of the Madonna. Her eyes became swirling pools of red and orange, her teeth darkened, become sharp and protruding; two were thickening, twisting into hooked, wicked tusks.

"Through her, the Black Bitch drained off our energy," Rathbone yelled bitterly.

"M . . . Mary?" Vince, trying to focus his eyes. He pushed himself up to sit on the matted grass. He stared at the transforming thing on the ground. "What's happening to Mary?" He started to reach for her.

"Stay away from her," Rathbone screamed. Vince yanked his hand back, shocked. The Druid turned away from the demons he was watching and leveled his hands at the creature on the ground.

"NO!" Vince's cried, trying to grab the Druid's arm. He sobbed as Rathbone let loose a long, powerful burst. The enormous bolt of energy was rapidly draining the power remaining between himself and Joshua.

The bolt sliced into the creature, driving into its heart like an azure lance.

The thing screamed and jerked, its twisted, blackened legs drummed the ground, its arms reached toward the cold, unforgiving moon. The pits of whirling fire which were its eyes flared and then flickered and then went slowly dark.

Its death cry was terrible, deafening. With a violent shudder, it was finally still.

The three humans watched in horror as the evil vestige of the Madonna vanished, replaced by the body of Mary Renata, a dark splotch of blood spreading over her torn and ragged white gown.

Vince rocked forward, his hand touching her still, peaceful face. He moaned softly and wept.

From beyond the trees there was a crack of thunder and

another unearthly, inhuman scream as the Occult Madonna rose into the silver and cobalt sky. Her ragged cloak lashed around Her unholy body, whipped by an unfelt wind.

"My God," breathed Agnes. "When will it end?"

"Now," roared the Druid. "It will end here and now!"

"We can't fight her anymore, Tobias," Joshua said, despairing.

"*We* won't! *I* will." Rathbone pulled away from Joshua and Agnes and stepped forward. The remaining demons danced and darted about in the distance, but none moved toward the Druid.

The Madonna hovered for a few seconds and then swooped low, diving at him, Her taloned hands thrust out. Rathbone stood his ground, a blue aura forming around his body.

"He's using the last of his power," Agnes said, dreading what was to follow. Knowing it was inevitable.

The dark thing landed in front the Druid and slashed at him with Her claws. He ducked the blow, but made no retaliatory move, simply stood, the aura around him growing brighter and increasingly more intense.

"Where's he finding the power?" Joshua whispered not taking his eyes away from the bizarre confrontation.

"His lifeforce, I think," Anges answered solemnly, tears flowing down her ink-marked cheeks, streaking them with muddy rivulets of black.

With an abrupt, lightning-fast move, the Madonna opened Her dark, tattered cloak and enveloped Rathbone in its folds. She roared a cry of triumph as the Druid's agonized voice spilled into the night.

"We've got to help him!" Joshua wailed, stepping forward.

Agnes clutched his arm, restraining him. "We can't. It's too late."

The Druid's screams continued for several blood-chilling seconds and then suddenly stopped.

"She's won," Joshua spat, his hand brushing at his

moustache. "That evil Bitch has beaten us . . . beaten him."

"Maybe not," Agnes cried, pointing.

Still clutching Rathbone to Her breast beneath the folds of Her cloak, the Madonna stiffened. Her hands dropped to Her sides. Her mouth fell open and a wail shattered the night. Her demonic creatures, too, wailed and howled as if in intense pain.

The night was washed away in a brilliant flash of blue energy, so intense Joshua and Agnes had to turn away for fear of being blinded. It consumed the pair in a flaring, radiating ball of energy. There was one more long undulating wail.

The light faded.

Tobias Rathbone or what had once been the Druid, stood where the two had met. He wavered, tottered and then tumbled backward.

Joshua and Agnes rushed past Vince, who still tearfully cradled Mary's lifeless body, and hurried to Rathbone. Agnes screamed when she looked upon the thing lying on the ground. Joshua drew in a ragged breath, as he dropped to his knees beside the Druid's ruined body.

"Tobias . . . ?" Joshua choked and bit his lip, the salty, coppery taste of blood filling his mouth.

Rathbone's flesh had been completely flayed from his body, exposing his raw, bleeding musculature. His lidless eyes, oddly soft, stared up at the pair and in spite of the pain that was tearing at him, he smiled.

"It is at an end. The Black Bitch is gone."

"Hush," Agnes sobbed. "We've got to get you out of there. Find you help . . ."

The grotesque head shook slowly, painfully. "No."

"But . . ."

"Too late, Aggie, my dear. Too late." Rathbone's voice was hoarse, little more than a ragged whisper. He looked at Joshua, his tongue flicking over his raw, bloody lips. "Do you remember what I told you about Timothy?"

Joshua mutely nodded.

"This is what She did to him. Neither of us understood. She can't directly attack a mortal. She can only harm them through her pawns. But Timothy and I are not . . . were not . . . mortals. She could attack us. Timothy didn't know what I know now. He and I were young then. He didn't know . . ." The Druid groaned.

"You *did* win, Tobias," Joshua said. "You beat Her."

"Yes. She is destroyed. No place for Her to go but back to Hell. No heir to accept her legacy. I'm sorry about the girl. I had no choice." His words came slowly, painfully. He paused and again looked at Joshua. "Now you have to send me on my way, too."

"Wh . . . what are you saying?"

"Kill me, Josh. For the love of God, kill me." Rathbone's voice was pitiful, pleading.

"I can't."

"You have to. Please."

Joshua shook his head. "How can I take your life? What gives me that right?"

"I . . . give it to you," the Druid answered.

"I'm not sure you have that right."

The Druid's ruined hand caught Joshua's wrist with an amazingly powerful grip. "It's *my* life. It's my right to say when it ends. For the love of God, Josh. Don't make me beg!"

Joshua looked around. He saw one of the demon's small dagger-like swords lying in the grass a few feet away. He reached for it, grasped it in a shaking hand.

"Do it, Josh," the Druid coaxed. "It's the kindest thing you could do."

Joshua blinked back tears. He looked at Agnes, who was watching him. She nodded and turned away.

"Aggie," Rathbone whispered. "You're one hell of a woman. I wish I had known you long ago."

She turned back, smiled weakly and nodded, wiping tears out of her eyes.

"Josh," the Druid said, forcing another weak smile. "You can do it."

Joshua lifted the small sword above his head, its hilt gripped in both of his trembling hands. Rathbone stared peacefully into Agnes's eyes.

The blade flashed in the moonlight.

Tobias Rathbone, who had lived for near half a millennium, died without a sound.

The cemetery was silent now. The screams and wails had ceased. The remaining demons had vanished, perhaps swept back to Hell with the Madonna. The raised dead had collapsed in heaps, their souls freed from their grotesque bodies. There was now only the rustle of leaves as a soft breeze moved through the trees.

Joshua and Agnes got slowly to their feet and left Rathbone's ravaged body. They returned to where Vince sat holding Mary.

"We have to go, Vince," Agnes said quietly. "We have to leave this place."

He looked up at her, his eyes wet. Agnes thought her old heart would break when she saw the pain and sadness in his face.

"I can't leave her here," he said, his voice flat, as lifeless as the body he clutched.

"We won't leave either her or Tobias," Joshua said. The old man stooped and with some effort, took the girl from Vince. Her body hung limp in his arms. He marveled at how light she felt.

Agnes helped Vince to his feet and together the three walked slowly toward the cemetery's gates. When they neared them, Joshua carefully placed Mary's body on the ground.

"I'll get my car. We'll put her and Tobias in it." He turned and walked out of the desecrated graveyard.

"I loved her, you know?" Vince told Agnes, as he stared down at the corpse.

"Yes, I know. It's hard to lose someone, hard to face

that *loss*. But it's as natural a part of life as being born." For Vince it would be a very long time before he could recall Mary's face or her touch without feeling his heart twist with longing and remorse.

There was a movement behind them. Startled, they both whirled around.

Oscar Bedlow came staggering out of the trees. His gaunt face shone pale in the moonlight and his eyes were wide, filled with madness. He carried the scimitar Terrance had used on the dais. Mumbling and cursing, he rushed at the pair.

"You ruined everything!" he shrieked. "Everything."

Vince, although weak and very stiff, still managed to grab Agnes and pulled her aside as the tall, crazed man swung the sword at them. It sliced harmlessly through the air and slashed into the grass. Bedlow turned and sprang again, this time narrowly missing Agnes's head with the blood-flecked blade.

"You son of a bitch!" Vince screamed. All the evil this man had brought on him and Mary had turned into a well of hate and rage. "You filthy bastard."

Bedlow was turning again as Vince lashed out with his foot, catching the man in the groin. Bedlow hissed, dropped the sword and clutched his crotch. As he bent forward, Vince kicked him in the face. Those huge teeth splintered against the hard toe of his boot.

Bedlow yelled and toppled over backward. Vince grabbed the sword and lifted it, ready to drive it into the man's heart.

"No, Vince," Agnes cried. "Don't, please."

Vince's hand waivered. For a long, breathless moment, he held the blade high. Finally, with a disgusted sigh, he lowered his arm.

Joshua's car came through the gates as Vince sent the sword spinning away into the darkness.

A hand covering his bloody mouth, Bedlow got unsteadily to his feet, turned and staggered away. They watched him until he vanished behind one of the now empty crypts.

Silently they loaded Mary's body into the trunk of Joshua's car. Rather than walk back to where they had left Rathbone, they drove. Joshua carried the ravaged body and placed it next to Mary's.

Vince sat in the back, his head leaning against the seat, his eyes squeezed shut. The pain in his body faded against the ache in his heart. He as so tired. So damned tired.

As Joshua drove slowly back down the road, Agnes touched his arm.

"Josh, stop for a minute, please," she said.

"Why, Aggie? We've got to get out of here."

"I know. I'll only be a minute."

Mystified, Joshua braked the car to a stop. Without another word, Agnes got out and walked into the shadows of the trees. In minutes she returned carrying a soiled bundle of rags.

"Okay, Josh," she said, settling in the seat, the dirty bundle on the floor between her feet. "Let's go home."

Silently, he nodded and drove out of Mansfield.

Oscar Bedlow, carrying a length of chain over one arm and a candle in the other fist, stumbled down the staircase and into the stone chamber where the Renata woman had been held. Blood streamed down his chin from the stubs of his shattered teeth and his abdomen still ached from the blow to his groin. His gaunt, pale face was lined with defeat.

He was a broken, ruined man.

Crossing the room, he fixed one end of the chain to the hook set in the ceiling. After struggling to uncover the pit wherein the bones of hundreds of sacrificed victims were heaped, not noticing the stench that quickly filled the room, he wrapped the free end of the chain around his neck.

With a curse, he leaned forward and then jumped into

the hole. He dropped a few feet and was jerked hard, his neck snapping.

Bedlow's body twitched an bucked on the chain. When it was finally still, it turned in slow, lazy circles above the yawning pit.

TWENTY-SIX

Agnes Hardwick sat on the couch in her ruined living room wiping the tears from her cheek as she handed the letter to Joshua. He took it and read Tobias Rathbone's fine, flared script.

Dear Aggie,

That you are reading this is proof that my premonitions were correct. Frankly, I don't expect to survive. If you're reading this, it is clear you did and I did not.

I understand the realities of tonight's confrontation with the evil in the cemetery. Even if we should somehow manage to defeat the Bitch—and I'm not sure that's a possibility—I know the cost will be high.

Perhaps now you understand the true nature of the Madonna's scheme. The dead rising as flesh and blood: a fool's dream. All the Madonna can offer is a parody of life, like that poor creature we saw last night at Mansfield. The Madonna and Her consort never intended to do anything for those they duped except capture their souls through greed and lust.

For a century, people—whole families—have sacri-

ficed and prepared for the return of their dead. But I now believe their long awaited ritual will be a sham, a fake. The Madonna's real motivation is, as always, to conquer souls. Aligning themselves with Her was all She required. It sealed their fate for eternity.

Enclosed with this letter is the key to my apartment and the combination to my safe. There is a considerable amount of money in it and a power of attorney in your name. Use the money for whatever purpose you deem appropriate. Give the Cord to Joshua.

If we managed to win at Mansfield, then revel in our victory; if we lost, know we made a good fight of it.

Don't mourn me. I've lived far too long and death isn't unwelcome at this advanced stage of my life. My only regret is that I did not get to know you and Josh. He's a good man, Aggie. Cherish his friendship.

Forever,
Tobias.

"He knew," Joshua sighed, staring at the sheet of paper.

Agnes felt sad and tired, overwhelmed by the events of the past few days.

After leaving the cemetery the previous morning, they had taken Vince to an emergency room to have his broken arm set. The attending physican had asked too many questions, but was finally convinced that Vince had simply taken a bad fall. Joshua had explained that Vince had landed on a pitchfork, thus accounting for the three puncture wounds in his back.

Exhausted, they had returned to Agnes's house and tumbled into their respective beds, sleeping until the early evening. Even the distraught Vince slept soundly.

After rising, they drove the still oddly marked car south out of Denver through the broad expanse of South Park and then west to Gunnison. From there it was a short trip to Crested Butte where they headed up the well-maintained gravel road over Kebler Pass, reaching a lush green meadow between the towering peaks shortly after midnight.

None of the three had spoken during the long drive. Vince, especially morose and grim, had sat in the back seat and stared blankly at the landscape sliding past his window until it was lost in darkness.

By the light of the brilliant moon, they toiled for several hours. By dawn, three fresh graves had been dug and covered with rock. They had carefully arranged the stones so as to appear natural.

Vince knelt at Mary's grave and laid a bouquet of freshly picked wild flowers atop it. He again wept; softly, silently, saying his final goodbyes.

Agnes and Joshua could think of nothing to say over the grave of Tobias Rathbone. He had been a good man and he had died following his destiny. There was nothing they could add to that.

The third grave held the bones of the murdered girl—the ragged bundle Agnes had retrieved from the cemetery. The poor, unfortunate girl had been brutally slain by her sick father and unjustly buried amid the evil of Mansfield. Now perhaps she would know a measure of peace surrounded by the wild beauty of the mountains.

They had decided to bury the remains of the three in secret to avoid a complex and complicated situation. They had no desire to explain their involvement with the disaster at Mansfield nor did any of them want the accompanying attention their revelations would undoubtedly generate. They had determined it was better to let sleeping dogs lie.

They had returned to Denver and Aggie's home in silence. She had found Rathbone's letter while inspecting the damaged rooms.

Well, she thought, there would be money to repair the house and maybe give some to a charity or set up a scholarship fund in Tobias's name. She would give Vince Cassidy enough to get a fresh start. Maybe she would be selfish and take just a little so she and Joshua could take a trip together. Maybe to England. To Stonehenge. To Rathbone's roots.

Maybe they would do that.

"I'm going to check on Vince," Joshua said, getting off the couch.

The young man was in the spare bedroom. He was propped up on pillows, his chest wrapped in bandages and his left arm in a cast. His right eye was bloodshot and swollen, but his vision was not impaired. He was ghostly pale and drawn and Joshua thought he knew what Vince would look like when he was old.

"How you feeling?" Joshua asked, forcing a smile.

Vince shrugged, continuing to stare out the bedroom window.

"It ain't easy, Vince," Joshua went on. "It never is."

"Yeah, right," Vince said bitterly. "What the hell am I supposed to do now?"

"What do you want to do?"

"Nothing," he answered. "Nothing seems worth doing."

Joshua sat on the edge of the bed and sighed, his hand brushing absently at his bushy moustache. "There's really nothing I can say to make it better. Just remember the good times, you know?"

"Yeah, I know." Joshua saw the tears forming in the younger man's eyes. "Maybe someday I'll forget what happened at that stinking cemetery. Maybe someday . . ."

Joshua patted Vince's leg. "You will. All those things that happened to you and to Mary was a part of the Madonna's plan. She wanted to disorient you. confusion, terror and deceit are . . . were Her chief weapons. You just have to remember it wasn't your fault."

"I wish I could believe that."

"You have to, Vince. I didn't know her, but I doubt Mary would want you to carry around that kind of baggage."

Vince looked at Joshua and shook his head. "It's still such a nightmare. Everything happened so fast." He sighed. "I just don't know what to do now."

"Maybe something will come up," the older man suggested, trying to sound hopeful. "A job."

Vince nodded, turning away as the tears came again. He choked back a sob and then covered his eyes with his right hand. "My God, I loved her."

Joshua stayed with him until he dropped into a shallow sleep. He left the room quietly.

"How is he?" Agnes asked, as he returned to the living room.

"Sleeping. He's depressed, broken-hearted."

"I wish there was something we could do," Agnes said.

"I made a call a while ago. I have a friend in California. An archaeologist. I gave him a story about this young man trying to piece his life back together and how going on a dig might really help the healing process." He sighed, reaching across Agnes to rub Solomon's big head. The cat sat purring, curled up next to his mistress.

"Will he help?" Agnes asked.

"I think so. He'll call me back tomorrow."

Agnes stroked the cat and shook her head. "All those people were betrayed for all those years."

Joshua snorted. "Betrayed by their own lusts." Again he saw the nightmare images of the undead falling on their ancestors, unleashing their terrible anger through acts of unspeakable violence.

"And out of all of it the only winner was the Devil," Agnes added.

"Yeah," her friend agreed. "A lot of souls lost. Although *we* survived. I sure wouldn't call that a loss."

They were both silent for a long time. Agnes finally spoke, her voice quiet and flat. "Mary, that poor child, never suspected her heritage."

Joshua nodded. "It was best that she didn't. And Tobias had no choice but to destroy her."

"I hope Vince understands that someday," Agnes sighed.

"Perhaps he will. Now, who was the spirit you contacted. The one you said sent Vince back?"

Agnes smiled. "I think it was Timothy. Tobias's long dead friend."

"Doing what he could to help?" Joshua asked rhetorically, reaching for the copy of the morning newspaper sitting on the coffee table.

As he had done a dozen times already, he scanned the article about the devastation at Mansfield. According to the report, Mansfield had been sealed off after a suspected natural gas explosion had virtually destroyed the entire cemetery. Officials were investigating.

It was a sensational story. Apparently numerous skeletons and hundreds of bodies were found and there was speculation that a cult had somehow set off the explosion while performing a bizarre ritual.

"What else *can* the authorities say?" Agnes said, glancing at the story.

"Yeah, it'll go down as another of those unexplained mysteries. They'll probably claim it was some sort of Guyanalike disaster. Mass hysteria and suicide. It'll be talked about for years, but no one will ever know the truth."

Agnes reached over and took his hand. "No one, except for us."

AUTHOR'S NOTE

The Occult Madonna was inspired by a poem of the same name written by the English poet J.C. Powys. It was originally published in *The Occult Review* (January, 1906), a psuedo-scientific journal issued in England.

Stanzas of the poem have been used to introduce each section of this book; however, its usage is in no way intended to suggest Powys envisioned the Occult Madonna as malevolent as the creature in this novel.

Maria Renata was, in fact, a nun in the Premonstratensian convent of Unterzell and she was a victim of the witchcraft hysteria. She was tortured into confessing, beheaded and her body burned. Her tale is a sad and disturbing one, but by no means unique to those terrible times.

All of the other characters are, of course, purely fictional.

Douglas D. Hawk
Denver, Colorado
October, 1987